SNOW

Orhan Pamuk, described as 'one of the freshest, most original voices in contemporary fiction' (*Independent on Sunday*) is the author of many books, including *The White Castle, The Black Book* and *The New Life*. In 2003 he won the International IMPAC Award for *My Name is Red*. His most recent book is *Istanbul* (2005), a cultural and personal history of his native city.

'One of the world's finest living writers.' *Independent*

'In this world of forgeries, where some might be in danger of losing their faith in literature, Pamuk is the real thing.' Savkar Altinel, *Observer*

'We in the West can only feel gratitude that such a novelist as Pamuk exists, to act as a bridge between our culture and that of a heritage quite as rich as our own.' Tom Holland, *Daily Telegraph*

ORHAN PAMUK

Snow

Translated by Maureen Freely

faber and faber

First published in 2004
by Faber and Faber Limited
3 Queen Square London WC1N 3AU
This open market edition first published in 2004

Published in the United States by Alfred A. Knopf
a division of Random House, Inc., New York

Originally published in Turkey as Kar by İletişim, Istanbul in 2002
© 2002 İletişim Yayincilik A.Ş.

Typeset by Faber and Faber Limited
Printed in England by Mackays of Chatham plc, Chatham, Kent

A CIP record for this book
is available from the British Library

ISBN 0–571–22299–4

To Rüya

Our interest's on the dangerous edge of things.
The honest thief, the tender murderer,
The superstitious atheist.
  Robert Browning, 'Bishop Blougram's Apology'

Politics in a literary work are a pistol-shot in the middle of a concert, a crude affair though one impossible to ignore. We are about to speak of very ugly matters.
  Stendhal, The Charterhouse of Parma

Well, then, eliminate the people, curtail them, force them to be silent. Because the European Enlightenment is more important than people.
  Fyodor Dostoevsky, Notebooks for The Brothers Karamazov

The Westerner in me was discomposed.
  Joseph Conrad, Under Western Eyes

SNOW

A Note on Pronunciation

Most Turkish letters are pronounced as in English.
The exceptions are as follows:

c – sounds like the 'j' in jelly
ç –   "   "   the 'ch' in chill
ğ – is a silent letter that lengthens the preceding vowel
ı – sounds like the 'u' in cranium
ö –   "   "   the 'ew' in jewel
ş –   "   "   the 'sh' in sheep
ü –   "   "   the first 'u' in usual

The Silence of Snow

The Journey to Kars

The silence of snow, thought the man sitting just behind the bus-driver. If this were the beginning of a poem, he would have called what he felt inside him 'the silence of snow'.

He'd boarded the bus from Erzurum to Kars with only seconds to spare. He'd just come into the station on a bus from Istanbul – a snowy, stormy, two-day journey – and was rushing up and down the wet, dirty corridors with his bag in tow, looking for his connection, when someone told him that there was a bus for Kars leaving immediately.

He'd managed to find the bus, an ancient Magirus, but the conductor had just shut the luggage compartment, and, being 'in a hurry', refused to open it again. That's why our traveller had taken his bag on board with him: the dark red suitcase was now wedged between his legs. He was sitting next to the window and wearing a thick charcoal coat that he'd bought at a Frankfurt Kaufhof five years earlier. We should note straight away that this soft, downy beauty of a coat would cause him shame and disquiet during the days he was to spend in Kars, while also furnishing a sense of security.

As soon as the bus set off, our traveller glued his eyes to the window next to him. Perhaps hoping to see something new, he peered into the wretched little shops, bakeries and broken-down coffee-houses that lined the streets of Erzurum's outlying suburbs, and, as he did, it began to snow. It was heavier and thicker than the snow he'd seen between Istanbul and Erzurum. If he hadn't been so tired, if he'd paid more attention to the snowflakes swirling out of the sky like feathers, he might have realised that he was travelling straight into a blizzard; he might have seen from the start that he had set out on a journey that would change his life for ever; he might have

3

turned back. But the thought didn't even cross his mind. As evening fell, he lost himself in the light still lingering in the sky above. In the snowflakes whirling ever more wildly in the wind he saw nothing of the impending blizzard, but rather a promise, a sign pointing back to the happiness and purity he had once known as a child.

Our traveller had spent his years of happiness and childhood in Istanbul; he'd returned a week ago, for the first time in twelve years, to attend his mother's funeral. Having stayed four days, he had decided to take this trip to Kars. Years later, he could still recall the extraordinary beauty of the snow that night: the pleasure it brought him was far greater than any he'd known in Istanbul. He was a poet, and, as he himself had written – in an early poem still largely unknown to Turkish readers – it snows only once in our dreams.

As he watched the snow outside the window fall as slowly and silently as the snow in his dream, the traveller fell into a long-desired, long-awaited reverie; cleansed by memories of innocence, he succumbed to optimism and dared to believe himself at home in this world. Soon afterwards, he did something else that he had not done for years and fell asleep in his seat.

So let us take advantage of this lull to whisper a few biographical details. Although he'd spent twelve years in political exile in Germany, our traveller had never been much of an activist. His real passion, his only thought, was for poetry. He was forty-two years old, single and never married. Although it might be hard to tell with him curled up in his seat, he was tall for a Turk, and had brown hair and a pallid complexion that had become even paler during this journey. He was shy and enjoyed being alone. Had he known what happened soon after he fell asleep – with the swaying of the bus his head would come to lean first on his neighbour's shoulder, and then on the man's chest – he would have been mortified. For the traveller we see leaning on his neighbour is an honest and well-meaning man, and – like those Chekhovian characters so laden with virtues that they never know success in life – full of melancholy. We'll have much to say about melancholy later. But as he is not likely to remain asleep for very long in that awkward position, for now suffice it to say that the traveller's name is Kerim Alakuşoğlu; that he doesn't like that name, preferring to be known by his initials, as Ka; and that I'll be complying with his wishes in this book. Even as a schoolboy our hero stubbornly insisted on writing 'Ka' on his homework and his exam papers; he signed in as Ka on university registration forms; he took every opportunity to defend his right to continue to do so, even if it meant coming into conflict with teachers and government officials. His mother, his family and his friends all knew him as Ka, and, having published some poetry collections under this name, he enjoyed some small, enigmatic fame as Ka in both Turkey and Turkish circles in Germany. That's all we have time for at present, so, just as the bus-driver wished his passengers a safe journey as we departed Erzurum station, let me add these words: 'May your road be open, dear Ka . . .' But I don't wish to deceive you: I'm an old friend of Ka's and I begin this story knowing everything that will happen to him during his time in Kars.

After leaving Horasan, the bus turned north, heading directly for Kars. As it climbed the winding road, the driver had to slam on the brakes to avoid a horse and carriage that had sprung out of nowhere on one of the hairpin bends, and Ka woke up. Fear had already fostered a strong fellow feeling among the passengers, and before long Ka also felt at one with them. Even though he was sitting just behind the driver, Ka was soon doing the same as the passengers behind him: whenever the bus slowed to negotiate a bend in the road or avoid going over the edge of a cliff, he stood up for a better view; when the zealous passenger who'd committed himself to helping the driver by wiping the condensation from the windscreen missed a corner, Ka would point it out to the man with his forefinger (which contribution went unnoticed); and when the blizzard became so bad that the wipers could no longer keep the snow from piling up on the windscreen, Ka would join the driver in trying to guess where the road was.

The road signs caked with snow were impossible to read. Once the snowstorm began to rage in earnest, the driver turned off his full beam and dimmed the lights inside the bus, hoping to conjure the road out of the semi-darkness. The passengers fell into a fearful silence, with their eyes on the scene outside: the snow-covered streets of derelict villages; the dimly lit, ramshackle, one-storey houses; the roads to farther villages that were already closed; and the ravines barely visible beyond the streetlamps. If they spoke, it was in whispers.

So it was in the gentlest of murmurs that Ka's neighbour asked him why he was travelling to Kars. It was easy to see that Ka was not a local.

5

'I'm a journalist,' Ka whispered in reply. This was a lie. 'I'm interested in the municipal elections – and also the women who've been committing suicide.' This was true.

'When the mayor of Kars was murdered, every newspaper in Istanbul ran the story,' Ka's neighbour replied. 'And it's the same for the women who've been committing suicide.'

It was hard for Ka to determine whether it was pride he heard in the man's voice . . . or shame. Three days later, while standing in the snow on Halitpaşa Avenue, with tears streaming from his eyes, Ka would see this slim, handsome villager again.

During the desultory conversation that continued intermittently for the rest of the bus journey, Ka learned that the man had just taken his mother to Erzurum because the hospital in Kars wasn't good enough; that he was a livestock dealer who served the villages in the vicinity of Kars; that he'd been through hard times but hadn't become a rebel; that – for mysterious reasons he did not disclose to Ka – he was sorry not for himself but for his country; and that he was happy to see a well-read, educated gentleman like Ka had taken the trouble to travel all the way from Istanbul to find out more about Kars' problems. There was something noble in the simplicity of his speech and the pride of his bearing, and Ka respected him for it.

His very presence was calming to Ka. Not once during his twelve years in Germany had Ka known such inner peace: it had been a long time since he had enjoyed the fleeting pleasure of empathising with someone weaker than himself. He remembered trying to see the world through the eyes of a man who could feel love and compassion. As he did the same now, he no longer felt so fearful of the relentless blizzard, for he knew that they were not destined to roll off a cliff: the bus would be late, but it would reach its destination.

When, at ten o'clock, three hours behind schedule, the bus began its crawl through the snow-covered streets of Kars, Ka didn't recognise the city at all. He couldn't see the station where he'd arrived twenty years earlier by steam engine, nor any sign of the hotel to which his driver had taken him that day after a full tour of the city – the Hotel Republic, with a 'telephone in every room'. It was as if everything had been erased, or lost beneath the snow. He saw a hint of the old days in the horse-drawn carriages here and there, sheltering in garages, but the city itself looked much poorer and sadder than he remembered. Looking through the frozen windows of the bus, Ka saw the same concrete apartments that had sprung up all over Turkey over the past ten years, the same plexiglass panels. He also saw, strung over every street, banners emblazoned with campaign slogans.

He stepped off the bus, and as his foot sank into the soft blanket of snow, a sharp blast of cold air shot under the cuffs of his trousers. He'd booked a room at the Snow Palace Hotel, and when he went to ask the conductor where it was, he thought a couple of the faces among the travellers waiting for their luggage looked familiar, but with the snow falling so thick and fast he couldn't work out who they were. He saw them again in the Green Pastures Restaurant, where he went after checking in to his hotel: a tired, careworn but still handsome and eye-catching man, and a fat but animated woman who seemed to be his lifelong companion.

Ka had seen them perform in Istanbul in the seventies, when they were leading lights of the revolutionary theatre world. The man's name was Sunay Zaim. As Ka let his mind wander, he watched the couple and was eventually able to work out that the woman reminded him of a classmate from primary school. There were a number of other men at the table with them, and they all had that deathly pallor that spoke of a life on the stage: what, he wondered, was this small theatre company doing in this forgotten city on a snowy night in February? Before leaving the restaurant, which twenty years before had been full of government officials wearing jackets and ties, Ka thought he saw one of the heroes of the seventies militant left of the seventies sitting at another table. But it was as if a blanket of snow had settled over his memories of this man, just as it had settled over the restaurant and the failing, gasping city of Kars.

Were the streets empty because of the snow, or were these frozen pavements always so desolate? As he walked, Ka studied the writing on the walls – the election posters, the advertisements for schools and restaurants, and new posters that the city officials hoped would end the suicide epidemic. Through the frozen windows of a half-empty tea-house, Ka saw a group of men huddled around a television. It cheered him just a little to see these old Russian stone houses still standing. In his memory they had made Kars such a special place.

The Snow Palace Hotel was one of those elegant Baltic buildings. It was two storeys high, with long, narrow windows that looked out on to a courtyard and an arch that led on to the street. The arch was a hundred and ten years old and high enough for horse-drawn carriages to pass through with ease. Ka felt a shiver of excitement as he passed under it, but he was too tired to ask himself why. Let's just say that it had something to do with one of Ka's reasons for coming to Kars. Three days earlier, Ka had paid a visit to the Istanbul offices of the *Republican* to see a friend from his youth. It was this friend, Taner, who had told him about the municipal elections coming up and how – just as in the city of Batman – an extraordinary number of girls in Kars had succumbed to a suicide epidemic. Taner went on to say that if Ka wanted to write about this subject and see what Turkey was really like after his twelve-year absence, he should think of going to Kars. With no one else available for this assignment, he thought he could provide Ka with a valid press card; and what's more, he said, Ka might be interested to know that their old classmate, the beautiful İpek, was now living in Kars. Although separated from her husband Muhtar, she'd stayed on in the city and was living with her father and sister in the Snow Palace Hotel. As Ka listened to Taner, who wrote political commentaries for the *Republican*, he remembered how beautiful İpek was.

Cavit, the receptionist, sat in the high-ceilinged lobby watching television. He handed Ka the key, and Ka went up to the second floor, to Room 203. Shutting the door behind him, he felt calmer. After a careful self-examination, he concluded that, notwithstanding the fears that had plagued him throughout his journey, neither his heart nor his mind was troubled by the possibility that İpek might be here in the hotel. After a lifetime whose every experience of affection was touched by shame and suffering, the prospect of falling in love filled Ka with an intense, almost instinctive dread.

In the middle of the night, before getting into bed, Ka padded across the room in his pyjamas and opened the curtains. He watched the thick, heavy snowflakes falling without end.

Our City Is a Peaceful Place

The Outlying Districts

Veiling as it did the dirt, the mud and the darkness, the snow would continue to speak to Ka of purity, but after his first day in Kars, it no longer promised innocence. The snow here was tiring, irritating, terrorising. It had snowed all night. It continued snowing all morning, while Ka walked the streets playing the intrepid reporter – visiting coffee-houses packed with unemployed Kurds, interviewing the voters, taking notes – and later, when he climbed the steep and frozen streets to interview the old mayor, the governor's assistant, and the families of the girls who had committed suicide. But it no longer took him back to the snowy streets of his childhood, no longer made him think, as he had done as a child standing at the windows of the sturdy houses of Nişantaş, that he was peering into a fairy tale, no longer returned him to a place where he could enjoy the middle-class life he missed too much even to visit in his dreams. Instead, it spoke to him of hopelessness and misery.

Early that morning, before the city had awoken and before he'd allowed the snow to get the better of him, he'd taken a brisk walk through the shanty town below Atatürk Boulevard to the poorest part of Kars, to the district known as Kalealti. The scenes he saw as he hurried under the ice-covered branches of the plane trees and the oleasters – the old, decrepit Russian buildings with stovepipes sticking out of every window, the thousand-year-old Armenian church towering over the wood depots and the electric generators, the pack of dogs barking at every passer-by from a five-hundred-year-old stone bridge as snow fell into the half-frozen black waters of the river below, the thin ribbons of smoke rising out of the tiny shanty houses of Kalealti sitting lifeless under their blanket of snow – made him

9

feel so sad that tears came to his eyes. On the opposite bank there were two children, a girl and a boy who'd been sent out early to buy bread, and as they danced along, tossing the warm loaves back and forth, clutching them to their chests, they looked so happy that Ka could not help smiling. It wasn't the poverty or the helplessness that disturbed him: it was what he would see time and again during the days to come; in the empty windows of the photography shops, in the frozen windows of the crowded tea-houses where the city's unemployed passed the time playing cards, and in the city's empty, snow-covered squares. These sights spoke of a strange and powerful loneliness. It was as if he were in a place that the whole world had forgotten; as if it were snowing at the end of the world.

Ka's luck stayed with him all morning. When people heard his reply after asking him who he was, they wanted to shake his hand; they treated him like a famous journalist from Istanbul; all of them – from the governor's assistant to the poorest man – opened their doors and spoke to him. He was introduced to the city by Serdar Bey, the publisher of *Border City News* (circulation: three hundred and twenty), who sometimes sent local news items to the *Republican* in Istanbul (mostly they didn't print them). Ka had been told to visit 'our local correspondent' first thing in the morning, as soon as he left the hotel, and the instant he found the old journalist ensconced in his office he realised that this man knew everything there was to know in Kars. It was Serdar Bey who was the first to ask him the question he would hear again hundreds of times during his three-day stay:

'Welcome to our border city, sir. But why are you here?'

Ka explained that he had come to cover the municipal elections and also perhaps to write about the suicide girls.

'As in Batman, the stories about the suicide girls have been exaggerated,' the journalist replied. 'Let's go over to meet Kasım Bey, the assistant chief of police. They should know you've arrived – just in case.'

That all newcomers, even journalists, should pay a visit to the police was a provincial custom dating back to the forties. Because he was a political exile who had just returned to the country after an absence of many years, and because – even though no one had mentioned it – he sensed the presence of the separatist Kurdish guerrillas (the PKK) in the city, Ka made no objection.

They set off into the blizzard, cutting through a fruit market and continuing past the stores of spare parts and hardware on Kâzım Karabekir Avenue, past tea-houses where gloomy unemployed men sat watching television or the falling snow, past dairy shops display-ing huge wheels of yellow cheese. It took them fifteen minutes to cut a diagonal across the city.

Along the way, Serdar Bey stopped to show Ka the place where the old mayor had been assassinated. According to one rumour, he'd been shot over a simple municipal dispute – the demolition of an illegal bal-cony. They'd caught the assailant after three days, in the village to which he'd fled; when they found him hiding in a barn, he was still holding the weapon. But there had been so much gossip during those three days before his capture that no one wanted to believe that this was indeed the culprit: the simplicity of his motive was disappointing.

The Kars Police Headquarters was in a long, three-storey building on Faikbey Avenue, where the old stone buildings that had once belonged to wealthy Russians and Armenians now mostly housed government offices. As they sat waiting for the assistant chief of police, Serdar Bey pointed out the high, ornate ceilings and explained that between 1877 and 1918, during the Russian occupation of the city, this forty-room mansion was first home to a rich Armenian and later to a Russian hospital.

Kasım Bey, the beer-bellied assistant chief of police, came into the corridor and ushered them into his room. Ka could see at once that they were in the company of a man who did not read national news-papers such as the *Republican*, considering them too left wing; that he was not particularly impressed to see Serdar Bey praising anyone simply for being a poet; but that he feared and respected him as the owner of the leading local paper. After Serdar Bey had finished speaking, the assistant police chief turned to Ka and asked, 'Do you want protection?'

'Pardon?'

'I'm only suggesting one plainclothes policeman. To set your mind at ease.'

'Do I really need it?' asked Ka, in the sort of agitated voice of a man whose doctor has just told him he should start walking with a cane.

'Our city is a peaceful place. We've caught all the terrorists who were driving us apart. But I'd still recommend it, just in case.'

'If Kars is a peaceful place, then I don't need protection,' said Ka. He was secretly hoping that the assistant chief of police would take this opportunity to reassure him once again that Kars was a peaceful place, but Kasım Bey did not repeat himself.

They headed north to Kalealtı and Bayrampaşa, the poorest neighbourhoods of the city. The houses here were shanties made of stone, brickettes and fluted aluminium siding. With the snow continuing to fall, they made their way from house to house: Serdar Bey would knock on a door, and, if a woman answered, he would ask to see the man of the house. If they recognised him, in a voice designed to inspire confidence he would say that his friend, a famous journalist, had come all the way to Kars from Istanbul to report on the elections, and also to learn more about the city; for example, why were so many women committing suicide? If these citizens could share their concerns, they would be doing a good thing for Kars. A few were very friendly, perhaps because they thought Ka and Serdar Bey might be candidates bearing tins of sunflower oil, boxes of soap or parcels full of cookies and pasta. If they decided to invite the two men in out of curiosity or simple hospitality, the next thing they did was tell Ka not to be afraid of the dogs. Some opened their doors fearfully, assuming, after so many years of police intimidation, that this was yet another search; even after they had realised that the visitors were not from the authorities, they would remain shrouded in silence. Every time they moved from one house to the next the number of dwellings seemed to have increased; they had to make their way past children kicking broken plastic cars, one-armed dolls, empty bottles or boxes of tea and medicine.

As for the families of the girls who had committed suicide (in a short time Ka had heard about six incidents), they all insisted that their daughters had given them no cause for concern, and so all were shocked and distressed by what had happened. The two men were shown to old divans and crooked chairs in tiny, icy rooms, with bare, earthen floors or cheap carpets. Sitting next to stoves that gave out no warmth unless stirred continuously or electric heaters that ran off illegal power lines, and silent televisions that no one ever turned off, they heard about the never-ending woes of Kars. They were informed of the high unemployment rate and the suicide epidemic. They listened to mothers who were in tears because their sons were out of work or in jail, and to bath attendants who worked twelve-hour shifts in the hamam but still could not earn enough to support a family of eight. They heard the laments of unemployed men who

could no longer afford to go to the tea-house. These people complained and moaned – about their bad luck, the city council and the
government – tracing their every problem to the nation and the state.

Listening to these tales of hardship, a moment arrived when, in
spite of the white light streaming in through the windows, Ka felt as
if he had entered a shadow world. The rooms were so dark that he
could barely make out the shape of the furniture, so when he was
compelled to look at the snow outside, it blinded him. It was as if a
tulle curtain had fallen in front of his eyes; as if he had retreated into
the silence of snow to escape from these stories of misery and
poverty.

But the suicide stories he heard that day would haunt him for the
rest of his life. It wasn't the poverty, or the helplessness, or the insen-
sitivity that Ka found shocking in these stories. Nor was it the constant
beatings to which the girls had been subjected; or the conservatism of
their fathers, who wouldn't even let them go outside; or the constant
surveillance of jealous husbands; or the lack of money. What shocked
and frightened Ka was the manner in which these girls had killed
themselves: abruptly, without ritual or warning, in the midst of their
everyday routines.

There was one girl, for example, who had been forced into an
engagement with an elderly tea-house owner. She had eaten her
evening meal with her mother, father, three siblings and paternal
grandmother, just as she had done every evening. After she and her
sisters had cleared the table with the usual amount of giggling and
tussling, she went from the kitchen into the garden to fetch the
dessert, and from there she climbed through the window into her
parents' bedroom, where she shot herself with a hunting rifle. The
grandmother heard the gunshot and ran upstairs to find the girl she
had thought was in the kitchen lying dead on the floor in her parents'
bedroom in a pool of blood. The old woman could not understand
how her granddaughter had managed to get from the kitchen to the
bedroom, let alone why she had committed suicide.

There was another sixteen-year-old girl who, following the usual
evening scuffle with her two siblings over what to watch on television, had managed to take possession of the remote control. Her
father came in to settle the matter by giving her two hard whacks.
The girl went straight to her room, found a big bottle of a veterinary
medicine, Mortalin, and knocked it back like a bottle of soda.

13

Another girl, who had married happily at the age of fifteen, had a six-month-old baby. Terrorised by the beatings of her depressed and unemployed husband, she locked herself in the kitchen after their daily quarrel. Her husband knew what she was up to, but she had earlier prepared the rope and the hook in the ceiling, so she was able to hang herself before he could break down the door.

Ka was fascinated by the desperate speed with which these girls had plunged from life into death. The care they had taken – the hooks they had screwed into the ceiling, the rifles they had loaded, the medicine bottles they had transferred from the pantry to their bedrooms – suggested that they had been carrying their suicidal thoughts around with them for some time.

The first stories of such suicides had come from a city called Batman, a hundred kilometres from Kars. All over the world men were three or four times more likely to kill themselves than women. It was a young civil servant in the National Office of Statistics in Ankara who had first noticed that in Batman the number of female cases was three times greater than the number for males, and four times greater than the world average for females. But when a friend of his at the *Republican* published this analysis in 'News in Brief', no one in Turkey took any notice. A number of correspondents for French and German newspapers, however, did pick up on the item, and after they had visited Batman and published stories in their papers the Turkish press began to take an interest: quite a few Turkish reporters travelled to the city. According to officials, the press interest had served only to push more girls over the edge.

The deputy governor of Kars told Ka that the local suicides had not reached the same statistical level as those in Batman. He had no objection 'at present' to Ka's speaking to the families, but went on to ask that Ka refrain from using the word 'suicide' too often when speaking to these people, and that he take care not to exaggerate the story when he wrote it up in the *Republican*. A committee of suicide experts – including psychologists, police officers, judges and officials from the Department of Religious Affairs – was already preparing to move from Batman to Kars. As a preliminary measure, the Department of Religious Affairs had plastered the city with the posters Ka had seen the day before. They proclaimed: 'Human beings are God's masterpieces and suicide is blasphemy'. The governor's office was soon to distribute a pamphlet with the slogan as its title. Still, the deputy governor was worried that these measures might produce the opposite result from the one intended.

'What is certain is that these girls were driven to suicide because they were extremely unhappy. We're not in any doubt about that,' the deputy governor told Ka. 'But if unhappiness were a genuine reason for suicide, then half the women in Turkey would be committing suicide.' The squirrel-faced man with a brush moustache went on to suggest that women might give in to the temptation of killing themselves because of a chorus of male voices – fathers, imams, the state – remonstrating: 'Don't commit suicide!' This, he told Ka proudly, was why he had written to Ankara asking that the Anti-Suicide Propaganda Committee include at least one woman.

The idea that suicide might spread contagiously like the plague had first been suggested after a girl had travelled all the way from Batman to Kars just to kill herself. Her family now refused to let Ka and Serdar Bey into the house, but the girl's maternal uncle agreed to speak to them outside. Smoking a cigarette, seated under the oleander trees in a snow-covered garden in the Atatürk District, he told her story. His niece had married two years earlier. Forced to do housework from morning till night, she had also endured incessant scolding by her mother-in-law for failing to conceive a child. The uncle believed this alone could not have been enough to drive the girl to suicide, so it was clear that she had copied the other women killing themselves in Batman. The dear-departed girl had seemed perfectly happy when visiting her family here in Kars, so it was all the more shocking when – on the very morning she was due to return to Batman – they found a letter in her bed saying that she had taken two boxes of sleeping pills.

One month after the suicide idea had, as it were, infected Kars, the girl's sixteen-year-old cousin committed her own 'copycat' suicide. With the uncle's coaxing, and having secured Ka's promise that he would include the full story in his report, her tearful parents explained that the girl had been driven to suicide after her teacher accused her of not being a virgin. Once the rumour had spread all over Kars, the girl's fiancé called off their engagement, and other young suitors – who had continued to come to the house to ask for this beautiful girl's hand despite the betrothal – stopped calling, too. At that point, the girl's maternal grandmother had started to say, 'Oh well, it looks like you're never going to find a husband.' Then, one evening, as the whole family was watching a wedding scene on television, and her father, drunk at the time, started to cry, the girl stole her grandmother's sleeping pills and swallowed them all (thus, not only the idea of suicide but the method had proved contagious). When the autopsy revealed that the girl had been a virgin, her father blamed not just the teacher who had spread the rumour but also his niece, who had come from Batman and committed suicide. It was out of a desire both to dispel the baseless rumour about their child's chastity and to expose the teacher who had started the malicious lie that the family had decided to tell Ka the full story.

Ka found it strangely depressing that the suicide girls had found hardly any privacy or time even to kill themselves. Even after swallowing their pills, even as they lay quietly dying, they'd had to share their rooms with others. Ka had grown up in Nişantaş reading Western literature, and in his suicide fantasies he had always thought it important to have a great deal of time and space: at the very least you needed a room you could stay in for days without anyone knocking on the door. In his fantasies suicide was a solemn ceremony with sleeping pills and whisky, a final act you performed alone and of your own free will. Every time he had ever imagined doing away with himself, it was the indispensable loneliness of it that scared him off; and so, he had to allow, he had never really been seriously suicidal.

The only suicide who had delivered him back to that loneliness was the covered girl who had killed herself five weeks earlier. This was one of the famous 'headscarf girls'. When the authorities had outlawed the wearing of headscarves in educational institutions across the country, many women and girls refused to comply. The rebels at the Institute of Education in Kars had been barred first from the classrooms, and then, following an edict from Ankara, from the entire institute. Among the families Ka met, that of the 'headscarf girl' was the most well off. The distraught father owned a little grocery store. Offering Ka a Coca-Cola from the shop's refrigerator, he told him his daughter's story. Regarding the headscarf, clearly the girl's mother, who wore one, had set the example, with the blessing of the whole family. But the real pressure had come from her schoolfriends who were running the campaign against the banishment of covered women from the institute. Certainly, it was they who taught her to think of the headscarf as a symbol of 'political Islam'. So, despite her parents' expressed wish that she remove her headscarf, the girl refused, thus ensuring that she would frequently be removed by the police from the halls of the institute. When she saw some of her friends giving up and uncovering their heads, and others forgoing their headscarves to wear wigs instead, the girl began to tell her father that life had no meaning and that she no longer wanted to live. She also discussed her feelings with her friends. But as the state-run Department of Religious Affairs and the Islamists had joined forces by now to condemn suicide as one of the greatest sins, and there were posters all over Kars proclaiming the same truth, no one expected a girl of such piety to take her own life.

The girl, Teslime, spent her last evening silently watching a series called *Marianna*. After making tea and serving it to her parents, she went to her room and readied herself for her prayers, washing her mouth, her feet and her hands. When she had finished her ablutions, she knelt down on her prayer rug, lost herself for some time in thought and prayer, then tied her headscarf to the lamp hook, from which she hanged herself.

3

Give Your Vote to God's Party

Poverty and History

Raised in Istanbul and surrounded by the middle-class comforts of Nişantaş – a lawyer for a father, a housewife for a mother, a beloved sister, a devoted maid, a radio, rooms full of furniture, curtains – Ka knew nothing of poverty; it was something beyond the house, in the outer world. Shrouded in a dangerous and impenetrable darkness, this other world took on a metaphysical charge in Ka's childhood imagination. Although it continued to cast its spell on him in later life, it is still hard to believe that Ka's sudden decision to travel to Kars was motivated even partly by a desire to return to his childhood. Returning to Istanbul after twelve years in Frankfurt, looking up old friends and revisiting the streets and shops and cinemas they'd shared as children, he found almost nothing he recognised. The landmarks that hadn't been torn down, had lost their souls. As for Kars, though he'd been living abroad for over a decade, he was still aware that it was the poorest, most overlooked corner of Turkey. For this reason, Ka may have been taken by a desire to look farther afield for childhood and purity: if the world he knew in Istanbul was no longer to be found, his journey to Kars could be seen as an attempt to step outside the boundaries of his middle-class upbringing, to venture at long last into the other world beyond. In fact, when he found the shop windows in Kars displaying things that he remembered from his childhood, items that you never saw in Istanbul any more – Gislaved gym shoes, Vesuv stoves and (the first thing any child learned about Kars) those round boxes of the city's famous processed cheese divided into six wedges – he felt happy enough even to forget the suicide girls: Kars brought him the peace of mind he'd once known.

Towards noon, once Serdar Bey and he had parted, he met with spokesmen for the People's Equality Party and for the Azeris; and after these interviews were over, he stepped out again into the flurry of snowflakes – how large they were – to take a solitary stroll through the city. Passing the barking dogs of Atatürk Avenue, he moved with sad determination towards the city's poorest neighbourhoods, through a silence broken only by more barking dogs. As the snow covered the steep mountains no longer visible in the distance, covered the Seljuk castle and the shanties that sprawled among the ruins, it seemed to have swept everything off to another world, a world beyond time. When it occurred to him that he might be the only person who had noticed, his eyes filled with tears. He passed a park in Yusuf Paşa that was full of dismantled swings and broken slides; next to it was an open lot where a group of teenage boys were playing football. The high lampposts of the coal depot gave them just enough light, and Ka stopped for a while to watch them. As he listened to them shouting and cursing, and watched them skidding in the snow, and gazed at the white sky and the pale yellow glow of the lamplights, the desolation and remoteness of the place hit him with such force that he felt God inside him.

It was less a certainty than a faint image at this point: like struggling to remember a particular picture after taking a swift tour through a gallery. You try to conjure up the painting only to lose it again. It wasn't the first time Ka had had this sensation. He had grown up in a secular, republican family and had taken no religious tuition outside school. Although he'd had similar visions on occasion over the past few years, they had caused him no anxiety nor inspired any poetic impulse. At most he would feel happy that the world was such a beautiful thing to behold.

When he returned to his hotel room for a bit of warmth and rest, he spent some time leafing happily through the histories of Kars he had brought with him from Istanbul, confusing what he read with the stories he had been hearing all day and with the tales from childhood that these books brought to mind.

Once upon a time in Kars, there had been a large and prosperous middle class, and, although it had been far removed from Ka's own world, it had engaged in all the rituals Ka remembered from childhood: there had been great balls in those mansions, festivities that went on for days. Kars was an important station on the trade route to Georgia, Tabriz and the Caucasus; and, being on the border between two defunct empires, the Ottoman and the Russian, the mountainous city also benefited from the protection of the standing armies each power had in turn placed here for that purpose. During the Ottoman period, many different peoples had made Kars their home. There had been a large Armenian community; it was now gone, but its thousand-year-old churches still stood in all their splendour. Many Persians fleeing first from the Mughal and later the Iranian armies had settled in Kars over the years. There were Greeks with roots going to the Byzantine and Pontus periods. There were also Georgians and Kurds and Circassians from various tribes. Some of the Muslims were driven out when the Russian army took possession of the city's five-hundred-year-old castle in 1878, and thereafter the Pasha's mansions and hamams and the Ottoman buildings on the slopes below the castle fell into decay. Kars was still prosperous and diverse when the Tsar's architects went to work along the southern bank of the Kars River, and soon they had built a thriving new city defined by five perfectly straight parallel avenues, and by streets that intersected these avenues at right angles, something never before seen in the East. Tsar Alexander came here for the hunting – and to meet secretly with his mistress. To the Russians, Kars was a gateway to the South and to the Mediterranean, and, with an eye to controlling the trade routes running through it, they invested a great deal in civic projects. These were the things that had so impressed Ka during his visit twenty years earlier – the streets and the large cobblestone pavements, the plane trees and the oleanders that had been planted after the founding of the Turkish Republic. They gave the city a melancholy air unknown in the Ottoman cities whose wooden houses were burned down during the years of nationalist struggle and tribal warfare.

After endless wars, rebellions, massacres and atrocities, the city was occupied alternately by Armenian and Russian armies; and even, briefly, by the British. For a short time, when the Russian and Ottoman forces had left the city following the First World War, Kars was an independent state; then in October 1920, the Turkish army entered under the command of Kâzım Karabekir, the general whose statue now stood in Station Square. This new generation of Turks made the most of the grand plan initiated by the Tsar's architects forty-three years earlier: the culture that the Russians had brought to

Kars fitted perfectly with the republic's Westernising project. But when it came to renaming the five great Russian avenues, they couldn't think of enough great men from the city's history who weren't soldiers, so they ended up naming them after five great pashas.

These were the city's Westernising years, as Muzaffer Bey, the ex-mayor from the People's Party, related with both pride and anger. He talked about the great balls in the civic centres, and the skating competitions held under the now rusty and ruined wrought-iron bridges Ka had crossed during his morning walk. When a theatre company from Ankara came to perform *Oedipus Rex*, the Kars bourgeoisie received them with great enthusiasm, even though less than twenty years had passed since the war with Greece. The elderly rich in coats with fur collars would go out for rides on sleighs pulled by hearty Hungarian horses adorned with roses and silver tassels. At the National Gardens balls were held under the acacia trees to support the football team, and the people of Kars would dance the latest steps as pianos, accordions and clarinets were played in the open air. In the summertime, girls could wear short-sleeved dresses and ride bicycles through the city without being bothered. Many lycée students who glided to school on ice-skates expressed their patriotic fervour by sporting bow ties. In his youth, Muzaffer Bey had been one of them, and when as a lawyer he eagerly returned to the city to run for office, he took to wearing them again. His party associates warned him that this fashion was a vote-loser, likely to inspire people to dismiss him as the worst sort of poseur, but Muzaffer Bey refused to listen.

Now they were lost, those endless cold winters, and, to listen to Muzaffer Bey, it was as if this loss explained the city's plunge into destitution, depression and decay. Having described the beauty of those winters – dwelling in particular on the powdered faces of the half-naked actors who had come all the way from Ankara to perform Greek plays – the old mayor went on to tell how in the late forties he himself had invited a youth group to perform a revolutionary play in the civic centre. 'This work tells of the awakening of a young girl who has spent her life enveloped in a black scarf,' he said. 'In the end she pulls it off and burns it.' In the late forties they had had to search the entire city for a black scarf to use in the play; in the end they had to phone Erzurum and ask for one to be sent. 'But now the streets of Kars are filled with women in headscarves of every kind,' Muzaffer Bey added. 'And now, because they've been barred from their classes

21

for brandishing this symbol of political Islam, they've begun committing suicide.'

Ka refrained from asking questions, as he would for the rest of his stay in Kars whenever anyone mentioned the rise of political Islam or the headscarf question. He also refrained from asking why it was, if indeed not a single headscarf could be found in Kars in the late forties, that a group of fiery youths had felt compelled to stage a revolutionary play urging women not to cover their heads. During his long walks through the city that day, Ka had paid little attention to the headscarves he saw and didn't attempt to distinguish the political kind from any other; having been back in the country for only a week, he had not yet acquired the secular intellectual's knack for detecting a political motive every time he saw a covered woman in the street. But it is also true that since childhood he had scarcely been in the habit of noticing covered women. In the Westernised upper-middle-class circles of the young Ka's Istanbul, a covered woman would have been someone who had come in from the suburbs – from the Kartal vineyards, say, to sell grapes. Or the milkman's wife, or someone else from the lower classes.

In time I was also to hear many stories about former owners of the Snow Palace Hotel, where Ka was staying. One was a westward-leaning professor whom the Tsar had exiled to Kars (a gentler option than Siberia); another was an Armenian in the cattle trade; subsequently the building housed a Greek orphanage. The first owner had equipped the hundred-and-ten-year-old structure with the sort of heating system typical of so many houses built in Kars at that time: the 'pech' stove was set behind the walls, to radiate heat to four surrounding rooms. It was only when Kars became part of the Turkish Republic, and had its first Turkish owner, that the building was converted into a hotel; but, being unable to figure out how to operate the Russian heating system, that owner installed a big brass stove beside the door opening on to the courtyard. Only much later was he converted to the merits of central heating.

Ka was lying on his bed with his coat on, lost in daydreams, when there was a knock on the door. He jumped up to answer it. It was Cavit, the receptionist who spent his days beside the stove watching television.

'I forgot to tell you when I gave you your key,' said Cavit. 'Serdar Bey, the owner of the *Border City Gazette*, wants to see you immediately.'

Ka was about to exit the lobby when he was stopped dead in his tracks; for just at that moment, coming through the door behind the reception desk, was İpek, even more beautiful than in Ka's memory. He'd forgotten just how stunning she had been during their university days. His heart began to pound. Yes, exactly – that's how beautiful she was. First they shook hands in the manner of the Westernised Istanbul bourgeoisie, but after a moment's hesitation they moved their heads forward, embracing without quite letting their bodies touch, and kissed on the cheeks.

'I knew you were coming,' İpek said as she stepped back. Ka was surprised to hear her speaking so openly. 'Taner called to tell me.' She looked straight into Ka's eyes when she said this.

'I came to report on the municipal elections and the suicide girls.'

'How long are you staying?' asked İpek. 'I'm busy with my father right now, but there's a place called the New Life Pastry Shop, right next door to the Hotel Asia. Let's meet there at half-past one – we can catch up then.'

If they'd run into each other in Istanbul – somewhere in Beyoğlu, say – this would have been a normal conversation. It was because it was happening in Kars that Ka felt so strange. He was unsure how much of his agitation had to do with İpek's beauty. After walking through the snow for some time, he found himself thinking: I'm so glad I bought this coat.

On the way to the newspaper office, his heart revealed a thing or two that his mind refused to accept: first, that in returning to Istanbul from Frankfurt for the first time in twelve years, Ka's purpose was not simply to attend his mother's funeral but also to find a Turkish girl to make his wife; second, it was because he secretly hoped that this girl might be İpek that he had travelled all the way from Istanbul to Kars.

If a close friend had suggested this second possibility, Ka would never have forgiven him; but the truth in it would cause Ka guilt and shame for the rest of his life. Ka, you see, was one of those moralists who believe that the greatest joy comes from never doing anything for the sake of personal happiness. On top of that, he did not think it appropriate for an educated, Westernised, literary man like himself to go in search of marriage to someone he hardly knew. In spite of all this, he was rather content when he arrived at the *Border City Gazette*. This was because his first meeting with İpek – what he had been dreaming of from the moment he stepped on the bus in Istanbul – had gone much better than he could have predicted.

The *Border City Gazette* was on Faikbey Avenue, one street down from Ka's hotel, and its offices and printing facilities took up only slightly more space than Ka's small hotel room. It was a two-room affair with a wooden partition on which were displayed portraits of Atatürk, calendars, sample business cards and wedding invitations (a printing sideline), and photographs of the owner with important government officials and other famous Turks who had paid visits to Kars. There was also a framed copy of the newspaper's first issue, published forty years before. In the background was the reassuring sound of the press's swinging treadle; a hundred and ten years old, it was manufactured in Leipzig by the Baumann Company for its first owners in Hamburg. After working it for a quarter-century, they sold it to a newspaper in Istanbul; this was in 1910, during the free-press period following the establishment of the second constitutional monarchy. In 1955 – just as it was about to be sold off as scrap – Serdar Bey's late father bought the press and shipped it to Kars. Ka found Serdar Bey's twenty-two-year-old son moistening his finger with spit, about to feed a clean sheet into the machine with his right hand while he skilfully removed the printed papers with his left; the collection basket had been broken during an argument with his younger brother eleven years earlier. But even while performing the complex manoeuvre he was able to wave hello to Ka. Serdar Bey's second son was seated before a jet-black table, its top divided into countless small compartments and surrounded by rows of lead letters, moulds and plates. The elder son resembled his father, but when Ka looked at the younger he saw the slant-eyed, moon-faced, short, fat mother. Hand-setting advertisements for the issue due out in three days, this boy showed the painstaking patience of a calligrapher who has renounced the world for his art.

'So now you see the difficult conditions under which we in the Eastern Anatolian press have to work,' said Serdar Bey.

At that very moment, the electricity cut out. As the printing press whirred to a stop and the shop fell into an enchanted darkness, Ka was struck by the beautiful whiteness of the snow falling outside.

'How many copies did you print?' Serdar Bey asked. Lighting a candle, he showed Ka to a chair in the front office.

'I've done a hundred and sixty, Dad.'

'When the electricity comes back on, bring it up to three hundred and forty. Our sales are bound to increase, what with the visiting theatre company.'

The *Border City Gazette* was sold at only one outlet, just across from the National Theatre, and this store sold on average twenty copies of each edition, but, including subscription, the paper's circulation was three hundred and twenty, a fact inspiring no little pride in Serdar Bey. Two hundred of these went to government offices and places of business – Serdar Bey was often obliged to report on their achievements. The other hundred went to 'honest and important people of influence' who had moved to Istanbul but still maintained their links with the city.

When the electricity came back on, Ka noticed an angry vein popping out of Serdar Bey's forehead.

'After you left us, you had meetings with the wrong people, and these people told you the wrong things about our border city,' said Serdar Bey.

'How could you know where I've been?' asked Ka.

'Naturally, the police were following you,' said the newspaperman. 'And for professional reasons, we listen in on police communication, with this transistor radio. Ninety per cent of the news we print comes from the Office of the Governor and the Kars Police Headquarters. The entire police force knows that you have been asking everyone why Kars is so backward and poor, and why so many of its young women are committing suicide.'

Ka had heard quite a few explanations for why Kars had fallen into such destitution. Business with the Soviet Union had fallen off during the Cold War, some said. The customs stations on the border had shut down. Communist guerrillas who had plagued the city during the seventies had chased away the money: the rich had pulled out what capital they could and moved to Istanbul and Ankara. The nation had turned its back on Kars, and so had God. And one must not forget Turkey's never-ending disputes with bordering Armenia . . .

'I've decided to tell you the real story,' said Serdar Bey.

With a clarity of mind and an optimism that he hadn't felt in years, Ka saw at once that the heart of the matter was shame. It had been for him, too, during his years in Germany, but he'd hidden it from himself. It was only now, having found hope for happiness, that he felt strong enough to admit this to himself.

'In the old days we were all brothers,' said Serdar Bey. He spoke as if betraying a secret. 'But in the last few years, everyone started saying, "I'm an Azeri, I'm a Kurd, I'm a Terekemian." Of course, we have people here from all nations. The Terekemians, whom we also call the Karapapaks, are the Azeris' brothers. The Kurds, whom we prefer to think of as a tribe, in the old days didn't even know they were Kurds. And it was that way through the Ottoman period; none of the people who chose to stay went around beating their chests and crying, "We are the Ottomans!" The Turkmens, the Posof Laz, the Germans who had been exiled here by the Tsar – we had them all, but none took any pride in proclaiming themselves different. It was the communists and their Tiflis Radio that spread tribal pride and they did it because they wanted to divide and destroy Turkey. Now everyone is prouder – and poorer.'

When he was confident that his point was not lost on Ka, Serdar Bey moved on to another subject. 'As for these Islamists. They go from door to door in groups, paying house visits: they give women pots and pans, and those machines that squeeze oranges, and boxes of soap, cracked wheat and detergent. They concentrate on the poor neighbourhoods, they ingratiate themselves with the women, they bring out hooked needles and sew gold thread on to children's shoulders to protect them against evil. They say, "Give your vote to the Prosperity Party, the party of God, we've fallen into this destitution because we've wandered off the path of God." The men talk to the men, the women talk to the women. They win the trust of the angry and humiliated unemployed; they sit with their wives, who don't know where the next meal is coming from, and they give them hope; promising more gifts, they get them to promise their votes in return. We're not just talking about the lowest of the low. Even people with jobs – even tradesmen – respect them, because these Islamists are more hardworking, more honest, more modest than anyone else.'

The owner of the *Border City Gazette* went on to say that the recently assassinated mayor had been universally despised. It was not because this man, having decided the city's horses and carriages were too old fashioned, had tried to ban them. (To no avail, as it turned out: once he was dead, the plan was abandoned.) No, Serdar Bey insisted that the people of Kars had hated this mayor because he took bribes and lacked direction. But the republican parties on both the right and the left had failed to capitalise on this hatred: divided as they were by blood feuds, ethnic issues and other destructive rivalries, they had failed to come up with a single viable candidate of their own. 'The only candidate the people trust is the one who is running for God's party,' said Serdar Bey. 'And that candidate is Muhtar Bey, the ex-husband of İpek Hanım, whose father Turgut Bey owns your hotel. Muhtar's not very bright, but he's a Kurd, and the Kurds make up forty per cent of our population. The new mayor will belong to God's party.'

Outside, the snow was falling thicker and faster than ever: just the sight of it made Ka feel lonely. He was also worried that the Western-ised world he had known as a child in Istanbul might be coming to an end. When he was in Istanbul, he had returned to the streets of his childhood, looking for the elegant old buildings where his friends had lived, buildings dating back to the beginning of the twentieth century, but he found that many of them had been destroyed. The trees of his childhood had withered or been chopped down; the cine-mas, shuttered for ten years, still stood there, surrounded by rows of dark, narrow clothing stores. But it was not just the world of his childhood that was dying: it was his dream of returning to Turkey one day to live. If the country were taken over by a fundamentalist Islamist government, he now thought, his own sister would be unable to go outside without covering her head.

The neon lights of the *Border City Gazette* had created a small pocket of light in the night outside. The giant snowflakes wafting slowly through the glow were the stuff of fairytales, and as Ka watched them continue to fall, he had a vision of himself with İpek in Frankfurt: they were in the same Kaufhof where he had bought the charcoal-grey coat he now wrapped so tightly around himself; they were shopping together on the second storey, in the women's shoe section.

'This is the work of the international Islamist movement that wants to turn Turkey into another Iran . . .'

'Is it the same with the suicide girls?' asked Ka.

'We're now gathering denunciations from people who say what a shame it was that these girls were so badly deceived, but because we don't want to put more pressure on the girls, thus perhaps driving more of them to suicide, we haven't yet printed any of the state-ments. They say that Blue, the infamous Islamist terrorist, is in our city; to advise the covered girls, and the suicide girls, too.'

'Aren't the Islamists against suicide?'

Serdar Bey did not answer this question.

When the printing press stopped and a silence fell over the room, Ka returned his gaze to the miraculous snow. The knowledge that he was soon to see İpek was making him nervous. The problems of Kars were a welcome distraction, but now Ka wanted to think only of İpek and to prepare for their meeting at the pastry shop. It was twenty-past one.

With the pomp and ceremony worthy of some precious handmade gift, Serdar Bey presented Ka with a copy of the front page that his huge older son had just printed. Ka's eyes, accustomed to scanning for his name in literary journals, were quick to spot the item in the corner:

KA, OUR CELEBRATED POET, COMES TO KARS

> KA, the celebrated poet whose fame now spreads throughout Turkey, has come to pay a visit to our border city. He first won the appreciation of the entire country with two collections entitled *Ashes and Tangerines* and *The Evening Papers*. Our young poet, who is also the winner of the Behçet Necatigil Prize, has come to Kars to cover the municipal elections for the *Republican*. For many years, the poet KA has been studying Western poetry in Frankfurt.

'My name is printed wrong,' said Ka. 'The "A" should be lower case.' He instantly regretted saying this. 'It looks good,' he now added, as if to make up for his bad manners.

'My dear sir, it was because we weren't sure of your name that we tried to get in touch with you,' said Serdar Bey. 'Son, look here, Son, you printed our poet's name wrong.' But as he scolded his son there was no surprise in his voice. Ka guessed that he was not the first to have noticed that his name had been misprinted. 'Fix it, right now.'

'There's no need,' said Ka. At the same moment, he saw his name printed correctly in the last paragraph of the new lead item.

NIGHT OF TRIUMPH FOR THE SUNAY ZAIM PLAYERS AT THE NATIONAL THEATRE

> The Sunay Zaim Theatrical Company, which is known throughout Turkey for its theatrical tributes to Atatürk, the republic and the Enlightenment, performed to a rapt and enthusiastic audience at the National Theatre yesterday evening. The performance, which went on until the

middle of the night and was attended by the deputy governor, the mayoral candidate and the leading citizens of Kars, was punctuated by thunderous applause. The people of Kars, who have long been yearning for an artistic feast of this calibre, were able to watch not just from the packed auditorium but from the surrounding houses. Kars Border Television worked tirelessly to organise the first live broadcast in its two-year history so that all of Kars would be able to see this splendid performance. Although it still does not own a live transmission vehicle, Kars Border Television was able to stretch a cable from its headquarters in Halitpaşa Avenue the length of two streets to the camera at the National Theatre. Such was the feeling of goodwill among the citizens of Kars that some residents were kind enough to take the cable into their houses to avoid snow damage. (For example, our very own dentist, Fadıl Bey and family, let them take the cable in through the window overlooking his front balcony and pass it into the gardens in the back.) The people of Kars now wish to have other opportunities to enjoy highly successful broadcasts of this order. The management of Kars Border Television also announced that in the course of the city's first live broadcast all of Kars' workplaces had been so kind as to broadcast advertisements. The show, which was watched by the entire population of our city, included republican vignettes, the most beautiful scenes from the most important artistic works of the Western Enlightenment, theatrical sketches criticising advertisements that aim to corrode our culture, the adventures of Vural, the celebrated goalkeeper, and poems in praise of Atatürk and the nation. Ka, the celebrated poet, who is now visiting our city, recited his latest poem, entitled 'Snow'. The crowning event of the evening was a performance of *My Fatherland or My Scarf*, the Enlightenment masterwork from the early years of the republic, in a new interpretation entitled *My Fatherland or My Headscarf*.

'I don't have a poem called "Snow", and I'm not going to the theatre this evening. Your newspaper will look like it's made a mistake.'

'Don't be so sure. There are those who despise us for writing the news before it happens; they fear us not because we are journalists but because we can predict the future. You should see how amazed they are when things turn out exactly as we've written them. And quite a few things do happen only because we've written them up first. This is what modern journalism is all about. I know you won't want to stand in the way of our being modern – you don't want to break our hearts – and that is why I am sure you will write a poem called "Snow", and then come to the theatre to read it.'

Scanning the rest of the paper – announcements of various campaign rallies, news of a vaccine from Erzurum that was now being administered in the city's lycées, an upbeat article describing how the city was granting all residents an additional two months to pay their water bills – Ka now noticed a news item he had missed earlier.

ALL ROADS TO KARS CLOSED

The snow that has been falling for two days has now closed all of our city's links to the outside world. The Ardahan Road closed yesterday morning, and the road to Sarıkamış was impassable by the afternoon. Due to excess snow and ice in the affected area, road closures forced a bus owned by the Yılmaz Company to return to Kars. The weather office has announced that the cold air coming straight from Siberia and the accompanying heavy snowfall will continue for three more days. And so for three days, the city of Kars will have to do as it used to do during the winters of old – stew in its own juices. This will offer us an opportunity to put our house in order.

Just as Ka was standing to leave, Serdar Bey jumped from his seat and held the door to ensure that his last words were heard.

'As for Turgut Bey and his daughters – who knows what they'll tell you?' he said. 'They are educated people who entertain many friends like me in the evening, but don't forget: İpek Hanım's ex-husband is the mayoral candidate for the Party of God. Her father is an old communist. And, to top it all off, her sister, who came here to complete her studies, is rumoured to be the leader of the headscarf girls. There is not a single person in Kars who has the slightest idea why they chose to come here during the worst days of the city four years ago.'

Ka's heart sank as he took in this disturbing news, but he showed no emotion.

Did You Really Come Here to Report on the Election and the Suicides?

Ka meets İpek in the New Life Pastry Shop

Why, despite the bad news he'd just received, was there a faint smile on Ka's face as he walked through the snow from Faikbey Avenue to the New Life Pastry Shop? Someone was playing Peppino di Capri's 'Roberta', a melodramatic pop song from the sixties, and it made him feel like the sad romantic hero of a Turgenev novel, setting off to meet the woman who had been haunting his dreams for years. But let's be honest: Ka loved Turgenev and his elegant novels; and, just like the Russian writer, Ka had tired of his own country's eternal troubles and had come to despise its backwardness, only to find himself gazing back with love and longing after he'd left for Europe. And Ka had not been haunted by İpek, even though in his mind was the vision of a woman very much like her. Perhaps İpek had crossed his mind from time to time, but it was only when he'd heard of her divorce that he'd begun to think of her. Indeed, it was precisely because he had dreamed of her so little that he was now so keen to stoke his feelings with music and Turgenevian romanticism.

But as soon as he entered the pastry shop and joined her at the table, all thoughts of Turgenevian romanticism vanished. For İpek seemed even more beautiful now than she had in the hotel; lovelier even than she had been at university. The true extent of her beauty – her lightly coloured lips, her pale complexion, her shining eyes, her open, intimate gaze – unsettled Ka. He had not expected such a sincere welcome, and he feared his studied composure would fail him. This was the worst of all his fears, save for writing bad poems.

'On the way here, I saw workmen drawing a live transmission cable all the way from Border City Television to the National Theatre. They were stretching it like a clothes line,' he said, hoping to break the awkward silence. But, not wanting to seem critical of the short-comings of provincial life, he was careful not to smile.

It took some effort to maintain the conversation, but they both applied themselves to the task with admirable determination. At least they could both discuss the snow with ease. And when they had exhausted this subject they moved on to the poverty of Kars. After that it was Ka's coat. Then two mutual confessions that each found the other quite unchanged, and that neither of them had been able to give up smoking. The next subject was distant friends: Ka had just seen many of them in Istanbul . . . But it was the discovery that both their mothers were now dead and buried in Istanbul's Feriköy Cemetery that induced the greater intimacy both were seeking. When they subsequently learned that they shared an astro-logical sign, the revelation – illusory or not – produced a *frisson* that brought them closer still. Relaxed now, they were able to chat (briefly) about their mothers and (at greater length) about the demolition of the old Kars train station. They soon turned to the pastry shop in which they were sitting: it had been an Orthodox church until 1967, when the door had been removed and gifted to the museum. A section of the same museum commemorated the Armenian Massacre. Naturally, she said, some tourists came expect-ing to learn of a Turkish massacre of Armenians, so it was always a jolt for them to discover that in this museum the story was the other way around. The next topic was the pastry shop's sole waiter, half deaf, half a ghost. Then the price of coffee, which was no longer sold in the city's tea-houses because it was too expensive for the unemployed clientele. They went on to discuss the political views of the newspaperman who had given Ka his tour of the city, those of the various local papers (all supporters of the military and the pre-sent government) and the next day's issue of the *Border City Gazette*, which Ka now fished out of his pocket.

As he watched İpek scan the front page, Ka was overcome by the fear that, like his old friends in Istanbul, she was so much consumed by Turkey's internal problems and miserable political intrigues that she would never even consider living in Germany. He looked for a long time at İpek's small hands and her elegant face – her beauty still shocked him.

'Under which article did they sentence you, and how long was your sentence?'

Ka told her. In the small political newspapers of the late seventies, they'd enjoyed considerable freedom of expression, much more than the Penal Code allowed. Anyone tried and found guilty of 'insulting the state' tended to feel rather proud of it, and no one ended up in prison, because the police made no serious effort to pursue the convicted editors, writers and translators in their ever-shifting locations. But after the military coup of 1980, the authorities slowly got around to tracking down everyone who'd earlier evaded prison simply by changing his address. It was in this period that Ka, having been tried for a hastily printed political article he had not even written, fled to Germany.

'Was it hard for you in Germany?' asked İpek.

'The thing that saved me was not learning German,' said Ka. 'My body rejected the language, and that was how I was able to preserve my purity and my soul.'

He was suddenly afraid that he was making a fool of himself, but in his delight to have İpek as his audience, he went on to tell her something he'd never told anyone – about the silence buried inside him, the silence that had kept him from writing a single poem for the past four years.

'I rented a small place next to the station; it had a window looking out over the rooftops of Frankfurt. In the evening, when I thought back on the day, I found that my memories were shrouded in a sort of silence. Out of this silence would come a poem. Over time, I gained some recognition in Turkey as a poet, and it was at this point that I began to get invitations to give readings. The approaches came from Turkish immigrants, from city councils, libraries and third-class schools hoping to draw in Turkish audiences, and also from Turks hoping to acquaint their children with a poet writing in Turkish.'

So when he was invited to give a reading, Ka would board one of those orderly, punctual German trains he so admired; through the smoky glass of the window, he'd watch the delicate church towers rising above remote villages. He'd peer into the beech forests, searching for the darkness at their heart. He'd see the hearty children returning home with their rucksacks on their backs, and that same silence would descend on him. Because he could not understand the language, he felt as safe, as comfortable, as if he were sitting in his own house, and this was when he wrote his poems. On days when he wasn't travelling, he'd leave home at eight in the morning, walk the length of Kaiserstrasse, go to the city library on the Zeil and read books: 'There were enough English books there to last me twenty lifetimes.' Here he read magnificent nineteenth-century novels, English romantic poetry, histories of engineering and related topics, museum catalogues. He read whatever he wanted, and he read it all with the pleasure of a child who knows death is too far off to imagine. As he sat in the library turning pages, stopping now and again to study the illustrations in old encyclopedias, rereading Turgenev's novels from cover to cover, he was able to block out the buzz of the city; he was surrounded by silence, just as he was on trains. Even in the evenings – when he would go by another route, walking in front of the Jewish Museum and the length of the River Main – even on weekends, when he walked from one end of the city to the other, this silence still enveloped him.

'Later, these silences took over my entire life. I needed noise. It was only by shutting out noise that I was able to write poetry,' said Ka. 'But now I lived in utter silence. I wasn't speaking with any Germans. And my relations with the Turks weren't good either – they dismissed me as a half-crazed, effete intellectual. I wasn't seeing anyone, I wasn't talking to anyone, and I wasn't writing poems.'

'But it says in the paper that you're going to be reading your latest poem tonight.'

'I don't have a latest poem, so how can I read it?'

There were only two other customers in the pastry shop. They were seated at a table on the other side of the room, in a corner next to the window. One was a tiny young man; his companion, old, thin and tired, was patiently trying to explain something to him. Behind them on the other side of the plate-glass window, great snowflakes were falling into the darkness: the pastry shop's neon sign tinged them with pink. Set against this backdrop, the two men, locked in intense conversation in the far corner of the pastry shop, looked like characters in a grainy black-and-white film.

'My sister Kadife was at university in Istanbul, but she failed her finals in the first year,' İpek now said. 'She managed to transfer to the Institute of Education here in Kars. The thin man sitting just behind me, way in the back, is the director of the institute. When my mother died in a car accident, my father, who adores my sister and didn't want to be alone, decided to move here and bring her along to live with us. But no sooner had my father moved here – this was three years ago – than Muhtar and I split up. So now the three of us live together. We own the hotel with some relatives; it's full of ghosts and tormented dead souls. We take up three rooms.'

During their years in the student left, Ka and İpek had nothing to do with each other. When, at seventeen, he first entered the high-ceilinged corridors of the Literature Department, Ka did not immediately single out İpek – there were plenty of others as beautiful as she. When he met her the following year, she was already Muhtar's wife. Muhtar was a poet friend of Ka's who belonged to the same political group; Kars was his home town, just as it was İpek's.

'Muhtar took over his father's Arçelik and Aygaz white-goods distributorship,' said İpek. 'And once we were settled here, I tried to get pregnant. When nothing happened, he started taking me to doctors in Erzurum and Istanbul, and when I still couldn't conceive we separated. But, instead of remarrying, Muhtar gave himself to religion.'

'Why are so many people turning to religion all of a sudden?' asked Ka.

İpek didn't answer, and for a while they just watched the black-and-white television on the wall.

'Why is everyone in this city committing suicide?' asked Ka.

'It's not everyone who's committing suicide, it's just girls and women,' said İpek. 'The men give themselves to religion, and the women kill themselves.'

'Why?'

İpek gave him a look that told him he would get nowhere pressing her for quick answers. He was left feeling that he had overstepped the mark. They were silent again.

'I have to speak to Muhtar, as part of my election coverage,' said Ka eventually.

İpek rose at once, went over to the cash register, and made a phone call. 'He's at the branch headquarters of the party until five,' she said on returning. 'He'll expect you then.'

As yet another silence fell, Ka began to panic. If the roads had not been closed, he would have jumped on the next bus out of Kars. He felt a pang of despair for this failing city and its forgotten people. Subconsciously, his eyes turned to look at the snow. For a long time, he and İpek watched the snow listlessly, as if they had all the time in the universe and not a care in the world. Ka felt helpless.

'Did you really come here for the election and the suicide girls?' asked İpek.

'No,' said Ka. 'I found out in Istanbul that you and Muhtar had separated. I came here to marry you.'

İpek laughed as if Ka had just told her an excellent joke, but before long her face turned deep red. During the long silence that followed, Ka looked into İpek's eyes and realised that she saw right through him: 'So you couldn't even take the time to get to know me,' her eyes told him. 'You couldn't even spend a few minutes flirting with me. You're so impatient that you couldn't hide your intentions at all. And don't try to pretend you came here because you always loved me and couldn't get me out of your mind. You came here because you found out I was divorced and remembered how beautiful I was and thought that I might be easier to approach now that I was stranded in Kars.'

By now Ka was so ashamed of his wish for happiness, and so determined to punish himself for his insolence, that he imagined İpek uttering the cruellest truth of all: 'The thing that binds us together is that we have both lowered our expectations of life.' But when she finally spoke, İpek didn't say that at all.

'I always knew you had it in you to be a good poet,' she said. 'I'd like to congratulate you on your books.'

The walls of the pastry shop, like the walls of every tea-house, restaurant and hotel lobby in the city, were decorated with photographs of mountain vistas. Not the beautiful mountains of Kars, but those of Switzerland. Stacked on the display counters were trays of chocolates and braided cakes; their oiled surfaces and their wrappings glittered in the pale light. The old waiter who had just served them tea was now sitting next to the till, facing Ka and İpek, his back to the other customers, happily watching the television that hung from the wall. Ka, who was eager to avoid İpek's eyes, gave his full attention to the film on the TV. A blonde, bikini-clad Turkish actress was running across a beach, while a man with a thick moustache chased her. At that very moment, the tiny man who had been sitting at the dark table at the far end of the pastry shop rose to his feet, and, pointing a gun at the director of the Institute of Education, muttered some words that Ka could not hear. He must have fired the gun while the director was speaking, but it made hardly any noise at all. It was only when Ka saw the director shudder violently and fall from his chair that he realised the man had been shot in the chest.

By then İpek had also turned around to watch.

Ka looked over to where the old waiter had been only a moment before, but he was gone. The tiny man, still standing in the same spot, was still pointing the gun straight at the director, who lay still on the ground. The director was trying to tell him something, but with the television turned up so high, it was impossible to make out what he was saying. Moments after pumping three more bullets into his victim, the tiny man made for the door behind him and disappeared. Ka had not seen his face.

'Let's go,' said İpek. 'We shouldn't stay here.'

'Help!' said Ka in a thin voice. Then he added, 'Let's call the police.' But he couldn't move a muscle.

Moments later, he was running behind İpek. As they rushed through the double doors of the pastry shop and down the stairs into the street, they did not see a soul.

On reaching the snowy pavement, they began to walk very fast. 'No one saw us leave,' Ka said to himself, and this brought him some comfort, because now he felt as if it was he who had committed the murder. This was what he got – what he deserved – for proposing to İpek. The mere memory made him cringe with shame. He couldn't bear to look anyone in the eye.

Ka's fears had not abated by the time they reached the corner of Kâzım Karabekir Avenue, but the shooting had given them a secret to share, and he was glad of having even this silent intimacy with İpek. But in the light shining on the orange and apple crates outside Halil Paşa Market and from the naked bulb reflected in the mirror in the neighbouring barber's, Ka was alarmed to see tears in İpek's eyes.

'The director of the Institute of Education wasn't letting covered girls into the classroom,' İpek explained. 'That's why they killed that poor, dear man.'

'Let's tell the police,' said Ka, even as he remembered that once upon a time, when he was a left-wing student, such an idea would have been unthinkable.

'There's no need, they'll find out anyway. They probably know all about it already. The branch headquarters of the Prosperity Party are on the second floor.' İpek pointed at the entrance to the market. 'Tell Muhtar what you've seen so that he won't be surprised when MİT pull him in. And there's something else I have to tell you: Muhtar wants to remarry me. So watch what you say.'

Excuse Me, Sir

*The First and Last Conversation between the Murderer
and his Victim*

When, in full view of Ka and İpek, the tiny man in the New Life Pastry Shop shot him in the head and the chest, the director of the Education Institute was wearing a concealed tape-recorder. The device – an imported Grundig – had been secured to his chest with duct tape by the diligent agents of the Kars branch of MİT, the national intelligence agency. The director had received a number of threats after barring covered girls from classes. When the agents who keep track of fundamentalist activities confirmed that these threats were serious, the Kars branch decided it was time to offer the potential victim some protection. But the director did not wish to have an agent trailing after him like an elephant. Although he identified himself with the secular political camp, he believed in fate just as much as any other religious man did. He preferred to record the death threats, with a view to having the guilty parties arrested later. He had stepped into the New Life Pastry Shop on a whim, to have one of those walnut-filled crescent rolls he loved so much. When he saw a stranger approach, he switched on the tape-recorder, as was now his practice in all such situations. The device took two bullets – not enough to save his life – but the tape survived intact. Years later, I was able to acquire a transcript from the director's widow (her eyes still not dry) and his daughter, who by then had become a famous model.

```
'Hello, sir. Do you recognise me?'/ 'No, I'm
afraid I don't.'/ 'That's what I thought you'd
say, sir. Because we haven't ever met. I did try
to come and see you last night and then again
this morning. Yesterday the police turned me
```

away from the school doors. This morning I managed to get inside but your secretary wouldn't
let me see you. I wanted to catch you before you
went into class. That's when you saw me. Do you
remember me now, sir?'/ 'No, I don't.'/ 'Are you
saying you don't remember me, or are you saying
you don't remember seeing me?'/ 'What did you
want to see me about?'/ 'To tell you the truth,
I'd like to talk to you for hours, even days,
about everything under the sun. You're an emi-
nent, enlightened, educated man. Sadly, I myself
was not able to pursue studies. But there's one
subject I know backwards and forwards. And
that's the subject I was hoping to discuss with
you. I'm sorry, sir. I hope I'm not taking too
much of your time?'/ 'Not at all.'/ 'Excuse me,
sir, do you mind if I sit down? We have a great
deal of ground to cover.'/ 'Please. Be my
guest.' (The sound of someone pulling out a
chair.)/ 'I see you're eating a pastry with
walnuts. We have lots of walnut trees in Tokat.
Have you ever been to Tokat?'/ 'I'm sorry to say
I haven't.'/ 'I'm so sorry to hear that, sir. If
you ever do come to visit, you must stay with
me. I've spent my whole life in Tokat. All
thirty-six years. Tokat is very beautiful.
Turkey is very beautiful, too. But it's such a
shame that we know so little about our own
country, that we can't find it in our hearts to
love our own kind. Instead we admire those who
show our country disrespect and betray its
people. I hope you don't mind if I ask you a
question, sir. You're not an atheist, are you?'/
'No, I'm not.'/ 'People say you are, but I
myself would find it hard to believe that a man
of your education would — God forbid — deny
God's existence. But you're not a Jew, either,
are you?'/ 'No, I'm not.'/ 'You're a Muslim.'/
'Yes. Glory be to God. I am.'/ 'You're smiling,
sir. I'd like to ask you to take my question
seriously and answer it properly. Because I've
travelled all the way from Tokat in the dead of
winter just to hear you answer this question.'/
'How did you come to hear of me in Tokat?'/
'There has been nothing in the Istanbul papers,

sir, about your decision to deny schooling to girls who cover their heads as dictated by their religion and the Holy Book. All those papers care about are scandals involving fashion models. But in beautiful Tokat we have a Muslim radio station called "Flag" that keeps us informed about the injustices perpetrated on the faithful in every corner of the country.'/ 'I could never do an injustice to a believer. I too fear God.'/ 'It took me two days to get here, sir. Two days on snowy, stormy roads. While I was sitting on that bus I thought of no one but you, and, believe me, I knew all along that you were going to tell me that you feared God. And here's the question I imagined asking you next, sir. With all due respect, Professor Nuri Yılmaz — if you fear God, if you believe that the Holy Koran is the Word of God, then let's hear your views on the beautiful 31st verse of the chapter entitled "Heavenly Light".'/ 'Yes, it's true. This verse states very clearly that women should cover their heads and even their faces.'/ 'Congratulations, sir! That's a good, straight answer. And now, with your permission, sir, I'd like to ask you something else. How can you reconcile God's command with this decision to ban covered girls from the classroom?'/ 'We live in a secular state. It's the secular state that has banned covered girls from schools as well as classrooms.'/ 'Excuse me, sir. May I ask you a question? Can a law imposed by the state cancel our God's law?'/ 'That's a very good question. But in a secular state these matters are separate.'/ 'That's a good, straight answer, sir. May I kiss your hand? Please, sir, don't be afraid. Give me your hand. Give me your hand and watch how lovingly I kiss it. Oh, God be praised. Thank you. Now you know how much respect I have for you. May I ask you another question, sir?'/ 'Please. Go right ahead.'/ 'My question is this, sir. Does the word "secular" mean "godless"?'/ 'No.'/ 'In that case, how can you explain why the state is banning so many girls from the classroom in the name of secularism, when all they are doing is obeying the laws

40

of their religion?'/ 'Honestly, my son. Arguing
about such things will get you nowhere. They
argue about it day and night on Istanbul
television, and where does it get us? The girls
are still refusing to take off their headscarves
and the state is still barring them from the
classroom.'/ 'In that case, sir, may I ask you
another question? I beg your pardon, but when I
think about these poor, hard-working girls of
ours who have been denied an education, who are
so polite and so diligent and who have bowed
their heads to God-only-knows how many decrees
already . . . The question I cannot help asking
is: How does all this fit in with what our con-
stitution says about educational and religious
freedom? Please, sir, tell me. Isn't your conscience bothering you?'/ 'If those girls were as
obedient as you say they are, then they'd have
taken off their headscarves. What's your name,
my son? Where do you live? What sort of work do
you do?'/ 'I work at the Happy Friends Tea-
house, which is just next door to Tokat's famous
Mothlight Hamam. I'm in charge of the stoves and
the teapots. My name's not important. I listen
to Flag Radio all day long. Every once in a
while I'll get really upset about something I've
heard, about an injustice done to a believer.
And because I live in a democracy, because I
happen to be a free man who can do as he
pleases, I sometimes end up getting on a bus and
travelling to the other end of Turkey to track
down the perpetrator wherever he is and have it
out with him, face to face. So please, sir,
answer my question. What's more important, a
decree from Ankara or a decree from God?'/ 'This
discussion is going nowhere, son. What hotel are
you staying at?'/ 'What — are you thinking of
turning me in to the police? Don't be afraid of
me, sir. I don't belong to any religious
organisations. I despise terrorism. I believe in
the love of God and the free exchange of ideas.
That's why I never end a free exchange of ideas
by hitting anyone, even though I have a quick
temper. All I want is for you to answer this
question. So please excuse me, sir, but when you

think about the cruel way you treated those poor
girls in front of your institute — when you
remember that these girls were only obeying the
Word of God as set out so clearly in the "Con-
federate Tribe" and "Heavenly Light" chapters of
the Holy Koran — doesn't your conscience trouble
you at all?'/ 'My son, the Koran also says that
thieves should have their hands chopped off. But
the state doesn't do that. Why aren't you oppos-
ing that?'/ 'That's an excellent answer, sir.
Allow me to kiss your hand. But how can you
equate the hand of a thief with the honour of
our women? According to statistics released by
the American Black Muslim Professor Marvin King,
the incidence of rape in Islamic countries where
women cover themselves is so low as to be non-
existent and harassment is virtually unheard-of.
This is because a woman who has covered herself
is making a statement. Through her choice of
clothing, she is saying, "Don't harass me." So
please, sir, may I ask you a question? Do we
really want to push our covered women to the
margins of society by denying them the right to
an education? If we continue to worship women
who take off their headscarves and just about
everything else, too, don't we run the risk of
degrading our women as we have seen so many
women in Europe degraded in the wake of the
sexual revolution? And if we succeed in degrading our women, aren't we also running the risk
of — pardon my language — turning ourselves into
pimps?'/ 'I've finished my roll, son. I'm afraid
I have to leave.'/ 'Stay in your seat, sir. Stay
in your seat and I won't have to use this. Do
you see what this is, sir?'/ 'Yes. It's a gun.'/
'That's right, sir. I hope you don't mind. I
came a long way to see you. I'm not stupid. It
crossed my mind that you might refuse to hear me
out. That's why I took precautions.'/ 'What's
your name, son?'/ 'Vahit Süzme. Salim Fesmekkan.
Really, sir, what difference does it make? I'm
the nameless defender of nameless heroes who
have suffered untold wrongs while seeking to
uphold their religious beliefs in a society that
is in thrall to secular materialism. I'm not a

member of any organisation. I respect human rights and I oppose the use of violence. That's why I'm putting my gun in my pocket. That's why all I want from you is an answer to my question.'/ 'Fine.'/ 'Then let us go back to the beginning, sir. Let's remember what you did to these girls whose upbringing took so many years of loving care. Who were the apples of their parents' eyes. Who were so very intelligent. Who worked so hard at their studies. Who were all at the top of the class. When the order came from Ankara, you set about denying their existence. If one of them wrote her name down on the attendance sheet, you'd erase it — just because she was wearing a headscarf. If seven girls sat down with their teacher, you'd pretend that the one wearing the headscarf wasn't there, and you'd order six teas. Do you know what you did to these girls? You made them cry. But it didn't stop there. Soon there was another directive from Ankara, and after that you barred them from their classrooms. You threw them out into the corridors and then you banned them from the corridors and threw them out into the street. And then, when a handful of these heroines gathered trembling at the doors of the school to make their concerns known, you picked up the phone and called the police.'/ 'We weren't the ones who called the police.'/ 'I know you're afraid of the gun in my pocket. But please, sir, don't lie. The night after you had those girls dragged off and arrested, did your conscience let you sleep? That's my question.'/ 'Of course, the real question is how much suffering we've caused our womenfolk by turning headscarves into symbols — and using women as pawns in a political game.'/ 'How can you call it a game, sir? When that girl who had to choose between her honour and her education — what a tragedy — sank into a depression and killed herself. Was that a game?'/ 'You're very upset, my boy. But has it never occurred to you that foreign powers might be behind all this? Don't you see how they might have politicised the headscarf issue so that they can turn Turkey into a weak and divided

nation?'/ 'If you'd let those girls back into
your school, sir, there would be no headscarf
issue.'/ 'Is it really my decision? These orders
come from Ankara. My own wife wears a headscarf.'/ 'Stop trying to mollify me. Answer the
question I just asked you.'/ 'Which question was
that?'/ 'Is your conscience bothering you?'/ 'My
child, I'm a father, too. Of course I feel sorry
for those girls.'/ 'Look. I'm very good at holding myself back. But once I blow my fuse, it's
all over. When I was in prison, I once beat up a
man just because he forgot to cover his mouth
when he yawned. Oh yes, I made men of all of
them in there. I cured every man in that prison
wing of all his bad habits. I even got them
praying. So stop trying to squirm out of it.
Let's hear an answer to my question.'/ 'What did
you ask, son? Lower that gun.'/ 'I can tell you
what I didn't ask. I didn't ask if you had a
daughter, or if you felt any remorse.'/ 'Pardon
me, son. What did you ask?'/ 'Don't think you
have to butter me up, just because you're afraid
of the gun. Just remember what I asked you.'
(Silence.)/ 'What did you ask me?'/ 'I asked you
if your conscience was troubling you, infidel!'/
'Of course it's troubling me.'/ 'Then why do you
persist? Is it because you have no shame?'/ 'My
son, I'm a teacher. I'm old enough to be your
father. Is it written in the Koran that you
should point guns at your elders and insult
them?'/ 'Don't you dare let the word "Koran"
pass your lips. Do you hear? And stop looking
over your shoulder like you're asking for help.
If you shout for help, I won't hesitate. I'll
shoot. Is that clear?'/ 'Yes, it's clear.'/
'Then answer this question: What good can come
to this country if women uncover their heads?
Give me one good outcome. Say something you
believe with all your heart. Say, for example,
that by uncovering themselves they'll get Europeans to start treating them like human beings.
At least then I'll understand what your motives
are and then I won't shoot you. I'll let you
go.'/ 'My dear child, I have a daughter myself.
She doesn't wear a headscarf. I don't interfere

with her decision, just as I don't interfere
with my wife's decision to wear a headscarf.' /
'Why did your daughter decide to uncover herself? Does she want to become a film star?' /
'She's never said anything of the sort to me.
She's in Ankara studying public relations. But
she's been a tremendous support to me since I've
come under attack over this headscarf issue.
Whenever I get upset about the things people
say, whenever I am slandered or threatened,
whenever I have to face the wrath of my enemies
— or people like you — who have every right to
be angry, she calls me from Ankara and . . .' /
'And she says, "Grit your teeth, Dad. I'm going
to be a film star."' / 'No, son, she doesn't say
that. She says, "Father dear, if I had to go
into a classroom full of covered girls, I would-
n't dare go in uncovered. I'd wear a headscarf
even if I didn't want to."' / 'So what if she
didn't want to cover herself — what harm could
come of it?'/ 'Honestly, I couldn't tell you.
You asked me to give you a reason.' / 'So tell
me, infidel, was this your thinking when you
allowed the police to club these devout girls
who have covered their heads at God's command?
Are you trying to tell me that you drove them to
suicide just to please your daughter?'/ 'There
are plenty of women in Turkey who think as my
daughter does.' / 'When ninety per cent of women
in this country wear headscarves, it's hard to
see who these film stars think they're speaking
for. You might be proud to see your daughter
exposing herself, infidel, but get this into your
head. I might not be a professor, but I know a
lot more about this subject than you do.' / 'My
good man, please don't point your gun at me.
You're very upset. If the gun goes off, you'll
live to regret it.' / 'Why would I regret it? Why
would I have spent two days travelling through
this miserable snow if not to wipe out an infidel? As the Holy Koran states, it is my duty to
kill any tyrant who visits cruelty on believers.
But, because I feel sorry for you, I'm going to
give you one last chance. Give me just one reason why your conscience doesn't bother you when

45

you order covered women to uncover themselves
and I swear I won't shoot you.'/ 'When a woman
takes off her headscarf, she occupies a more
comfortable place in society and gets more
respect.'/ 'That might be what that film-star
daughter of yours thinks. But the opposite is
true. Headscarves protect women from harassment,
rape and degradation. It's the headscarf that
gives women respect and a comfortable place in
society. We've heard this from so many women
who've chosen later in life to cover themselves.
Women like the old belly-dancer Melahat Şandra.
The veil saves women from the animal instincts
of men in the street. It saves them from the
ordeal of entering beauty contests to compete
with other women. They don't have to live like
sex objects, they don't have to wear make-up all
day. As Professor Marvin King has already noted,
if the celebrated film star Elizabeth Taylor had
spent the last twenty years covered, she would
not have had to worry so much about being fat.
She would not have ended up in a mental hospital. She might have known some happiness. Pardon
me, sir. May I ask you a question? Why are you
laughing, sir? Do you think I'm trying to be
funny? (Silence.) Go ahead and tell me, you
shameless atheist. Why are you laughing?'/ 'My
dear child, please believe me, I'm not laughing!
Or, if I did laugh, it was a nervous laugh.'/
'No! You were laughing with conviction.'/
'Please believe me, I feel nothing but compassion for all the people in this country — like
you, like those covered girls — who are suffering for this cause.'/ 'I told you, kind words
will get you nowhere. I'm not suffering one bit.
But you're going to suffer now for laughing
about those girls who committed suicide. And now
that you've laughed at them, there's no chance
you'll show remorse. So let me tell you where
things stand. It's quite some time now since the
Freedom Fighters for Islamic Justice condemned
you to death. They reached their verdict in
Tokat five days ago and sent me here to execute
the sentence. If you hadn't laughed, I might
have relented and forgiven you. Take this piece

of paper. Let's hear you read out your death sentence . . . (Silence.) Stop crying like a woman. Read it out in a good, strong voice. Hurry up, you shameless idiot. If you don't hurry up, I'm going to shoot.'/ '"I, Professor Nuri Yılmaz, am an atheist . . ." My dear child, I'm not an atheist.'/ 'Keep reading.'/ 'My child, you're not going to shoot me while I'm reading this, are you?'/ 'If you don't keep reading it, I'm going to shoot you.'/ '"I confess to being a pawn in a secret plan to strip the Muslims of the secular Turkish Republic of their religion and their honour and thereby to turn them into slaves of the West. As for the girls who would not take off their headscarves, because they were devout and mindful of what is written in the Koran, I visited such cruelty on them that one girl could bear it no more and committed suicide . . ." My dear child, with your permission, I'd like to make an objection here. I'd be grateful if you could pass this on to the committee that sent you. This girl didn't hang herself because she was barred from the classroom. And it wasn't because of the pressure her father put on her, either. As MİT has already told us, she was suffering from a broken heart.'/ 'That's not what she said in her suicide note.'/ 'Please forgive me, but my child, I think you should know — please lower that gun — that even before she got married, this uneducated girl was naïve enough to give herself to a policeman twenty-five years her senior. And — it's an awful shame — but it was after he'd told her he was married and had no intention of marrying her . . .'/ 'Shut up, you disgrace. That's something your whore of a daughter would do.'/ 'Don't do this, my son. My child, don't do this. If you shoot me, you're only darkening your own future.'/ 'Say you're sorry.'/ 'I'm sorry, son. Don't shoot.'/ 'Open your mouth. I want to shove the gun inside. Then put your finger on top of mine and pull the trigger. You'll still be an infidel, but at least you'll die with honour.' (Silence.)/ 'My child, look what I've become. At my age, I'm crying.

I'm begging you, take pity on me. Take pity on yourself. You're still so young. And you're going to become a murderer.'/ 'Then pull the trigger yourself. See for yourself how much suicide hurts.'/ 'My child, I'm a Muslim. I'm opposed to suicide.'/ 'Open your mouth. (Silence.) Don't cry like that. Didn't it ever cross your mind that one day you'd have to pay for what you've done? Stop crying, or I'll shoot.'/ (The voice of the old waiter in the distance.) 'Should I bring your tea to this table, sir?'/ 'No, thank you. I'm about to leave.'/ 'Don't look at the waiter. Keep reading your death sentence.'/ 'My son, please forgive me.'/ 'I said read.'/ '"I am ashamed of all the things I have done. I know I deserve to die and in the hope that God Almighty will forgive me . . ."'/ 'Keep reading.'/ 'My dear, dear child. Let this old man cry for a few moments. Let me think about my wife and my daughter one last time.'/ 'Think about the girls whose lives you destroyed. One had a nervous breakdown, four were kicked out of school in their third year. One committed suicide. The ones who stood trembling outside the doors of your school all came down with fevers and ended up in bed. Their lives were ruined.'/ 'I am so very sorry, my dear, dear child. But what good will it do if you shoot me and turn yourself into a murderer? Think of that.'/ 'All right. I will. (Silence.) I've given it some thought, sir. And here's what I've worked out.'/ 'What?'/ 'I'd been wandering around the miserable streets of Kars for two days and getting nowhere. And then I decided it must be fate, so I bought my return ticket to Tokat. I was drinking my last glass of tea when . . .'/ 'My child, if you thought you could kill me and then escape on the last bus out of Kars, let me warn you: the roads are closed due to the snow. The six o'clock bus has been cancelled. Don't live to regret this.'/ 'Just as I was turning around, God sent you into the New Life Pastry Shop. And if God's not going to forgive you, why should I? Say your last words. Say, "God is great."'/ 'Sit down, son. I'm warning you, this state of ours will catch you all. And hang you all.'/ 'Say, "God is great."'/ 'Calm down, my child. Stop. Sit down. Think it over one more time. Don't pull that trigger. Stop. (The sound of a gunshot. The sound of a chair pushed out.) Don't, my son!'/ (Two more gunshots. Silence. A groan. The sound of a television. One more gunshot. Silence.)

6

Love, Religion and Poetry

Muhtar's Sad Story

After İpek left him at the entrance to Halil Paşa Arcade and returned to the hotel, Ka waited before climbing the stairs to the second-floor branch headquarters of the Prosperity Party. He spent some time mingling with the apprentices, the unemployed and the idle poor who were loitering in the corridors on the ground floor. In his mind's eye he kept seeing the director of the Education Institute lying on the floor in his death throes. Racked by remorse and guilt, he told himself that he should be phoning some of the contacts he'd made that morning – the assistant chief of police perhaps, or someone in Istanbul, or the news desk of the *Republican*. But even though the arcade was packed with tea-houses and barbers' shops, he couldn't find a single place with a telephone.

It was while he was still searching that he went into an establishment whose door bore the sign 'The Society of Animal Enthusiasts'. There was a telephone inside, but someone was using it. And by now he was no longer sure that he even wanted to make a call. He walked through to a hall with pictures of roosters on the walls; in the centre of the hall was a small cock-fighting ring. At this moment Ka realised he was in love with İpek. And, sensing that this love would determine the rest of his life, he was filled with dread.

Among the wealthy animal enthusiasts who enjoyed cock-fights, there was one man who would remember very well how Ka came into the society at that time, sat down on one of the empty benches in the viewing area and appeared to lose himself in thought. He drank a glass of tea as he read the list of sporting rules posted in big letters on the wall:

- No rooster touched without permission of its owner.

- A rooster that goes down 3 times in a row and doesn't peck its beak will be declared a loser.

- Owners may take 3 minutes to treat a wounded spur and 1 minute to dress a broken claw.

- In the event a rooster falls down and his rival steps on his neck, the fallen rooster will be brought back to his feet and the fight will continue.

- In the event of an electricity blackout there will be a 15-minute time-out, by which time, if power is not restored, the match will be cancelled.

When he left the Society of Animal Enthusiasts at two-fifteen, Ka was trying to figure out how he might induce İpek to escape from Kars with him. The lights were out in Muzaffer Bey's office, which Ka now noticed was only three doors down from the Prosperity Party – separated by the Friend's Tea-house and the Green Tailor. So much had happened to Ka since his visit to the lawyer that morning that even as he entered the branch headquarters of the Prosperity Party, he could scarcely believe he was back on the same floor.

Ka had not seen Muhtar for twelve years. After embracing him and kissing him on both cheeks, Ka noticed that he now had a large belly and that his hair was thinning and turning grey, but this was more or less what Ka had expected. Even in their university days, there had been nothing special about Muhtar, and now, as then, one of those cigarettes he chain-smoked was hanging from the corner of his mouth.

'They've killed the director of the Education Institute,' said Ka.

'He didn't die. They just announced it on the radio,' said Muhtar. 'How do you know this?'

'He was sitting right next to us in the place İpek called you from,' said Ka. 'The New Life Pastry Shop.' He told Muhtar exactly what they'd seen.

'Have you called the police?' asked Muhtar. 'What did you do?'

Ka told him that İpek had gone back to the hotel and he had come straight here.

'There are only five days until the election, and everyone knows we're going to win, so the state is knitting a sock to pull over our heads. It's prepared to say anything to bring us down,' said Muhtar. 'All across Turkey, our support of the covered girls is the key expression of our political vision. Now someone's tried to assassinate the wretch who refused to let those girls past the entrance of the Education Institute; and now a man who was at the scene of the crime comes straight to our party headquarters without even stopping to call the police.' Muhtar paused to compose himself, and then added, with some delicacy, 'I'd appreciate it if you called the police right now. Please tell them everything.' He passed Ka the receiver as a proud host might offer an hors d'oeuvre. Once Ka had taken it, Muhtar looked up and dialled the number.

'I've already met the assistant chief of police. His name's Kasım Bey,' said Ka.

'Where do you know him from?' asked Muhtar in a suspicious tone of voice that Ka found irritating.

'He was the first person Serdar Bey, the newspaper proprietor, took me to meet this morning,' said Ka.

Before he could continue, he was connected to the assistant chief of police. Ka told him exactly what he had seen at the New Life Pastry Shop. Muhtar lurched towards him and, with a clumsy gesture that was faintly flirtatious, he pressed his ear up next to Ka's and tried to listen in. To help him hear better, Ka lifted the receiver from his ear and held it closer to Muhtar's. Now they were so close that each man could feel the other's breath on his face. Although Ka had no idea why Muhtar would want to be part of his conversation with the assistant chief of police, his instincts told him that it was best not to ask. After explaining that he had not seen the assailant's face, and describing his build as tiny, Ka took care to repeat the facts twice.

'We'd like you to come right over so that we can take your statement,' said the assistant chief of police in a friendly voice.

'I'm at the headquarters of the Prosperity Party,' said Ka. 'It won't take me long to reach you.'

There was silence at the other end of the line.

'Just a moment,' said Kasım Bey.

Ka and Muhtar could hear him covering the phone and whispering to his colleagues.

'I hope you don't mind, but I've ordered a patrol car for you,' the police chief continued. 'This snow just isn't letting up. We can send a car in a few minutes. They can pick you up from the party head-quarters.'

'It's good you told them that you were here,' Muhtar said when Ka had hung up. 'In any case, they already knew. They have surveillance everywhere. And I don't want them to get the wrong idea about the possibly suspicious things I just said to you.'

A wave of anger swept over Ka: this took him back to his first polit-ical encounters during his bourgeois days in Nişantaş. The game then was to get people to denounce each other as informers. It was the fear of patrol cars – and the fear of being caught in a situation in which he'd be forced to tell the police which houses to raid – that had put Ka off politics for good. Now here was Muhtar, running on the Islamic fundamentalist ticket – something he would have found despicable ten years earlier – and here was Ka, still making excuses for this and so much else. They could almost have been back in school, getting their asses pinched by the bigger boys, turning against each other to avoid being branded as queers.

The phone rang. Muhtar resumed a respectable pose and set about bargaining with someone from Kars Border Television over the price for a commercial for his family's domestic appliance dealership that was to run during that evening's live transmission.

After he had hung up, Muhtar and Ka fell into silence, like two peeved children with nothing to say to each other. As they sat there, Ka imagined their discussing everything that had happened to them during the twelve years since they'd last met. First he imagined each describing what was on his mind: 'Now that we've both been forced into exile, without having managed to achieve much, or succeed at anything, or even find happiness, we can at least agree that life's been hard! It wasn't enough even to be a poet . . . That's why poli-tics still casts such a shadow over our lives.' But, even having said this, neither would find it in him to add what he could not admit even to himself: 'It's because we failed to find happiness in poetry that we have found ourselves hiding in the shadow of politics.' Now Ka despised Muhtar more than ever.

But then Ka reminded himself that Muhtar might have found a little happiness having brought himself to the brink of an election victory, just as he, Ka, had found some having gained a middling reputation as a poet. And a middling reputation was better than no reputation at all. But as neither was ever going to admit to happiness with these things, they could not broach the big subject, the bitter truth that stood between them. The worst of it was that they had both inured themselves to defeat and to the pitiless unfairness of life. Ka was afraid that both longed for İpek just to escape from this defeatist state of mind.

'I hear you're going to be reading your latest poem at the city cinema this evening,' said Muhtar with a barely perceptible smile on his lips.

For a few moments Ka stared fiercely into the beautiful hazel eyes of this man who had once been married to İpek. He could not detect even a trace of a smile in them.

'Did you see Fahir while you were in Istanbul?' asked Muhtar, this time with something closer to a grin.

Now Ka was able to smile with him, and not disingenuously: he respected Fahir. He was a contemporary of theirs, and for twenty years had been a staunch defender of Western modernist poetry. He'd studied at St Joseph, the French lycée, and once a year would dip into the inheritance from his crazy but rich grandmother who was said to have come from the Sultan's harem and head off to Paris. There he would fill his suitcase with poetry collections from the booksellers of St Germain. Back in Istanbul, he would translate them into Turkish, for publication either in the magazines he'd founded or as volumes for the poetry lists of foundering publishing houses. He also secured the same accommodations for his own poems and those of several other Turkish poets in the modernist camp. But while everyone respected him for his efforts, Fahir's own poetry – written as it was under the influence of the poems he'd translated into affected 'pure Turkish' – was generally, at best, devoid of inspiration, or, at worst, incomprehensible.

Ka told Muhtar that he had been unable to see Fahir in Istanbul.

'There was a time when I really wanted Fahir to like my poetry,' said Muhtar. 'Sadly, he despised poets like me who were interested not in pure poetry but in folklore and the "beauties of the home-land". Years went by, the military took over and we all went to prison. And, like everyone else, when I was released I drifted like an idiot. The people I had once tried to imitate had changed; those whose approval I had once sought had disappeared; and none of my dreams had come true, not in poetry or life. So, rather than con-tinue my abject, penniless frenzy in Istanbul, I came back to Kars to take over my father's shop, which had once caused me such shame. But, even with all these changes, I was still not happy. I couldn't take the people here seriously, and when I saw them, I did just as Fahir had done when he saw my poems: I turned up my nose. It was as if the city of Kars and the people in it were unreal. Everyone wanted either to die or leave. But I had nowhere left to go. It was as if I'd been erased from history, banished from civilisation. The civilised world seemed so far away that I couldn't even imitate it. God wouldn't even give me a child who might do all the things I had not done, who might release me from my misery by becoming the Westernised, modern and self-possessed individual I had always dreamed of becoming.'

Ka was impressed by the way Muhtar could occasionally mock himself with a faint smile that seemed to radiate from within.

'In the evenings I would drink, and, to avoid arguing with my beautiful İpek, I would come home late. Once, on one of those Kars nights when everything, even the birds in the sky, seems to have frozen, it was very late and I was the last patron to leave the Green Pastures Restaurant. I was heading towards Army Avenue, where İpek and I were living then, not more than a ten-minute walk away but a long distance by Kars standards. The raki had gone to my head, so I hadn't gone more than two steps before I lost my way. There wasn't a soul on the streets; Kars looked abandoned, as it always does on such cold nights. Even when I knocked on a door there was no answer, either because it was one of those Armenian houses no one's lived in for eighty years or else because the people inside were buried under many quilts and, like hibernating animals, were unwilling to leave the warmth of their holes.

'It pleased me, in a way, to see the whole city looking abandoned and unpopulated. Soon a sweet drowsiness was spreading through my body, thanks to the drink and the cold. I silently decided to leave this life, so I took three or maybe five more steps before stretching out on the frozen pavement under a tree to wait for sleep and death to take me. In a drunken stupor you can withstand that sort of cold for three or maybe five minutes before freezing to death. As the soft drowsiness spread through my veins, I saw before me the child I never had. What a joy it was to see this child, a boy, already grown, and wearing a tie, but his manner nothing like that of our tie-wearing bureaucrats. No, this son of mine was a true

European. Just as he was about to tell me something, he stopped and kissed the hand of an old man. Light radiated from the old man in all directions. At the same moment, a shaft of light pierced the place where I lay; shining right into my eyes, it went straight through me and woke me up. Feeling shame and hope in equal measure, I rose to my feet and looked around. Just across from me, I saw light pouring through an open door as people came and went. The voice inside my head told me to follow them through that door. I was accepted into the group and taken into this bright and warm little house. Inside, the people were nothing like the hopeless and downtrodden folk who populate Kars: they were happy and, even more amazing, they were all from this city. I even knew some of them. I realised now that this was the secret lodge of His Excellency Saadettin Efendi, the Kurdish sheikh. I'd heard so many rumours about him: that he had many disciples in the civil service and also among the wealthy; that the number was growing daily; and that, at their invitation, he had come down from his village in the mountains to perform his rites for the city's poor, unemployed and disconsolate. But, knowing the police would never permit such an anti-republican display, I had paid little attention to these stories. Now, here I was, climbing the sheikh's staircase step by step, tears streaming from my eyes. Something was happening that I had secretly dreaded for a long time, and that in my atheist years I would have denounced as weakness and backwardness: I was returning to Islam. You know those caricatures you see of sheikhs with their long robes and their round-trimmed beards? The truth is that I found them frightening; which was why, as I climbed those stairs of my own free will, I began to cry.

'The sheikh was kind. He asked me why I was crying. Of course, I was not about to say, "I'm crying because I've fallen among reactionary skeikhs and their disciples." I was also deeply ashamed of the raki fumes coming from my mouth like smoke from a chimney. So I said I'd lost my key. I had in fact let my keyring drop in the place where I'd stretched out to die. My declaration led to his sycophantic followers launching into a discussion of the possible metaphorical meanings of "the key", but the sheikh soon sent them all out to look for the actual key. Once we were alone, he smiled sweetly, and I realised that he was the good-hearted old man in my dreams. With that, I relaxed.

'I felt such awe at this august man with his saintly expression that I kissed his hand. Then he did something that shocked me greatly: he kissed my hand, too. A feeling of peace spread through me. I had not felt that way for years and immediately understood that I could talk to him about anything, tell him all about my life. And he would bring me back to the path I had always believed in, deep down inside, even as an atheist: the road to God Almighty. Just the promise of salvation brought me joy.

'Meanwhile, they had found my key. I left, went home and slept, and in the morning I remembered what had happened and felt ashamed. My memories were vague, not least because I didn't *want* to remember any of it. I promised myself I would never return to the sheikh's lodge, but I was worried about what might happen if I were to run into one of the disciples who'd seen me there.

'Then, one night, again on my way home from the Green Pastures Restaurant, my feet took me back to the lodge. And, despite my nightly crises of shame, this kept happening, evening after evening. The sheikh would seat me right beside him; as he listened to my sorrows, he filled my heart with God's love. I kept crying, which made me feel at peace. By day, I would keep the secrets of the lodge by carrying around the *Republican*, the most secular newspaper in Turkey, and rail against the religious revivalists who were taking over the country as enemies of the republic. I'd ask why the Atatürk Thought Association didn't have meetings here any more.

'The double life went on until the night İpek asked me if there was another woman. I burst into tears and told her everything. She cried, too. "Now that you've gone religious, are you going to wrap a scarf around my head?" she asked. I promised her I would make no such demand. And, as I was worried that she might think my change might be due to economic reasons, I was quick to assure her that everything was going well at the store. In spite of all the electricity blackouts, the new Arçelik cookers were selling well. I said all this to calm her down. To tell the truth, I was happy that I would now be able to pray at home. I bought myself a how-to-pray manual at the bookseller's. My new life stretched out before me.

'Soon after that I was filled with inspiration and wrote an important poem. I described the entire crisis, my shame, the love of God growing inside me, the peace, the first time I climbed the sheikh's staircase, even the real and metaphorical meanings of my key. As a poem, it was flawless. I swear to you, it was as good as those fashionable Western poems Fahir translated into Turkish. I immediately posted it to him with a covering letter. I waited six months, but the poem never appeared in his magazine at the time, *Achilles's Ink*. Over that half-year I had written three more poems. Every two months, I had sent them to him. For a year I waited impatiently, but he still didn't publish a single one.

'My unhappiness at this time had nothing to do with our remaining childless, or with İpek's continuing resistance to the teachings of Islam, or even with the taunts of my old secular and leftist friends who made fun of me for turning to religion. Anyway, so many were now doing the same themselves with equal ardour that they scarcely had time to pay much attention to me. No, most upsetting for me was that the poems I'd sent to Istanbul weren't being published. At the beginning of every month, with the appearance of the new issue of *Achilles's Ink*, time stood still. Every time I would tell myself that this month, at last, they would publish a poem. The truths in these poems deserved to stand alongside the truths in Western poetry. In my view, the only person in Turkey who could make this happen was Fahir.

'The injustice of his continuing indifference began to anger me and to poison the happiness I had found through Islam. It got so that I was thinking about him even when I was praying in the mosque. Once again, I was miserable. One night I decided to disclose my sorrow to the sheikh, but he knew nothing of modernist poetry, René Char, the broken sentence, Mallarmé, Joubert, the silence of an empty line. This undermined my confidence in my sheikh. After all, he hadn't been offering me anything new for some time, just "Keep your heart clean, and God's love will deliver you from oppression," and eight or ten other lines like that. I don't want to be unfair, he is not a simple man, it's just that he had a simple education.

'It was at this point that some devil within – half utilitarian, half rationalist – a remnant of my atheist days, began to goad me. People like me find peace only when fighting for a cause in a political party with like-minded people. Which is why I joined this party – I knew it would give me a deeper and more meaningful spiritual life than I had found with the men in the lodge. This is, after all, a religious party, a party that values the spiritual side. My experience as a party member during my Marxist years prepared me well.'

'In what ways?' asked Ka.

The lights went out. There was a long silence.

'The electricity's gone off,' said Muhtar finally in a mysterious voice.

Ka did not answer him. He sat in the darkness, perfectly still.

7

'Political Islamist' Is Only a Name That Westerners and Secularists Give Us

At the Party Headquarters, the Police Headquarters and Once Again in the Streets

It was spooky sitting in darkness and total silence, but Ka preferred it to sitting in a well-lit room and chatting with Muhtar as if they were old friends. Now all they had in common was İpek, and, while one part of Ka was very eager to discuss her, another was just as keen to conceal his feelings. He also feared that Muhtar might tell more stories that would reveal him to be even more stupid than he currently appeared. If that happened, Ka would be forced to wonder why İpek had stayed married to this man for so many years, and he had no wish to discover her unworthy of his devotion.

This was why he relaxed when Muhtar, having become bored of his own story, changed the subject to left-wing friends and political exiles who had fled to Germany. Ka smiled and told him what he'd heard about Tufan, their curly-haired friend from Malatya, who had once written about 'Third World issues' for various periodicals: he'd lost his mind. Ka had last seen him in the central station in Stuttgart, a long pole with a wet cloth tied to the end in his hands, racing back and forth mopping the floor, whistling as he worked. Then Muhtar asked about Mahmut. Never one to mince words, Mahmut had once caused much upset. Ka explained how he had joined the fundamentalist group of Hayrullah Efendi; he now devoted himself to its internal wranglings with the same argumentative fury he had shown as a leftist, except that now his issue was who got to control which mosque. As for the lovable Süleyman, Ka smiled as he told how he had been living off the support of a church charity that had given refuge to many political exiles from the Third World. But, having grown bored of life in the small town of Traunstein, he'd returned to Turkey, even knowing full well he'd be thrown into prison the moment he arrived.

Ka went on to talk about Hikmet, who had died under mysterious circumstances while working as a chauffeur in Berlin; and Fadıl, who had married the elderly widow of a Nazi officer and now ran a small hotel with her; and 'Tarık, the theoretician', who had made a fortune working with the Turkish mafia in Hamburg. As for Sadık – who, alongside Muhtar, Ka, Taner and İpek, had once folded periodicals fresh off the press – he was now running a gang that smuggled illegal immigrants over the Alps and into Germany. Muharrem, the famous sulker, was now living a happy underground life with his family in the Berlin metro, in one of those ghost stations abandoned in the time of the Cold War and the Wall. As the train sped between Kreuzberg and Alexanderplatz stations, the retired Turkish socialists on board would stand to attention, just as the old bandits of Istanbul would salute whenever passing through Arnavutköy, gazing into the swirling waters where a legendary gangster had driven over the edge and perished. Even if they didn't recognise one another, the political exiles standing to attention in the carriage would cast furtive looks about them to see whether any fellow passengers might also be honouring the legendary hero of their secret cause. It was in such a metro carriage that Ka met up with Ruhi, who had once been so critical of his leftist friends for their refusal to engage with psychology. It was also there that Ka learned that Ruhi was now working as a test subject in a study measuring the effectiveness of an advertising campaign for a new type of lamb pastrami pizza marketed to Turkish workers in the lowest income bracket.

Of all the political exiles Ka had met in Germany, the happiest was Ferhat, who had joined the PKK and was now attacking various offices of Turkish Airlines with revolutionary fervour. He'd also been seen on CNN, throwing Molotov cocktails at Turkish consulates. Apparently he was now learning Kurdish and dreaming of a second career as a Kurdish poet.

As for the few others Muhtar asked about, with a strange note of concern in his voice, Ka had long forgotten them. He could only guess that they had followed the path of so many others, who had joined small gangs, worked for the secret service, played some part in the black market, or otherwise vanished or went underground. Some, no doubt, had ended up via quiet yet violent means at the bottom of a canal.

His old friend had lit a match by now, so Ka was able to see the ghostly furniture of the branch headquarters, and once he had located the old coffee table and the gas stove, he stood up and moved to the window, where he gave his rapt attention to the falling snow.

How large the flakes were. Ka found a soothing elegance in their slow, white fullness, which was all the more luminous when a bluish light from an unknown source shone through them. His mind returned to the snowy evenings of his childhood, when storms caused power cuts and all through the house he would hear fearful whispers: 'God save the poor!'. His childish heart would beat faster, and he was very glad to have a family. He watched sadly as a horse and carriage struggled through the snow. In the darkness he could see only the heads of the agitated horses swinging from side to side.

'Muhtar, do you still pay visits to your sheikh?'

'Do you mean His Excellency Saadettin Efendi?' asked Muhtar. 'Yes, I do, every once in a while. Why do you ask?'

'What does this man have to offer you?'

'A little companionship and, even if it doesn't last very long, a little compassion. He's well informed.'

Ka heard not serenity but disillusionment in Muhtar's voice. 'I live a very solitary life in Germany,' Ka said, determined to keep the conversation going. 'When I look over the rooftops of Frankfurt in the middle of the night, I sense that the world and my life are not without purpose. I hear all sorts of sounds inside me.'

'What sorts of sounds?'

'It may just have to do with fear of getting old and dying,' Ka said with embarrassment. 'If I were an author and Ka were a character in a book, I'd say, "Snow reminds Ka of God!" But I'm not sure that would be accurate. What brings me close to God is the silence of snow.'

'The religious right, this country's Muslim conservatives . . .' Muhtar was speaking rapidly, as though willing himself to be carried away by a false hope. 'After my years as a leftist atheist, these people come as such a great relief. You should go and meet them. I'm sure you'll warm to them, too.'

'Do you really think so?'

'Well, for one thing, all these religious men are modest, gentle, understanding. Unlike Westernised Turks, they don't instinctively despise the common folk. They're compassionate and wounded themselves. If they got to know you, they'd like you. There would be no sharp words.'

As Ka had always known, in this part of the world faith in God was not something achieved by thinking sublime thoughts and stretching one's creative powers to their limits; nor was it something one could do alone. Above all, it meant joining a mosque, becoming part of a community. Nevertheless, Ka was still disappointed that Muhtar could talk so much about his group without once mentioning God or his own private faith. More than disappointed, in fact, he despised Muhtar for it. But as he pressed his forehead against the window, something prompted him to say something altogether different.

'Muhtar, if I started to believe in God, you would be disappointed, and I think you'd despise me.'

'Why?'

'The idea of a solitary, Westernised individual whose faith in God is private is very threatening to you. An atheist who belongs to a community is far easier for you to trust than a solitary man who believes in God. For you a solitary man is far more wretched and sinful than a non-believer.'

'I'm a solitary man,' said Muhtar.

The fact that he could say these words with such sincerity and conviction made Ka feel both rancour and pity for him. It seemed to him that the darkness had given them both a certain drunken confidence. 'I know I'm not going to be one, but say I did become the sort of believer who prays five times a day, why would that disturb you? Perhaps because you can embrace your religion and your community only if godless secularists like me are overseeing business and government affairs. A man can only pray to his heart's content in this country because he depends on the efficiency of the atheist who's an expert at managing the West and all other aspects of worldly business.'

'But you're not one of those godless businessmen. I can take you to see His Excellency whenever you like.'

'I think our friendly policemen have arrived,' said Ka.

Through the icy window they saw two plainclothes policemen struggling to get out of a patrol car parked just below, at the entrance to the arcade.

'I'm going to ask a favour now,' said Muhtar. 'In a moment these men are going to come upstairs and take us off to the station. They won't arrest you. They'll just take your statement and let you go. You can go back to your hotel and in the evening Turgut Bey will invite you to supper and you'll join him at his table. Of course, his devoted daughters will be there, too. I'd like you to say the following things to İpek. Are you listening to me? Tell İpek that I want to marry her again. It was a mistake for me to ask her to cover herself in accordance with the sharia. Tell her I'm through acting like a jealous provincial husband; that I'm ashamed and sorry for the pressures I put her under during our marriage.'

'Haven't you already said all of this to İpek?'

'I have, but I got nowhere. It's possible that she didn't believe me, seeing as I'm the district head of the Prosperity Party. But you're a different sort of man. You've come all the way from Istanbul, all the way from Germany even. If you tell her, she'll believe it.'

'As you're the district head of the Prosperity Party, though, won't it cause you political difficulties if your wife isn't covered?'

'With God's permission, I'm going to win the election in four days' time and become the mayor,' said Muhtar. 'But it's far more important to me that you tell İpek how sorry I am. When you do, I'll probably still be behind bars. Brother, could you do this for me?'

Ka had a moment of indecision before saying, 'I'll do it.'

Muhtar embraced him and kissed him on both cheeks. Ka felt a mixture of pity and revulsion; he despised himself for not being pure and open-hearted like Muhtar.

'And I'd be very grateful if you could take this poem to Istanbul and deliver it by hand to Fahir,' said Muhtar. 'It's the one I just mentioned to you. Its title is "The Staircase".'

Ka was putting the poem into his pocket when three plainclothes policemen entered the darkened room; two were carrying huge torches. They were capable and efficient, obviously from MİT, and it was clear from their demeanour that they knew exactly what Ka was doing there with Muhtar. They insisted all the same on seeing Ka's identity card and asking him his business. Ka said once again that he had come to cover the municipal elections and the suicide girls for the *Republican*.

'It's because people like you are writing about them in the Istanbul papers that these girls are committing suicide in the first place,' barked one of the policemen.

'No, it's not,' said Ka stubbornly.

'So what's your explanation, then?'

'They're committing suicide because they're unhappy.'

'We're unhappy, too, but we don't commit suicide.'

While this conversation was going on, they were combing the branch headquarters with their torches, opening cabinets, pulling out drawers, dumping their contents on to tabletops, and leafing through files. They turned Muhtar's table upside down to look for weapons underneath, and they shifted one of the heavy filing cabinets to look behind that. They treated Ka much better than they treated Muhtar.

'After you saw the director of the Education Institute being shot, why did you come here instead of going straight to the police?'

'I had an appointment here.'

'Why?'

'We're old friends from university,' said Muhtar apologetically. 'And the daughter of the owner of the Snow Palace Hotel, where he's staying, was my wife. Just before the incident, they called me and made an appointment. Our phones here at the party headquarters are tapped, so you'll have no trouble verifying this.'

'What do you know about our surveillance operations?'

'I beg your pardon,' said Muhtar without the slightest annoyance. 'I don't know for sure – I was only guessing. Maybe I'm wrong.'

Ka felt a tinge of respect for Muhtar, who had ingratiated himself with the bullying policemen; who was taking their pushing and shoving with equanimity; who, like the rest of Kars, shrugged off the power cuts and the dreary muddiness of the roads.

Having searched every corner of the branch headquarters, over-turned every drawer and emptied every file folder, the policemen bound a sheaf of papers together with string, noting them for the official record, and threw the bundle into a sack. Then they took Ka and Muhtar down to the patrol car.

As they sat in the back with an officer, side by side like a mother and two guilty children, Ka watched Muhtar's huge white hands go limp and fall to his lap. They looked like two old, fat dogs. While the patrol car inched its way through the dark, snow-covered streets, the two men stared miserably at the weak orange lights shining through the half-drawn curtains of old Armenian mansions, at pensioners clutching plastic bags as they struggled down the icy pavements, at the dark, old, empty houses, lonely as ghosts. On the billboard in front of the National Theatre a poster announced that evening's performance. The workmen were still out on the streets installing the cable for the live transmission. The crowds milling around the bus station looked more impatient than ever with the roads still closed.

The snowflakes now seemed as large as the snowstorms Ka had played with as a child. As a police car trundled through the snow he imagined himself inside a plastic dome. Because the driver was taking great care, what should have been a short trip took seven or eight minutes, but in all that time he exchanged only one look with Muhtar. He could tell from the latter's look of miserable resignation that when they reached the police headquarters, Muhtar knew he would get a beating, while Ka himself would be spared.

He read something else into the look Muhtar gave him, and it would stay with him for many years: Muhtar thought he deserved to be beaten. He seemed to be thinking: I deserve this beating not just for insisting on settling in this godforsaken city, but for having succumbed once again to the desire for power. I won't let them break my spirit, but I still hate myself for knowing all this, and so I feel inferior to you. So, please, when you look me straight in the eye, don't throw my shame back at me.

While they didn't separate Ka from Muhtar after parking the patrol car in the inner courtyard of police headquarters, there was nevertheless a marked difference in the treatment of the two men. Ka was a journalist from Istanbul who could, if he wrote something critical, cause them a great deal of trouble, so they treated him like a witness who was there to help them with their inquiries. If they showed any disrespect towards him, he presumed it stemmed only from them wondering what a man like him was doing with a man like Muhtar. But with Muhtar himself, the police's attitude was one of 'Not you again!' Innocently, Ka assumed that Muhtar's ingratiating replies caused the detectives to find him, on the one hand, stupid ('Do you really think they're going to let you take over the country?') or, on the other, confused ('You should get your own life in order first!'). Only much later would Ka learn that the police were implying something much more serious.

Hoping that he might be able to identify the tiny man who had shot the director of the Education Institute, the police took Ka into a side room to peruse an archive of about a hundred black-and-white photographs. Here was every political Islamist from Kars and the surrounding areas who had ever been detained, even once, by the police. Most of them were young Kurds, from the villages or unemployed, but there were also mug shots of street vendors, students attending religious high schools or universities, teachers and Sunni Turks. As Ka looked at photograph after photograph of doleful youth staring miserably into the police camera, he thought he recognised two teenagers from his walk around the city earlier in the day, but he saw no one who resembled the tiny and – from what he could tell from the assassin's back – older man who'd shot the director.

Ka was returned to the interview room, where he found Muhtar hunching on a stool; his nose was bleeding and one eye was shot with red. Muhtar made one or two shameful gestures and then hid his face behind a handkerchief. In the silence, Ka imagined that Muhtar had found redemption in this beating, that it might have released him from the guilt and spiritual agony he felt at the misery and stupidity of his country. Two days later, just before receiving the unhappiest news of his life – and having by then fallen into the same state as Muhtar – Ka would have reason to recall this foolish fantasy.

Moments after reuniting the two men, Ka was removed again to the side room to make his statement. Sitting across from a young policeman who was using the same old Remington typewriter Ka's father had used when he brought work home, Ka recounted the attack on the director. As he spoke, it occurred to him that the police had shown him Muhtar in order to frighten him into telling the truth.

He was released soon afterwards, but Muhtar's beaten face remained in his mind for some time. In the old days, the provincial police weren't quite so ready to beat up religious conservatives. But Muhtar was not from one of those wishy-washy centre-right parties; he was a proponent of radical Islam. Once again Ka wondered if this stance had something to do with Muhtar's personality.

He walked through the snow for a long time. At the end of Army Avenue, he sat down on a wall, and while he watched a group of children slipping and sliding on a side street in the lamplight, he smoked a cigarette. The poverty and the violence he had seen that day had tired him, but he was buoyed by the hope that, with İpek's love, he would be able to begin a new life.

Later, still walking through the snow, he ended up on the pavement across the street from the New Life Pastry Shop. The window was broken and the navy-blue light atop the police patrol car parked out front was flashing. The glow it cast over the people who had gathered around the car seemed almost spiritual, and the falling snow spoke to Ka of a divine patience. When he joined the crowd, the police were still interrogating the old waiter.

Someone tapped timidly on Ka's shoulder. 'You're Ka, the poet, aren't you?' It was a teenage boy with large green eyes and a good-natured, childish face. 'My name is Necip. I know that you've come to Kars to report on the elections and the suicide girls for the *Republican* and you've already met with quite a few people. But there's one more important person in Kars that you need to meet.'

'Who?'

'Could we move a little to the side?'

Ka liked the teenager's air of mystery. They moved in front of the Modern Buffet, with its boastful sign: 'World-famous sherbets and saleps'.

'My instructions are such that I cannot give you the name of the person you need to meet unless you agree to meet him.'

'How can I agree to see someone without first knowing who he is?'

'You're right,' said Necip. 'But this person is in hiding. I can't tell you whom he's hiding from or why unless you agree to see him.'

'All right, I agree to see him,' said Ka. Striking a pose that came straight out of an adventure comic, he added, 'I hope this isn't a trap.'

'If you can't put your trust in people, you'll never get anywhere in life,' said Necip, also striking a pose straight out of a comic-book.

'I trust you,' said Ka. 'Who is this person I need to see?'

'After you find out his name, you'll meet him. But you must also keep his hiding-place a secret. Now think about it one more time. Shall I tell you who he is?'

'Yes,' said Ka. 'You have to trust me, too.'

'This person's name is Blue,' said Necip, his voice full of awe. He looked disappointed when Ka offered no reaction. 'Did you never hear about him when you were in Germany? In Turkey, he's famous.'

'I know,' said Ka in a soothing voice. 'I'm ready to meet him.'

'But I don't know where he is,' said Necip. 'What's more, I myself have never seen him even once in my whole life.'

For a moment they smiled at each other suspiciously.

'Someone else is going to take you to see Blue. My job is to help you make contact with that person.'

They walked together down Little Kâzımbey Avenue, under the small campaign banners and amid the posters. There was something about Necip's wiry body and his nervous, childish manner that reminded Ka of himself at that age, so he warmed to the boy. For a moment, he found himself trying to imagine what the world looked like through Necip's eyes.

'What did you hear about Blue in Germany?' asked Necip.

'I read in the Turkish papers that he was a militant political Islamist,' said Ka. 'I read other nasty things about him, too.'

Necip quickly interrupted him. '"Political Islamist" is just a name that Westerners and secularists give to us Muslims who are ready to fight for our religion,' he said. 'You're a secularist, but please don't let yourself fall for the lies about him in the secular press. He hasn't killed anyone, not even in Bosnia, where he went to defend his Muslim brothers, nor in Grozny, where a Russian bomb left him crippled.'

They came to a corner, where Necip stopped Ka.

'You see that store across the street? The Communication Bookstore? It belongs to the Followers, but all the Islamists in Kars use it as a gathering-place. The police know this, and so does everyone else. Some of the shop assistants spy for them. I'm a pupil at the religious high school. It's against the rules for me to go in there. If I do, I'll be disciplined, but I'm going to let the people inside know you're here. In three minutes, you'll see a tall, bearded young man wearing a red skullcap coming out of the door. Follow him. When you've gone two streets, if there aren't any plainclothes police around, he'll approach you and take you where you need to go. Do you understand? May God be your helper.'

With that, Necip vanished into a cloud of snowflakes. Ka's heart went out to him.

8

Girls Who Commit Suicide Are Not Even Muslims

Blue and Rüstem

Ka stood across the street from the Communication Bookstore. The snowfall was heavier, and by now he was tired of waiting and of dusting snow off his head, his coat, his shoes. He was about to return to his hotel when he looked across the street and in the dim light of the streetlamp saw a tall, bearded youth walking along the pavement. When he realised that the snow had turned the boy's skullcap from red to white, Ka's heart began to race and he set off after him.

After walking all the way down Kâzım Karabekir Avenue – which the mayoral candidate of the Motherland Party, following the new fashion set by Istanbul, had promised to turn into a pedestrian precinct – they turned into Faikbey Avenue and then took the second right into Station Square. The statue of Kâzım Karabekir that Ka had seen earlier in the middle of the square was now buried and looked like a giant ice-cream. In spite of the darkness, Ka caught sight of the bearded youth entering the station; he hurried after him. Finding no one in the waiting hall, he imagined that his guide must have gone out to the platform, so Ka did the same. At the end of the platform, he was just able to see someone moving away in the shadows. Fearfully, he followed him on to the tracks. Just as Ka was considering that, were he to be shot dead here, his body would probably lie undiscovered till the spring, he came face to face with the bearded youth.

'No one's following us,' said the boy. 'Though you can still change your mind. But if you decide to continue, you must keep your mouth shut from here on. You can never tell anyone how you got here. The penalty for treachery is death.'

This threat didn't scare Ka, if only because the youth's high-pitched voice made it sound almost funny.

They continued along the tracks, passing a silo and then turning into Stew Street, which was right next to the military barracks. It was here that the bearded youth with the high-pitched voice pointed to an apartment building and told Ka which bell to ring. 'Don't be insolent to the Master,' he said. 'Don't interrupt him. And when you're finished, don't hang around, just get up and leave.'

This was how Ka discovered that Blue was also known as 'the Master' among his admirers. But it was just about the only thing Ka knew about Blue – aside from his being a political Islamist of some notoriety. He remembered reading in the Turkish newspapers in Germany that, years ago, Blue had been involved in a murder. Still, plenty of Islamic terrorists committed murders, but few of them became famous. Blue's fame derived from the fact that he was held responsible for the murder of an effeminate, exhibitionist TV personality named Güner Bener, on whose quiz show, broadcast on a minor channel, contestants had competed for cash prizes. He'd worn gaudy suits and had a penchant for indecent remarks, favouring jokes about 'the uneducated'. One day, during a live broadcast, this freckled master of sarcasm was making fun of one of his poorer and clumsier contestants when, by some slip of the tongue, he uttered an inappropriate remark about the Prophet Mohammed. It was probably noticed by only a few devout men dozing in front of their televisions, and most would have forgotten the quip a second after they'd heard it, but Blue sent a letter to all the Istanbul papers threatening to kill the host unless he made a formal apology on the next show and promised never to make such a joke again. The Istanbul press receives threats like this all the time and might well have paid no attention, but the television station had such a commitment to its provocative secularist line – and to showing just how rabid these political Islamists could be – that the managers invited Blue to appear on the show. He took this opportunity to make even fiercer threats, and he was such a hit as the 'wild-eyed, scimitar-wielding Islamist' that he was invited to repeat his performance on other channels.

Around this time, the public prosecutor issued a warrant for Blue's arrest on the charge of making a public death threat, so Blue marked his first burst of celebrity by going into hiding. Meanwhile, Güner Bener, whose own profile had mushroomed alongside Blue's, appeared on his daily live TV show to defy would-be assassins, proclaiming on one occasion with unexpected vehemence that he was 'not afraid of Atatürk-hating, anti-republican perverts'. The next day, in his luxury hotel room in Izmir where he stayed when making the show, the police found him strangled with the same loud tie festooned with beachballs he'd been wearing during the broadcast.

Blue had an alibi – he'd been attending a conference in Manisa in support of the headscarf girls – but he stayed in hiding to avoid the press, which by now had made sure that the whole country knew about the incident and Blue's part in it. Some of the Islamist press were as critical as the secularists. They accused Blue of 'bloodying the hands' of political Islam, of allowing himself to become the plaything of the secularist press, of enjoying his media fame in a manner unbefitting a Muslim, of being in the pay of the CIA. This may explain why Blue had stayed underground ever since.

Soon tales spread in Islamist circles that Blue had gone to Bosnia to fight the Serbs and had been heroically wounded fighting the Russians in Grozny, but there were also those who claimed that these rumours were false. Those who are interested in Blue's own version of these matters might like to consult his short autobiography, *My Execution*. Details can be found on the fifth page of the book's thirty-fifth chapter, 'I'm Not an Agent for Anyone', subtitled 'Ka with Blue in His Cell', though it is impossible to know how much of what is written there is true.

Many lies were certainly told about Blue. The fact is that some of them fed his legend, and it could be said that Blue was nourished by his own mysterious reputation. It was also suggested that, by his later silence, Blue had tacitly agreed with all the barbs he attracted in some Islamist circles for his proclamations. Many would even suggest that a Muslim appearing so much in the secularist, Zionist, bourgeois media had got exactly what he deserved.

As for why he was in Kars, as is so often the case with rumours in small towns, the theories spread fast but just didn't add up. Some said he had come to shore up the local operations of a Kurdish Islamist group: with the government having crushed the Diyarbakır-based national operations centre, Blue, it was said, had been dispatched to Kars to 'secure the organisation's secrets'. Others discounted this theory, as the faction in question had no members in Kars, apart from one or two raving lunatics.

Some said Blue had come to repair relations between the Marxist revolutionary Kurds and the Islamist Kurds. There was increasing conflict between them in the cities of the East and, according to this rumour, Blue was trying to create an atmosphere of peaceful, well-behaved militancy. The tension between the Islamist Kurds and the Marxist revolutionary Kurds had begun with violent arguments, exchanges of insults, beatings and street fights, but then in many cities matters had escalated to knifings and attacks with meat cleavers. In recent months, partisans had been shooting one another, taking hostages and interrogating them under torture (with both sides using familiar methods such as pouring melted plastic on to a prisoner's skin or squeezing his testicles). There were also reports of strangulations. It was said that a secret group of mediators who believed this factional conflict was playing into the hands of the state had formed. In a bid to end the war, they had dispatched Blue as their emissary, but, according to his enemies, his black past and relative youth disqualified him from such an important mission.

Among the other rumours, spread by young Islamists, was one that he had come to Kars to 'straighten out' Hakan Özge, Kars Border Television's camp, boyish, shiny-suit-wearing presenter, who had been making mischievous jokes and sly insinuations about Islam, and who now continually referred to God and prayer-time on his programme. Others still imagined that Blue was a go-between for an international Islamist terrorist ring. It was said that the Kars intelligence and security units were taking seriously the rumours about this Saudi-backed network that supposedly planned to murder some of the thousands of women who were pouring into Turkey from the old Soviet Union to work as prostitutes.

Blue had done nothing to deny any of the rumours. His refusal to respond to what was said about him, coupled with his determination to remain in hiding, gave him an air of mystery that appealed to the students at the religious high school and the young in general. He wasn't just hiding from the police: he stayed off the streets to boost his legend, and it suited him to keep people guessing whether he was in their city.

Ka rang the doorbell that the youth with the skullcap had indicated. When the door opened, he immediately recognised the short man who welcomed him inside as the one who had shot the director of the Education Institute at the New Life Pastry Shop. Ka's heart began to beat faster.

'I hope you won't take offence,' said the small man, raising his arms in the air, as a prompt for his guest to do likewise. 'Over the past two years they've made three attempts to assassinate the Master, so I'm going to have to frisk you.'

Ka held out his arms to be searched – it took him back to his university days. As the little man's little hands passed carefully over his shirt, Ka was afraid that he would notice how fast his heart was beating. But once the search was over, Ka felt calmer and his heartbeat returned to normal. Now he realised that this was not in fact the assassin. This pleasant, middle-aged man, who rather resembled Edward G. Robinson, seemed neither decisive nor strong enough to shoot anyone.

Ka heard the sobs of a baby and the sweet sound of a mother tenderly trying to comfort it.

'Shall I take off my shoes?' he asked, and removed them without waiting for an answer.

'We're guests here,' said a second voice. 'We don't want to be a burden to our hosts.'

Although Ka knew at once that the voice belonged to Blue, a part of him was confused, perhaps because he had expected the meeting to be far more carefully staged. He followed Blue into a sparsely furnished room, where a black-and-white television set was on. Here, a tiny infant, his fist in his mouth, was staring with happy and deeply serious eyes at his mother, who was changing him and whispering sweetly in Kurdish. The baby's eyes then fixed on Blue and Ka as they entered the room. But they weren't staying: they continued on to an adjoining room.

Ka's mind was on Blue. He saw a bed made so well that it would have passed military inspection, and a pair of striped pyjamas neatly folded beside the pillow. Sitting on the bed was an ashtray inscribed 'Ersin Electric', and on the wall a calendar showing scenes of Venice. There was a large window giving a view of the melancholic lights of the snow-covered city. Blue closed the shutters and turned to face Ka.

His eyes were deep blue – almost midnight blue – a colour you never saw in a Turk. He was brown-haired and beardless, much younger than Ka had expected; he had an aquiline nose and breathtakingly pale skin. He was also extraordinarily handsome, his gracefulness born of self-confidence. In his manner, expression and appearance, there was nothing of the truculent, bearded, provincial fundamentalist whom the secular press had depicted with a gun in one hand and a string of prayer beads in the other.

'Please don't remove your coat until the room has warmed up. It's a beautiful coat. Where did you buy it?'

'In Frankfurt.'

'Frankfurt . . . Frankfurt,' Blue murmured, and he lifted his eyes to the ceiling and lost himself in thought.

He explained that 'some time ago' he had been found guilty under Article 163 of the Penal Code of promoting the establishment of a state based on religious principles and had for that reason escaped to Germany.

Ka did not reply. He knew that he should take this opportunity to establish a cordial relationship, so when his mind went blank, he began to panic. He sensed that Blue was talking to calm himself.

'When I was in Germany, at whatever Muslim association I happened to be visiting, in whatever city – it could be Frankfurt, or Cologne, somewhere between the cathedral and the station, or in one of the wealthy neighbourhoods of Hamburg – wherever I happened to be walking, there was always one German who stood out from the crowd as an object of fascination for me. The important thing was not what I thought of him, but what I thought *he* might be thinking about *me*. I'd try to see through his eyes and imagine what he might be thinking about my appearance, my clothes, the way I moved, my history, where I had just been and where I was going, who I was. It made me feel terrible but it became a habit. I grew used to feeling degraded and I came to understand how my brothers felt. Most of the time it's not the Europeans who belittle us. What happens when we look at them is that we belittle ourselves. When we undertake the pilgrimage, it's not just to escape the tyranny at home, but to reach to the depths of our souls. The day arrives when the guilty must return to save those who could not find the courage to leave. Why did *you* come back?'

Ka remained silent. The threadbare room, with its unpainted walls and its flaking plaster, did not invite confidences; nor did the naked bulb that hung from the ceiling, its light piercing his eyes.

'I don't want to bore you with questions,' said Blue. 'When the dear-departed Mullah Kasım Ensari received visitors at his tribal encampment on the banks of the Tigris River, this was always the first thing he'd say: "I'm very glad to meet you, sir, and now would you tell me who you're spying for?"'

'I'm spying for the *Republican*,' said Ka.

'That much I know. But I still have to ask why they're so interested in Kars as to have taken the trouble to send someone all the way out here.'

'I volunteered. I'd also heard that my old friend Muhtar and his wife were living here.'

'But they've separated,' Blue corrected him, looking straight into Ka's eyes. 'Hadn't you heard?'

'I had heard,' said Ka. He blushed. Thinking of everything that Blue must be noticing right then, Ka hated him.

'Did they beat Muhtar at the police station?'

'Yes, they did.'

'Did he deserve to be beaten?' asked Blue suggestively.

'No, of course he didn't,' replied Ka angrily.

'And why didn't they beat you? Are you pleased with yourself?'

'I have no idea why they didn't beat me.'

'Of course you know why – you belong to the Istanbul bourgeoisie. Anyone can tell, just by looking at your skin and the way you hold yourself. "He must have friends in high places" – that's what they said to one another, there's no doubt about it. As for Muhtar, one look and you know he has no connections, no importance whatsoever. In fact, Muhtar only went into politics in the first place so that he could stand up to those people in the same way you can. But even if he wins the election, to take office he still has to prove to them that he's the sort of person who can take a beating from the state. That's why he was probably glad to be given a beating.' Blue was not smiling; his expression was even sad.

'No one can be happy about a beating,' said Ka, feeling ordinary and superficial next to Blue.

Blue's expression said: Let's move on to the subject we're really here to discuss. 'You've been meeting with the families of the girls who committed suicide,' he said. 'Why did you want to talk to them?'

'To research an article.'

'For newspapers in the West?'

'Yes, for newspapers in the West,' said Ka, with a certain pride, even though he had no contacts in the German press. 'And also in Turkey, for the *Republican*,' he added with embarrassment.

'The Turkish press is interested in this country's troubles only if the Western press takes an interest first,' said Blue. 'Otherwise it's offensive to discuss poverty and suicide. They talk about these things as if they happen in a land beyond the civilised world. Which means that you, too, will be forced to publish your article in Europe. This is why I wanted to meet you: you are not to write about the suicide girls for a Turkish paper or for a European paper! Suicide is a terrible sin! It's an illness that grows the more you focus on it! Particularly this most recent case. If you write that she was a Muslim girl making a political statement about headscarves, it will be more lethal for you than poison.'

'But it's true,' said Ka. 'Before she committed suicide, this girl did her ritual ablutions and then said her prayers. I understand that the headscarf girls have a lot of respect for her because she did that.'

'Girls who commit suicide are not even Muslims,' shouted Blue. 'And it's wrong to say they're taking a stand over headscarves. If you publish lies like this, you'll only spread more rumours – about quarrels among the headscarf girls, about the poor souls who have resorted to wearing wigs, about how they've been destroyed by the pressure put on them by the police and their parents. Is that what you came here for? To encourage more poor girls to commit suicide? These girls who for the love of God find themselves caught between their schools and their families are so miserable and so alone that they see no course of action but to imitate the suicidal martyrs.'

'The deputy governor said that the Kars suicides have been exaggerated.'

'Why did you meet the deputy governor?'

'For the same reason I went to see the police: so that they wouldn't feel obliged to follow me around all day.'

'When they heard the news that "the covered girls thrown out of school are committing suicide" they were very pleased,' said Blue.

'I will write things as I see them,' said Ka.

'Your insinuation is directed not just against the state and the deputy governor, but against me. When you say, "Neither the secular governor nor the political Islamists want anything written about the suicide girls," I know you're trying to provoke me.'

'Yes, I am.'

'That girl didn't kill herself because they threw her out of school. She killed herself over a love affair. But if you write that a covered girl killed herself – sinned against God – all on account of a broken heart, the boys at the religious high school will be furious. Kars is a small town.'

'I was hoping to discuss all this with the girls themselves.'

'Fine,' said Blue. 'Why don't you ask these girls whether they'd like you to write in the German press about their sisters who, having stood up for the right to cover their heads, were so devastated by the repercussions that they departed this world in a state of sin.'

'I'd be more than happy to ask them,' said Ka stubbornly, even as he was beginning to feel afraid.

'I had another reason for inviting you here,' said Blue. 'A few hours ago, you witnessed the shooting of the director of the Education Institute. This was a direct result of the anger of our believers over the cruelty that the state has visited on our covered girls. But, of course, the whole thing is a state plot. First they used this poor director to enforce their cruel measures; then they incited some madman to try to kill him so that they could pin the blame on the Muslims.'

'Are you claiming responsibility or are you condemning the attack?' asked Ka, sharply, as if he really were a journalist.

'I haven't come to Kars for political reasons,' said Blue. 'I came, perhaps, to stop this suicide epidemic.' Suddenly he put his hands on Ka's shoulders, pulled him close, and kissed him on both cheeks. 'You are a modern-day dervish. You've withdrawn from the world to devote yourself to poetry. You would never want to be the pawn of those who would denigrate innocent Muslims. Just as I've decided to trust you, you've decided to trust me – and you came through all this snow that we might meet. Now, to show my gratitude, I'm going to tell you a morality tale.' Again he looked Ka straight in the eye. 'Shall I tell you this story?'

'Tell me the story.'

'Long, long ago, there was a tireless warrior of unequalled bravery who lived in Iran. Everyone who knew him loved him. They called him Rüstem, and so shall we. One day, while hunting, he lost his way. Then, as he slept in his camp that same night, he lost his horse, Raksh. While he was looking for Raksh, Rüstem wandered into Turan, with whom Iran was at war. But, because his reputation preceded him, the locals treated him well. The Shah of Turan welcomed him as a guest and arranged a feast in his honour. After the feast, the Shah's daughter paid Rüstem a visit in his room to proclaim her love for him. She told him that she wished to have his child, seduced him with her beauty and her fine words, and before long they were making love. The following morning, Rüstem returned to his own country, but he left a token – a wristband – for his future child.

'When the child was born, they called him Suhrab, so let's call him that, too. Years later, his mother told him that his father was none other than the legendary Rüstem, and the boy said, "I'm going to Iran to depose the wicked Shah Keykavus and install my father as his successor. Then I'll return to Turan and do exactly the same thing to the wicked Shah Efrasiyab. And when I've done that, I'll install myself as *his* successor. Then my father and I will bring just rule to Iran and Turan, in other words to the entire universe!"

'So said the pure and good-hearted Suhrab, little knowing that his enemies were far more cunning and sly than he. For while Efrasiyab, the Shah of Turan, lent his support to the war with Iran, he also placed spies in the army to make sure Suhrab wouldn't recognise his father. After many tricks and ruses, and cruel twists of fate and coincidence (engineered, for all he knew, by the Sublime Almighty), the day arrived when Rüstem and his son Suhrab came face to face on the battlefield, each with his army behind him. Neither could have known the other's face, and they were covered from head to toe in armour anyway. Rüstem of course wanted to remain anonymous inside his armour, otherwise he knew that this hero facing him would unleash the full fury of his force against him in particular. As for Suhrab, his childish heart allowed him only one vision – that of his father on the throne of Iran – so he never even stopped to wonder who his adversary might be. So it came to pass that these two great and good-hearted warriors who were father and son stood before their respective armies, strode forward and drew their swords.'

Blue paused. Before looking into Ka's eyes, he added in a childish voice: 'Although I've read this story hundreds of times, I always shudder when I get to this part, and my heart starts to pound. I don't know why, but for some reason I identify with Suhrab as he prepares to kill his father. Who would want to kill his own father? What soul could bear the pain of that crime, the weight of that sin? Especially Suhrab, with his innocent heart. The only hope at this point is that Suhrab will kill his foe without discovering his identity.

'As these thoughts pass through my mind, the two warriors begin to fight, and in a struggle that goes on for hours neither is able to better the other. Soaked and exhausted, they sheathe their swords. When we come to the evening of this first day of the battle, I'm as troubled for the father as I am for Suhrab, and when I continue the story, it's as if I'm reading it for the first time. I dare to dream that father and son will be unable to kill each other and will find some way out of their predicament.

'On the second day, the two armies line up once more, and once again father and son face each other in their armour and engage in merciless combat. After a long struggle, luck smiles on Suhrab – but can we even call this luck? – and he throws Rüstem off his horse and pins him to the ground. He takes out his dagger but, as he prepares to bring it down on his father's neck, his lieutenants say: "In Iran, it is not the tradition for enemy heroes to take away a head on the first occasion. Don't kill him – that would be too crude." So Suhrab does not kill his father.

'When I read this part, I become very confused. I'm full of love for Suhrab. What fate has God arranged for this father and his son?

'The third day of the battle is one I have awaited with great trepidation, but, against all my expectations, it's over in a moment. Rüstem knocks Suhrab off his horse and, leaping forward, plunges his sword into him and kills him. The speed of the event is horrifying, shocking. Then he sees the wristband and realises he has killed his own son. Rüstem kneels down, takes his son's bloody corpse on to his lap and weeps.

'At this point in the story, I always cry, too, not just because I share Rüstem's grief, but because I now understand the meaning of Suhrab's death: it is Suhrab's love for his father that kills him. But now I move beyond the childish and good-hearted love Suhrab felt for his beloved father. What I feel most acutely now is the deeper and far more dignified anguish of the father as he struggles to honour both his son and the codes that define him. My sympathies, which throughout have been with the rebellious and individualistic Suhrab, transfer to Rüstem, the strong, responsible father who is his own man.'

Blue paused for a moment, and Ka felt very jealous of his ability to tell this story, or indeed any story, with such conviction.

'But I didn't tell you this beautiful story to show you what it means to me, or how I relate it to my life. I told it to point out that this thousand-year-old story, which comes from Firdevsi's *Shehname*, is now forgotten,' said Blue. 'Once upon a time, millions of people knew it by heart – from Tabriz to Istanbul, from Bosnia to Trabzon – and when they recalled this story, they found the meaning in their lives. The story spoke to them in just the same way that Oedipus' murder of his father and Macbeth's obsession with power and death speak to people throughout the Western world. But now, because we've fallen under the spell of the West, we've forgotten our own stories. They've removed all the old stories from our children's textbooks. These days, you can't find a single bookseller who stocks the *Shehname* in all of Istanbul! How do you explain that?'

Ka didn't reply.

'Let me guess what you're thinking,' said Blue. 'Is this story so beautiful that a man could kill for it? That's what you're thinking, isn't it?'

'I don't know,' said Ka.

'Then think about it,' said Blue, and he left the room.

9

Are You an Atheist?

A Non-Believer Who Does Not Want to Kill Himself

After Blue left the room, Ka was unsure what to do. At first he thought Blue would return to quiz him on his 'thoughts'. But it soon dawned on him that he had misread this man. In his posturing, insinuating way, Blue had given him a message. Or was it a threat?

In either case, it wasn't danger that Ka felt as he sat waiting for Blue, but rather a sense of not belonging there. The room in which he had seen the mother and the baby was now empty; so, too, was the entrance hall. As he closed the front door behind him, he felt so unwelcome that it was all he could do not to run down the stairs.

When he looked up at the sky, Ka's first thought was that the snowflakes were no longer descending: as he watched them seem to hover in midair, it was as if time itself had stopped. It also seemed that much had changed and a great deal of time had elapsed while he'd been inside. But Ka's meeting with Blue had lasted only twenty minutes.

He made his way back along the railway tracks, past the snow-covered silo that loomed like a great white cloud, and was soon back inside the station. As he passed through the filthy concourse, he saw a black dog wagging its curly tail in a friendly way. Then, in the dirty waiting hall, he saw three teenage boys. One of them was Necip, who broke away from his friends and ran towards Ka.

'On no account are you to let my classmates know how I knew you'd be coming through here,' he said. 'My best friend has a very important question to ask you. If you can give Fazıl a moment of your time, he'll be very happy.'

'All right,' said Ka, and he walked over to the bench where the other two teenagers were sitting.

One poster on the wall behind them urgently reminded travellers how important the railroads had been for Atatürk; another sought to strike fear in the heart of any girl contemplating suicide. The boys rose to their feet to shake Ka's hand, but then shyness overtook them.

'Before Fazıl asks his question, Mesut would like to tell you a story he's heard,' said Necip.

'No, I can't tell it myself,' said Mesut, hardly able to contain his excitement. 'Please, could you tell it for me?'

While Necip told the story, Ka's eyes strayed to the black dog frolicking in the shadows of the filthy station.

'The story takes place in a religious high school in Istanbul, or that's what I heard,' Necip began. 'A typically slapdash place in one of those suburbs on the edge of the city. The director of this school had an appointment with a city official in one of those new Istanbul skyscrapers that we've seen on television. He got into an enormous lift and began to go up. There was another man in the lift – a tall man, younger than he. This man showed the director the book in his hand, and, as some of the pages in the book were still uncut, he took out a knife with a mother-of-pearl handle while he recited a few lines. When the lift stopped on the nineteenth floor, the director got out and attended his meeting.

'However, in the days that followed, he began to feel very strange. He became obsessed with death, couldn't find the will to do anything and couldn't stop thinking about the man in the lift. The director was a devout man, so he went to a Cerrahi lodge in the hope of finding solace and guidance. He sat there until morning, pouring out all his woes. After he had done this, the celebrated sheikh made the following diagnosis: "It seems you've lost your faith in God," he said. "What's worse, you don't even know it. And, as if that isn't bad enough, you're even proud of not knowing it! You contracted this disease from the man in the lift. He's turned you into an atheist." The director rose to his feet in tears to deny what the sheikh had said, but there was still a part of his heart that was pure and honest, and this part assured him that the illustrious sheikh was telling the truth.

'Infected by the disease of atheism, he began to put unreasonable pressure on his lovely little pupils: he tried to spend time alone with their mothers; he stole money from another teacher whom he envied. And the worst of it was that he felt proud for having committed these sins. He would assemble the whole school to accuse them of blind faith; he told them that their traditions made no sense and asked why they couldn't be free, as he was; he couldn't utter a sentence without stuffing it with French words; he spent all the money he had stolen on all the latest European fashions. And wherever he went, he made sure to let people know how much he despised them for being "backward".

'Before long, the school descended into anarchy: one group of pupils raped a beautiful classmate, another group beat up an elderly teacher of the Koran, and the whole place was on the brink of revolt. The director would go home in tears, part of him contemplating suicide, but, because he lacked the courage to follow this through, he kept hoping that someone else would kill him. To make this happen, he – God forbid – cursed His Excellency the Prophet Mohammed in front of one of his most God-fearing pupils. But, knowing by now that he had lost his mind, the pupil didn't lay a finger on him. The director took to the streets to proclaim – God forbid – that God did not exist, that mosques should be turned into discos, and that we'd only become as rich as people in the West if we all converted to Christianity. But still everyone, even the young Islamists, merely treated him as a lunatic.

'Hopeless and unable to find any way to satisfy his death wish, the director returned to the same fateful skyscraper in Istanbul. Stepping into the same lift, he found himself face to face once again with the tall man who had first exposed him to atheism. The man smiled knowingly, and then presented to the director the book he'd held before. The cure for atheism was to be found in it, too. As the director stretched out his trembling hands, the man took out the knife with the mother-of-pearl handle, as if preparing to cut the pages of the book again, but, with the lift still ascending, he plunged it into the director's heart.'

At this, the story's conclusion, Ka realised that he'd heard it before, from Islamist Turks in Germany. In Necip's version, the mysterious book remained untitled, but Mesut now named one or two Jewish writers known to be agents of atheism, as well as a number of columnists who had led the media campaign against political Islam (one of these would be assassinated three years later): 'The director is not alone in his anguish – there are many atheists in our midst. They've been seduced by the devil and now roam among us, desperate for peace and happiness,' he said. 'Do you share this view?'

'I don't know.'

'What do you mean, you don't know?' asked Mesut with some annoyance. 'Aren't you an atheist, too?'

'I don't know,' said Ka.

'Then tell me this: do you or don't you believe that God Almighty created the universe and everything in it, even the snow that is falling from the sky?'

'The snow reminds me of God,' said Ka.

'Yes, but do you believe that God created snow?' demanded Mesut.

Ka did not reply. He watched the black dog run through the door to the platform to play in the snow under the dim halo of neon light.

'You're not giving me an answer,' said Mesut. 'If a person knows and loves God, he never doubts God's existence. It seems to me that you're not giving me an answer because you're too timid to admit that you're an atheist. But we knew this already. That's why I wanted to ask you a question on my friend Fazıl's behalf. Do you suffer the same terrible pangs as the poor atheist in the story? Do you want to kill yourself?'

'No matter how unhappy I was, I'd still find suicide terrifying,' said Ka.

'But why?' asked Fazıl. 'Is it because it's against the law? But when the state talks about the sanctity of human life, they get it all wrong. Why are you afraid of committing suicide? Please explain this.'

'Please don't take offence at my friend's insistence,' said Necip. 'Fazıl's asking you this question for a reason – a very special reason.'

'I wanted to ask,' said Fazıl: 'aren't you so troubled and unhappy that you want to commit suicide?'

'No,' said Ka. He was becoming annoyed.

'Please, don't try to hide anything from us,' said Mesut. 'We won't do anything bad to you just because you're an atheist.'

There was a tense silence. Ka rose to his feet. He had no desire to let them know how he felt. He started to walk.

'Where are you going? Please don't go,' said Fazıl.

Ka stopped in his tracks but said nothing.

'Maybe I should speak instead,' said Necip. 'The three of us are in love with "covered girls" who have put everything at risk for the sake of their faith. But it's the secular press that calls them "covered girls". For us, they are simply Muslim girls, and what they do to defend their faith is what all Muslim girls must do.'

'And men, too,' said Fazıl.

'Of course,' said Necip. 'I'm in love with Hicran. Mesut is in love with Hande. Fazıl was in love with Teslime, but now she's dead. Or she committed suicide. But we can't bring ourselves to believe that a

Muslim girl ready to sacrifice everything for her faith would be capable of suicide.'

'Perhaps she could no longer bear her suffering,' suggested Ka. 'After all, she'd been thrown out of school, and her family was putting pressure on her to take off her headscarf.'

'No amount of suffering can justify a believer's committing this sin,' said Necip excitedly. 'If we even forget or miss our morning prayers, we're so worried about our sinful state that we can hardly sleep at night. The more it happens, the earlier we run back to the mosque. When someone's faith is this strong, he'll do anything to stop committing this sin, even submit to a life of torture.'

'We know that you went to see Teslime's family,' said Fazıl. 'Do they think she committed suicide?'

'They do. She'd just watched *Marianna* on TV with her parents and washed herself and said her prayers.'

'Teslime never watched soap operas,' said Fazıl softly.

'How well did you know her?' asked Ka.

'I didn't know her personally, we never actually spoke,' said Fazıl with some embarrassment. 'I saw her once from a distance, but she was pretty well covered. But, as a soulmate, of course I knew her very well. When you love someone above all others, you know everything there is to know about her. The Teslime I knew would never have committed suicide.'

'Maybe you didn't know her well enough.'

'And maybe the Westerners sent you here to cover up Teslime's murder,' said Mesut, now with a swagger.

'No, no, we trust you,' said Necip. 'Our leaders say you're a dervish, a poet. It's because we trust you that we wanted to talk to you about something that's making us very unhappy. Fazıl would like to apologise for what Mesut has just said.'

'I apologise,' said Fazıl. His face was bright red. Tears were forming in his eyes.

Mesut remained silent as peace was restored.

'Fazıl and I are blood brothers,' said Necip. 'Most of the time, we think identical thoughts, we can read each other's mind. However, unlike me, Fazıl has no interest in politics. And now we'd like to know if you could do us both a favour. The thing is, we can both accept that Teslime might have been driven to the sin of suicide by the pressures from her parents and the state. It's very painful, but

Fazıl can't stop thinking that the girl he loved committed the sin of suicide. If Teslime was a secret atheist, like the man in the story, if she was one of those unlucky atheists who didn't even know she was an atheist, or if she committed suicide because she was an atheist, then this is a catastrophe for Fazıl. Because that means he was in love with an atheist. You're the only one who can answer this terrible suspicion that's plaguing us. You're the only one who can offer Fazıl some comfort. Do you understand what I'm saying?'

'Are you an atheist?' asked Fazıl with imploring eyes. 'If you are an atheist, do you want to kill yourself?'

'Even on days when I am most certain that I'm an atheist, I feel no urge to commit suicide,' said Ka.

'Thank you for giving us a straight answer to our question,' said Fazıl. He looked calmer now. 'Your heart is full of goodness, but you're afraid of believing in God.'

Seeing that Mesut was still glaring at him, Ka was eager to put some distance between them. His mind was already far away. He felt a desire stirring inside him, and a dream connected to that desire, but he was unable to focus on the dream because of the activity around him. Later, when he could concentrate, he would understand that this dream centred on his yearning for İpek, but also his fear of dying and his failure to believe in God. And in a moment Mesut would add another element.

'Please don't misunderstand us,' said Necip. 'We have no objection to anyone becoming an atheist. There's always room for atheists in Muslim societies.'

'Except that the cemeteries have to be kept separate,' said Mesut. 'It would bring disquiet to the souls of believers to lie in the same cemeteries with the godless. When people go through life concealing their lack of faith, they bring turbulence not only to the land of the living, but also to the cemeteries. It's not just the torment of having to lie beside the godless till Judgement Day. The worst horror would be to rise up on Judgement Day only to find ourselves face to face with a luckless atheist. Mr Poet, Mr Ka, you've made no secret of the fact that you were once an atheist. Maybe you still are one. So tell us, who is it who makes the snow fall from the sky? What is the snow's secret?'

For a moment they all looked across the empty concourse to watch the snow falling on to the tracks.

What am I doing in this world? Ka asked himself. How miserable these snowflakes look from this perspective; how miserable my life is.

A man lives his life, and then he falls apart and soon there is nothing left. Ka felt as if half his soul had just abandoned him, but still the other half remained. He still had love in him. Like a snowflake, he would fall as he was meant to fall; he would devote himself heart and soul to the melancholy course on which his life was set. His father had a certain smell after shaving, and this came back to him now. Then he thought of his mother making breakfast, her feet aching inside her slippers on the cold kitchen floor. He had a vision of a hairbrush; he remembered his mother giving him sugary pink syrup when he woke up coughing in the middle of the night; he felt the spoon in his mouth. As he gave his mind over to all such little things that make up a life, as he thought how they all added up to a unified whole, he saw a snowflake . . .

And so it was that Ka heard the call from deep inside him, the call he heard at moments of inspiration, the only sound that could ever make him happy: the sound of his muse. For the first time in four years, a poem was coming to him. Although he had yet to hear the words, he knew that it was already written. Even as it lurked in its hiding-place, it radiated the power and beauty of destiny. Ka's heart rejoiced. He told the three youths that he was in a hurry and left the deserted, filthy station. He hurried through the snow, thinking all the while of the poem he would write when he was back in the hotel.

10

What Makes This Poem Beautiful?

Snow and Happiness

Ka threw off his coat the moment he entered his room. He opened the green notebook he'd brought with him from Frankfurt and wrote down the poem as it came to him, word by word. It was as easy as following a dictation whispered into his ear, but nevertheless he gave the words on the page his full attention. Because he'd never before written a poem like this – in one flash of inspiration, without a single pause – there was a corner of his mind that doubted its worth. But as line followed line, it seemed to him that the poem was perfect in every way, and this made his joyful heart beat faster still. So he carried on writing, hardly even pausing, leaving spaces only here and there for the words he had not quite heard, until he had written thirty-four lines.

The poem comprised many of the thoughts that had come to him in a rush a short while earlier: the falling snow, cemeteries, the black dog that had been frolicking happily around the station, an assortment of childhood memories, and the image that had lured him back to the hotel, İpek – how happy it made him just to imagine her face. But also how terrified! He called the poem 'Snow'.

Much later, when he thought about how he'd written this poem, he had a vision of a snowflake. This snowflake, he decided, was his life writ small; the poem that had unlocked the meaning of his life he now saw sitting at its centre. But – just as the poem itself defies easy explanation – it is difficult to say how much he decided at that exact moment, and how much of his life was determined by the hidden symmetries that this book is seeking to reveal.

Just as he was finishing the poem, Ka went over to the window and silently watched the scene outside – the large snowflakes floating so elegantly through the air. He had the feeling that simply by watching the snow he would be able to bring the poem to its pre-determined conclusion. There was a knock on the door and, just as he opened it, the last two lines came to him, but then somehow he lost them again. They would remain lost for the duration of his stay in Kars.

It was İpek. 'I have a letter for you,' she said, handing it to him.

Ka took the letter and, without even looking at it, threw it aside. 'I'm very happy,' he said. He'd always thought that only vulgar people boasted about how happy they were, but when he said it now, he felt no shame at all. 'Come inside,' he said to İpek. 'You're looking very beautiful.'

She entered nonchalantly, as if she knew the rooms of the hotel as well as her own home. The time they had spent apart seemed to Ka to have intensified their intimacy.

'I can't say how it happened,' he said, 'but it's possible that this poem came to me thanks to you.'

'The condition of the director of the Education Institute has worsened,' said İpek.

'That's good news, considering we thought at first that he was dead.'

'The police are widening their net. They've raided the university dormitories and now they're doing the hotels. They came here and looked at our books, and asked about each and every one of our guests.'

'What did you tell them about me? Did you tell them that we're getting married?'

'You're very sweet. But my mind's on other things at the moment. We've just heard that they picked up Muhtar and beat him. But apparently they've released him now.'

'He asked me to pass on a message: he's ready to do anything to get you to marry him again. He apologises a thousand times over for trying to force you to wear a headscarf.'

'Muhtar's already said this to me. He says it every day,' said İpek. 'After the police let you go, what did you do?'

'I wandered around the city,' said Ka. He had a moment of indecision.

'Go on, tell me.'

'They took me to see Blue. I was told not to tell anyone.'

'You shouldn't tell anyone,' said İpek. 'You shouldn't say anything to him about us, or about my father, either.'

'Have you ever met him?'

'For a while, Muhtar was very much taken with him, so he paid a few visits to our house. But when Muhtar decided he wanted a more moderate and democratic form of Islam, he distanced himself.'

'He says he came here for the suicide girls.'

'Be afraid that you heard that, and don't discuss it with anyone,' said İpek. 'There's a high probability that his hiding-place is bugged by the police.'

'Then why can't they catch him?'

'They will when it suits them.'

'Why don't you and I just get out of this city right now?' asked Ka.

Rising up inside him was that sensation he had always felt as a child and as a young man at moments of extraordinary happiness: the prospect of future misery and hopelessness. In a panic, he tried to bring this happy moment to a close. This, he hoped, would lessen the impact of the unhappiness he knew would follow. The surest way to calm himself, he thought, would be simply to accept the inevitable: that the love he felt for İpek – the source of his anxiety – would be his undoing; that any intimacy he might enjoy with her would undo him, as salt dissolves ice; that he didn't deserve this happiness but rather the disgrace and denigration that would result. He braced himself.

But it didn't happen. Instead, İpek wrapped her arms around him. First they just held each other, and then their friendly embrace turned to passion. They began to kiss, and soon they were lying side by side on the bed. His pessimism was no match for his sexual excitement: soon he had given himself over to boundless desire. Soon enough, he dreamed, they would be taking off each other's clothes and making love for hours.

But İpek suddenly stood up. 'I find you very attractive and I, too, want to make love, but I haven't been with anyone for three years, and I'm just not ready,' she said.

I haven't made love with anyone for *four* years, thought Ka. He was sure that İpek could see these words on his face.

'And even if I were ready,' said İpek, 'I could never make love with my father so near, in the same house.'

'Does your father have to be out of the hotel for you to get into bed with me naked?' asked Ka.

'Yes. And he hardly ever leaves the hotel. He doesn't care for the icy streets of Kars.'

'All right then, let's not make love now. But let's kiss some more,' said Ka.

'OK.'

İpek leaned over Ka, who was sitting on the edge of the bed, and they enjoyed a long and sensual kiss.

'Let me read you my poem,' he said when he felt sure the kiss was over. 'Don't you want to hear it?'

'Read this letter first. A young man delivered it to the door.'

Ka opened the letter and read it in a loud voice.

Ka, my dear son. If you'd prefer me not to call you my son, I offer my sincere apologies. Last night I saw you in my dreams. It was snowing in my dream and every snowflake that fell to the earth shone with divine radiance. I asked myself if it was a sign and then this afternoon I saw the same snow that I'd seen in my dream falling right in front of my window. You walked past our humble home, 18 Baytarhane Street. Our esteemed friend Muhtar, whom God Almighty has just subjected to a severe test, has explained to me the meaning you take from this snow. We are travellers on the same road. I am waiting for you, sir. Signed: Saadettin Cevher.

'Sheikh Saadettin,' said İpek. 'Go to him at once. Then you can come back and have supper with my father this evening.'

'Am I supposed to pay my respects to every lunatic in Kars?'

'I told you to be afraid of Blue, but don't be so quick to dismiss him as a lunatic. The sheikh is cunning too, and he isn't stupid.'

'I want to forget about all of them. Shall I read you my poem now?'

'Go ahead then.'

Ka sat down at the little table and began to read in an excited yet confident voice, but then he stopped. 'Go over there,' he said to İpek. 'I want to see your face while I'm reading.' When he was sure he could see her in the corner of his eye, he started again. 'Is it beautiful?' he asked her a few moments later.

'Yes, it's beautiful!' said İpek.

Ka read out a few more lines, and then he asked her again: 'Is it beautiful?'

'It's beautiful,' replied İpek.

When he finished, he asked, 'So what was it that made it beautiful?'

'I don't know,' replied İpek, 'but I did find it beautiful.'

'Did Muhtar ever read you a poem like this?'

'Never,' she said.

Ka began to recite the poem again, this time with growing force, but still he stopped at all the same places to ask, 'Is it beautiful?' He also stopped at a few new places to say, 'It really is very beautiful, isn't it?'

'Yes, it's very beautiful!' replied İpek.

Ka was so happy that he felt (as he had felt once before, early in his career, when he had written a poem for a child) as if a strange and beautiful light were enveloping him, and, seeing in a shaft of this light the reflection of İpek, he was even happier. Taking it as a sign that the rules were suspended, he began to embrace İpek again, but this time she gently pulled away.

'Now listen: go to our esteemed sheikh at once. He is a very important person here, much more important than you think: many people in this city go to see him, even people who see themselves as secularists. It's even said the governor's wife goes there, and lots of rich people, lots of army officers. He's on the side of the state. When he said that the covered girls in the university should remove their headscarves, the Prosperity Party didn't make a peep. In a place like Kars, when a man this powerful invites you over, you can't turn him down.'

'Was it you who sent poor Muhtar to see him?'

'Are you worried that the sheikh will discover a God-fearing part of you and send you scurrying back into the fold?'

'I'm very happy right now. I have no need for religion,' said Ka. 'And anyway, that's not what brought me back to Turkey. Only one thing could have brought me back: your love . . . Are we going to get married?'

İpek sat down on the edge of the bed. 'Come on, go,' she said. She gave Ka a warm and bewitching smile. 'But be careful, too. There's no one better at finding the weak point in your soul and working his way inside you like a genie.'

'What will he do to me?'

'He'll speak to you and then all of a sudden he'll throw himself on the floor. He'll take some ordinary thing you said and say how wise it is. He'll insist you're a real man. Some people even think he's making fun of them at this point. But that's His Excellency the

Sheikh's special gift. He does it so convincingly you end up believing that he really thinks what you've said is wise, and that he thinks as you do, with all his heart. He acts as if there is someone much greater inside you. After a while, you begin to see this inner beauty, too, and, because you have never before sensed the beauty within yourself, you think it must be the presence of God, which makes you happy. In other words, the world becomes a beautiful place when you're near this man. And you'll love our esteemed sheikh because he's brought you to this happiness. All the while another voice whispers inside your head that this is all a game the esteemed sheikh is playing and that you are a miserable idiot. But, as far as I could figure out from what Muhtar told me, it seems you no longer have the strength to believe in that miserable idiot. You're so wretchedly unhappy that all you want is for God to save you. Now, your mind – which knows nothing of your soul's desires – objects a little, but not enough: you embark on the road the sheikh has shown you because it is the only road in the world that will let you stand on your own two feet. Sheikh Saadettin Efendi's greatest gift is to make the wretch sitting before him feel special; even more at one with the universe than His Excellency himself. To most men in Kars, this feels like a miracle. For they know only too well that no one in Turkey could be as wretched, poor and unsuccessful as they. So you come to believe first in the sheikh, and then in the long-forgotten teachings of your Islamic faith. Contrary to what they think in Germany, and to the pronouncements of secular intellectuals, this is no bad thing. You can become like everyone else, you can become one with the people, and, even if it's only for a short while, you can escape from unhappiness.'

'I'm not unhappy,' said Ka.

'In fact, someone that unhappy is not unhappy at all. Even the most miserable people have hidden consolations and hopes they secretly embrace. It's not like Istanbul – there are no mocking non-believers. Things are simpler here.'

'I'm going now, but only because you want me to. Which one was Baytarhane Street? How long should I stay there?'

'Stay there till your soul finds some solace,' said İpek. 'And don't be afraid to believe.' She helped Ka put on his coat. 'Is your knowledge of Islam fresh in your mind?' she asked. 'Do you remember the prayers you learned at primary school? You might embarrass yourself.'

'When I was a child, our maid used to take me to Teşvikiye Mosque,' said Ka. 'It was more a chance for her to get together with the other women who worked as maids than it was to worship. They would have a good long gossip waiting for the prayers to begin, and I would roll around on the carpets with the other children. At school, I memorised all the prayers very well, to ingratiate myself with the teacher. He helped us memorise the *fatiha* by hitting us, picking us up by the hair, squeezing our heads under the lids of our desks. All the while the Koran stood open. I learned everything they taught us about Islam, but then I forgot it all. Now it's as if everything I know about Islam is from *The Call* – you know, that film starring Anthony Quinn.' Ka smiled. 'It was showing not long ago on the Turkish channel in Germany, but for some strange reason dubbed into German. You're here this evening, aren't you?'

'Yes.'

'Because I want to read you my poem again,' said Ka as he put his notebook into his pocket. 'Do you think it's beautiful?'

'Yes, really, it's beautiful.'

'What's beautiful about it?'

'I don't know, it's just beautiful,' said İpek. She opened the door to leave.

Ka threw his arms around her and kissed her on the mouth.

11

Do They Have a Different God in Europe?

Ka with Sheikh Saadettin Efendi

Ka left the hotel at a gallop (a number of people remember seeing him race through the snow under the long line of propaganda banners in the direction of Baytarhane Street). He was so happy that, just as in his most joyful moments of childhood, two films were running simultaneously in the cinema of his imagination. In the first, which ran in a loop, he was usually somewhere in Germany – though not at his Frankfurt house – making love to İpek. Sometimes they were not in Germany but in his hotel room in Kars. On the second imaginary screen, the words and visions relating to the last two lines of his poem, 'Snow', were playing.

He stopped first at the Green Pastures Restaurant to ask for directions. There, inspired by a row of bottles on the shelf beside the picture of Atatürk and the Swiss vistas, he took a table, and with the decisiveness of a man in a great hurry he ordered a double raki and a plate of white cheese and roasted chickpeas. According to the announcer on the TV, despite the heavy snowfall, preparations for Kars' first live broadcast were almost complete. There then followed a summary of local and national news. It seemed that in the interests of peace and to avoid any further trouble for the deputy governor, the authorities had contacted the station to bar them from mentioning the shooting of the director of the Education Institute. While he was taking this in, Ka downed his double raki like a glass of water.

After polishing off a third raki, he headed for the sheikh's lodge, and four minutes later he was buzzed in. As he climbed the steep steps, he remembered that he was still carrying 'Staircase', Muhtar's poem, in his jacket pocket. He was sure everything would go well here, but still felt that spine-tingling chill that a child suffers on his way to the doctor's surgery, even when he knows he's not going for a jab. Having reached the top of the stairs, Ka regretted coming.

The sheikh sensed the fear in Ka's heart the moment he set eyes on him. And Ka knew that the sheikh sensed it. But there was something about the man that stopped Ka feeling ashamed. On the wall of the landing there was a mirror with a carved walnut frame. Ka's first glimpse of Sheikh Saadettin was in this mirror. The house itself was so crowded that it was warm with breath and body heat. Scarcely a moment later, Ka was kissing the sheikh's hand, before he'd even taken in his surroundings or looked to see who else was in the room.

There were twenty others who had come to attend the simple ceremony held every Tuesday, to listen to the sheikh in conversation, and to unburden their hearts. Five or six were tradesmen or tea-shop or dairy owners – they took every opportunity to spend time with the sheikh for the happiness it gave them. Also present were a young paraplegic, a cross-eyed bus-company manager, an elderly man who was the manager's friend, a nightwatchman from the Electricity Board, a man who had been the caretaker of Kars Hospital for forty years, and a few others.

Reading the confusion in Ka's face, the sheikh gestured expansively and kissed the new arrival's hand. There was something almost childlike in this, as if he were paying his respects. And, although it was exactly what Ka had expected from the sheikh, he was still astonished. Fully aware that everyone else in the room was watching them, the two men began to converse.

'May God bless you for accepting my invitation,' said the sheikh. 'I saw you in my dream. It was snowing.'

'I saw you in *my* dream, Your Excellency,' said Ka. 'I came here to find happiness.'

'It makes us happy to know that it was here in Kars that your happiness was born,' said the sheikh.

'This place, this city, this house . . . they make me afraid,' said Ka. 'Because you all seem so strange to me. Because I've always shied away from these things. I never wanted to kiss anyone's hand . . . or let anyone kiss mine.'

'It seems that you spoke most openly of the beauty within you to our brother Muhtar,' said the sheikh. 'So tell us, of what does this blessed snowfall remind you?'

At the far end of the divan on which the sheikh sat, right next to the window, Ka now noticed Muhtar. There were a few bandages on his forehead and nose. To hide the purple bruises around his eyes, he wore big, dark sunglasses, like those of pensioners blinded by smallpox. He was smiling at Ka, but his expression was far from friendly.

'The snow reminded me of God,' said Ka. 'The snow reminded me of the beauty and mystery of creation, of the essential joy that is life.' He fell silent for a moment, and noticed that all the eyes in the crowded room were still on him. The sheikh's continued serenity was starting to annoy him. 'Why did you summon me here?' he asked.

'Please don't ask such a thing!' cried the sheikh. 'After Muhtar Bey told us what you had said to him, it seemed to us that you might want to open your heart to us, talk to us, find a friend.'

'All right, let's talk then,' said Ka. 'Before I came here, I had three glasses of raki.'

'Why are you so afraid of us?' asked the sheikh, his eyes widening, as if he were very surprised. He was a sweet, fat man, and those around him sported the same sincere smiles. 'Aren't you going to tell us why you're so afraid of us?'

'I'll tell you, but I don't want you to take offence.'

'We won't take offence,' said the sheikh. 'Please, come over here, sit right next to me. It's very important for us to understand why you're afraid of us.'

The sheikh's expression was half serious, half joking – he was ready to make his disciples laugh at a moment's notice. Ka liked his host's demeanour and, as soon as he had taken his place next to the sheikh, he was tempted to imitate it.

'I've always wanted this country to prosper, to modernise . . . I've wanted freedom for its people,' said Ka. 'But it seemed to me that our religion was always against all this. Maybe I'm mistaken. I beg your pardon, maybe I'm saying all of this just because I've had too much to drink.'

'Please don't say such a thing!'

'I grew up in Istanbul, in Nişantaş, among society people. I wanted to be like the Europeans. Because I couldn't see how I could reconcile my becoming a European with a God that required women to wrap themselves up in scarves, I kept religion out of my life. But when I went to Europe, I realised there could be a God who was different from the God of the bearded provincial reactionaries.'

'Do they have a different God in Europe?' asked the sheikh jokingly, and he patted Ka's back.

'I want a God who doesn't ask me to take off my shoes in His presence, and who doesn't make me fall to my knees to kiss people's hands. I want a God who understands my need for solitude.'

'There is only one God,' said the sheikh. 'He sees everything, understands everyone. Even your need for solitude. If you believed in Him, if you knew He understood your need for solitude, you wouldn't feel so alone.'

'That's very true, Your Excellency,' said Ka, feeling as if he were speaking to everyone in the room. 'It's because I'm solitary that I can't believe in God. And because I can't believe in God, I can't escape from solitude. What should I do?'

Although he was drunk and unexpectedly pleased to be speaking with such courage to a real sheikh, part of him still knew that he was entering dangerous territory. So when the sheikh fell silent, he was afraid.

'Do you really want guidance from me?' asked the sheikh. 'We are just like those people you mentioned – bearded provincial reactionaries. Even if we shaved off our beards, there is no cure for being provincial.'

'I'm provincial, too, and I want to become even more provincial. I want to be forgotten in the most unknown corner of the world under a blanket of snow,' said Ka. He kissed the sheikh's hand again. The ease with which he could do this pleased him, but he knew that one part of his mind still operated in a different way, in a Western way, and he despised himself for that.

'I hope you will forgive me, but, before I came here, I had something to drink,' he reiterated. 'I felt guilty about having refused all my life to believe in the same God as the uneducated, as the aunties with their heads wrapped in scarves, as the uncles with prayer beads in their hands. There's a lot of pride involved in my refusal to believe in God. But now I want to believe in that God who is making this beautiful snow fall from the sky. There's a God who pays careful attention to the world's hidden symmetry, a God who will make us all more civilised and refined.'

'Of course there is, my son,' said the sheikh.

'But that God is not among you. He's outside, in the empty night, in the darkness, in the snow that falls inside the hearts of outcasts.'

'If you want to find God by yourself, then go ahead – walk out into the darkness, revel in the snow, use the snow to fill yourself with God's love. We have no desire to divert you from this path. But don't forget that arrogant men who think too much of themselves always end up alone. God doesn't have any time for pride. Pride was what got Satan expelled from Heaven.'

Once again, Ka was overcome with a fear that he would find so shaming later. He also dreaded what he knew they would say about him if he left. 'So what shall I do, Your Excellency?' he asked. He was just about to kiss the sheikh's hand again, but changed his mind. He could tell that everyone around him knew how confused he was, and how drunk he was, and pitied him for this. 'I want to believe in the God you believe in and be like you, but, because there's a Westerner inside me, my mind is confused.'

'If your intentions are this good, then it's a fine beginning,' said the sheikh. 'The first thing you need to learn is humility.'

'How can I do that?' asked Ka. Once again, he could feel the mocking devil inside him.

'After the evening meal, anyone who wants to talk comes to join me in this corner, on the divan where you're sitting right now,' said the sheikh. 'Everyone here is a brother.'

It now dawned on Ka that the great crowd of men sitting on the chairs and cushions around him were queuing up to sit on the corner of the divan that he occupied. He guessed that the sheikh now wanted him to step back, make his way to the end of the queue and wait patiently, like a European. With this in mind, he rose to his feet. He kissed the sheikh on the hand one more time and went to sit on a cushion in the far corner.

Sitting next to him was a short, kindly man with gold-capped teeth who worked at one of the tea-houses on İnönü Avenue. He was so small (and Ka so addled) that Ka found himself wondering whether the man had come to see the sheikh to obtain a cure for his shortness. When he was a child in Nişantaş, there'd been a very elegant dwarf who every evening would visit the gypsies in the square to buy a bouquet of violets and a single carnation. The man on the cushion told Ka that he had seen him passing in front of his tea-house earlier in the day, that he was sorry Ka hadn't come in, and that he would be very happy if Ka dropped by in the morning. At this point, the cross-eyed bus-company manager chimed in. He told Ka in a whisper of having gone through a very bad spell on account of a girl, that he had given himself to drink and become rebellious to the point of losing all sight of God, but that in the end he had been able to put all that behind him. Before Ka could ask, 'Did you marry the girl?' the cross-eyed manager added, 'We had come to see that this girl was not right for us.'

The sheikh then said a few words against suicide. All the men around them listened in silence, some nodding at the wisdom of his words, but Ka and his two companions in the corner continued with their whispering. 'There have been a few more suicides,' the tiny man said, 'but the authorities have decided not to tell us, for the same reason as when they keep quiet about the temperature dropping – they don't want to upset us. But here's the real reason for this epidemic: they're selling these girls to elderly clerks, men they don't love.'

The manager objected: 'When my wife first met me,' he said, 'she didn't love me, either.' He went on to declare that the epidemic had many causes, for example unemployment, high prices, immorality and lack of faith.

Because he agreed with everything both men said, Ka felt rather two-faced as they sat in silence for several minutes. When his elderly companion began to nod off, the cross-eyed manager woke him up, but the silence continued, and a feeling of peace rose inside Ka: they were so far from the centre of the world, so far that one couldn't even imagine going there, and as he fell under the spell of the snowflakes that seemed to hang in the sky outside, he began to wonder if he had entered a world without gravity.

At that point, with no one now focused on Ka, another poem came to him. He had his notebook with him, and, as with 'Snow', he gave himself fully to the voice within him. But this time he wrote down all thirty-six lines in one go. Because his mind was still foggy with drink, he was not sure the poem was any good, but when a new rush of inspiration overtook him, he rose to his feet, begged the sheikh's pardon, rushed out of the room and sat down on the stairs. Reading what he had written, he could see that this poem was as flawless as the first.

It draws upon the events Ka had just experienced and witnessed. Four lines allude to a conversation with a sheikh about the existence of God. There is a reference to Ka's shameful look following the mention of 'the poor man's God', and then some discussion of solitude, the world's secret symmetry and the creation of life. A man with gold teeth, one who is cross-eyed and a gentle dwarf holding a carnation all tell their life stories. Shocked by the beauty of his own words, he asked himself, 'What does it all mean?' It seemed to be a poem someone else had written, which, he thought, was why he was able to appreciate its beauty. But finding it beautiful was also disturbing, considering its contents, and considering his own life. How could he understand the beauty in this poem?

The light timer in the stairwell clicked off and Ka was plunged into darkness. When he found the button and turned the light back on, he took one last look at the notebook and found a title: 'Hidden Symmetry'. Later, he would point to the speed with which this title came to him as proof that this and all the poems that followed it were – like the world itself – not of his own creation. With this in mind, he would move it to what might be called the most prominent position on the 'Logic' axis.

12

If God Does Not Exist, Then How Do You Explain All the Suffering of the Poor?

The Sad Story of Necip and Hicran

On leaving the sheikh's lodge, Ka headed back to the hotel. As he trudged through the snow, his mind returned to İpek: it wouldn't be long before he'd see her again. On his way down Halitpaşa Avenue he passed first a group of People's Party campaigners and then a crowd of students on their way out of a university entrance-exam course. They were talking about what they were going to watch on television that night, and about how easy it was to fool their chemistry teacher; and they were needling one another just as mercilessly as Ka and I had done when we were their age. He saw two parents leading their tearful child by the hand from an apartment building where they'd just paid a visit to the dentist upstairs. It was clear from their clothes that this couple could barely make ends meet, but they had decided to take their beloved child to a private dentist rather than the state dispensary, presumably to spare the child some pain. Through the open door of a shop that sold women's stockings, bolts of cotton, coloured pencils, batteries and cassettes, he heard once again the strains of Peppino di Capri's 'Roberta'. He recalled hearing it on the radio when he was a child and his uncle had taken him out for a drive to the Bosphorus. As his heart began to soar, it occurred to Ka that there might be a new poem coming to him, so he stepped into the first tea-house he could find and, sitting down at an empty table, took out his pencil and notebook.

After gazing through moist eyes at the empty page for some time, he revised his forecast – there was no poem coming to him – but this didn't dampen his spirits in the slightest. The tea-house was packed with unemployed men and students, and all around him the walls were plastered not just with scenes of Switzerland but with theatrical posters, newspaper cartoons, assorted clippings, an announcement of the terms and conditions of the civil service exam and a schedule of the matches to be played by Karsspor that year. The results of past matches – most of them losses – were pencilled in by various hands – and next to the 6–1 loss to Erzurumspor someone had written the lines that Ka would incorporate into 'All the People and the Stars', the poem he would write the following day while sitting in the Lucky Brothers Tea-house:

> Even if our mother came back from Heaven to take us into her arms,
> Even if our wicked father spared her a beating for just one night,
> You'd still end up penniless, your shit would still freeze, your soul
>   would still wither, there is no hope!
> If you're unlucky enough to live in Kars, you might as well flush
>   yourself down the toilet.

Smiling happily as he copied these words into his notebook, he was soon joined by Necip, who had been sitting at a table in the back. It was clear from his expression that he was stunned to see Ka in this place, but also delighted.

'I'm so happy you're here,' said Necip. 'Are you writing a poem? I would like to apologise for my friend, the one who called you an atheist. It's the first time in their lives they've come face to face with an atheist. But it seems to me that you couldn't really be an atheist, because you're such a good person.' He went on to talk about a few other things that he'd felt unable to mention during their earlier meetings: he and his friends had sneaked out of school to attend the show at the theatre that evening, but they were going to sit right at the back, because, of course, they didn't want the school directors to spot them on live TV. Necip was elated to have escaped from school and excited about meeting his friends at the National Theatre. They all knew that Ka was going to read a poem there. Everyone in Kars wrote poems, but Ka was the first person he had ever met to have had his poems published. Could he offer Ka a glass of tea? Ka explained that he was short of time.

'In that case, I'll just ask you one question, one last question,' said Necip. 'I'm not like my friends, I'm not trying to show you disrespect. I'm just very curious.'

'Yes?'

Before speaking, Necip lit his cigarette with shaky hands. 'If God does not exist, then that means that Heaven does not exist, either. And that means that the world's poor, those millions who live in poverty and oppression, will never go to Heaven. And if that is so, then how do you explain all the suffering the poor have to endure? What are we here for, and why do we put up with so much suffering, if it's all for nothing?'

'God exists. So does Heaven.'

'No, you're just saying that to console me, because you feel sorry for us. As soon as you're back in Germany, you'll start thinking that God doesn't exist – just as you did before.'

'For the first time in years, I'm very happy,' said Ka. 'Why shouldn't I believe the same things as you?'

'Because you belong to high society,' said Necip. 'People in high society never believe in God. They believe in what Europeans do, so they think they're better than ordinary people.'

'I may belong to high society,' said Ka. 'But in Germany I'm a worthless nobody. I was falling apart there.'

Necip's beautiful eyes clouded over, and Ka could see that the teenager was considering his case, trying to put himself in Ka's shoes. 'Then why did you become angry with your country and flee to Germany?' he asked. Seeing Ka's face fall, he said, 'Never mind! Anyway, if I were rich, I'd be so ashamed of my situation that I'd believe in God even more.'

'One day, God willing, we'll all be rich,' said Ka.

'Nothing is quite as simple as you think, I reckon. I'm not so simple, either, and I don't want to be rich. I want to be a poet, a writer. I'm writing a science-fiction novel. It might get published – in one of the Kars papers, *Lance* – but I don't want to be published in a paper that sells seventy-five copies. I want to be published in an Istanbul paper that sells thousands. I have a synopsis of the novel with me. If I read it to you, could you tell me whether you think an Istanbul paper might publish it?'

Ka looked at his watch.

'It's very short!' said Necip.

The electricity cut out and all of Kars was plunged into darkness. The only light in the tea-house was coming from the stove. Necip ran over to the counter and grabbed a candle. He lit it and dripped a few drops of wax on to a plate, a seal by which to affix the burning candle, and set the plate on the table. Retrieving a few sheets of crumpled paper from his pocket, he began to read in a hesitant voice, stopping from time to time to gulp with excitement.

In the year 3579, there was a planet we haven't even discovered yet. Its name was Gazzali and its people were rich, and their lives were much easier than our lives are today, but, contrary to what the materialists would have predicted, their rich and easy lives did not bring the inhabitants of this planet any spiritual satisfaction. Rather, everyone was deeply anxious about being and nothingness, man and the universe, God and His people. And so it came to pass that a number of Gazzalians travelled to the most remote corner of their red planet to set up the Islamic Lycée for the Study of Science and Oration. It took only the cleverest and most hard-working students. Two close friends attended this lycée. Inspired by books written 1600 years earlier, books that illuminated this East–West problem so beautifully that they could have been written yesterday, they too called each other Necip and Fazıl. Together they would repeatedly read The Great East, their great master's greatest book. And in the evenings they would meet secretly in Fazıl's bed, the highest bunk, where under the covers they would lie side by side watching the blue snowflakes fall on to the glass roof above them and disappear just like planets. And they would whisper into each other's ear, whisper about the meaning of life and what they hoped to do when they were older.

The evil-hearted tried in vain to tarnish this pure friendship with snide, jealous jokes. But then one day the two came under a cloud. It so happened that they had simultaneously fallen in love with the same girl, a virgin called Hicran. Even when they discovered that Hicran's father was an atheist, they couldn't cure themselves of this hopeless longing – on the contrary, their love intensified. In this way they came to realise that there was no longer enough room on the red planet for both of them: they both knew in their hearts that one of them must die. But they made the following promise: after spending some time in the next world, no matter how many light years away it was, the one who died would have to return to this world to visit his surviving friend and answer their most urgent questions – about life after death.

As for the question of who would kill whom, and how it would be done, they just couldn't make up their minds – mainly because they both knew that true happiness could come only from one sacrificing his own happiness for that of the other. So, for example, if one of them, let's say it was Fazıl, said, 'Let's both stick our hands into electricity sockets at the same time,' Necip would see it at once for what it was – a clever trick Fazıl had invented to sacrifice himself for his friend. Clearly, Fazıl would have arranged for Necip's socket to be disconnected. After many months of hemming and hawing, months that caused both boys great pain, the question was decided in a matter of seconds: one night Necip returned from his evening lessons to discover his dear friend lying dead in his bed, riddled with bullets.

The following year, Necip married Hicran, and on their wedding night he told her what had passed between him and his friend, and how one day Fazıl would return from the spirit world. Hicran told him that she really loved Fazıl, that after his death she had cried for days, cried so much that blood had run from her eyes, and that she had married Necip only because he was Fazıl's friend and reminded her of him. They were unable to consummate their marriage, and agreed that the ban on love should continue until Fazıl had returned from the other world.

But, as the years passed, they began to long for each other. First their longing was spiritual, and then it became physical. One night, during an interplanetary inspection, while the beams were illuminating a city on earth that went by the name of Kars, they were no longer able to control themselves: they fell upon each other like lunatics and made passionate love. You might think this meant they had forgotten Fazıl, whose memory had for so long plagued them like a toothache. But they had not. The shame in their hearts grew with every day, and it scared them. A night arrived when they awoke suddenly, having both decided at the exact same time that this strange cocktail of fear and other emotions was going to destroy them. Then the television across the room turned on by itself, and there, shining brightly, the ghostly form of Fazıl took shape. The deadly bullet holes in his forehead were still fresh, and his lower lip and other wounds were dripping with blood.

'I am racked with pain,' he said. 'There is not a single corner of the other world I have not seen. ['I will write about these travels in full detail using Gazzali's Victories of Mecca and Ibn Arabi as my

107

inspirations,' said Necip.] I have earned the highest compliments of God's angels, and I have travelled to what is thought to be the summit of the highest plain of Heaven. I have seen the terrible punishments meted out in Hell to tie-wearing atheists and arrogant colonial positivists who make fun of the common people and their faith. But everywhere happiness eluded me, because my mind was here with you.'

Husband and wife were overwhelmed with a fearful admiration as they listened to the sad ghost.

'The thing that made me so unhappy all those years was not the thought that I might one day see you two sitting so happily together, as I am seeing you tonight. On the contrary, I longed for Necip's happiness more than I longed for my own. It was because of the profound feeling between us that we had been unable to find any way to kill ourselves or each other. Because each valued the other's life more than his own, it was as if we were both wearing protective armour that made us immortal. How happy that made me feel! But my death proved to me that I had been wrong to believe in this feeling.'

'No!' cried Necip. 'Not once did I give my own life more value than I gave yours!'

'If this had been true, then I never would have died,' said Fazıl's ghost. 'And you would never have married the beautiful Hicran. I died because you harboured a secret wish, a wish so secret you hid it even from yourself: to see me dead.'

Necip objected violently to this accusation, but the ghost refused to listen.

'It was not just the suspicion that you wished me dead that deprived me of peace in the other world,' said the ghost. 'It was also that you had a hand in my murder, for it was you who so treacherously shot me in the head, and here, and here, as I lay in my bed sleeping. And there was another fear, too: that you acted as an agent for the enemies of the Holy Koran.'

By now Necip had given up objecting and fallen silent.

'There is only one way for you to deliver me from my suffering and restore me to Heaven, and only by following this same path can you deliver yourself from suspicion in this heinous crime,' said the ghost. 'Find my killer, whoever he might be. In seven years and seven months, they haven't had a single suspect. And when you've found whoever killed me or wanted me dead, I want to see the crime avenged: an eye for an eye. While that villain remains unpunished, there is no peace for me in this life; nor will there be any peace for you in the transitory realm that you still insist on calling the 'real world'.

Neither the man nor his wife could think of anything to say. They watched in tearful amazement as the ghost vanished from the screen.

'And then what? What happened next?' asked Ka.

'I haven't decided yet,' said Necip. 'But if I wrote the whole story, do you think I could sell it?' When he saw Ka hesitating, he added, 'Listen, every line I write comes from the bottom of my heart. They all express my deepest convictions. What does this story mean to you? What did you feel when I was reading it to you?'

'It shook me to the core, because it showed me that you believe with all your heart that this world is nothing more than a preparation for the next.'

'Yes, I believe so,' said Necip excitedly. 'That's not enough, though. God wants us to be happy in this world, too. But that's the hardest thing.'

They fell silent as they pondered the 'hardest thing'.

At this moment, the lights came back on, but the people in the tea-house remained silent, as they had been in the darkness. The TV did not come back to life, and the owner began to hit it with his fist.

'We've been sitting here together for twenty minutes now,' said Necip. 'My friends must be dying of curiosity.'

'Who are your friends?' asked Ka. 'Is one of them Fazıl? And are those your real names?'

'No, of course not. I'm using an assumed name, just like the Necip in the story. You're not a policeman – stop interrogating me! As for Fazıl, he refuses to come to places like this,' Necip told him, becoming quite mysterious. 'Fazıl is the most religious person in our group, and I trust him more than anyone else in the world. But he's worried that if he gets involved in politics, he'll end up with a police file and might get kicked out of school. He has an uncle in Germany who might send for him, but even if he does, we love each other just as much as the two boys in the story; so, if someone killed me, I'm certain he would come back and take revenge. In fact, it's just as in the story – we're so close that no matter how far apart we are, we can always tell what the other is doing.'

'So what's Fazıl doing right now?'

'Hmmm,' said Necip, assuming a strange pose. 'He's in the dormitory, reading.'

'Who is Hicran?'

'That's not her real name, either. But it's not a name she took herself; it's a name we've given her. Some of us write her love letters and poems non-stop, but we're too afraid to send them. If I had a daughter, I'd want her to be as beautiful, as intelligent and as courageous as she is. She's the leader of the headscarf girls, and she's afraid of nothing. Her mind is her own. To tell you the truth, in the beginning she was an infidel, because she was under the influence of her atheist father. She modelled in Istanbul – she'd go on television and bare her bottom, and flaunt her legs. She came here to do a shampoo commercial for TV. In it she was going to be walking along Ahmet Muhtar Pasha the Conqueror Avenue – the meanest, dirtiest avenue in Kars, but also the most beautiful. Then, when she stopped in front of the camera, she was to swing her magnificent, waist-length brown mane and say, "Even in the filth of the beautiful city of Kars, my hair is still sparkling clean – thanks to Blendax." The commercial was going to be shown everywhere; the whole world was going to laugh at us.

'At that time, the headscarf business at the Education Institute was just getting started, and two of the girls had seen Hicran on television and also recognised her from photographs in gossip magazines that had reported on her scandals with rich kids in Istanbul. Secretly the girls admired her, so they invited her for tea. Hicran accepted, though for her it was a big joke. She grew bored with the girls almost immediately, and do you know what she said? "If our religion" – no, she didn't say "our religion", she said "your religion" – "If your religion requires you to hide your hair, and the state forbids you to wear a headscarf, then why don't you do like So-and-So?" – and here she gave the name of a foreign rock star – "Why don't you just shave off all your hair and wear a nose-ring? Then the whole world would stand up and take notice!" Our poor girls were so taken aback to hear these affronts that they couldn't even stop themselves laughing with her! This made Hicran even bolder, so she said, "These scarves are sending you back to the Middle Ages – why don't you take them off

and flaunt your beautiful hair?' But, as Hicran was about to remove
the scarf from the silliest girl among them, suddenly her hand froze.
At this moment Hicran threw herself at the silly girl's feet – this girl's
brother is one of our classmates, and he's so stupid that even the
morons call him a moron – and begged her pardon.

'Hicran returned the next day, and the day after that, and in the
end she joined them instead of going back to Istanbul. She's one of
the saints who's helped turn the headscarf into the flag of Anatolia's
oppressed Muslim women – mark my words!'

'Then why is it that you said nothing about her in your story except
that she was a virgin?' asked Ka. 'Why didn't Necip and Fazıl ask for
her opinion before deciding to kill themselves for her sake?'

There was a tense silence, during which Necip raised his beautiful
eyes (one of which, in two hours and three minutes, would be shattered by a bullet). He looked up at the dark street to watch the snow
fall silently, layer upon layer, like the stanzas of a poem. Then he
whispered, 'There she is. It's her!'

'Who?'

'Hicran! She's out there in the street.'

13

I'm Not Going to Discuss My Faith with an Atheist

A Walk through the Snow with Kadife

She was wearing a purple raincoat; her eyes were hidden behind futuristic dark glasses; and on her head was one of those nondescript headscarves Ka had seen thousands of women wearing since child-hood and which were now the symbol of political Islam. When he saw that this young woman entering the shop was walking directly towards him, Ka jumped to his feet as though the teacher had just entered the classroom.

'I'm İpek's sister, Kadife,' said the woman, smiling faintly. 'Every-one's expecting you for supper. My father sent me to find you.'

'How did you know I was here?' asked Ka.

'In Kars everyone always knows about everything that's going on,' said Kadife. She wasn't smiling at all now. 'If it's happening in Kars, of course.'

Ka detected some pain in her expression, but he could not guess its cause. Necip made the introductions: 'Meet my poet–novelist friend!' he said. They looked each other over but did not shake hands. Ka took it for a sign of tension. Much later, looking back on these events, he would realise that the omission was out of deference to Islamic convention. Necip turned ghostly white looking at Kadife, as if Hicran had just arrived from outer space, but Kadife's manner was so matter-of-fact that not a single man in the crowded tea-house even turned around to look at her. She wasn't as beautiful as her sister, either.

But as he walked with her through the snow and down Atatürk Avenue, Ka felt very happy. She was wrapped up in a scarf, and, though plainer than her sister, she was fresh-faced, and when he looked right into her eyes–hazel, like İpek's – he was able to talk to her with great ease. He found her so attractive because of this that he felt as if he were betraying her older sister.

First, to Ka's surprise, they discussed meteorology. Kadife knew everything there was to know about it – she rattled off details like one of those old people who do nothing all day but listen to the radio. She told him that the low-pressure system coming down from Siberia was going to last two more days; that, if this snow continued, the roads would be closed for another two days, too; that 160 centimetres had fallen in Sarıkamış; and that the inhabitants of Kars no longer believed the weather reports. In fact, she said, everyone was talking about how the state, wishing not to upset the populace, routinely announced air temperatures 5 or 6 degrees higher than they were (but no one else had mentioned this to Ka). She talked about how, as children in Istanbul, when she and İpek would always want the snow to continue, the sight of it made her think about how beautiful and short life was, and about how, in spite of all their enmities, people had so much in common. Measured against eternity and the greatness of creation, the world in which they lived was narrow. That's why snow drew people together. It was as if snow cast a veil over hatreds, greed and wrath and made everyone feel close to one another.

They fell silent for a while. All the shops along Şehit Cengiz Topel Street were closed, and they didn't see a soul. This walk with Kadife through the snow brought Ka as much anxiety as happiness. He locked his eyes on the lights in the window of a shop at the very end of the street: it was as if he were afraid that if he kept turning to look into Kadife's face, he would fall in love with her. Was he really in love with her older sister? He had a rational desire to fall madly in love, that much he knew.

When they reached the end of the street, Ka stopped to look at the sign in the window of the Beerhall of Joy, written on a piece of notepaper: 'Due to tonight's theatrical event, the honourable Zihni Sevuk, candidate for the Free People's Party, has postponed this evening's meeting'. Through the window of the small and narrow Beerhall of Joy, he could see Sunay Zaim sitting at the head of a table with his entire troupe; with only twenty minutes to go before the show began, they were all drinking thirstily.

As he perused the campaign posters in the window of the beerhall, his eye fell on the yellow one announcing that 'Human beings are

God's masterpieces and suicide is blasphemy', and this prompted him to ask Kadife what she thought of Teslime's suicide.

'I'm sure you know enough already to turn Teslime into a very interesting story for your friends in Germany – not to mention the Istanbul press,' she said, sounding faintly annoyed.

'I'm new to Kars,' said Ka. 'Even as I come to understand how things work here, I'm beginning to think I'll never be able to make it clear to anyone on the outside. My heart breaks to see these people's fragile livelihoods, and their needless suffering.'

'The only people who worry about needless suffering are atheists who've never suffered a thing,' said Kadife. 'Because, after all, it takes only the tiniest discomfort for atheists to decide that they can't bear life without faith any more, and the next thing you know they've returned to the fold.'

'But Teslime's suffering was so great that she left the fold and committed suicide,' said Ka. The alcohol that was still in his system had made him stubborn.

'Well, if Teslime did indeed kill herself, then it's possible to say that she committed a terrible sin. If you turn to the twenty-ninth line of the Nisa verse of the Glorious Koran, you'll see that suicide is clearly prohibited. But the thought that she might have sinned and killed herself is nothing next to the love we feel for her: there is still a corner of our hearts where we remember her with deep love and affection.'

'So you mean to say that even if this luckless girl has committed an insult against our faith, we still love her,' said Ka, like a barrister asking a leading question. 'We don't believe in God with our whole hearts any more. We no longer need to, because now, as in the West, we confirm our beliefs by reason and logic. Is that what you're saying?'

'The Holy Koran is the Word of God, and when God makes a clear and definite command, it's not a matter for ordinary mortals to question,' said Kadife. She sounded very sure of herself. 'But do not assume from this that our religion leaves no room for discussion. I will say that I'm not prepared to discuss my faith with an atheist – or even a secularist. I beg your pardon.'

'You're right.'

'And I'm not one of those Islamist toadies who go around trying to convince secularists that Islam can be a secular religion,' added Kadife.

'Right again,' said Ka.

'That's the second time you've said I'm right,' said Kadife with a smile, 'but I don't think you really mean it.'

'No, you are right again,' said Ka, but he wasn't smiling.

For a time they walked in silence. Could it be that he would fall in love with Kadife and not her sister? Ka knew only too well that he could never feel sexually attracted to a woman in a headscarf, but still he couldn't stop flirting with this secret thought.

As they joined the crowds on Black Mountain Avenue, he brought the conversation around to his poetry. Then, in an awkward aside, he mentioned that Necip was also a poet, and asked whether Kadife was aware of having quite a few admirers in the religious high school who worshipped her by the name of 'Hicran'.

'They call me *what*?'

Ka told her a few of the stories he'd heard about Kadife in her role as the leader of the headscarf girls: Hicran, 'Sadness'.

'None of these stories are true,' said Kadife. 'I haven't heard any of the religious high-school boys of my acquaintance telling them.' She walked a few more steps and then said, 'But I've heard that shampoo story before.' She smiled. In fact it hadn't been her but rather a rich and much-hated Istanbul journalist who had first suggested to the headscarf girls that they shave their heads – and this had been done just to attract media attention in the West, to make the girls seem important. 'There's only one thing that's true in these stories,' continued Kadife. 'The first time I went to see the headscarf girls, I did go to make fun of them. But I was also curious. Put it like this: I went out of devilish curiosity.'

'And then what happened?'

'I came to Kars because the Education Institute would take me, and also because my sister was here already. So, in the end, these girls were my classmates, and if you still don't believe me, go and visit them in their homes when they invite you. Their mothers and fathers brought them up to be as they are. So did the religious instruction they received during their state education. Then suddenly, having been told all their lives to keep their heads covered, these girls were now hearing, "Take off those scarves, because that's what the state wants you to do." As for me, I just put on a headscarf one day to make a political statement. I did it for a laugh, but it was also frightening. Maybe it was because I remembered that I was the daughter of a man who has been an enemy of the state since the beginning of time. I'm certain that I intended it to last for only one day: it was one of those "revolutionary gestures" that you laugh about years later, when you're remembering the good old days when you were political. But the state, the police and the local press came down on me so hard that I could scarcely think of it as a joke any more – and also I had painted myself into a corner and I couldn't get out. They arrested us – the excuse was that we had staged a demonstration without a permit. But when they released us the next day, if I had said, "Forget the veil! I never really meant it anyway!" the whole of Kars would have spat in my face. Now I've come to see that God put me through all this suffering to help me find the true path. Once I was an atheist, like you. Don't look at me like that, you look at me as if you pity me.'

'I'm not looking at you in that way.'

'Yes, you are. I don't think my situation is any funnier than yours. I don't feel superior to you, either – you should know this, too.'

'What does your father say about all this?'

'So far we're managing. But the way things are going, I'm not sure how much longer we will – and this scares us, because we love each other very much. In the beginning, my father was proud of me – the day I went to school wearing that headscarf, he acted as if I had found a special new form of rebellion. He stood with me in front of my mother's old mirror with the brass frame as I tried on the headscarf, and while we were still in front of the mirror, he gave me a kiss. Although we never talked about it a great deal, this much was clear: what I was doing was worthwhile not as a defence of Islam but as defiance of the state. He made as if to say, "My daughter looks just fine like this," but deep down inside, he was as scared as I was. I knew he was worried when they threw us in jail, and I knew he felt guilty. He insisted that MİT didn't care about me but were still interested in him. But it was in the old days that they kept files on leftists and democrats; now they're mostly interested in the Islamists. Still, you could imagine why he saw it as the same old gun now being turned on his daughter. It all got more difficult when I began to take my stance seriously. My father went out of his way to support me in every step I took but it was difficult for him. You know how it is sometimes with old people – no matter how much noise there is in the house, no matter how much the stove clatters, no matter how loudly the wife complains, no matter how much the door hinges creak, whatever reaches their ears, it's as if they've heard nothing. Well, that's my father when it comes to the headscarf issue. If one of those girls comes to the house, he'll sometimes play the atheist bastard, but before long he's encouraging them to stand up to the state. And because I've seen that these girls are mature enough to stand up to him, I have meetings at home. One of them is joining us tonight – her name is Hande. After Teslime committed suicide, Hande's parents pressured her to take off her headscarf, and she agreed, but she's having a hard time carrying it through.

'My father sometimes says it all reminds him of his old communist days. There are two kinds of communists: the arrogant ones who enter the fray hoping to make men out of the people and bring progress to the nation; and the innocent ones who get involved because they believe in equality and justice. The arrogant ones are obsessed with power, they presume to think for everyone and only bad can come of them. The innocents harm only themselves; but that's all they ever wanted in the first place. They feel so guilty about the suffering of the poor, and are so keen to share it, that they deliberately make their lives miserable. My father was a teacher, but they removed him from his post. During one torture session they pulled out one of his fingernails; after another session they threw him into prison. Still he did what he could. For years he and my mother ran a stationery store. They did photocopying. They even translated a few novels from French into Turkish. At times they would go door to door selling encyclopedias on the instalment plan. When the poverty was just too much to bear, he'd put his arms around us and cry. He was always so afraid something bad would happen to us. And so, when the police came to see us after the director of the Education Institute was shot, he grew very frightened – even though he grumbled at them, too.

'I've heard that you went to see Blue. Please don't tell my father.'

'I won't tell him,' said Ka. He stopped to brush the snow off his coat. 'Aren't we going this way – straight to the hotel?'

'You can go this way, too. The snow doesn't end, and neither will the list of things we have to discuss. Besides, I'd like to show you Butcher Street . . . What did Blue want from you?'

'Nothing.'

'Did he say anything about us – my father or my sister?'

Ka saw an anxious expression on Kadife's face. 'I can't remember,' he said.

'Everyone's afraid of him. We are, too . . . These are the most famous butchers' shops in the city.'

'How does your father spend his days?' asked Ka. 'Does he ever leave the house – the hotel?'

'He manages the hotel. He gives orders to the housekeeper, the cleaner, the laundrywoman and the porters. My sister and I help out. But my father almost never goes out. What's your sign?'

'Gemini,' said Ka. 'Geminis are supposed to tell lots of lies, but I'm not so sure.'

'Are you saying that you don't know whether Geminis tell a lot of lies or that you don't know whether you have?'

'If you believe in astrology, you must be able to figure out why today is such a special day for me.'

'Yes, my sister told me: today you wrote a poem.'

'Does your sister tell you everything?'

'We have two diversions here. We talk about everything that happens to us, and we watch television. We even talk while watching television. And while we're talking, we watch television, too. My sister is very beautiful, don't you think?'

'Yes, she's very beautiful,' said Ka reverently. 'But you're also beautiful,' he added politely. 'And now are you going to tell her that, too?'

'No, I'm not going to tell her. Let's have one secret we can share. It's the best way to begin a friendship.'

She brushed off the snow that had piled up on her long, purple coat.

How Do You Write Poems?

*As Supper is Served, the Conversation Turns to Love,
Headscarves and Suicide*

They saw a crowd milling in front of the National Theatre; in just a few minutes, the show would begin. The relentless snowfall seemed to have deterred no one, or perhaps the snow itself had made people decide that, with so much going wrong, they might as well seize this chance for an enjoyable evening out. Many of those gathered on the pavement in front of the 110-year-old building came from the ranks of the unemployed: there were youths who had left their homes and their dormitories in shirts and ties, and boys who had snuck out of the house. Many older people had brought their children. For the first time since arriving in Kars, Ka saw an open black umbrella. Kadife knew that Ka was scheduled to appear on the programme to recite a poem, but when Ka said that he had no intention of taking part, and had no time for it anyway, she made no attempt to persuade him.

He could feel another poem coming, so he cut their conversation short and rushed back to the hotel as fast as he could. He excused himself by saying that he needed to nip back to his room to collect himself; no sooner had he opened the door than he threw off his coat, sat down at the small table and began to scribble furiously. The poem's main themes were friendship and secrecy. Snowflakes and stars also featured, as did a number of motifs that suggested special, happy days. A number of Kadife's remarks went straight into the verse, without alteration, and, as one line followed another, Ka surveyed the page with the pleasure and excitement of a painter watching a picture appear on his canvas.

He could see now that his conversation with Kadife had a hidden logic. In this poem, entitled 'Stars and Their Friends', he elaborated the theory that every person had a star, every star had a friend, and for every person carrying a star there was someone else who reflected it, and everyone carried this reflection as a secret confidant in his heart. Although he could hear the poem's music in his head and exalted in its perfection, he had to skip a word that eluded him here and there; there were a few lines missing, too. He would later say that this was because of his preoccupation with İpek, his not having had his supper yet, and his being happier than he had ever been.

As soon as he finished the poem, he rushed down to the lobby and into the owner's private quarters. Sitting at a bountifully set table in the middle of a spacious room with high ceilings, flanked on either side by his daughters Kadife and İpek, was Turgut Bey. There was a third girl too, sitting to one side. She wore a stylish purple headscarf, and Ka knew her at once to be Kadife's friend Hande. Across from her was Serdar Bey, the newspaperman. He seemed at home in this group. As Ka surveyed all the dishes on the table – what a strange and beautiful disorder – and watched the Kurdish maid, Zahide, gracefully darting in and out of the back kitchen, he imagined that Turgut Bey and his daughters were accustomed to spending long evenings at this supper table.

'I've been thinking about you all day; all day I've been worrying about you,' said Turgut Bey. 'Why are you so late?' He rose to his feet and leaned over to wrap his arms around Ka in such a way that Ka thought his host was about to cry. 'Terrible things can happen at any time,' he said with a tragic air.

Ka sat down in the place Turgut Bey indicated, directly across from him. The maid served him a bowl of lentil soup, which he devoured hungrily. As the two other men returned to their raki, their eyes drifted towards the television behind Ka, and when he saw that everyone else had done the same, he did something he'd been dreaming of for a long time: he stared at İpek's beautiful face.

Because he would later vividly describe his boundless ecstasy in his notebook, I know exactly how he felt at that moment – like a happy child, he couldn't keep his arms or legs still. His jittery impatience was such as he would feel if he and İpek were rushing to catch the train that would take them back to Frankfurt. He looked at Turgut Bey's work-table – piled high with books, newspapers, receipts, hotel record-books – and as he gazed at the circle cast by the lamp below its shade, he conjured up the vision of another circle of light, one on his own work-table, in the little office he would share with İpek when they returned to live happily ever after in Frankfurt.

Just then he saw that Kadife's eyes were on him. Meeting her gaze, Ka thought he saw a flash of jealousy in her face, which was not as beautiful as her sister's, but she managed to conceal it with a conspiratorial smile.

His dinner companions remained mesmerised by the television set; even in the midst of conversation, they kept glancing at it out of the corners of their eyes. The live telecast from the National Theatre had begun: the very tall, very thin presenter swaying this way and that on the stage was one of the actors Ka had seen while getting off the bus the previous evening. They had not been watching him long when Turgut Bey picked up the remote control and changed the channel. For an age they sat staring at a fuzzy picture flecked with white dots: they had no idea what they were watching, but it seemed to be in black and white.

'Father,' said İpek, 'why are you watching this?'

'It's snowing here . . .' said Turgut Bey. 'If nothing else, this is an accurate description. This counts as real news. And anyway, you know that if I watch one channel for too long, I feel robbed of my dignity.'

'Then, Father, why don't you just turn off the television? Something else is going on here that's robbing us all of our dignity.'

'Tell our guest what's happened,' said Turgut Bey, looking rather shame-faced. 'It makes me uneasy that he doesn't know.'

'That's how I feel, too,' said Hande. There was anger in her large and beautiful black eyes.

For a moment everyone fell silent.

'Why don't you tell the story, Hande?' said Kadife. 'There's nothing to be ashamed of.'

'No, that's not true. There's a great deal to be ashamed of, and that's why I want to talk about it,' said Hande. Her eyes flashed with a strange joy. She smiled as if recalling a happy memory and said, 'It's forty days exactly since our friend Teslime's suicide. Of all the girls in our group, Teslime was the one most dedicated to the struggle for her religion and the Word of God. For her, the headscarf did not just stand for God's love; it also proclaimed her faith and preserved her honour. None of us could ever have imagined she would kill herself. Despite pressure both at school and at home to take off her scarf – her father and her teachers were relentless – Teslime held her ground. She was about to be expelled from school – in her third year of study, just on the verge of graduating. Then, one day her father had some visitors from the police headquarters; they told him that if he didn't send his daughter to school scarfless, they would "close down his shop and run him out of Kars". Now, the father threatened to throw Teslime out of the house, and when this tactic failed, he entered into negotiations to marry her off to a forty-five-year-old policeman who had lost his wife. Things had gone so far that the policeman was coming to the grocery store with flowers. Teslime told us that she was so revolted by this "grey-eyed widower" that she was thinking of removing her headscarf, if it would save her from this marriage. But she just couldn't bring herself to do it. Some of us agreed that she should take off the headscarf to avoid marrying the widower, while others of us said, "Why don't you threaten your father with suicide?" I was the one who urged this most strongly. I really didn't want Teslime to give up her headscarf. I don't know how many times I said, "Teslime, it's far better to kill yourself than to uncover your head." But I was just making a point. I never thought she'd actually do it. We believed what the papers said – that the suicide girls had killed themselves because they had no faith, because they were slaves to materialism, because they had been unlucky in love – and so all I was trying to do was give Teslime's father a fright. Teslime was a devout girl and so I assumed she would never seriously consider suicide. But when we heard she had hanged herself, I was the first to believe it. And, what's more, I knew that, had I been in her shoes, I would have done the same thing.'

Hande began to cry. İpek went to her side, gave her a kiss and began to caress her. Kadife joined them. With the girls wrapped in one another's arms, Turgut Bey was waving the remote control and soon also trying to comfort Hande. Before long, they were all telling jokes to keep Hande from crying. As though trying to distract a weeping child, Turgut Bey pointed out the giraffes on television: then, like the child not yet certain she's ready to relent, Hande tearfully gazed at the screen. For a very long while, they forgot their own lives as they watched two giraffes in slow motion, in a faraway land, in a field shaded by the heavy growth of trees.

'After Teslime's suicide, Hande decided to take off her headscarf and return to school – she didn't want to cause her parents any more distress,' explained Kadife. 'They'd made so many sacrifices, gone without so much, to give her the right sort of upbringing. The things most people would do for their only son, they did for her. Her parents have always assumed that Hande would be able to support them one day, because she is very clever.' Kadife was speaking softly, almost whispering, but still loud enough for Hande to hear her, and, like everyone else in the room, Hande was listening, even with her tear-filled eyes still fixed on the television screen. 'At first the rest of us tried to talk her out of removing her scarf, but when we realised that her going uncovered was better than her committing suicide, we decided to support her decision. When a girl has accepted the headscarf as the Word of God and the symbol of faith, it's very difficult for her to take it off. Hande spent days locked up inside her house trying to "concentrate".'

Like everyone else in the room, Ka was cowering with embarrassment at this deeply disturbing story, but when his arm brushed against İpek's arm, a wave of happiness spread through him. As Turgut Bey jumped from channel to channel, Ka tried to find more happiness by pressing his arm against İpek's. When İpek did the same, he forgot all about the sad story he'd just heard.

Once again, the television was tuned to the programme coming from the National Theatre. The tall, thin man was saying how proud he was to be taking part in Kars' first live telecast. He announced the schedule for the evening, promising spectacular renditions of the world's greatest legends, secret confessions of our national goalkeeper, shocking revelations that would bring shame to our political history, unforgettable scenes from Shakespeare and Victor Hugo, amorous disasters, the greatest, most glittering stars of Turkish film and theatre, jokes, songs and earth-shattering surprises. Then Ka heard himself described as 'our greatest poet, who has returned to our country in silence after many years'. Reaching under the table, İpek took hold of his hand.

'I understand that you don't want to take part in the performance,' said Turgut Bey.

'I'm very happy where I am, sir. Very happy indeed,' said Ka, pressing his arm harder against İpek.

'I really wouldn't want to do anything to disrupt your happiness,' said Hande, setting everyone in the room on edge. 'But I came here tonight to meet you. I haven't read any of your books, but it's enough for me that you're a poet and have been to places like Germany. Do you mind if I ask whether you've written any poems lately?'

'Quite a few have come to me since I arrived in Kars,' said Ka.

'I wanted to meet you because I thought you could tell me how I might learn to concentrate. May I ask, how do you write poems? Isn't it through concentration?'

Whenever he gave readings for Turks in Germany, this was the most common question from women in the audience; but every time they asked, Ka recoiled, as if having been quizzed on something very personal. 'I have no idea how poems are written,' he said. 'A good poem always seems to come from outside, from far away.' He saw suspicion in Hande's eyes. 'Why don't you explain to me what you mean by "concentrate"?'

'I try all day, but I can't conjure up the vision I want to see, the vision of myself without a headscarf. Instead I keep seeing all the things I want to forget.'

'For example?'

'When they first noticed how many of us were wearing head-scarves, they sent us a woman from Ankara to try to talk us out of it. This "agent of persuasion" sat in the same room for hours on end, talking to each of us alone. She asked things like, "Did your parents beat you? How many children are there in your family? How much does your father earn? What sort of clothes did you wear before you adopted religious dress? Do you love Atatürk? What sort of pictures do you have hanging on the walls at home? How many times a week do you go to the movies? In your view, are men and women equals? Is God greater than the state, or is the state greater than God? How many children do you want to have? Have you ever suffered from abuse in the home?" She asked us hundreds of questions like these, and she wrote down all our answers, filling out a long form for each of us. She was a very stylish woman – painted nails, dyed hair, no headscarf, of course, and she wore the sort of clothes you see in mag-azines – but at the same time she was – how should I put this? – plain. Even though some of her questions made us cry, we liked her . . . we even hoped that the muddy streets of Kars weren't causing her too much trouble. Afterwards I began to see her in my dreams. At first I didn't read too much into it, but now, whenever I try to imagine myself walking through crowds with my hair flying all around me, I see myself as the "agent of persuasion". In my mind's eye I'm as stylish as she is, wearing stilettos, and dresses even shorter than hers. And men are staring at me. I find this pleasing – and at the same time shameful.'

'Hande, you don't have to describe your shame unless you want to,' said Kadife.

'No, I'm going to talk about it. Even though I feel shame in my dreams, that doesn't mean I'm ashamed *of* my dreams. Even if I did take off my headscarf, I don't think I'd become the kind of woman who flirts with men, or who can't think of anything but sex. After all, when I do take off my headscarf, I won't be doing it of my own free will. Still, I know people can be overcome by sexual feelings even when they do something like this without conviction, without even wanting it. There's one thing all men and women have in common – we all sin in our dreams with people who wouldn't remotely interest us in our waking lives. Isn't that true?'

'That's enough, Hande,' said Kadife.

'But isn't it?'

'No, it isn't,' said Kadife. She turned to Ka. 'Two years before all this happened, Hande got engaged to a very handsome Kurdish teenager. But the poor boy got mixed up in politics and they killed him . . .'

'That has nothing to do with my reluctance to bare my head,' Hande said angrily. 'The true reason is that I can't concentrate, I can't imagine myself without a headscarf. Whenever I try to concentrate, I turn into either an evil stranger like the "agent of persuasion" or a woman who can't stop thinking about sex. If I could close my eyes just once and imagine myself going bare-headed through the doors of the school, walking down the corridor, and going into class, I'd find the strength to go through with this, and then, God willing, I'd be free. I would have removed the headscarf of my own free will, and not because the police have forced me. But for now I just can't concentrate, I just can't bring myself to imagine that moment.'

'Then stop making so much of that moment,' said Kadife. 'Even if you collapse there and then, you'll still be our beloved Hande.'

'No, I won't,' said Hande. 'That's what's caused me the most anguish since I left you and decided to bare my head – knowing that you despise me.' She turned to Ka. 'Sometimes I can conjure up an image of a girl walking into school with her hair flying all around her. I can see her walking down the hall and entering my favourite classroom–oh, how I miss that classroom. I can even imagine the smell of the hallway and the clamminess of the air. Then I look through the pane of glass that separates the classroom from the hallway and I see that this girl is not me but someone else, and I start to cry.'

Everyone thought that Hande was about to start crying again.

'I'm not all that afraid of becoming someone else,' said Hande. 'What scares me is the thought of never being able to return to the person I am now – and even forgetting who that person is. That's the sort of thing that makes people commit suicide.' She turned again to Ka. 'Have you ever wanted to commit suicide?' She sounded almost flirtatious.

'No, but after hearing about the women of Kars, you can't help asking yourself difficult questions.'

'If a lot of girls in our situation are thinking about suicide, you could say it has to do with wanting to control our own bodies. That's what suicide offers girls who've been duped into giving up their virginity, and it's the same for virgins who are married off to men they don't want. For girls like that, a suicide wish is a wish for innocence and purity. Have you written any poems about suicide?' She instinctively turned to İpek. 'Have I gone too far now, am I really bothering your friend? All right then, if he would just tell me *where* they've come from, these poems that have "come" to him in Kars, then I promise to leave him alone.'

'When I sense a poem coming to me, my heart is full of gratitude for the sender, because I feel so very happy.'

'Is that the same person who makes your poems more intense? Who is that person?'

'I can't be sure of this, but I think it is He who is sending me the poems.'

'Is it that you can't be sure of God, or simply that you can't be sure it's God who is sending them?'

'It's God who sends me poems,' said Ka fervently.

'He's seen the rise of political Islam,' said Turgut Bey. 'Maybe that's even threatened him, scared him into becoming a believer.'

'No, it comes from inside,' said Ka. 'I want to join in, be just like everyone else here.'

'I'm sorry: you're afraid, and I'm reprimanding you.'

'Yes, of course I'm scared,' said Ka, raising his voice. 'I'm very scared.' Then Ka jumped to his feet fast, as if someone were pointing a gun at him.

Or so it seemed to everyone else at the table. 'Where is he?' cried Turgut Bey – as if he, too, sensed someone were about to shoot them.

'I'm not afraid,' said Hande. 'I couldn't care less what happens to me.'

Everyone was looking at Ka and trying to figure out where the danger was.

Years later, Serdar Bey told me that Ka's face turned ashen at this point, but there was nothing in his expression to suggest either fear or dizziness. What Serdar Bey recalled seeing was sublime joy. The maid went further and told me that a light had entered the room and bathed all those present with divine radiance. In her eyes, he achieved sainthood. Apparently someone then said, 'A poem has arrived' – an announcement that caused more fear and amazement than the imaginary gun. According to the more measured account in Ka's notebook, the tense, expectant air in the room brought back memories of the seances we had witnessed as children a quarter-century ago in a house in one of the back streets of Nişantaş. These evenings were organised by a friend's fat mother, who had been widowed at an early age. Most of her guests were unhappy house-wives, but other regulars were a pianist with paralysed fingers, a neurotic middle-aged film star (but only because we kept asking for her), her sister (forever yawning), a retired pasha who was 'wooing' the fading star, and, when our friend could sneak us in, Ka and myself. During the uneasy waiting period, someone would say, 'Oh soul, if you've come back to us, speak!' and after a long silence there would be an almost imperceptible rattling, the scraping of a chair, a moan, and sometimes the sound of someone giving a swift kick to a leg of the table, whereupon a trembling voice would announce: 'The soul has arrived.'

But as he headed towards the kitchen, Ka was not at all like a man who'd made contact with the dead. His face was radiating joy.

'He's had a lot to drink,' said Turgut Bey. 'Go and help him.'

He said this so that it would look as if he had sent İpek running after Ka, who had hurled himself on to a chair next to the kitchen door. He took out his notebook and his pen.

'I can't write with you all standing around watching me,' he said.

'Let me take you to another room,' said İpek.

Ka followed İpek through the kitchen, which was full of the sweet smell of a syrup Zahide was pouring over bread pudding. Then they passed through a cold room and into another which was half in darkness.

'Do you think you can write here?' asked İpek, as she turned on a lamp.

Around him, Ka saw a tidy room with two perfectly made beds. There was a low table and a nightstand on which the sisters had arranged various pots of cream, lipsticks, small bottles of perfume, a modest collection of other substances in bottles that had once held alcohol and cooking oil, books, a zippered pouch, and an old Swiss chocolate box filled with brushes, pens, charms against the evil eye, necklaces and bracelets. He sat on the bed, beside the frozen window pane.

'I can write here,' he said. 'But don't leave me alone.'

'Why not?'

'I don't know,' he said, before adding, 'I'm worried.'

He set to work on the poem, which began with a description of the chocolate box his uncle had brought from Switzerland when Ka was a child. The box was decorated with the same Swiss landscapes he'd been seeing all day in the tea-shops of Kars. According to notes Ka would make later on – when he went back to interpret, classify and organise the poems that had 'come' to him in Kars – the first thing to emerge from this box was a toy clock. Two days later he would discover that İpek had played with this clock as a child. And Ka would use it to travel back in time and say a few things about childhood and life itself . . .

'I don't want you ever to leave me,' Ka told İpek. 'I've fallen wildly in love with you.'

'But you hardly know me,' said İpek.

'There are two kinds of men,' said Ka didactically. 'The first kind does not fall in love until he's seen how the girl eats a sandwich, how she combs her hair, what sort of nonsense she cares about, why she's angry with her father, and what stories people tell about her. The second type of man – and I am in this category – can fall in love with a woman only if he knows next to nothing about her.'

'In other words, you've fallen in love with me because you know nothing about me? Do you really think you can call this love?'

'If you fall head over heels, that's how it happens,' said Ka.

'So once you know how I eat a sandwich and what I wear in my hair, you'll fall right out of love.'

'No, by then the intimacy that's built up between us will deepen and turn into a desire that wraps itself around our bodies – we'll be bound together by our happy memories.'

'Don't get up – sit there on the bed,' said İpek. 'I can't kiss anyone when my father is under the same roof.' In spite of these words, though, she did not reject his first kisses. But then she pushed him away, saying, 'When my father is in the house, I don't like it.'

Ka tried to plant one more kiss on her lips before sitting back down on the edge of the bed. 'We're going to have to get married and run away from this place as soon as is humanly possible. Do you know how happy we could be in Frankfurt?'

İpek did not reply immediately. Then she asked, 'How can you fall in love with me without even knowing me?'

'Because you're so beautiful . . . Because I've already seen in my dreams how happy we will be together . . . Because I can tell you anything without a hint of shame. In my dreams I can never stop imagining us making love.'

'What did you do while you were in Frankfurt?'

'I'd think a lot about the poems I wasn't able to write . . . I masturbated . . . Solitude is essentially a matter of pride; you bury yourself in your own scent. The issue is the same for all real poets. If you've been happy too long, you become banal. By the same token, if you've been unhappy for a long time, you lose your poetic powers . . . Happiness and poetry can only coexist for the briefest time. Afterwards either happiness coarsens the poet or the poem is so true that it destroys his happiness. I'm terribly afraid of the unhappiness that could be waiting for me in Frankfurt.'

'Then stay in Istanbul,' said İpek.

Ka looked at her carefully. 'Is Istanbul where you want to live?' he asked in a whisper. His greatest wish just then was for İpek to ask something of him.

İpek sensed this, too. 'I don't want anything,' she said.

Ka knew he was rushing. But something told him he wasn't going to be in Kars much longer, that soon he would be unable to breathe here – so he had to rush, as if his life depended on it. For a few moments they listened to snatches of a distant conversation; then a

129

horse and carriage passed under the window and they listened to the wheels rolling over the snow. İpek was standing in the doorway, slowly and meticulously removing the hair that had collected in the brush in her hand.

'Life here is so poor and hopeless that people, even people like you, forget what it's like to want something,' said Ka. 'One cannot think of life here, only death . . . Are you coming with me?' İpek didn't answer. 'If you're going to say no, then don't answer me at all,' added Ka.

'I don't know,' said İpek, her eyes on the brush. 'They're waiting for us in the other room.'

'There's some sort of intrigue going on in there, but I have no idea what it's about,' said Ka. 'Why don't you explain it to me?'

The lights went off. When İpek didn't move, Ka wanted to embrace her, but he was so wrapped up in fearful thoughts about returning to Frankfurt alone that he couldn't move himself.

'You're not going to be able to write a poem in this pitch darkness,' said İpek. 'Let's go.'

'What do you want most from me? What can I do to make you love me?'

'Be yourself,' said İpek. She stood up and headed for the door.

Ka had been so happy sitting on the edge of the bed that it took a great effort to stand. He sat down again in the cold room next to the kitchen and in the flickering candlelight penned the poem entitled 'The Chocolate Box' in his green notebook.

When he rose again, he found İpek right in front of him. He rushed forward to embrace her and bury himself in her hair, but his thoughts got in the way, it was almost as if they, too, were stumbling in the dark.

There, glowing in the candlelight from the kitchen, were İpek and Kadife. With their arms around each other's neck, they were embracing like lovers.

'Father sent me to find you,' said Kadife.

'That's fine, dear,' replied İpek.

'Wasn't he able to write his poem?'

'I did write it,' said Ka, coming out of the shadows. 'But now I was hoping to help you.'

He went into the kitchen; in the light cast by his candle, he saw no one. He quickly filled a glass with raki and drank it neat. When the tears began to stream down his face, he poured himself a glass of water.

When he left the kitchen, he found himself plunged into a menacing darkness. Then he saw the distant candle on the supper table and headed towards it. The people at the table turned to look at him, and the gigantic shadows he cast on the wall.

'Were you able to write your poem?' asked Turgut Bey. He prefaced the question with a few moments of silence, as if to convey a slight air of mockery.

'Yes.'

'Congratulations.' He'd pressed a raki glass into Ka's hand and began to fill it. 'What's it about?'

'Everyone I've interviewed since coming here, everyone I've talked to. I agree with them all. The fear I used to feel in Frankfurt when I was walking in the street, that fear is now inside me.'

'I understand you perfectly,' said Hande with a knowing look.

Ka smiled gratefully. 'Don't bare your head, my little beauty,' he wanted to say.

'If, when you say you believe everyone you've heard here, you mean to tell me that you believed in God while you were in the company of Sheikh Efendi,' said Turgut Bey, 'then let me make one thing clear: Sheikh Efendi does not speak for God in Kars!'

'So who does speak for God here?' asked Hande.

Turgut Bey didn't snap at her. Stubborn and quarrelsome though he was, he was too soft-hearted to be an implacable atheist. Ka also sensed that, as much as Turgut Bey worried about his daughters' unhappiness, he worried even more that his habits and his world might disintegrate. This wasn't a political anxiety but the anxiety of a man who, more than anything, feared losing his place at the table, whose only pleasure was spending his evenings with his daughters and his guests, arguing for hours about politics and the existence or non-existence of God.

The electricity came back on, and suddenly the room was bright. They were so accustomed by now to the lights' random coming and going that no one here bothered with the rituals of power cuts that had been practised in Ka's childhood in Istanbul: no one cheered when the lights returned or asked if the washing-machine was stuck in the middle of a cycle; there was none of the joy he had once felt saying, 'Let me be the one to blow out the candles' – instead, he simply acted as if nothing had happened. Turgut Bey turned the television back on and, having taken possession of the remote control, began to surf the channels.

Ka whispered to the girls that Kars was an extraordinarily quiet city.

'That's because we're afraid of even our own voices,' said Hande.

'That', said İpek, 'is the silence of snow.'

Feeling defeated, they stared grimly at the ever-changing television screen. As he held hands with İpek under the table, it occurred to Ka that if he spent his days doing nothing much at all, and his evenings holding hands with İpek and watching satellite TV, he would live in bliss for the rest of his life.

15

There's One Thing We All Want out of Life

At the National Theatre

Exactly seven minutes after deciding that he and İpek could live happily ever after in Kars, Ka was racing through the snow to the National Theatre, his heart pounding as if he were heading alone into a war zone. Everything had changed during those seven minutes, with a speed possessed of its own logic.

It began when Turgut Bey switched back to the broadcast of the performance at the National Theatre; it was clear from the roar of the audience that something extraordinary had just happened. Although this awakened in the viewers a longing for excitement, a desire to step outside their little provincial routines, if only for one night, it also created anxiety that something might go very wrong. As they watched the restless audience clap and shout, they sensed a certain tension between the VIPs sitting in the front rows and the youths at the back. With the camera showing only part of the hall, they were all very curious to know what was happening.

On stage was a goalkeeper who had once been a household name all over Turkey, talking about a tragic match fifteen years earlier in which England had managed to score eleven goals. He had barely finished the sad tale of the first goal when the tall, thin presenter appeared on screen. Realising that they must be pausing for a commercial break, the goalkeeper stopped speaking. The presenter grabbed the microphone and, after rattling off two advertisements (the Tadal Grocery Store on Fevzi Pasha Avenue was proud to announce that the spiced beef from Kayseri had finally arrived, and the Knowledge Study Centre had opened registration for their university preparation course), he reminded the audience of the delights still to come. When he announced Ka's name again, he looked mournfully into the camera.

'Missing this chance to see our great poet, who travelled all the way from Frankfurt to visit our border city, is a great sadness.'

'Well, that does it,' said Turgut Bey at once. 'If you don't go now, you'll cause terrible offence.'

'But they never even asked me if I'd like to take part,' said Ka.

'That's the way things are done here,' said Turgut Bey. 'If they'd invited you, you'd have declined. But now you *will* go, because you don't want it to seem as if you look down on them.'

'We'll watch you from here,' said Hande, with an enthusiasm that no one could have predicted.

At that moment, the door opened. It was the boy who was the night receptionist. 'The director of the Institute of Education has just died in hospital,' he said.

'Poor fool,' said Turgut Bey. Then he fixed his eyes on Ka. 'The Islamists have embarked on a clean-up operation. They're taking care of us one by one. If you want to save your skin, I would advise that you increase your faith in God at the earliest opportunity. It won't be long, I fear, before a moderate belief in God will be insufficient to save the skin of an old atheist.'

'I think you're right,' said Ka. 'As it happens, I've already decided to answer the call that's been coming from deep within me my whole life and open my heart to God.'

They all caught his sarcastic tone. Knowing he was very drunk, they all suspected that this witticism might well have been prepared in advance.

Then Zahide breezed in with a huge pot and an aluminium ladle that glistened in the lamplight. Smiling at the table like a proud mother, she said, 'One more portion of soup left; let's not waste it, which girl would like it?'

İpek had been advising Ka not to go to the National Theatre for fear of what might happen there, but now she turned around to smile with Kadife and Hande at the Kurdish maid.

If İpek says, 'I do!' thought Ka, it means we're getting married and going back together to Frankfurt. In that case, I'll go to the National Theatre to read 'Snow'.

'I do!' said İpek, holding out her bowl somewhat joylessly.

As he walked among the giant snowflakes, Ka remembered that he was an outsider in Kars, and for a moment he felt sure he'd forget this city the second he left it, but the feeling didn't last long. Now suddenly he had intimations of destiny; he could see that life had a secret geometry on which his rational mind had no purchase. But even as he was overcome with a desire to subdue his reason and find happiness, he also sensed that – for the moment at least – his yearning for happiness was not yet strong enough.

He looked ahead, at the line of waving campaign banners stretching as far as the National Theatre; there wasn't a soul beneath them anywhere on the wide, snow-covered avenue. As he gazed at the grand old buildings on either side, admiring their handsome doors, their generously proportioned eaves, their beautiful friezes, and their dignified but time-worn façades, Ka had a strong sense of the people (Armenians who traded in Tiflis? Ottoman pashas who collected taxes from the dairies?) who had once led happy, peaceful and even colourful lives here. Gone now were all the Armenians, Russians, Ottomans and early republican Turks who had made this city a modest centre of civilisation; and since no one had come to replace them, the streets were deserted. But, unlike those in most deserted cities, these empty streets did not inspire fear. Ka marvelled at the snow-laden branches of the oleanders and the plane trees, and at the icicles hanging from the sides of the electricity poles feeding the pale orange light of the streetlamps, and the dying neon bulbs behind the icy shop windows. The snow was falling into a magical, almost holy silence, and aside from his own, virtually silent footsteps and rapid breathing, Ka could hear nothing. Not a single dog was barking. He had arrived at the end of the earth, the whole world apparently mesmerised by the falling snow. As he watched the snowflakes fall through the halo of light, he saw how some fell heavily earthward while others wheeled around to fly back up into the darkness.

Standing under the eaves of the Palace of Light Photo Studio, with the help of the red light from its ice-covered signboard, he studied a snowflake that had landed on the sleeve of his coat.

There was a gust of wind; something moved. As the red light on the sign of the Palace of Light Photo Studio went out, the oleander tree opposite seemed to go out with it. He looked towards the National Theatre and saw crowds around the entrance; just beyond them he could see a police minibus. There were more crowds gathering outside the coffee-houses across the road.

The moment he stepped into the theatre, the wave of noise and motion coming from the audience overwhelmed him. The air was thick with alcohol fumes, cigarette smoke and exhaled breath. They were standing shoulder to shoulder in the aisles; in one corner was a tea stand selling soft drinks and sesame rolls. From the door to the toilets came the whiff of something like a corpse, and Ka spotted a group of whispering youths. On one side he saw uniformed policemen in blue, and further ahead he passed a few in plain clothes listening to their police radios. A child holding his father's hand studied the dried chickpeas he'd dropped into his soda bottle, totally oblivious to the noise behind him.

Someone was waving vigorously from the aisle, but Ka was not sure whether this person was waving at him.

'I recognised you from all the way over there – just by your coat.'

When he saw Necip's face emerge from the crowd, Ka felt his heart leap. They embraced warmly.

'I knew you would come,' said Necip. 'I'm so glad to see you. Do you mind if I ask you one thing right now? I have two very important things on my mind.'

'So do you want to ask me one thing, or two things?'

'You're very intelligent, so intelligent that you know that intelligence is not everything,' said Necip. He took Ka over to a corner where it was calmer. 'Did you tell Hicran, or Kadife, that I was in love with her, and that she was my whole life?'

'No, I didn't.'

'You left the tea-house with her. Didn't you mention me at all?'

'I said you were a student at the religious high school.'

'And then what? Didn't she say anything?'

'No, she didn't.'

After a pause, and with some effort, Necip said, 'I know the real reason why you didn't mention me again.' He gulped. 'Because Kadife is four years older than me – so she probably hasn't even noticed me. Maybe you discussed private matters with her. Maybe even secret, political matters. I'm not asking you to tell me one way or the other. I'm concerned about one thing only and this thing is extremely important for me. The answer you give will affect the rest of my life. Even if Kadife hasn't yet noticed me – and it might take her years, and by then she could be married – your answer now could lead me to spend the rest of my life loving her, or it could lead me to forget her from this moment on. So please, without hesitation, give me your answer now.'

'I'm still waiting for your question,' said Ka, officiously.

'Did you talk about superficial things at all? Things like the nonsense on television, or meaningless titbits of gossip, or the little things money can buy. Do you know what I mean? Is Kadife the sort of serious person who has no time for such superficialities, or have I fallen in love with her for nothing?'

'No, we didn't talk about anything superficial,' said Ka. In the teenager's face he could see evidence of a superhuman effort to recover his strength.

'But you did decide that she is an extraordinary person.'

'Yes.'

'Could you yourself fall in love with her? She is very beautiful, after all. She's beautiful, and she's independent – more than any other Turkish woman I've ever seen.'

'Her sister's even more beautiful,' said Ka. 'If beauty's what we're discussing.'

'What are we really discussing, though?' asked Necip. 'What does God in His wisdom intend by making me think so much about Kadife?' With a childishness that amazed Ka, he opened his large green eyes (one of which would be shattered in fifty-one minutes).

'I don't know,' said Ka.

'You do, you're just not telling me.'

'I don't know.'

'A writer should be able to talk about everything that's important,' said Necip encouragingly. 'If I were a writer, I'd want to talk about everything that people didn't talk about. Can't you tell me everything, just this once?'

'So ask.'

'There's one thing we all want out of life, one main thing, isn't there?'

'That's right.'

'So what is it would you say?'

Ka remained silent, and smiled.

'For me, it's very simple,' said Necip, with pride. 'I want to marry Kadife, live in Istanbul, and become the world's first Islamist science-fiction writer. I know none of this is possible, but I still want it. If you can't tell me what you want, it's OK, because I understand you. You are my future. And my instinct also tells me this: when you look at me, you see your own youth, and that's why you like me.'

A happy, cunning smile began to take form on Necip's lips, and it made Ka uneasy.

'So, you think you're the person I was twenty years ago?'

'Yes. There's going to be a scene exactly like this in the science-fiction novel I'm going to write one day. Excuse me, may I put my hand on your forehead?'

Ka tilted his head slightly forward. With the ease of a well-practised gesture, Necip put his palm on Ka's forehead.

'Now, I'm going to tell you what you were thinking twenty years ago.'

'Is this what you were doing with Fazıl?'

'We think the same thing at the same time. But with you and me, there's a time difference. Now, listen to me, please: on a winter day, when you were a lycée student, it was snowing, and you were lost in thought. You could hear God inside you, and you were trying to forget Him. You could see that the world was a unified entity, but you thought that if you could close your eyes to this vision, you could be more unhappy and also more intelligent. And you were right. Only people who are very intelligent and very unhappy can write good poems. So you heroically undertook to endure the pains of faithlessness, just to be able to write good poems. But you didn't realise then that when you lost that voice inside you, you'd end up all alone in an empty universe.'

'All right. You're right. I was thinking this,' said Ka. 'So tell me, is this what you're thinking right now?'

'I knew you were going to ask me that,' said Necip uneasily. 'Don't you *want* to believe in God? You do, don't you?' His hand was so cold that it was making Ka shiver, but now Necip took it off Ka's forehead. 'I could tell you a lot more about this. There's another voice inside me that tells me, "Don't believe in God," because, when you devote so much of your heart to believing something exists, you can't help having a little suspicion, a little voice that asks, "What if it doesn't?" You understand, don't you? Just at those times when I realised my belief in my beautiful God sustained me, I would sometimes ask myself, just as a child would wonder what would happen if his parents died, What if God doesn't exist, what happens then? At those times a vision would appear before my eyes: a landscape. Because I knew that this landscape was made by God's love, I felt no fear and looked at it. I wanted to look at it carefully.'

'Tell me about this landscape.'

'Are you going to put it into a poem? If you do, you don't need to mention my name. I want only one thing from you in exchange.'

'Yes?'

'In the last six months, I've written three letters to Kadife. I couldn't bring myself to post any of them. It's not because I'm ashamed: I didn't send them because I knew they would be opened and read at the post office, because half the people in Kars are working as undercover policemen. Half the people in this hall are, too. They follow us everywhere we go. Even our people are following us.'

'Who are "our people"?'

'All the young Islamists of Kars. They were very curious to know what I was going to say to you. They came here to make trouble, because they knew that the military and the secularists were going to turn this evening into a public demonstration. They're going to put on that old play we've heard so much about – *Headscarf*. And we hear they are going to use it to belittle our headscarf girls. To tell you the truth, I can't stand politics, but my friends are right to be enraged by this. They're suspicious of me though, because I'm not as fired up as they are. I can't give you those letters. I mean, not right now, with everyone watching. I want you to give them to Kadife.'

'No one's looking now. Give them to me quickly, and then tell me about that landscape.'

'The letters are here, but I don't have them on me. I was afraid they'd search me at the door. My friends might have searched me, too. If you go through that door next to the stage, you'll see a toilet at the far end of the corridor – meet me there in exactly twenty minutes.'

'Will you tell me about the landscape then?'

'One of them is coming towards us now,' said Necip, looking away. 'I know him. Don't look in his direction, just act like we're having a normal, casual conversation.'

'All right.'

'Everyone in Kars is very curious to know why you've come here. They think you're on a secret government mission, or else you've been sent here by the Western powers. My friends sent me over to ask you if these rumours are true. Are they?'

'No, they're not.'

'What shall I tell them, then? Why have you come?'

'I don't know.'

'You do know, but once again you're too ashamed to admit it.' He paused before continuing. 'You came here because you were unhappy.'

'How can you tell?'

'From your eyes: I've never seen anyone look so unhappy . . . I'm not at all happy right now, either; but at least I'm young. Unhappiness gives me strength. At this age, I'd rather be unhappy than happy. The only people who can be happy in Kars are the idiots and the villains. But by the time I'm your age, I want to be able to wrap my life in happiness.'

'My unhappiness protects me from life,' said Ka. 'Don't worry about me.'

'How nice. You're not angry with me for what I said, are you? There's something so nice in your face, it makes me think I can tell you whatever comes into my head, even if it's really stupid. If I said things like this to my friends, they'd mock me without mercy.'

'Even Fazıl?'

'Fazıl's different. If someone does something bad to me, he goes after them and he always knows what I'm thinking. Now you say something – someone's watching us.'

'Who's watching us?' asked Ka. He scanned the crowds milling behind the stalls: a man with a pear-shaped head, two pimply youths, beetle-browed teenagers in ragged clothes. They were all facing the stage now, and some were swaying like drunks.

'Looks like I'm not the only one who's had too much to drink tonight,' muttered Ka.

'They drink because they're unhappy,' said Necip. 'But you got drunk so you could resist the hidden happiness rising inside you.'

As he uttered these words, Necip plunged back into the crowd. Ka wasn't sure he'd heard him correctly. But, despite the noise and commotion around him, his mind was still; he felt relaxed, as if he were listening to his favourite music. Someone waved at him, drawing his eye to a few empty seats reserved for the 'performing artists'. Someone from the theatre troupe – a well-mannered but rather rough-looking stagehand – showed him where to sit.

Years later, in a video I found in the archives of Kars Border Television, I was able to see what Ka then saw on stage. It was a send-up of a well-known bank advertisement, but as it had been years since Ka had watched Turkish television, he could not tell whether it was poking fun or just imitating. Even so, he could tell that the man who had gone into the bank to make a deposit was an outrageous poseur, a parody of a Westerner. When it performed in towns even smaller and more remote than Kars, in tea-houses never frequented by women or government officials, Sunay Zaim's Brechtian and Bakhtinian theatre company made this piece much more obscene, with the bankcard-carrying poseur played as a raving queen who reduced audiences to helpless laughter. The next sketch featured a mustachioed man dressed up as a woman pouring Kelidor shampoo and conditioner on to her hair and it took Ka some time to work out that the actor was Sunay Zaim himself. Just as he did in those remote tea-houses when he decided to bring some relief to his poor and angry all-male audiences with an 'anti-capitalist catharsis', he treated tonight's audience to a string of obscenities as he pretended to stick the long Kelidor shampoo bottle into his back passage. Later still, Sunay's wife Funda Eser did a spoof of a much-loved sausage advertisement. Weighing a coil of sausages in her hand in a decidedly lewd fashion, she asked, 'Is it a horse or a donkey?' and then she ran off stage before taking things further.

The famous goalkeeper from the sixties now returned to the stage to continue his account of the infamous match in Istanbul when the English put eleven goals past him, as well as detailing various allegations of match-fixing and the love affairs he'd had with famous film stars during the same period. His stories gave the audience a rich source of masochistic pleasure, as everyone took the chance to smile at the misery of the Turk.

16

Where God Doesn't Exist

Necip Describes His Landscape and Ka Recites His Poem

Twenty minutes later, Ka went down the chilly corridor to the men's room, where Necip was standing among the men facing the urinals. For a time they stood together at the back of a line for the locked stalls in front of them, acting as if they'd never met. Ka took this opportunity to admire the moulding of the high ceiling: garlands of roses and leaves.

When their turn came, they went into the same stall. Ka noticed that a toothless old man was watching them. After bolting the door from the inside, Necip said, 'They didn't see us.' He gave Ka a warm but quick embrace. Hoisting himself up the wall of the stall, he reached up and retrieved several envelopes from atop the cistern. Back on the floor, he gently blew dust off the envelopes.

'When you give these letters to Kadife, I want you to say just one thing,' he said. 'I've given this a great deal of thought. From the moment she reads these letters, I will neither hope nor expect to have anything to do with her for the rest of my life. I want you to say this to her – make it clear to her, so that she understands exactly what I mean.'

'If she is to find out that you're in love with her at the very moment she discovers that there isn't any hope in it, then why tell her at all?'

'Unlike you, I'm not afraid of life or my passions,' said Necip. Worried that he might have upset Ka, he added, 'These letters are all I care about: I can't live without being passionately in love with someone, or something, beautiful. Now I have to find love and happiness elsewhere. But first I have to get Kadife out of my head. Shall I tell you who it is I plan to love with all my heart after Kadife?' He handed the letters to Ka.

'Who?' asked Ka as he put the letters into his pocket.

'God.'

'Tell me about that landscape you see.'

'First open that window! It smells really bad in here.'

Ka fiddled with the rusty latch until it opened. For a time they both stood there dumbstruck, as if witnessing a miracle, watching the endless stream of snowflakes sailing silently through the night.

'How beautiful the universe is!' whispered Necip.

'What would you say is the most beautiful part of life?' asked Ka.

'All of it!' said Necip after a pause, as if he were betraying a secret.

'But doesn't life make us unhappy?'

'We do that to ourselves. It has nothing to do with the universe or its Creator.'

'Tell me about that landscape.'

'First, put your hand on my forehead and tell me my future,' said Necip. His eyes opened wide (one of them to be shattered twenty-six minutes later, along with his brain). 'I want to live a long, full life and I know many wonderful things are going to happen to me. But I don't know what I'll be thinking twenty years from now, and that's what I'm curious about.'

Ka pressed the palm of his right hand against Necip's smooth forehead. 'Oh my God!' He mockingly pulled away his hand, as if he'd touched something burning hot. 'There's a lot going on in there.'

'Tell me.'

'In twenty years' time – in other words, when you're thirty-seven years old – you will have understood at last that all the evil in the world, I mean the poverty and ignorance of the poor and the cunning and extravagance of the rich, and all the vulgarity in the world, and all the violence and all the brutality – I mean all the things that make you feel guilty and think of suicide – by the time you're thirty-seven, you'll know that all these things are the result of everyone thinking alike,' said Ka. 'Therefore, just as so many in this place have done idiotic things and died "decently", you'll discover that you can become a good person while appearing to be shameless and evil. But you know this may have terrible consequences, because what I feel under my trembling hand is –'

'What?'

'You're very bright and even at this age you know what I'm talking about. And that's why I want you to tell me first.'

'Tell you what?'

'The reason why you feel so guilty about the misery of the poor. I know *you* know what it is, but you must say it.'

'You're not saying – God forbid – that I will no longer believe in God, are you?' said Necip. 'If that's what you mean, I'd rather die.'

'It's not going to happen overnight, the way it did to that poor director in the lift! It's going to happen so slowly you'll hardly even notice. And because you'll have been dying so slowly, having been in this other world so long, you'll be just like the drunk who realises he's dead only after he's had one raki too many.'

'Is that what you're like?'

Ka took his hand off Necip's forehead. 'No, I'm just the opposite. I must have started believing in God years ago. This happened so slowly, it wasn't until I arrived in Kars that I noticed it. That's why I'm so happy here, and why I'm able to write poems again.'

'You seem so happy right now, and so wise,' said Necip, 'so I'm wondering if you can answer this question. Can a human being really know the future? And even if he can't, can he find peace by convincing himself that he knows the future? This is perfect for my first science-fiction novel.'

'Some people know the future,' said Ka. 'Take Serdar Bey, the owner of the *Border City Gazette*. He printed the story of this evening way in advance. Ka fished his copy of the paper from his pocket and together they read: '. . . the entertainments were punctuated by enthusiastic applause'.

'This must be what they mean by happiness,' said Necip. 'We could be the poets of our own lives if only we could first write about what shall be and later enjoy the marvels we have written. In the paper it says you read your most recent poem. Which one is that?'

Someone banged on the door of the stall. Ka asked Necip to tell him quickly about 'that landscape'.

'I'll tell you now,' said Necip. 'But you have to promise not to tell anyone else. They don't like my fraternising with you.'

'I won't tell anyone,' said Ka. 'Tell me what you see.'

'I love God a great deal,' said Necip in an agitated voice. 'Sometimes, when I ask myself what would happen if – God forbid – God didn't exist – I do this sometimes without even meaning to – a terrifying landscape appears before my eyes.'

'Yes?'

'I see this landscape at night, in darkness, through a window. Outside there are two white walls, as tall as the walls of a castle. Like two castles back to back! There is only the narrowest passageway between them, which stretches into the distance like a road, and when I look down this road I am overcome with fear. The road where God does not exist is as snowy and muddy as the roads in Kars, but it's purple! There's something in the middle of the road that tells me, "Stop!" but I still can't keep myself from looking right down to the end of the road, to the place where this world ends. Right at the end of this world, I can see a tree, one last tree, and it's bare and leafless. Then, because I'm looking at it, it turns bright red and bursts into flames. It's at this point that I begin to feel very guilty for being so curious about the land where God does not exist. So, just as suddenly, the red tree turns back to black. So I tell myself I'd better not look again, but then I can't help it, I do look again, and the tree at the end of the world starts burning red once more. This goes on until morning.'

'What is it about this landscape that scares you so much?'

'I can't help thinking that it's the Devil making me think such a landscape could be of this world. But if I can make something come to life before my eyes, the source must be my own imagination. Because, if there really were a place like this on earth, then it would mean that God – God forbid – didn't exist. And since this can't be true, the only possible explanation is that I myself don't believe in God. And that would be worse than death.'

'I understand,' said Ka.

'I looked it up in an encyclopedia once, and it said that the word "atheist" comes from the Greek word *athos*. But that word doesn't refer to people who don't believe in God: it refers to the lonely ones, the people whom the gods have abandoned. And so this proves that people can't ever really be atheists. Because, even if we wanted Him to, God would never abandon us here. To become an atheist, then, you must first become a Westerner.'

'I'd prefer to be a Westerner *and* a believer,' said Ka.

'A man could be at the coffee-house every evening laughing and playing cards with his friends, he could have so much fun with his classmates that there is never a moment they aren't exploding into laughter, he could spend every hour of the day chatting with his intimates, but if that man has been abandoned by God, he'd still be the loneliest man on earth.'

'It might be of some consolation to have a true love,' said Ka.

'But she, too, should love you as much as you love her.'

There was another knock on the door, and Necip put his arms around Ka, then kissed him like a child on both cheeks before he left the stall. Ka caught a glimpse of the man who had been waiting running into the other toilet, so, bolting the door again, he lit a cigarette and watched the wondrous snow still falling outside. He thought about Necip's landscape – he could remember his description word for word, as if it were already a poem – and, if no one came from Porlock, he would, he was now sure, soon be writing that poem in his notebook.

The man from Porlock! During our last years in school, when Ka and I would stay up half the night talking about literature, this was one of our favourite topics. Anyone who knows anything about English poetry will remember the note at the start of Coleridge's 'Kubla Khan'. It explains how the work is a 'fragment of a poem, from a vision during a dream', how the poet had fallen asleep after taking medicine for an illness (actually, he'd taken opium for fun) and how he'd seen, in his deepest sleep, sentences from the book he'd been reading just before losing consciousness, except that now each sentence and each object had taken on a life of its own in a magnificent dreamscape to become a poem. Imagine, a magnificent poem that had created *itself*, without the poet exerting any mental energy! Even more amazing, when Coleridge woke up, he could remember this splendid poem word for word. He got out his pen and ink and some paper and carefully began to write it down, line by line, as if he were taking dictation. He had just written the last line of the poem we all know when there came a knock at the door. He rose to answer it, and it was a man from the nearby town of Porlock, come to collect a debt. As soon as he'd dealt with this man, he rushed back to his desk, but he'd forgotten the rest of the poem, except for a few half-remembered words and the general atmosphere.

As no one arrived from Porlock to break his concentration, Ka still had the poem clear in his mind when he was called on stage. He was taller than everyone else there. He also stood out on account of his German charcoal-grey coat.

There had been a great deal of noise in the audience, but now they fell silent. Some of them – the unruly schoolboys, the unemployed, the Islamist protesters – fell silent because they were no longer quite sure what they should be laughing at, or objecting to. The very important officials in the front rows, the officers who'd been following Ka all day long, the deputy governor, the assistant chief of police and the teachers, all knew he was a poet. The tall, thin master of ceremonies seemed unnerved by the silence. So he asked Ka the only question that came to mind. 'So, you're a poet,' he said. 'You write poems. Is it difficult to write poems?' By the end of this awkward interview (and every time I watch the tape, I wish I could forget it), the audience had no idea whether Ka found it hard writing poems, but they did know he had just arrived from Germany.

'How do you like our beautiful Kars?' the host now asked.

After a moment of indecision, Ka said, 'Very beautiful, very poor and very sad.'

At the back of the hall, two students from the religious high school burst out laughing. Someone else cried out, 'It's your own soul that's poor!' Encouraged by this taunt, six or seven others stood up and started shouting. Some were heckling Ka, and who knows what the others were saying? Long after the events in question, during my own visit to Kars, Turgut Bey told me that when Hande heard Ka say his piece on television, she began to cry.

'In Germany, you were representing Turkish literature . . .' said the host, trying to press on.

'Why doesn't he tell us why he's here?' shouted someone.

'I came here because I was desperately unhappy,' said Ka. 'I'm much happier here. Listen, please, I'm going to read my poem now.'

For a few moments, there was confusion. Then the shouting stopped, and Ka began to speak. Only years later, when the videotape of that evening passed into my hands, was I able to watch my friend's moving performance. It was the first time I had ever seen him read a poem to a large audience. He moved forward cautiously, silently, like someone with a great deal on his mind, but there wasn't a hint of pretension in his bearing. Aside from one or two moments when he paused, slightly uncertain as to what came next, he recited the poem right through to the end without trouble.

When Necip realised that Ka's description of 'the place where God does not exist' matched his own description of his 'landscape' word for word, he rose from his seat, but he did not break Ka's concentration as the latter described the falling snow. There was a smattering of applause. Someone in the back rows stood up and shouted and was soon joined by a few others. It was hard to know whether they were responding to the poem or were simply bored.

Unless you count his fleeting appearance a short while later – his falling silhouette, set against a green backdrop – this was my last sighting of my friend of twenty-seven years.

17

My Fatherland or My Headscarf

A Play about a Girl who Burns Her Headscarf

After Ka had finished reading his poem, the master of ceremonies bowed with an exaggerated flourish and, making the most of every word in the title, announced the evening's main event: '*My Fatherland or My Headscarf.*'

From the middle and back rows, where the boys from the religious high school were seated, there came a few shouts of protest, one or two whistles, and a fair amount of booing. A couple of the officials sitting up front clapped approvingly. The rest of the packed hall waited to see what would happen next, their curiosity tempered with a fair amount of awe. The 'light sketches' the troupe had performed earlier in the evening – Funda Eser's shameless parodies of familiar commercials, her rather gratuitous belly-dancing, her impression with Sunay Zaim of an ageing prime minister and her corrupt husband – had caused remarkably little offence, and had even gone down rather well among the dignitaries at the front.

Most in the audience would also enjoy the next offering, though they'd soon had enough of the taunts and endless disruptions from the religious high-school students. At times you couldn't hear a word of what was being said on stage. But this desperately old-fashioned, even primitive, twenty-minute play had such a sound dramatic structure that even a deaf mute would have had no trouble following it.

1 A woman draped in a jet-black scarf is walking down the street; she is talking to herself and thinking. Something is troubling her.

2 The woman takes off her scarf and proclaims her independence. Now she is scarfless and happy.

3 The woman's family, her fiancé, her relatives and several bearded Muslim men oppose her independence and demand that she put her scarf back on, whereupon in a fit of righteous rage the woman burns her scarf.

4 The neatly bearded, prayer-bead-clutching religious fanatics, outraged by this show of independence, turn violent, but just as they are dragging her off by her hair to kill her . . .

5 The brave young soldiers of the republic burst on to the scene to save her.

From the mid-thirties through the early years of the Second World War, when it was known as *My Fatherland or My Scarf*, this short play was performed frequently in lycées and town halls all over Anatolia, and it was very popular with Westernising state officials eager to free women from the scarf and other forms of religious coercion. But, after the fifties, when the ardent patriotism of the Kemalist period had given way to something less intense, the piece was forgotten. When I caught up with her years later in a sound studio, Funda Eser, who played the woman that night in Kars, told me of her great pride in recreating the same role her own mother had played at Kütahya Lycée in 1948, and of her disappointment that the events following her own performance denied her the righteous exultation her mother had enjoyed. Ravaged though she was by drugs, fatigue and fear, vapid though her face had become, in the manner so common in actors, I nevertheless pressed her to tell me exactly what had happened that evening. Having also interviewed quite a few other witnesses to the events of that night, I can describe them in some detail:

Most of the locals in the National Theatre were shocked and confused by the first scene. When they had heard that the play was entitled *My Fatherland or My Headscarf*, they assumed it would be a consideration of contemporary politics, but, aside from one or two octogenarians who remembered the original from the old days, no one expected to see an actual woman on stage wearing a headscarf. So when she appeared, they took the headscarf to be of the type that has become the respected symbol of political Islam. And, as they watched this mysterious covered woman wandering up and down the stage, it was not immediately clear that she was meant to be sad:

many in the audience saw her as proud, even arrogant. Even those officials well known for their 'radical' views on religious dress felt respect for this woman. So, when one alert student from the religious high school guessed who was hiding underneath the scarf, his hoots of laughter were greeted with great annoyance by those in the front rows.

In the second scene, when the woman made her grand gesture of independence, launching herself into enlightenment as she removed her scarf, the audience was at first terrified. We might say that even the most Westernised secularists in the hall were frightened by the sight of their own dreams coming true. Fear of the political Islamists was so great that they had long ago accepted that the city must remain as it always had been. I say 'dreams', but not even in their sleep could they have imagined the state forcing women to remove their headscarves as it had done in the early years of the republic. They were prepared to live with the practice, 'as long as the Islamists don't use intimidation or force to make Westernised women wear scarves, as we've seen in Iran'.

'But the truth of the matter is this: all those fervent secular Kemalists in the front rows weren't really Kemalists at all – they were cowards!' said Turgut Bey to Ka after it was all over. It was not only religious extremists who objected to a covered woman baring her head; everyone else in the theatre was afraid that this spectacle might enrage the unemployed men witnessing it, not to mention the youthful horde milling at the back of the hall. And, when one of the men in the front row rose from his seat to applaud Funda Eser as she elegantly shed her scarf, a handful of youths at the back jeered this poor, forlorn teacher with catcalls. Mind you, according to some witnesses, the teacher was not making a political statement about modern womanhood, but rather succumbing to dizzy admiration of Funda's plump arms and famously beautiful neck.

As for the republicans in the front rows, they weren't too happy with what the uncovering revealed, either. Having expected a bespectacled village girl, pure-hearted, bright-faced and studious, to emerge from beneath the scarf, they were greatly perturbed to see it was the lewd belly-dancer Funda Eser instead. Was this suggesting that only whores and fools take off their headscarves? If so, then it was precisely what the Islamists had been saying all along. The deputy governor was heard to shout, 'This is wrong – all wrong.' While a number of others joined the chorus – perhaps to curry favour – Funda Eser persevered. Still, most of those in the front rows, however anxiously, continued to watch with quiet appreciation as this enlightened republican secular girl stood up for the freedoms they all hoped to enjoy, and, while a few protests continued to issue from the religious high-school boys, no one felt intimidated by them. Certainly not the deputy governor, flanked on all sides by other top officials, who saw little to fear in the antics of a few boys who ought to have known better. The deputy governor's retinue included Kasım Bey, the courageous assistant chief of police, who in his day had made life so difficult for the PKK; a number of army officers in civilian clothing, accompanied by their wives; the branch manager of the Ordnance Survey office, joined by his wife, two daughters, four sons in suits and ties, and three nephews; and the city's cultural director, whose main job was to seize tapes of banned Kurdish music and send them to Ankara. It could be said that all put their faith in the plainclothes officers stationed throughout the hall, the uniformed officers lined up along the walls, and the soldiers they'd heard were waiting backstage. Their only real concern was the fact that the performance was being broadcast live: although it was going out only locally, these grandees could not help feeling as if all of Ankara, all of Turkey, was watching them. The great and the good in the front rows, like all those behind them, could not quite forget that the scenes playing out before their eyes were simultaneously appearing on TV; this alone may explain why the vulgarities, political provocations and nonsense they'd witnessed seemed to the audience more elegant and magical than they really were. Some were so concerned to know whether the cameras were still running that they were turning their heads at every opportunity just to check. While those at the back were continually waving at the camera, and others were shouting, 'Oh my God, they can see me on TV!' the front row found the filming so exciting that they could barely move, even if they were sitting in the most secluded corner of the hall. As for those citizens not in attendance, the city's first live broadcast did not inspire a desire to see the stage on screen; rather, it made them long to be in the theatre watching the television crews in action.

By now, Funda Eser had removed her scarf and tossed it like dirty laundry into a copper basin. She then sprinkled it with petrol –

carefully, as if adding detergent – and plunged her hands into the basin, as though wringing the wash. By a strange coincidence, they'd put the petrol into an old bottle of Akif liquid detergent – a brand much favoured by Kars housewives (at the time) – and this was why everyone in the auditorium, everyone in Kars for that matter, took it that the freedom-fighter girl had changed her mind: seeing her plunge her hands into the basin, they all relaxed.

'That's the way to do it!' someone shouted from the back. 'Scrub out all that dirt!'

There was a ripple of laughter, annoying some of the officials at the front. Still, everyone in the hall thought they were simply watching a woman doing laundry. 'So where's the Omo?' shouted one of the religious high-school boys.

Although some were becoming annoyed by the noise the boys were making, no one was very angry. Most of the audience, including the officials up front, were just hoping that this dated, provocative work of republican theatre would end without incident. Quite a few of those I interviewed years later, from the most august official to the poorest Kurdish student, told me that most of the Kars residents in the National Theatre had come to the performance hoping for one thing: to be transported from their everyday lives for a few hours, and maybe even to enjoy themselves.

Meanwhile, Funda Eser was 'doing her laundry' with as much relish as the happy housewife in the commercials. And, like all happy housewives, she refused to rush. But when the time came to remove the black scarf from the basin and shake out the wrinkles to prepare it for the clothes line, she unfurled it like a flag before the audience. While everyone was still exchanging glances, struggling to work out what was going on, she produced a lighter from her pocket and lit one of the scarf's corners. For a moment, there was silence. They all heard the breath of the flame as the burning scarf cast the entire hall in a strange and fearsome light.

Quite a few leaped to their feet in horror. Even the most steadfast secularists were badly shaken. When the woman threw the burning scarf on to the stage, many were principally worried about the theatre's 110-year-old fixtures; the filthy, patched, velvet curtains, dating back to the richest days of the city, seemed particularly in danger of igniting. But the greatest cause for concern, justifiably, was that the trouble had only started. It seemed that anything could happen.

And now, from the boys at the back, there rose a terrible din of boos, catcalls and angry whistles.

'Down with the enemies of religion!' shouted one. 'Down with atheists! Down with infidels!'

The front-row dignitaries were still in shock. Although the solitary courageous teacher stood up again to cry, 'Be quiet and watch the show,' no one paid him the least attention. With the realisation that the booing, shouting and chanting was not going to stop, and that the situation was spiralling out of control, a ripple of panic spread across the hall. At this point, Dr Nevzat, the branch health director, was first to head for the exit; he was followed by his sons in their suits and ties, his daughter, whose hair was neatly pulled into two braids, and his wife, in her very best outfit, a crêpe dress in all the colours of a peacock. Sadık Bey, one of the rich leather manufacturers from the old days, who had returned to Kars to oversee some work, and his classmate from primary school, Sabit Bey, now a lawyer affiliated to the People's Party, also rose to their feet. Ka saw dread in the faces of everyone in the front rows, but, uncertain what to do, he stayed in his seat: his main concern was that, in the confusion, he might forget the poem still only recorded in his mind, waiting to be transcribed into his green notebook. At the same time, he wanted to leave, to join İpek. At that moment, Recai Bey, director of the telephone company, a gentleman respected throughout Kars for his erudition, made his way towards the smoke-filled stage.

'My dear girl,' he cried, 'we have all enjoyed your tribute to the ideals of Atatürk. But we've had enough now. Look – the audience is upset, we're in danger of inciting a riot.'

By now, the scarf had stopped burning and Funda Eser was standing amid the smoke, reciting the same monologue I would later find in the 1936 Townhall edition of *My Fatherland or My Scarf*. The author claimed that it was the passage of which he was most proud. Four years after the events I describe in this book, I had the opportunity to meet the author, then ninety-two years old but still very energetic. During our interview, while most of his energy was focused on scolding his naughty grandchildren, or great-grandchildren, who wouldn't sit still, he nevertheless also found the strength to tell me how sorry he was that, of all his works (*Atatürk is Coming, Atatürk Plays for High Schools, Our Memories of Him*, and so on), it was *My Fatherland or My Scarf* that would be forgotten. Unaware of its revival in Kars, or indeed of the events it precipitated, he went on to tell me how, during the thirties, it was this play that had the same remarkable effect on lycée girls and state officials alike – it had moved them to tears and standing ovations wherever it was performed.

But now, no one could hear anything but the booing and the catcalls and the angry whistles from the religious high-school boys. Despite the guilty, fearful silence at the front of the auditorium, few could hear what Funda Eser was saying. When the angry girl tore the scarf off her head, she was not just making a statement about people, nor about national dress; she was talking about our souls, because the scarf, the fez, the turban and the headdress were all symbols of the reactionary darkness in our souls, from which we should liberate ourselves and run to join the modern nations of the West. Although few could make out *her* words, everyone heard one taunt from the back very clearly: 'So why not take off everything and run to Europe stark naked?'

This brought laughter even from the front rows, and some applause around the hall, but soon those at the front became disconcerted and scared again. Like many others, Ka chose this moment to stand. Noise was coming from every mouth by now, competing with the voluble shouting from the back rows. Some who had headed for the doors were looking back over their shoulders. Funda Eser continued to recite the poem that almost no one could hear.

18

Don't Fire, the Guns Are Loaded!

A Revolution on Stage

From this point on, the situation escalated very quickly. Two religious fanatics sporting round beards and skullcaps appeared on stage. They carried ropes and knives and left no one in any doubt that they were there to punish Funda Eser for burning her scarf and defying God's law.

Once they'd captured her, Funda Eser writhed provocatively as she struggled to break free.

By now, she had given up any pretension to being a heroine of the Enlightenment: she had switched to the role she always found most comfortable, 'the woman about to be raped'. But her practised, self-abasing entreaties did not arouse the men in the audience as much as she expected. One of the bearded fanatics (rather clumsily made-up, having played the father in the previous scene) yanked at her hair and threw her to the ground; the other laid a dagger on her throat in a manner suggesting a Renaissance tableau of the 'Sacrifice of Isaac'. This perfectly illustrated the fears of a reactionary religious backlash felt in Westernised circles in the early years of the republic. The older officials in the front rows and the conservatives in the back were the first to become truly alarmed.

For exactly eighteen seconds, Funda Eser and the 'fundamentalists' held their grand pose without moving a muscle. Though quite a few of the people I interviewed were sure that the trio had remained immobile for much longer. The crowd was out of control by then. It was not just the play's affront to covered women that bothered the schoolboys; nor was it simply the caricature of fanatics as ugly, dirty dolts. They also suspected the whole thing had been staged to provoke them. So, every time they heckled the players, every time they threw half an orange or a cushion on to the stage, they were one step closer to a trap that had been laid just for them. The knowledge of their helplessness in this matter made them even angrier, which was why the most politically astute member of the group, a short, broad-shouldered boy named Abdurrahman Öz (although his father, who came from Sivas to collect his body three days later, would give a different name), did everything he could to settle and quieten his companions, but to no avail. Egged on by the clapping and booing from other sectors of the auditorium, the angry students assumed that there were allies in the anxious crowd who felt as they did. Even more important, for the first time, the young Islamists, who were weak and disorganised compared with their peers in the areas surrounding Kars, had found the courage to speak with one voice, and they were pleased to see how much they could scare the officials and army officers in the front rows. And they were all the more heartened to know that their show of solidarity was being broadcast to the entire city. They were not just angrily shouting and stamping; they were enjoying themselves. This is one thing that everyone later forgot. Having seen the video many times, I can also say that a number of the ordinary citizens were even laughing at times at the students' slogans and curses. If, at other moments, they also clapped and jeered along with the students, that was because they were a little bored, though still determined to make the most of a 'theatrical evening' that had turned out to be something of a mystery to them. One witness claimed, 'If the people at the front had not overreacted to this feeble commotion, everything that followed would have been prevented.' Still, others insisted that 'The rich men and high-ranking officials in the front rows who panicked during those eighteen seconds already knew what was going to happen. Why else would they have gathered up their families and headed for the door? Ankara', they said, 'had planned the whole thing in advance.'

Fearful of losing the poem in his head, now Ka also left the auditorium. At the same moment, a man came on to the stage to rescue Funda Eser from the two round-bearded reactionaries: this man was Sunay Zaim. He was wearing an army uniform from the thirties with the fur hat in the style of Atatürk and the heroes of the War for Independence. As he strode purposefully across the stage (no one could have known he had a slight limp), the two 'fundamentalists' took fright and threw themselves at his feet. Yet again the brave teacher stood up and applauded Sunay's heroism with all his might. One or two others shouted, 'Bless you! Bravo!' Standing in the centre of the spotlight, Sunay seemed to all of Kars to be a wondrous creature from another planet. Everyone noticed how handsome and enlightened he looked. The long and punishing years spent touring Anatolia may have left him lame, but they had not diminished his attraction: he still had the hard, decisive, tragic air and faintly feminine good looks that had made him such a sensation among leftist students when he played Che Guevara, Robespierre and the revolutionary Enver Pasha. Instead of bringing the index finger of his white-gloved hand to his lips, he rested it elegantly on his chin and said, 'Quiet!'

There was no need for this word, which wasn't in the script: everyone in the auditorium was already silent. Those who'd stood up were now back in their seats and heard him say: 'They're in torment!'

Probably this is only half of what he meant to say, because no one had the faintest idea who was meant to be in torment. In the old days, this would have been a reference to the people or the nation; but now, the people of Kars weren't sure if Sunay was referring to them, or Funda Eser, or the entire republic. Still, the feeling evoked by the remark was precise: the entire audience fell into an uneasy hush.

'Oh, honourable and beloved citizens of Turkey,' said Sunay Zaim. 'You've embarked on the road to enlightenment and no one can turn you back from this great and noble journey. Do not fear. The reactionaries who want to turn back time, those vile beasts with their cobwebbed minds, will never be allowed to crawl out of their hole. Those who seek to meddle with the republic, with freedom, with enlightenment will see their hands crushed.'

Everyone in the hall heard the taunt from the boy two seats away from Necip. Then a deep silence fell over the crowd again: awe mixed with fear. They all sat as still as candles, as if hoping to hear one or two whispers, a few clues to help them make sense of the evening when they went home, and perhaps a story or two. At that moment, a detachment of soldiers appeared on either side of the stage. Three more entered through the main doors and marched down the aisle to join them. The people of Kars, unaccustomed to the modern technique of sending actors among the audience, were first alarmed and then amused. A bespectacled messenger boy came running on to the stage and, when they saw who it was, everyone laughed. It was

'Glasses', the sweet and clever nephew of the city's main newspaper distributor. Everyone knew him as a constant presence in the shop just across the street from the National Theatre. Glasses ran over to Sunay Zaim, who bent down to allow the boy to whisper a few words in his ear.

All of Kars could see that the news had made Sunay Zaim very sad.

'We have just learned that the director of the Education Institute has passed away,' Sunay Zaim told the audience. 'This lowly murder will be the last assault on the republic and the secular future of Turkey!'

Before the audience had had a chance to digest the news, the soldiers on stage cocked their rifles and took aim straight at the audience. They opened fire at once; the noise was thunderous.

It was unclear whether this was an honour guard requested by the company to mark the sad news. A number of Kars residents – out of touch as they were with modern theatrical conventions – took it for yet another piece of experimental staging.

A roar rose as a strong vibration rippled through the hall. Those frightened by the noise of the weapons thought the vibration had issued from the agitation in the audience. Just as one or two were standing up, the bearded 'fundamentalists' on stage ducked for cover.

'No one move!' said Sunay Zaim.

Once again, the soldiers cocked their guns and took aim at the crowd. At the exact same time, the short, fearless boy two seats away from Necip stood up and shouted, 'Damn the godless secularists! Damn the fascist infidels!'

Once again, the soldiers fired.

As the shots rang in the air, another strong vibration trembled through the hall.

Just then, those in the back rows saw the boy who had made the taunt collapse into his chair, before rising up again, with his arms and legs jerking wildly. Among those who had been enjoying the antics of the religious high-school students and laughing all evening at comments they couldn't understand, several took this as yet another joke. And when the student's jerking continued – as violent as death throes – they laughed some more.

It was only with the third volley that a few members of the audience realised that the soldiers were firing live rounds. They could tell

– just as one could tell on those evenings when soldiers rounded up terrorists in the streets – because these shots could be heard in one's stomach as well as in one's ears. A strange noise emanated from the huge German-made stove that had been heating the hall for forty-four years; the stovepipe had been pierced and was now spewing smoke, like an angry kettle at full boil. As someone from the back rows stood up and made straight for the stage with blood streaming from his head, the smell of gunpowder became overpowering. The audience looked ready to erupt in panic, yet almost everyone remained sitting still, in silence. As in a bad dream, everyone felt very alone. Even so, Nuriye Hanım, a literature teacher who attended the National Theatre every time she visited Ankara, and who was full of admiration for the beauty of the theatrical effects, rose to her feet for the first time to applaud the actors. At precisely that moment, Necip rose to his feet, too, like an agitated student trying to catch the teacher's attention.

The soldiers launched their fourth volley. According to the inspector colonel subsequently sent by Ankara to oversee the inquiry, a man who would spend many weeks secretly compiling his meticulous report, this fourth volley killed two people. He named one of them as Necip, adding that one bullet had entered his forehead and the other his eye, but, having heard a number of rumours to the contrary, I can't say for sure that this was when Necip died. One thing is certain, though: after the third volley, Necip must have seen the bullets flying through the air, and, though realising what was happening, he utterly misjudged the soldiers. Two seconds before being hit, he'd risen to his feet to utter the words heard by many, though not registered on the tape: 'Stop! Don't fire, the guns are loaded!'

His words gave voice to what everyone in the hall knew but could not quite believe. Of the five shots in the first volley, one had hit the plaster laurel leaves above a box where, a quarter-century earlier, the last Soviet consul in Kars had watched films in the company of his dog. This bullet went wide because the soldier who had fired the shot – a Kurd from Siirt – had no desire to kill anyone. Another round, fired with similar care though somewhat less skilfully, had hit the ceiling, sending a blizzard of 120-year-old lime and paint dust snowing down on the anxious crowd below. Another bullet overflew the nest where the TV camera was perched to hit the wooden balustrade that demarcated the standing room from which poor, romantic

Armenian girls who could afford only the cheapest tickets had once watched theatre troupes, acrobats and chamber groups from Moscow. The fourth flew into the outer reaches of the hall, beyond the range of the camera; through the back of a seat, it went into the shoulder of a dealer in spare parts for tractor and agricultural equipment named Muhittin Bey, who was sitting with his wife and his widowed sister-in-law. He, too, having seen the shower of lime dust, then stood up to see whether something had fallen from the ceiling. The fifth bullet hit a grandfather sitting just behind the Islamist students. He had come from Trabzon to see his grandson, who was doing his military service in Kars. After the bullet shattered the left lens of his spectacles, it entered his brain. The old man, luckily asleep at the time, died silently, never knowing what had happened to him; the bullet then exited from his neck, and, passing through the back of his seat, pierced a bag belonging to a twelve-year-old Kurdish egg and bread vendor. The boy had been passing between seats to give a customer his change and so was not holding the bag at the time (later, the bullet was recovered inside one of his boiled eggs).

These details explain why it was that most people in the audience stayed so still when the soldiers opened fire. When bullets from the second volley hit a student in the temple, the neck and the upper chest, just above the heart, most assumed that he was putting on another show, an encore to his terrifying but entertaining display of courage moments earlier. One of the two remaining bullets went into the chest of a relatively subdued religious high-school student sitting at the back (it was later revealed that his aunt's daughter was the city's first 'suicide girl'). The last struck two metres over the projection booth, hitting the face of the clock, which, having stopped working sixty years earlier, was now covered with dust and cobwebs. According to the colonel in charge of the inquiry, the fact that one of the bullets had hit the clock was proof that one of the marksmen chosen that evening at sunset for the assignment had violated the oath he'd sworn with his hand on the Koran: clearly he had gone out of his way to avoid killing someone. As for the fiery Islamist student killed in the third volley, the colonel would mention parenthetically that careful consideration had been given to the lawsuit the family had brought against the state, in which it had been alleged that the lad had been not merely a student, but a hard-working, devoted agent of the Kars branch of MİT. In the end, though, the colonel found insufficient grounds for the award of damages. Of the last two bullets in this same volley, one hit Reza Bey, who had built the fountain in the Kalealtı district and was much loved by all the conservatives and Islamists in the city; the other struck the servant who served as his walking stick.

By now, it is difficult to explain why so many in the audience remained still, watching these two lifelong friends moaning and dying on the floor as the soldiers on stage cocked their rifles for the fourth time. Years later, a dairy owner who still refuses to let me use his name, explained it as follows: 'Those of us who were sitting at the back knew something terrible had happened, but we were afraid that if we moved from our seats to get a better look, the terror would find us, so we just sat there watching, without making a sound.'

Some of the bullets from the fourth volley were never found. One wounded a young salesman who had come to Kars from Ankara to sell parlour games and encyclopedias on an instalment plan (he would bleed to death in hospital two hours later). Another blew a huge hole in the lower facing wall of a private box where, in the first decade of the twentieth century, Kirkor Çizmeciyan, a wealthy leather manufacturer, had sat with his family, dressed from head to toe in fur. According to one tall tale, neither the bullet that hit one of Necip's green eyes nor the other that hit his wide, smooth forehead killed him instantaneously. Some eyewitnesses claimed that, for a moment, the teenager looked at the stage and cried, 'I can see!'

By the time the shouting and screaming had stopped, almost everyone – including those rushing for the door – had collapsed. Even the TV cameraman was forced to throw himself against a back wall; his camera, which had been panning right and left all evening, now stood still. The viewers at home could see only the crowd on the stage and the silent, respectful notables in the front rows. Even so, most Kars residents had heard enough shouting, screaming and gunfire to realise that something very strange was going on at the National Theatre. As for those who had grown bored with the play towards midnight and had begun to doze off in front of their televisions, by the last eighteen seconds of the gun battle, even their eyes were glued to their screens.

Sunay Zaim was experienced enough to notice the renewed interest. 'Oh, heroic soldiers, you have done your duty,' he said. Then, with an elegant gesture, he turned to Funda Eser, still lying on the floor, and made an exaggerated bow. Taking the hand of her saviour, the woman rose to her feet.

A retired civil servant in the front row stood to applaud them. A few others sitting near by joined him. There was scattered applause from the back, from people presumably in the habit of clapping at anything . . . or perhaps they were scared. The rest of the hall was silent. It was as if they'd woken up after a long night on the town; a few even appeared to be relaxed and allowed themselves weak smiles. They seemed to have decided that even the dead bodies before their very eyes belonged to the dream world of the stage. A number of those who had ducked for cover had their heads in the air, but then cowered in fear again at the sound of Sunay's voice.

'This is not a play – it is the beginning of a revolution,' he said reproachfully. 'We are prepared to go to any lengths to protect our fatherland. Put your faith in the great and honourable Turkish army! Soldiers, bring them over.'

Two soldiers escorted the two round-bearded 'fundamentalists'. As the other soldiers cocked their guns and descended into the auditorium, a strange man rushed forward on to the stage. It was clear from the unbecoming speed of his approach and his awkward body language that he was neither a soldier nor an actor. But he still had everyone's attention – quite a few were hoping he would reveal that it had all been one great big joke.

'Long live the republic!' he cried. 'Long live the army! Long live the Turkish people! Long live Atatürk!' Very slowly, the curtains began to close. He took two steps forward, as did Sunay Zaim; the curtain closed behind them. The strange man was carrying a gun manufactured in Kırıkkale; he was wearing civilian clothes but military boots. 'To Hell with the fundamentalists!' he cried as he walked down the steps into the auditorium. Two armed guards appeared to follow him. But the threesome did not head to the back of the hall where the soldiers were busy arresting boys from the religious high school. Ignoring the terrified audience, the three men continued to shout slogans as they rushed for the exits and disappeared into the night.

They were in tremendously high spirits, for it had been only at the very last minute, after lengthy discussion and bargaining, that they had been allowed to take part in the performance that was to begin 'the little revolution of Kars'. They'd met with Sunay Zaim on the night of his arrival, and he had resisted their proposal for a whole day, fearing that the involvement of the shady, armed adventurers would ruin the artistic integrity of the piece. But, in the end, he could not counter the argument that he might need a man experienced with guns to control the lowlifes in the audience who were unlikely to appreciate the nuances of 'modern art'. It was later said that he felt great remorse about his decision in the hours that followed, and great pangs of passion in the face of the bloodshed caused by this band in tramps' clothing. But, as is so often the case, this was only a rumour.

When I visited Kars years later, I had a tour of what had once been the National Theatre. Half the building had been torn down; the other half turned into a warehouse. The owner, Muhtar Bey, was my guide. Presumably to deflect my questions about the evening of the performance and the ensuing terror, he told me how Kars had been witness to an endless string of murders, massacres and other evils dating all the way back to the time of the Armenians. If I wanted to bring some happiness to the people of Kars, I should, upon returning to Istanbul, ignore the sins of the city's past and write instead about the beautiful, clean air and the inhabitants' kind hearts. As we stood in the dark, mildewy auditorium-turned-warehouse surrounded by the ghostlike forms of fridges, stoves and washing-machines, he pointed out the sole remaining trace of that last performance: the huge, gaping hole made by the bullet that had hit Kirkor Çizme-ciyan's private box.

19

How Beautiful, This Falling Snow

The Night of the Revolution

The leader of the boisterous trio who ran shouting into the auditorium as the curtains closed, waving their pistols and rifles at the cowering audience before they vanished into the night, was a journalist and an old communist. His alias was Z Demirkol. During the seventies, he had belonged to various pro-Soviet communist organisations, and, although known as a writer and poet, he was most renowned as a bodyguard. He was a rather large man. He'd escaped to Germany after the military takeover in 1980, and after the Berlin Wall came down, he received a special pardon and returned to Turkey to help defend the secular state and the republic against Kurdish separatist guerrillas and Islamist 'fundamentalists'. The two men behind him had once been Turkish nationalist militants, former comrades of Z Demirkol himself in night-time street battles in Istanbul during his Marxist years, in 1979 and 1980, but now they had put all that behind them, galvanised by their adventurism and their mission to protect the nation state. Some cynics claimed that the threesome had been agents of the state from the very beginning. When they rushed down from the stage and bolted from the National Theatre, no one made much of it, assuming they were simply part of the play.

When Z Demirkol saw how much snow there was on the ground, he jumped up and down like a child, fired two shots in the air, and cried, 'Long live the Turkish people! Long live the republic!' The crowd who had gathered at the entrance retreated to the sides. A few stood watching the men and smiling fearfully. Some seemed embarrassed, as if they were about to apologise for not staying longer. Z Demirkol and his friends ran straight up Atatürk Avenue. They were still shouting slogans and calling to one another like giddy drunks. A few old people struggling through the snow and some of the fathers who were guiding their huddled families home decided, after a few moments of indecision, to applaud them.

The happy trio caught up with Ka at the corner of Küçük Kasımbey Avenue. They could see that he had seen their approach: he had stepped under the oleander trees, as if to let a car pass.

'Mr Poet,' cried Z Demirkol, 'you've got to kill them before they kill you. Do you understand?'

Ka still had had no opportunity to write down the poem to which he would later give the title 'The Place Where God Does Not Exist', and it was at this moment that he forgot it.

Z Demirkol and his friends continued running straight up Atatürk Avenue. Not wishing to follow them, Ka turned right into Karadağ Avenue, and it was now that he realised the poem had vanished, leaving not a fragment in its wake.

He felt the sort of guilt and shame he had once felt as a young man leaving political meetings. Those political meetings had disturbed him not only because he was an upper-middle-class boy, but because the discussions were so full of childish posturing and exaggeration. Hoping to find a way to bring back his forgotten poem, he decided to continue walking instead of going straight back to the hotel.

A few people, alarmed at what they'd just seen on television, were at their windows. It's difficult to say how much Ka was aware of the terrors at the theatre. The volleys had begun before he left, but it's possible he too thought they were part of the performance, and that Z Demirkol and his friends were part of it, too.

His mind was focused on his forgotten poem. But, sensing another coming in its stead, he willed it to the back of his mind to give it time to ripen.

Then he heard two gunshots in the far distance. They were lost in the snow.

How beautiful, this falling snow. How large the snowflakes were and how *decisive*. It was as if they knew their silent procession would continue until the end of time. The wide avenue was buried knee-deep; white and mysterious, it climbed up a slope and disappeared into the night. There wasn't a soul in the beautiful three-storey Armenian building that now housed the city council. The icicles from one of the oleander trees reached down as low as the snow blanket draping an invisible car; the snow and ice had merged to form a tulle curtain. Ka passed an empty, one-storey Armenian house, its windows boarded up. As he listened to his footsteps and the sound of his own short breath, he could feel the call of life and happiness as if for the first time, and yet he also felt strong enough to turn his back on it.

Across the street from the governor's residence, the little park with the statue of Atatürk was empty. And Ka could not see any sign of life in the residence itself, which dated back to the Russian period and was still Kars' grandest building. Seventy years earlier, after the First World War, when both the Ottoman and Imperial Russian armies had withdrawn and the Turks of Kars had established an independent state, this building had housed both the secretariat and the assembly. Just across the street was the old Armenian building that had been attacked by the English army because it was the same doomed republic's presidential palace. The governor's residence was well guarded, so Ka avoided the building by turning right and looping back towards the park. A little farther down the road, in front of yet another old Armenian building, just as peaceful and beautiful as the rest, he saw a tank gliding past, slow and silent, as if in a dream. Ahead, he saw an army truck parked near the religious high school. There was almost no snow on it, so Ka deduced that it had only just arrived.

There was a gunshot. Ka turned back. The sentry station in front of the governor's residence was full of policemen trying to warm themselves, but with the windows iced over, no one saw Ka walking by on Army Avenue. He knew now that if he could remain within the silence of the snow until he reached his hotel room, he'd be able to preserve not just the new poem in his head but the memory that had emerged with it.

Halfway down the slope, he heard a noise on the opposite pavement and slowed his pace. Two people were trying to kick in the door of the telephone office. Ka saw the headlights of a car beaming through the snow and then heard the satisfying rattle of snow chains. As a black unmarked police car pulled up in front of the telephone office, Ka saw two men in the front seat; he remembered having seen one of them in the theatre only minutes earlier, just as he'd begun to think about leaving. That man now remained seated as his partner, in a woollen beret and armed, stepped out of the car.

There followed a discussion among those assembled outside the door of the telephone office. They were standing under the streetlamp and Ka could hear their voices, so it wasn't long before he had worked out that they were Z Demirkol and his friends.

'What do you mean, you don't have a key?' one of them was saying. 'Aren't you the head manager of the telephone office? Didn't they send you here to cut the lines? How could you have forgotten your keys?'

'We can't cut off the phones from this office. We'll have to go to the new centre on Station Avenue,' said the head manager.

'This is a revolution and we want to get into this office,' said Z Demirkol. 'If we decide to go to the other office later, then we'll do that. Understand? Now, where's the key?'

'My child, this snow will be gone in two days' time and then the roads will be open. And when they are, the state will call us all to account.'

'So, you're afraid of the state. Well, hear this: we *are* the state you fear!' Z Demirkol bellowed. 'So are you going to open the door for us or what?'

'I can't open that door for you without a written order.'

'We'll see about that,' said Z Demirkol. He took out his gun and fired two shots in the air. 'Take this man and spread him against the wall,' he said. 'If he makes any more trouble, we'll execute him.'

No one believed him, but Z Demirkol's two assistants dutifully took Recai Bey and spread him against the wall. Not wishing to damage any windows, they pushed him slightly to their right, but, because the snow was very soft in that corner, the manager tripped and fell. The men apologised and helped him back to his feet. They removed his tie and bound his arms behind him with it. Meanwhile, they announced that this was a clean-up operation and that all the enemies of the fatherland would be eliminated from the streets of Kars by morning.

When Z Demirkol gave the order, they cocked their rifles and lined up in front of Recai Bey, like a firing squad. Just then there were gunshots in the distance. (These came from the dormitory garden of the religious high school, where soldiers were firing shots into the air to frighten the students.) They all fell silent and waited. For the first time all day, the snow was abating. The silence was extraordinarily beautiful, bewitching even. After a few moments, one of the men said that the 'old man' (who wasn't old at all) was entitled to a last cigarette. They put a cigarette into Recai Bey's mouth and lit it for him. Then, perhaps having grown restless while the manager was smoking, they started kicking the door of the telephone office again and ramming it with the butts of their rifles.

'I can't bear to see you destroy state property,' said the manager from the wall. 'Undo my hands and I'll let you in.'

Once the men were inside, Ka went on his way. He continued to hear the odd gunshot, but he now paid no more attention than he gave to howling dogs. His mind filtered out everything but the beauty of the night. For a time, he tarried before an empty old Armenian house. Then he stopped at an Armenian church to pay his respects: the trees in its gardens were dripping with icicles and looked like ghosts. The pale yellow streetlamps cast such a deathly glow over the city that he felt himself in some strange, sad dream, and, for some reason, it made Ka feel guilty. Still, he was mightily thankful for this silent and forgotten country now filling him with poems.

A little further on, he happened on an agitated mother standing at a window and calling for her son to come home; the boy had told her that he was 'just going out to see what's happening'. Ka passed between them. At the corner of Faikbey Avenue, he saw two men about his age rushing out of a shoemaker's shop; one was rather large, the other as slim as a child. Twice a week for the past twelve years, each of these two lovers had been telling his wife that he was 'going to stop in at the coffee-house' and they would then meet secretly in this shop that reeked of glue. But, hearing on the upstairs neighbours' television set that a curfew had been announced, the couple had panicked.

Ka turned into Faikbey Avenue. Two blocks down, opposite a shop he remembered from his morning walk – he had stopped at the trout counter just outside its doors – he saw a tank. Like the street, the tank seemed shrouded in a magical silence; it was so still and deathly that he thought it must be empty. But then the door opened, and a head popped out to tell him to go home at once. Ka asked the head if it could direct him to the Snow Palace Hotel, but, before the soldier could answer, he noticed across the street the darkened offices of the *Border City Gazette*, and from this he worked out where he had to go.

The lights in the hotel lobby were blazing; walking into that warmth was like coming home. A number of guests were in pyjamas and puffing on cigarettes, watching the lobby television, and it was clear from their expressions that something extraordinary had happened. But, like a child eager to avoid a dreaded subject, Ka refused to notice. After letting his eyes skate swiftly over the scene, he proceeded light-heartedly into Turgut Bey's apartment. The whole group was still at the table and still watching the TV. When Turgut Bey saw Ka, he jumped to his feet, scolded him for being so late and told him how worried they'd all been. He went on to say a few other things, but by now Ka's gaze had met İpek's and he was no longer listening.

'You read your poem very beautifully,' said İpek. 'I felt so proud.'

Ka knew at once that he would remember this moment until the day he died. He felt such joy that, even amid the other girls' tedious questions and Turgut Bey's hectoring, he had to fight back tears.

'It looks as if the army is up to something,' said Turgut Bey. To judge from his voice, he was in a foul temper, and was unable to decide whether this was good or bad.

The table was in disarray. Someone had stubbed out a cigarette in an orange peel – most probably that had been İpek. Ka remembered seeing Aunt Munire, a distant young relative of his father, doing the same thing when he was a child, and, although she had never once forgotten to say 'madam' when speaking to Ka's mother, everyone despised her for her bad manners.

'They've just announced a curfew,' said Turgut Bey. 'Tell us what happened at the theatre.'

'I have no interest in politics,' said Ka.

Although everyone, and especially İpek, was aware that he'd spoken without thinking, Ka still felt sorry.

All he wanted to do now was sit silently and look at İpek, but he knew it was out of the question. The house was ablaze with 'revolutionary fever' and he felt uncomfortable, not just because he was reminded of the military takeovers of his childhood, but because everyone was talking at once, except for Hande, who'd fallen asleep in the corner. Kadife returned to the television screen that Ka refused to watch, and Turgut Bey seemed simultaneously pleased and disturbed that these were interesting times.

For a while, Ka sat next to İpek and held her hand. He asked her to come up to his room, and when it became too difficult to keep his distance, he went up alone. There was a familiar smell of wood there. He hung his coat with great care on the hook behind the door, and as he lit the small lamp at the head of the bed a wave of sleep passed over him. He could barely keep his eyes open; he felt himself floating, as if the whole room, the whole hotel, were floating with him. This is why the new poem, which he jotted down in his notebook line by line as it came to him, portrayed the bed, the hotel in which he lay and the snowy city of Kars as a single divine entity.

The title he gave the poem was 'The Night of the Revolution'. It began with his childhood memories of coups, when the whole family would sit around the radio, listening to military marches. Then the poem went on to describe the holiday meals they'd had together. This was why he would later decide this poem was not about a coup at all and would assign it to the axis of the snowflake entitled 'Memory'. One of the important themes in the poem is the poet's ability to shut off part of his mind even while the world is in turmoil. But this meant that a poet had no more connection to the present than a ghost did. Such was the price a poet had to pay for his art!

After he finished his poem, Ka lit a cigarette and went to the window.

20

A Great Day for Our Nation!

*While Ka Slept that Night and When He
Woke the Next Morning*

Ka slept for exactly ten hours and twenty minutes without stirring once. In one of his dreams he watched the snow falling. Just before, through the gap in the half-drawn curtains, the snow had begun to fall again on to the white street below, and it looked exceptionally soft where the lamp lit the pink signpost of the Snow Palace Hotel. Perhaps it was because this strange and magically soft snow absorbed the sound of the gunfights occurring all over Kars that night that Ka was able to sleep so soundly.

Only two streets away, a tank and two army trucks attacked the religious high-school dormitory. There was a skirmish – not next to the main iron door, where the fine Armenian craftsmanship is visible to this day, but outside the wooden door leading to the common rooms and the seniors' dormitory. Hoping to frighten the boys, the soldiers who had gathered in the snow-covered garden fired straight up into the night sky. All the hardened political Islamists in the student body had attended the performance at the National Theatre, and they had all been arrested on the spot, so the only boys in the dormitory were either raw recruits or had no interest in politics. But the scenes on television had made them all rather giddy, so, barricading the door with tables and desks and shouting such slogans as 'God is great!', they'd holed up to wait. One or two of the crazy ones, though, having stolen a few knives and forks from the kitchen, decided to throw the utensils at the soldiers from the bathroom window. Then, because they began to brandish and horse around with the sole gun in their possession, the stand-off ended in gunfire. One beautiful slip of a boy – nothing but innocence in his face – fell to his death, a bullet in his forehead.

Most of the inhabitants of the city were still awake, their eyes glued not to the windows and the streets below but to their television sets. The live broadcast had not ended when Sunay Zaim had announced that this was not a play but a revolution. As the soldiers were rounding up the troublemakers and carrying out the dead and wounded, on to the stage came a man well known to all of Kars: Umman Bey, the deputy governor. In a formal and uneasy voice that nevertheless inspired confidence, he expressed perhaps for the first time a certain impatience about the broadcast and announced a curfew in all of Kars until twelve o'clock the following day. When he left the stage, no one else appeared, so, for the next twenty minutes, the people of Kars saw only the curtains of the National Theatre on their screens. There was then a break in transmission, after which the same old curtains reappeared. Some time later, Kars' populace saw the curtains opening again, very slowly, as the whole performance was repeated from the very beginning.

Seated in front of their sets, struggling to work out what was going on, most people in the city began to fear the worst. The very tired or half drunk found themselves revisiting earlier times of civic turmoil; others feared a return to death, disappearance and the rule of night. Those viewers with no interest in politics saw the repeat as an opportunity to make some sense of what had happened in Kars that night (just as I would attempt to do many years later), so they just concentrated once more on watching the screen.

As the people of Kars watched Funda Eser's portrayal of the prime minister, and later her riotous belly-dance, a specially trained security team raided the branch headquarters of the People's Freedom Party in the Halil Paşa Arcade, arrested the Kurdish caretaker who was the only person there at that hour, searched the filing cabinets and desks, and confiscated every piece of paper they could find. The same police unit rounded up the party's executive committee – they knew all the identities and addresses from an earlier raid – and, charging them with subversion and Kurdish nationalism, took them all into custody.

These were not the only Kurdish nationalists in Kars that night. The three corpses discovered early the next morning in a burned-out Murat taxi not yet covered with snow on the road to Digor were – according to official reports – Kurdish nationalist guerrillas. The police claimed that the three young men had been trying to infiltrate the city for months, but, having panicked during the events of the previous evening, they had decided to jump into the taxi and escape into the mountains. When they discovered the road closed they lost hope and, in an ensuing quarrel, one of them detonated a bomb that killed him and his two companions. The mother of one of the boys, a cleaner at the hospital, later submitted a petition alleging that unidentified armed agents had rung the doorbell and taken away her son. And the taxi-driver's older brother filed his own charge to the effect that his brother was no nationalist, nor even a Kurd. Both petitions were ignored.

By this time, everyone in Kars had become aware of the unrest in the city. If it wasn't a full-blown coup, the two tanks wandering the city like dark and ponderous ghosts were enough to confirm at least that something very odd was happening. But, as most of the populace was watching the whole performance on their television screens, and as the snow continued to fall apparently without end outside their windows like a scene from an old fairy tale, the tanks provoked little fear. Anxiety afflicted only the politically active.

Consider, for example, Sadullah Bey. A journalist held in the highest esteem by the Kurds of Kars, and a well-known collector of folklore, he'd seen his share of military takeovers, so the moment he heard of the curfew, he began to prepare for the days in prison he knew lay ahead. After packing his bag with essentials – the blue pyjamas he couldn't sleep without, the medicine for his prostate problem, his sleeping pills, his woollen cap and socks, the photograph of his daughter in Istanbul (with his smiling grandson on her lap), and the painstaking notes he had taken for a book on Kurdish dirges – he sat down for a glass of tea with his wife. They watched Funda Eser do her second belly dance, and they waited. When the doorbell rang much later, in the middle of the night, he bade his wife farewell, picked up his suitcase and headed for the door. Seeing no one, he stepped into the street, where in the sulphurous light of the street-lamps he let his mind return to the glorious winters of his childhood, when he would skate across the frozen Kars River, when the silent streets were covered with this same beautiful snow. As he stood there, someone pumped two bullets into his head and his chest, killing him on the spot.

Months later, when most of the snow had melted, the remains of a number of others similarly murdered that night were discovered, but –

like the Kars press in the wake of the revolution – I don't want to upset my readers any more than is necessary, so I'll gloss over the details. As for the rumours that the 'unknown perpetrators' of these murders were Z Demirkol and his friends – at least in respect of whatever may have occurred in the early hours of the evening – these allegations are untrue. Although it took longer than expected, they managed to sever the phone lines and safeguard the Kars Border Television transmission in support of the revolution. By dawn, all their energy was channelled into what had by then become their main obsession – finding a 'deep-voiced folk singer to celebrate the heroes of the borderlands'. After all, this would never measure up as a real revolution until all the radio and television stations in the city were broadcasting folk songs celebrating the heroes of the borderlands.

After asking at the barracks, the hospitals, the science high school and the tea-houses, they finally found a folk singer among the firemen on duty at the fire station. He was sure they would either arrest him or riddle him with bullets, but they whisked him down to the TV studio, and when Ka awoke the next morning, it was the fireman's sonorous voice he heard coming through the walls from the television in the lobby. Through the half-drawn curtains came an extraordinarily bright and wonderfully strange shaft of sunlight that had reflected off the settled snow. He awoke relaxed and refreshed, but he'd not even risen from the bed before feeling a pang of guilt for having slept so soundly. He rallied by pretending he was just an ordinary hotel guest in another city. After he had washed, shaved and changed, he picked up his doorkey by its heavy copper fob and went down to the lobby.

When he saw the folk singer on the screen and the other guests conversing in whispers as they watched, Ka had a measure of the silence that now engulfed the city. His thoughts returned to the previous evening, and only then did he begin to piece together everything his mind had ignored until that moment. He smiled coolly at the boy behind the reception desk. Then, like a harried traveller, vexed with the city's violent political in-fighting and determined to leave at the first opportunity, he headed straight for the adjoining dining room and ordered breakfast. In the corner an enormous teapot was steaming above a samovar; on the serving table was a plate of Kars cheese sliced very thin and a bowl of olives that, having long since lost their shine, looked rather deathly.

Ka sat down at a table next to the window. Through the gaps in the tulle curtain he gazed out at the snow-covered street in all its beauty. The peacefulness of the empty street took Ka back to the curfews of his childhood, the census days, the days devoted to checking the electoral roll, the days given over to hunting for enemies of the state, the days when the military marched in and everyone would gather around the television and radio. He recalled them all, one by one. As they'd sat listening to the military tunes on the radio, as they'd listened to the news bulletins reporting the imposition of martial law and the list of prohibitions, all Ka had wanted was to go outside and play in the empty streets. As a child he'd loved those martial law days like holidays, when his aunts, uncles and neighbours would come together in a common cause. It was perhaps to hide the fact that they felt happier and more secure during military coups that the middle- and upper-middle-class families of Ka's childhood in Istanbul were in the habit of quietly ridiculing the silly actions that inevitably attended any military takeover – the whitewashing of the cobblestones to make the whole city look like a barracks, and the rough-handed soldiers and policemen who'd seize anyone with long hair or a beard. While the Istanbul rich had a terrible fear of the soldiers, they also knew the deprivations under which they lived – the harsh discipline, the low wages. The soldiers were peasants, and the rich despised them for it.

The street outside looked as if it had been abandoned for centuries, so when Ka looked down to see an army truck turning into it, this sight also took him back to his childhood. Like the boy he'd once been, he sat transfixed.

A man who looked like a cattle dealer had just entered the room and he came over to Ka, threw his arms around him, and kissed him on both cheeks. 'Congratulations! This is a great day for our nation!'

Ka remembered how the grown-ups in his childhood would congratulate one another after military coups, in much the same way that they congratulated one another during the old religious holidays. He returned the compliment, muttering a few words.

The door to the kitchen swung open and Ka felt all the blood in his body rise to his head. İpek walked into the room. They came eye to eye, and for a moment Ka had no idea what to do. He decided he should stand, but just then İpek smiled at him and turned to the man who had just sat down. She was carrying a tray with a cup and a plate, which she then set on the man's table. Like a waitress.

Ka's spirits sank. He hated himself for failing to greet İpek as he should have done, but there was something else going on, too, and he knew instantly that he wouldn't be able to hide from it. Everything he'd done the day before had been wrong, and now he hated himself for abruptly proposing to a woman he hardly knew. He hated himself for kissing her (as fine as that had been), and for losing control, and for holding her hand at the supper table. Most of all he hated himself for behaving like a common Turk, for getting drunk and shamelessly letting everyone know that he was sexually attracted to her. He had no idea what to say to her now; his only hope was that İpek would keep playing the waitress for ever.

The man who looked like a cattle dealer shouted, 'Tea!' in a coarse voice. İpek turned smoothly towards the samovar, the empty tray in her hand. After she had given the man his tea, she approached Ka's table. He felt the pulse of his heartbeat even in his nose.

'So what happened?' asked İpek with a smile. 'Did you sleep well?'

This reference to the previous night, to yesterday's happiness, made Ka uneasy. 'It looks like this snow isn't going to stop,' he stammered.

They observed each other in silence. Ka knew he had nothing to say; anything he might utter right now would be counterfeit. And so, staring into her big, hazel, slightly cast eyes, he told her wordlessly that he had no choice but to remain silent. İpek sensed now that Ka's frame of mind was very different from that of the day before, that he had become a very different sort of person. Ka could tell that İpek sensed a darkness inside him and that she accepted it. This, he thought, would bind him to her for life.

'This snow is going to last some time,' she said carefully.

'There's no bread,' said Ka.

'Oh, I'm so sorry.' She went straight over to the table next to the samovar, put down the tray and began slicing a loaf.

Ka had asked for bread because he couldn't bear the tension. Now, as he gazed at her back, he assumed a pensive pose. 'Actually, I could have sliced that bread myself.'

İpek was wearing a white pullover, a long brown skirt and a thick belt of a type Ka remembered as being fashionable in the seventies; he hadn't seen such a belt since. Her waist was slim, her hips perfect. She was just the right height for Ka. He even liked her ankles. He knew that if he returned to Germany without her, he would dwell for the rest of his life on painful memories of how happy he'd been here, holding hands, exchanging half-playful, half-serious kisses and telling each other jokes.

Ka saw İpek's bread-slicing arm fall still, and, before she turned around, he looked away.

'I'm putting cheese and olives on your plate,' said İpek. Her tone was formal, Ka realised, because she wanted to remind him there were people watching them.

'Yes, please,' answered Ka, and as he spoke he looked around the room.

When their eyes met again, her expression was enough to tell him that she was aware he'd been staring at her the whole time her back had been turned. Ka was unnerved by her familiarity with the sub-tleties of male–female relations – that diplomacy at which he himself had always been clumsy. And he was already worried that she might be his only chance for happiness.

'The bread came in on an army truck just a few minutes ago,' said İpek, flashing a smile that broke Ka's heart. 'I'm looking after the kitchen because Zahide Hanım couldn't make it here this morning, because of the curfew . . . I was worried when I saw the soldiers.'

Because the soldiers could have been coming for Kadife or Hande. Or even for her father . . .

'They've sent in the hospital caretakers to wipe up the blood at the National Theatre,' whispered İpek. She sat down at his table. 'They've raided the university hostels, the religious high school, the party headquarters . . .' And in the course of these raids, there'd been more deaths, she said. Hundreds had been arrested, although some had already been released that morning. She told him all this in the particular hushed tone people saved for political emergencies.

It took Ka back twenty years; he remembered how he and his friends would sit in the university canteen exchanging similar tales of torture and brutality in whispers that were angry and woeful, but also strangely proud. It was at times like these that he had felt most guilty: all he'd wanted was to forget about Turkey and everything in it and go home and read books. So now, to help İpek close the subject, he felt the impulse to say something like 'This is terrible, absolutely terrible!' But, though the words were in his mouth, he refrained from comment, knowing he would sound pretentious, no matter how hard he tried not to. Instead, he just sat there, sheepishly eating his bread and cheese.

While he ate, İpek carried on whispering, recounting how they'd loaded the dead boys from the religious high school into army trucks and sent them out to the Kurdish villages for their relatives to identify them. But the trucks had got stuck in the snow. The authorities had granted a day-long amnesty for everyone to surrender their weapons; Koran instruction had been suspended, and so had all political activity. As she told him all this, Ka looked at her arms, looked into her eyes, admired the fine colour of her long neck, admired the way her brown hair brushed against her nape. Could he love her? For a while he tried to imagine them together in Frankfurt, walking down the Kaiserstrasse, going home after an evening at the cinema. But dark thoughts were taking over his soul. All he could see was that this woman had cut the bread into thick slices just as they did in the poorest houses, and, even worse, that she had arranged these thick slices in a pyramid, in the manner of fishermen's soup kitchens.

'Please, talk to me about something else now,' said Ka carefully.

İpek had been telling him about a man two houses down who'd been arrested on his way through the back gardens after someone had denounced him, but now she gave him a knowing look and stopped.

Ka saw fear in her eyes. 'I was very happy yesterday, you know. For the first time in years I was writing poems,' he explained. 'But I can't bear to hear these stories right now.'

'The poem you wrote yesterday was very beautiful,' said İpek.

'Can I ask you to do something for me, before this despair overtakes me?'

'Tell me what I can do.'

'I'm going up to my room now,' said Ka. 'Come up in a little while and hold my head between your hands. Just for a while – no more than that.'

Before he had even finished speaking, he could tell from İpek's frightened eyes that she wasn't going to oblige, so he rose to leave. She was a provincial, a stranger to Ka, and he had asked her for something no stranger could understand. He could have spared himself this woman's uncomprehending look; he ought to have known better than to make this asinine request. As he ran up the stairs, he was full of self-reproach for having made himself believe he loved her. Throwing himself on the bed, he mused about what a fool he'd been to leave Istanbul for Kars in the first place, and then concluded it had been a mistake even to leave Germany and return to Turkey. He thought of his mother, who had so wanted him to have a normal life and tried so hard to keep him away from poetry and literature. If she could have known his happiness depended on a woman from Kars who helped out in the kitchen and cut bread in thick slices, what would she have said? What would his father have said on learning that Ka had knelt before a village sheikh and talked with tears in his eyes about his faith in God? Outside, the snow had started falling again; the snowflakes he could see from his window were large and dreary.

There was a knock, and he rushed to the door, suddenly full of hope. It was İpek, but she was wearing a very different expression now. An army truck had just arrived, with two men, one of them a soldier, and they'd asked for Ka. She'd told them he was here and that she would let him know they were waiting for him.

'All right,' said Ka.

'If you want, I can give you that two-minute massage you wanted,' said İpek.

Ka pulled her inside, closed the door, kissed her once, and then sat her down at the head of the bed. He lay down, putting his head on her lap. They stayed like this for a time, saying nothing as they gazed out of the window at the crows walking over the snow on the roof of the 110-year-old building that now housed the police headquarters.

'That's fine, I've had enough now, thank you,' said Ka. Carefully lifting his charcoal-grey coat off the hook on the door, he left the room. As he went down the stairs, he smelled the coat to remind himself of Frankfurt, and for a few minutes he could see the city in full colour in his mind and wished he was there. The day he'd bought the coat at the Kaufhof, he'd been helped by an assistant, whom he'd seen again two days later when he'd gone to collect it after it had been shortened. His name was Hans Hansen. It may have been because his name was so Germanic and because he had blond hair that Ka also remembered thinking about him when he woke up in the middle of the night.

21

But I Don't Recognise Any of Them

Ka in the Cold Rooms of Terror

The men sent out to pick up Ka came in one of those old army trucks – rarely seen these days, even in Turkey. A young, hook-nosed, fair-skinned plainclothes policeman met him in the lobby and sat him down in the middle of the front seat, taking the space by the door for himself, as if to block Ka's possible escape. But his manner was polite enough – he addressed Ka as 'sir', and this, Ka decided, meant that he was not a policeman after all, but a MİT agent, perhaps under instructions not to harm him.

They moved slowly through the city's empty white streets. The dashboard of the army truck was covered with dials, but none of them was working. Because the cab was high off the ground, Ka could see into the handful of houses whose curtains were open: the televisions were on everywhere, and, for the most part, the city of Kars had drawn its curtains and turned in on itself. It was as if they were moving through another city altogether. As the windscreen wipers went about their monotonous work, it seemed to Ka that the dreamlike streets, the old Baltic-style houses and the beautiful snow-covered oleander trees had cast a spell that was bewitching even the driver and his hook-nosed companion.

They stopped in front of police headquarters; by now they were all freezing, so they lost no time making their way inside. It was much more crowded and frenetic than it had been the day before, and even though he'd been expecting this, Ka still felt uneasy. The animated disorder was typical of so many Turkish bureaucratic offices. It made Ka think of courthouse corridors, turnstiles at football stadiums, bus stations. But there was also a whiff of iodine and hospitals, terror and death. Somewhere very close to where he was standing, someone was being tortured. The very thought of what was going on in there made him feel inadequate and guilty for not trying to stop it. Fear gripped his soul.

As he climbed the same stairs he had climbed with Muhtar the day before, instinct told him to follow the example of the men in charge, so he did his best to adopt an air of authority. Passing open doors, he heard the rapid tap-tap-tap of old typewriters. Everywhere men were barking into walkie-talkies or calling down the stairs for the tea-boy. On the benches outside closed doors he saw lines of young men awaiting interrogation. They were handcuffed to each other, and it was obvious they had been badly roughed up; their faces were covered with bruises. Ka tried not to look them in the eye.

They took him into a room rather like the one he'd sat in with Muhtar, and here they informed him that, despite his statement to the effect that he had not seen the man who had murdered the director of the Education Institute and his inability to identify the assailant from the photographs they'd shown him the day before, they now hoped he would be able to recognise the culprit among the religious high-school boys in the cells downstairs. From this, Ka deduced that MİT had asserted their authority over police following the 'revolution' and that relations between the two groups were tense.

A round-faced intelligence agent asked Ka where he'd been at around four o'clock the previous afternoon.

For a moment, Ka's face turned grey. 'They told me it would also be a good idea to pay a visit to His Excellency Sheikh Saadettin,' he began.

His round-faced interrogator cut him short. 'No, before that!' he said.

When Ka remained silent, the round-faced agent reminded him of his meeting with Blue. He did it in such a way as to suggest that he already knew all about it and even regretted having to cause Ka such embarrassment. Ka struggled to see this as a sign of good intentions. An ordinary police officer would have accused Ka of trying to conceal the meeting, and then he would have relished humiliating him, bragging that the police know everything.

In an almost apologetic voice, the round-faced agent explained that Blue was a dangerous terrorist and a formidable conspirator. He was a certified enemy of the republic and in the pay of Iran. It was certain that he had murdered a television presenter, so a warrant had been issued for his arrest. He'd been sighted all over Turkey. He was organising the fundamentalists. 'Who arranged your meeting?'

'A boy from the religious high school – I don't know his name,' said Ka.

'We want to see if you can identify him now,' said the agent. 'Look at them very carefully; you're going to be using the observation windows in the doors to their cells. Don't be afraid, they won't see your face.'

They took Ka down a wide staircase to the basement. A hundred-odd years ago, when this fine building housed an Armenian hospital, this basement served as a woodstore and a dormitory for the care-takers. Much later, in the 1940s, when the building was turned into a state lycée, they had knocked down the basement walls and turned the space into a cafeteria. Quite a few Kars youths who would go on to become Marxists and sworn enemies of the West during the 1960s had swallowed their first cod-liver oil capsules in this place; they'd washed them down with powdered milk sent by UNICEF, a vile-smelling drink that turned their stomachs. Now this spacious basement comprised a corridor and four cells.

With a careful confidence that revealed a practised routine, a policeman placed an army cap on Ka's head. The hook-nosed MİT agent who'd picked him up at the hotel gave him a knowing look and said, 'These people are terrified of army caps.'

When they reached the first of the two cells on the right, the policeman slid open the little observation window and bellowed, 'Attention! Officer!' Ka peered in through the window, which was no bigger than his hand.

The cell itself was about the size of a double bed; Ka could see five people inside. Perhaps there were more: it was hard to tell because they were all crowded into a single mass. They were propped up against the filthy wall on the far side; and, although they'd done no military service, they knew how to stand, however awkwardly, to attention, their eyes shut. (It seemed to Ka that a few had their eyes half open and were looking at him.) The 'revolution' had begun only ten hours earlier, but already the suspects' heads were shaven, their faces and eyes swollen from beatings. There was more light in the cells than in the hallway, but to Ka's eyes all the boys looked alike. His head began to spin as fear engulfed him. He was glad not to see Necip among these boys.

After Ka had failed to identify any of the boys in the second and third cells, the hook-nosed MİT agent said, 'There's nothing to be afraid of. After all, when the roads open again you're going to be straight out of here.'

'But I don't recognise any of them,' said Ka, stubbornly.

However, he *did* recognise a few of them: he had a very clear memory of one boy he'd seen heckling Funda Eser and another who'd been chanting slogans. And if he denounced these boys now, it would prove his willingness to cooperate, which would mean that later, if he saw Necip, it would be easier to pretend that he didn't know him. (It wasn't as if these boys were charged with anything serious.)

But he didn't denounce anyone.

One youth, whose face was streaked with blood, looked straight at Ka and pleaded, 'Sir, please don't tell our mothers.'

These boys had probably been beaten in the heat of the revolution's early hours: the officers had not used any weapons, just their boots and their fists. Ka was now up to the fourth cell, and once again he failed to see anyone who resembled the man who had assassinated the director of the Education Institute. Once he was sure that Necip was not sitting among these terrified boys, he began to relax.

By the time they returned upstairs, it was clear that the round-faced agent and his superiors were under great pressure to find the director's assassin, so that they could parade him as the revolution's first achievement. Ka suspected that they even had a mind to hang the culprit there and then. Now a retired major entered the room. Despite the curfew, he had somehow managed to find his way to the police headquarters to ask for his grandson to be released from detention. The major begged them not to torture the boy, who had no grievances against the state, and had been sent to the religious high school only because his impoverished mother wanted her child to have the promised free woollen coats and suits. In fact, the family were staunch supporters of Atatürk and the republic. The round-faced agent interrupted the major mid-sentence.

'My dear sir, no one here gets treated badly,' he said.

He then took Ka to one side. There was, he said, a chance that the murderer and Blue's men (Ka had the feeling that the culprit was thought to be one of them) might be with those they'd detained from the veterinary school.

This is how Ka ended up back in the army truck with the hook-nosed agent who'd picked him up at the hotel. En route, as he admired the beauty of the empty streets and smoked a cigarette, he was thankful to have made it out of the police headquarters. A small part of him was secretly relieved that the military had taken charge and the country wasn't bending to the will of the Islamists. But with most of his heart he vowed to himself that he would refuse to cooperate with the police or the army. Just then a new poem came rushing into his mind; it was so powerful, so strangely exhilarating, that Ka now turned to the hook-nosed agent and asked, 'Might it be possible to stop off at a tea-house along the way?'

You couldn't walk two feet in this city without passing a tea-house full of unemployed men. Although most such establishments were closed this morning, one on Canal Street was managing to do business without attracting the attention of the army jeep stationed on the kerb. Inside, a young apprentice was awaiting the end of the curfew, and three other young men were sitting at another table. They all stirred to see a man in an army cap and a plainclothes officer coming through the door.

Without missing a beat, the hook-nosed agent drew a pistol from his coat and, with a professionalism Ka could not help but admire, he lined up the young men with their faces to a huge picture of a Swiss landscape hanging on the wall; then, just as efficiently, he searched them and checked their identity cards. Ka was sure he was just going through the motions, so he sat down at the table next to the cold stove and effortlessly transcribed his latest poem.

He would later give it the title 'Dream Streets'. It opens with the snowy streets of Kars, but its thirty-six lines also contain numerous references to the streets of old Istanbul, the Armenian ghost town of Ani and the wondrous, fearsome, empty cities Ka had seen in his dreams.

When he had finished the poem, Ka looked up at the black-and-white television to see that the folk singer had gone, and in his place they were repeating the first moments of the revolution at the National Theatre. Vural the goalkeeper had just begun to recount his past loves and lost goals, and by Ka's calculations it would be twenty minutes before he could watch himself reading his poem on television. This was the poem that had been erased from his mind before he'd had a chance to write it down. He was determined to record it.

Four more people entered the tea-house, through the back door. The hook-nosed MİT agent again drew his gun and lined them up against the wall. The tea-house owner, a Kurd, tried to explain to the agent, whom he addressed as 'my commander', that these men had not broken the curfew, having come in from the courtyard via the garden.

The MİT agent decided to check their stories anyway. After all, one of them didn't have his identity card on him, and he was quaking with fear. The agent announced that he would take the man home by the same route he had come. He called in his chauffeur, whom he assigned to watch the other youths still lined up against the wall. Ka, putting his poetry notebook back into his pocket, then followed the two men through the back door and into the icy, snow-covered courtyard. They went over a low wall, down three icy steps, and were lunged at by a barking dog on a chain before entering a ramshackle cement building similar to most others in Kars. In the basement was a foul stench of mud and dirty bedclothes. The man at the front slipped past a humming furnace and into an area furnished with boxes and vegetable crates. There, in a shabby bed, slept an exceptionally beautiful, fair-skinned woman. Ka could not stop himself from staring. The man without the identity card produced a passport for the MİT agent. The furnace was making such a clatter that Ka couldn't hear their words, but as he peered through the shadows he saw that the man then produced a second passport.

It turned out that the man and the woman in the bed were a Georgian couple who had come to Turkey looking for work. Back in the tea-house, the unemployed youths whose identity cards the MİT agent had checked earlier were full of complaints about these Georgians. The woman was tubercular, but still working as a prostitute; her customers were the dairy owners and leather merchants who came down to the city to do business. As for the husband, like so many other Georgians, he was willing to work for half pay in the markets, so was depriving Turkish citizens of job opportunities at a time when work was already scarce. The couple were so poor, and so stingy, that they wouldn't even pay for a hotel; instead, they paid the caretaker from the Water Department five dollars a month to let them live in this furnace room. They were said to be saving up for a house to be bought when they returned to their own country, after which they planned never to work again for the rest of their lives. The boxes

186

were full of leather goods they had bought cheaply with an eye to selling back in Tiflis. They had already been deported twice, but both times had found their way back 'home' to the furnace room. Now, having assumed control, it was up to the army to do what the corrupt municipal police had failed to accomplish – tackle these parasites, clean up the city.

Back at the tea-house the owner was only too happy to be serving guests and listening to this table of feeble, unemployed youths who, with a little prompting from the MİT agent, began to speak, if somewhat haltingly, about what they hoped for from the coup. Mixed with their complaints about rotten politicians was quite a bit of hearsay strident enough to count as denunciation: the unlicensed slaughter of animals, the scams in the warehouse where state-owned commodities were stored, the crooked contractors who were smuggling in Armenian illegals on meat trucks and housing them in barracks, working the men all day long and paying them peanuts . . . These unemployed youths gave no hint of understanding that the military had stepped in to make a stand against Kurdish nationalism and keep the 'religious fanatics' from winning the municipal elections. Instead, they seemed to think that last night's events marked the beginning of a new age in which immorality and unemployment would no longer be tolerated. They seemed to think that the army had stepped in expressly to find them jobs.

Back in the army truck once again, Ka observed the hook-nosed MİT agent taking out the Georgian woman's passport. Sensing the agent's purpose was to ogle her photograph, Ka felt strangely embarrassed.

The moment they stepped into the veterinary faculty, Ka could see how relatively benign things had been at police headquarters. As he walked down the corridors of this ice-cold building, he sensed at once he was in a place where no one gave a moment's thought to other people's pain. This was where they'd brought all the Kurdish nationalists they'd rounded up, along with all those left-wing terrorists who proudly took responsibility for bombings, not to mention all those listed in the MİT files as these people's supporters. The police, soldiers and public prosecutors all took a very dim view of any participant in the events these groups had organised, and the same went for anyone who aided or abetted the Kurdish guerrillas who came down from the mountains to infiltrate the city. For these people there was no mercy; they were interrogated far more brutally than those with suspected links to political Islam.

A tall, powerfully built policeman took Ka by the arm and walked him down the corridor, lovingly, as if Ka were an old man unsteady on his feet. Together they visited three classrooms where terrible things were taking place. I will follow the lead of my friend here. Just as he decided not to record them in his notebook, I will try not to dwell on them for too long.

After staring for a few seconds at the suspects in the first classroom, Ka's immediate thought was of the shortness of mankind's journey from birth to death. One look at these freshly interrogated suspects was enough to conjure up fond, longing dreams of distant civilisations and countries he'd never visited. Ka knew with absolute certainty that he and all the others in the room were fast approaching the end of their allotted time: their candles would soon be extinguished. In his notebook, Ka would call this place the yellow room.

In the second classroom he had a simpler vision. He remembered these men from a tea-house he'd passed the day before during his strolls around the city; their eyes were now blank with guilt. They had drifted off into some faraway dreamworld, or so it now seemed to Ka.

Moving on to the third classroom, in the mournful darkness that overtook his soul Ka felt the presence of an omniscient power whose refusal to disclose all he knew made a torment of life on earth. His eyes were open, but he could not see what was in front of him; all he could see was the colour inside his head. Because this colour was something close to red, he would call this the red room. Here, the thoughts he'd had in the two first rooms – that life was short, that mankind was awash with guilt – came back to haunt him, but even faced with this fearsome landscape in front of him, he still managed to remain calm.

As they left the veterinary faculty, Ka was aware that his companions were losing faith in him and beginning to wonder about his motives. After all, he had failed, yet again, to make an identification. But he was so relieved not to have seen Necip that when the hook-nosed agent suggested that they continue on to the Social Insurance Hospital morgue to take a look at the corpses, Ka agreed at once.

When they reached the morgue, located in the basement of the hospital, they showed him their most suspicious corpse first. This was the slogan-chanting Islamist militant who'd taken three bullets of the soldiers' second volley. But Ka had never seen him before. He approached this corpse with caution, and as he looked it seemed to him that the dead youth was offering a sad and respectful greeting. The corpse laid out on the second slab of marble seemed to be shivering from the cold; this was the body of the little grandfather. They showed it to Ka because they hadn't yet established that this man had come from Trabzon to see a grandson who was doing his military service in Kars, and because his tiny frame suggested he might be the man they were seeking for the assassination of the director of the Education Institute. As he approached the third corpse, Ka was already happily dreaming of seeing İpek again. This corpse had a shattered eye. For a moment, Ka thought this was a feature of all the corpses in the room. Then, as he looked more closely at the dead boy's white face, something inside him shattered and disappeared.

It was Necip. That same impish face, his lips still pushed forward, as if to ask one more childish question. Ka felt the cold and the silence of the hospital. He could see the same little pimples he'd noticed earlier on the boy's face. The same aquiline nose. The same grimy school jacket. For a moment, he thought he was going to cry, which made him panic. But the rising panic distracted him long enough for him to hold back the tears. There, in the middle of the forehead on which he'd pressed the palm of his hand only twelve hours earlier, was a bullet hole. But the most deathly thing about Necip was not the bullet hole, not his pale, bluish complexion, but the frozen stiffness with which he lay on the slab.

A wave of gratitude swept over Ka; he was glad to be alive. This distanced him from Necip. He leaned forward, separated the hands he'd been clasping behind his back, placed them on Necip's shoulders and kissed him on both cheeks. The boy's cheeks were cold but had not yet hardened. His remaining green eye was still half open, and it was looking straight at Ka, who stood upright and told the hook-nosed agent that this was a 'friend' who had stopped him in the street the day before to describe his efforts as a science-fiction writer. He then disclosed that Necip had later taken him to see Blue. He had kissed him, he explained, because this teenager had had a very pure heart.

22

'The People's Choice' for the Role of Atatürk

Sunay Zaim's Military and Theatrical Careers

After Ka had identified Necip at the Social Insurance Hospital morgue, an official hastily drew up a report, signed it and passed it on to be certified. Then Ka and the hook-nosed agent got back into the army truck and set off down the road. A pack of timid dogs walked alongside them, but the only other signs of life were the election banners and the anti-suicide posters. As they continued along their way, Ka's eyes were drawn to the restless children and anxious fathers twitching their closed curtains to catch a glimpse of the passing truck, but they scarcely registered with him. All he could think about, all he could see, was Necip's face, and Necip's stiff body. He imagined İpek consoling him when he got back to the hotel, but after the truck had crossed the empty city centre, it carried on straight down Atatürk Avenue before stopping just beyond a ninety-year-old Russian building two streets on from the National Theatre.

This was one of the beautiful, run-down single-storey mansions that Ka had been so happy to see on his first night in Kars. After the city had passed over to the Turks and joined the republic, the mansion passed into the hands of one Maruf Bey, a well-known merchant who sold wood and leather to the Soviet Union. For forty-three years, he and his family had lived magnificently there, their every need met by cooks and servants, conveyed in horse-drawn sleighs and carriages. After World War Two, at the start of the Cold War, the National Security Agency had rounded up all the merchants who did business with the Soviet Union, charged them with spying, and carted them off to prison. None ever returned. So, for the next twenty years, Maruf Bey's mansion sat empty, first because it had no owner and then because there was a dispute over its inheritance. In the mid-seventies, a club-wielding Marxist splinter group had seized the building as its headquarters, and from there had planned a number of political assassinations (including that of Muzaffer Bey, in which attempt the lawyer and former mayor had been wounded, but survived). After the 1980 coup the building was empty again for a time, and then the enterprising white-goods dealer who owned the small shop next door converted half of it into a warehouse, while a visionary tailor – who had returned to his home town three years earlier with an impossible dream, having made his money in Istanbul and Saudi Arabia – turned the other half into a sweatshop.

When Ka walked into the house, he saw button machines, big, old-fashioned sewing-machines, and giant pairs of scissors hanging from nails on the wall; in the soft, orange glow of the rose-patterned wallpaper they resembled strange instruments of torture.

Sunay Zaim was still dressed in the ragged coat, pullover and army boots he'd been wearing two days earlier, when Ka had first seen him. He was pacing up and down the room with an unfiltered cigarette wedged between his fingers. When he saw Ka, his face lit up as if he'd spied a dear old friend, and he ran across the room to embrace him and kiss him on both cheeks. Ka almost expected him to say, 'Congratulations! This is a great day for our nation.' as the cattle dealer at the hotel had done; there was something in his excessive friendliness that put Ka on his guard. He would describe his dealings with Sunay favourably: they were just two men from Istanbul, thrown together in a remote and impoverished city, who had found a way to work together under difficult conditions. But he was well aware of Sunay's part in helping to create those difficult conditions.

'Not a day passes when the dark eagle of depression doesn't take flight in my soul,' said Sunay, infusing his words with a mysterious pride. 'But I cannot catch myself. So hold yourself in. All's well that ends well.'

In the white light pouring through the huge windows, Ka surveyed the spacious room: the large stove and the friezes in the corners of its high ceilings bore witness to a glorious past; now it was crawling with men carrying walkie-talkies and there were two massive guards clocking Ka's every movement; on the table by the door leading into the corridor was a map, a gun, a typewriter and a pile of dossiers. Ka deduced that this was the centre of operations for the revolution, and that Sunay was the most powerful man in the room.

'There were times, and these were the worst of times,' said Sunay as he paced back and forth, 'when we would arrive in some wretched, godforsaken town in the middle of nowhere – still not knowing if we would find a place to stage our plays, or even a hotel room to rest our weary heads – when I would go out in search of an old friend, only to discover that he had long since left that small town. At such times depression – *grief* – would overtake me. To keep it at bay, I would rush about the streets of the city, knocking on the doors of the local doctors, lawyers and teachers in search of *someone* who might be interested in hearing the news we had brought from the frontiers of modern art and contemporary culture. When I found no one living at the only address I had to hand, when the police informed us that they would not, after all, give us permission to put on a performance, or when – and this was always my last hope – I took my humble request to the mayor, only to learn that he, too, was unwilling to accommodate us, I began to fear that darkness might engulf me. At moments like this the eagle in my chest would come to life; it would spread its wings and – just before it smothered me – it would take flight. And it didn't matter where we performed – we could be in the most wretched tea-house the world has ever seen, we could be in a train station courtesy of some stationmaster who had his eye on one of our actresses, we could be in a fire station or an empty classroom in the local primary school, or in a humble shack of a restaurant, we could be playing in the window of a barber's shop, or on the stairs of a shopping arcade, or in a barn, or on the pavement – I would refuse to succumb to depression.'

When the door opened and Funda Eser came in to join them, Sunay switched from 'I' to 'we'. This couple were so intimate that Ka saw nothing contrived in the shift to the plural. Funda Eser moved her great bulk across the room with considerable grace, and, after giving Ka a quick handshake, she whispered something into her husband's ear and then left the room looking very preoccupied.

'Yes, those were our worst years,' said Sunay. 'Social unrest and the combined stupidities of Istanbul and Ankara had taken their toll, and our fall from favour had been well documented in the press. I had seized the great opportunity that comes only to those graced with genius – yes I had – and on the very day when I was going to use my art to intervene in the flow of history, suddenly the rug was pulled out from under me and I found myself trudging through the worst imaginable mud. Although it had failed to destroy me, my old friend depression now returned to haunt my soul. But no matter how long I languished in the mire, no matter how much filth, wretchedness, poverty and ignorance I saw around me, I never lost my belief in my own guiding principles, never doubted that I had reached the summit. Why are you so frightened?'

A doctor wearing a white smock and carrying a bag appeared at the door. With a hurried air that seemed only half genuine, he pulled out a blood-pressure gauge and wrapped it around Sunay's arm. As he did so, Sunay gazed at the white light pouring through the windows, his air so tragic that Ka thought he might still be thinking about his 'fall from favour' in the early eighties. For his part, Ka remembered Sunay more for his roles in the seventies, for the roles that had made him famous. That was the golden age of leftist political theatre. If Sunay stood out in this still rather small theatrical society, it was not only for being a hard-working and accomplished actor who could rise to the challenge of a demanding role; no, what audiences most admired his leadership qualities. Young Turkish audiences warmed to his portrayals of such powerful leaders as Napoleon, Lenin and Robespierre, as well as to his roles as local folk heroes with whom they could identify. When he raised his commanding voice to rail against oppression, when, after a stage beating at the hands of some wicked oppressors he raised his proud head to cry, 'The day will come when we will call them to account,' when, on the worst day of all (the day he knew, when everyone knew, that his arrest was imminent), he gritted his teeth and, wishing his friends luck, told them that no matter what suffering lay ahead, he remained certain they would and could bring happiness to the people through the exercise of merciless violence – it was then that the lycée students and 'progressive' university students in the audience would always respond with tearful and thunderous applause. Especially impressive was his decisiveness in the final acts of these plays, when power had passed into his hands and the time had come to mete out punishments to the wicked oppressors. Here many critics saw the influence of his military training. He'd studied at Kuleli Military Academy, but had been expelled in his final year for slipping over to Istanbul in a rowing-boat to perform in various Beyoğlu theatres and also for staging a secret performance of a play called *Before the Ice Melts*.

When the military took over in 1980, all left-wing plays were banned, and it was not long afterwards that it was decided a major new television drama about Atatürk would be commissioned to celebrate the hundredth anniversary of his birth. In the past, no one had thought a Turk could be equal to the challenge of playing this blond, blue-eyed westward-looking national hero. The predominant view was that great national films called for great international stars like Laurence Olivier, Curt Jurgens and Charlton Heston. But this time, *Hürriyet*, the biggest Turkish newspaper, entered the fray to promote the view that 'for once' a Turk should be allowed to play the role. It even went so far as to provide ballots that readers could cut out and send in with their suggestions. Sunay was among those nominated by this popular jury; in fact, as he was still well known for his fine work during the democratic era, he was the clear front runner from day one. He had, after all, been playing revolutionaries for years. Turkish audiences had no doubt that the handsome, majestic, confidence-inspiring Sunay would make an excellent Atatürk.

The actor's first mistake was to take this public vote seriously. He went straight to the papers and the television networks, and made grand pronouncements to any who would listen. He had himself photographed relaxing at home with Funda Eser. He spoke openly about his domestic life, his daily routines and his political views, remaking himself in the great revolutionary's image. He was at pains to show that, like Atatürk, he was a secularist. He also emphasised that he and his wife enjoyed the same pastimes and pleasures (raki, dancing, fine clothes and 'good breeding'). He took to posing with volumes of Atatürk's classic work, *Orations*, and claiming that he was rereading his oeuvre from start to finish. (When one unsupportive columnist who entered the fray early on ridiculed him for reading not the original version of *Orations* but an abridged, pure Turkish edition, Sunay took the original out of the library and posed with it. Sadly, his efforts to get the new photographs published in the columnist's paper proved fruitless.) Undaunted, Sunay continued to appear at grand openings, concerts and important football matches, and, wherever he went, he answered each question of every third-rate reporter about Atatürk and art, Atatürk and music, Atatürk and Turkish sport. With an eagerness to please rather unbecoming in a political radical, he even did interviews with the anti-Western religious newspapers.

During one of these, he said, in answer to a fairly mundane question, 'Perhaps one day, when the public deems fit, I might be able to play the Prophet Mohammed.' With this offhand remark, his trouble really began.

The small Islamist periodicals went on the rampage: God forbid, they wrote, that any mortal should presume to play the Great Prophet. The swarm of angry columnists who had initially accused Sunay of 'showing disrespect for our Prophet' were soon writing that he was 'actively discrediting the Prophet'. When even the army proved reluctant to silence the political Islamists, it was left to Sunay himself to put out the fire his careless comment had started. Hoping to assuage their fears, he took to carrying around a copy of the Holy Koran and telling its conservative readers how much he loved this book, which in so many ways was really rather modern. But this only created an opportunity for Kemalist columnists who had taken offence at his preening as 'the people's choice' for the role of Atatürk. Never once, they wrote, had Atatürk tried to curry favour with religious fanatics. The newspapers supporting the military coup kept printing a picture of Sunay in a spiritual pose with a copy of the Koran. Underneath would be the caption, 'Is this how you see Atatürk?' Then the Islamist press lashed back. They ran pictures of Sunay drinking raki with captions like 'He's a raki drinker, just like Atatürk!' and 'Is this the man who is to play the Great Prophet?' This sort of war flared up between the Islamist press and the secular press every couple of months, but this time Sunay was caught in the crossfire.

For a week, you couldn't open a paper without seeing him: one picture had him guzzling beer in a commercial he'd made years earlier; others showed him receiving a beating in a film he'd made in his youth, defiantly raising his fist before a flag emblazoned with a hammer and sickle, and watching his wife kissing the male leads in various plays . . . And page after page of innuendo followed the pictures: his wife was a lesbian; he was still as much of a communist as ever; he and Funda had done the voice-overs for contraband porn films. It was suggested that he would do anything if the money was right. After all, East German funding had made it possible for him to perform Brecht. And, after the coup, he had insulted the state by telling 'women from a Swedish association that torture was endemic to Turkey'.

Finally, a 'high-ranking officer' summoned Sunay to army headquarters to inform him rather curtly that he should withdraw from the race to play Atatürk. This was not the same good-hearted officer who had invited several uppity Istanbul journalists to Ankara to scold them for criticising the army's involvement in politics, before then offering them chocolates, but another, less jovial major from the same public relations department. He didn't soften one bit when he saw Sunay quaking with remorse and fear; rather, he ridiculed the actor for propounding his own political views in the guise of the 'man chosen to be Atatürk'. He alluded to Sunay's short visit two days earlier to the town of his birth, during which he had played the 'people's politician'. Cheered on by convoys of cars and crowds of tobacco manufacturers and unemployed men, he had climbed up to the statue of Atatürk in the town's main square and inspired even more applause by squeezing the statue's hand. When a reporter from a popular magazine then asked him whether he thought he might leave the stage one day to enter politics, Sunay answered, 'If the people want me.' The prime minister's office announced that the Atatürk film was to be 'postponed indefinitely'.

Sunay was experienced enough to endure this defeat. His real undoing came with what followed. During his month-long campaign to land the role, he'd had so much television exposure that everyone associated him only with Atatürk, so now no one would give him dubbing work. The TV advertisers who had once been happy to have him play the reasonable father with a knack for buying only the best and healthiest products turned their backs on him: they thought their viewers would find it strange to see a failed Atatürk brandishing a brush and holding a can of paint, or explaining why he was so satisfied with his bank. But even worse for Sunay was that many people believed everything they read in the papers. So he was accused of being both an enemy of Atatürk *and* an enemy of religion. Some even believed that he had kept quiet when his wife kissed other men. Or, if they didn't believe it, there was still a lot of muttering about no smoke without fire.

The chief effect of all this was the declining box office for Sunay's theatre troupe. Quite a few people stopped him in the street to say, 'I expected better from you!' A young religious high-school student, convinced that Sunay had stuck his tongue out at the Prophet (and motivated also no doubt by his own desire to get into the papers), stormed into one theatre waving a knife and spat in several people's faces. This happened over the course of five days. Sunay and Funda then disappeared.

And in their absence the gossip grew even wilder. One rumour had it that they'd joined the Brechtian Berliner Ensemble, ostensibly to teach drama, though really they were learning how to be terrorists. According to another account, the French Ministry of Culture had given them a grant and refuge at the French Mental Hospital in Şişli.

In fact, they had decamped to the house of Funda Eser's artist mother on the Black Sea coast. A year later, they finally found work as activity directors at an undistinguished hotel in Antalya. They spent their mornings playing volleyball in the sand with German grocers and Dutch tourists. In the afternoons they dressed up as the shadow-theatre characters Karagöz and Hacivat and performed in butchered German for the amusement of the children. In the evenings they sailed on stage dressed as a sultan and the belly-dancing darling of his harem. This was the beginning of Funda Eser's belly-dancing career, which she would continue to develop during their tours of the provinces over the next ten years. For three months, Sunay managed to play the clown, until a Swiss barber crossed the line, interrupting their act with jokes about Turks with harems and fezes, which continued the next morning on the beach, where he began to flirt with Funda. Sunay beat him up in full view of a shocked and terrified crowd of tourists.

After that, it seems that the couple worked as freelance masters of ceremonies, dancers and 'theatrical entertainers' at weddings and dance halls throughout the Antalya area. Even when he was introducing cheap singers, fire-eating jugglers and third-rate comedians, Sunay would make short speeches about Atatürk, the republic and the institution of marriage. Funda Eser would do a belly-dance, and then the couple, now assuming an austere and highly dignified air, would do something like the murder of Banquo, stopping after eight or ten minutes for a round of applause. During these evenings the seeds were planted for the touring theatre troupe they would later take all over Anatolia.

While having his blood pressure checked, Sunay had one of his bodyguards bring over a walkie-talkie. After issuing a few orders into it and reading a message a factotum had abruptly pushed in front of him, his face crumpled with revulsion. 'They're all denouncing one another,' he said. He went on to mention that during his years of touring the remote towns of Anatolia, he had come to the conclusion that all the men in the country were paralysed by depression. 'For days on end, they sit in those tea-houses; day after day they go there and do nothing,' he said. 'You see hundreds of these poor jobless, luckless, hopeless, motionless creatures in every town. In the country as a whole there must be hundreds of thousands of them, if not millions. They've forgotten how to keep themselves presentable; they've lost the will to button up their stained, oily jackets; they have so little energy they can hardly move their arms and legs; their powers of concentration are so weak they can't even follow a story to its conclusion; and they've forgotten how to laugh at a joke, these poor brothers of mine.'

Most of them were too unhappy to sleep; they took pleasure in knowing that the cigarettes they smoked were killing them; they began sentences only to let their voices trail off as they remembered how pointless it was to carry on; they watched television not because they liked or enjoyed the programmes, but because they couldn't bear to hear about their friends' depression and TV helped to drown them out. What they really wanted was to die, but they didn't even think themselves worthy of suicide. During elections, masochistically they voted for the most wretched parties and the most loathsome candidates. Sunay insisted that these men preferred the generals at the head of the military coup over politicians because the former spoke with honest realism about the need for punishment while the latter just endlessly promised hope.

Funda Eser, who had re-entered the room by now, added that there were also many unhappy women who'd all worn themselves out by having too many children, curing tobaccco, weaving carpets and working as nurses for pitiful wages while their husbands were who knew where. These women who shouted and wailed at their children all day long were the ones who kept life going. If they ceased to exist, it would be the end of the line for the millions of joyless, jobless, aimless men all over Anatolia. They all looked the same, these men: unshaven, their shirts dirty. But, without the women looking after them, they would end up like the beggars who froze to death on street corners during cold snaps, or the drunks who staggered out of taverns to fall into open sewers, or the senile grandfathers sent off to the grocery store in their pyjamas and slippers to buy a loaf of bread only to lose their way. Yet these men were all too numerous, 'as we've seen in the wretched city of Kars'. Although they owed their lives to their women, the love they felt for their wives made them so ashamed that they tortured them.

'I gave ten years to Anatolia because I wanted to help my unhappy friends out of their misery and despair,' said Sunay. There was no self-pity in his voice. 'They accused us of being communists, perverts, spies working for the West, even Jehovah's Witnesses. They said I was a pimp and my wife a prostitute. Time and again they threw us into jail, beat and tortured us. They tried to rape us; they stoned us. But they learned to love my plays and the freedom and happiness that my theatre company brought them. So now, as I am handed the greatest opportunity of my life, I shall not weaken.'

Two men entered the room. As before, one of them handed Sunay a walkie-talkie. The channel was open and Ka could hear people talking: they'd surrounded one of the shanties in the Sukapı district, and, after someone inside had fired at them, they'd gone in to find one of the Kurdish guerrillas and a family. On the same frequency a soldier was giving orders; his subordinates addressed him as 'my commander'. Then the soldier addressed Sunay, to give him advance notice of their plans and to seek his views; he sounded more like an old school friend than the leader of a revolution.

'There's a little fellow who's a brigade officer here in Kars,' Sunay said when he noticed Ka's interest. 'During the Cold War, the military command had the very best forces amassed further inland, in Sarıkamış, in anticipation of a Soviet incursion. At most, the people here would be staging diversions during the first attack. These days, they're mostly here to guard the border with Armenia.'

Sunay now told him that on the night when he and Ka had come in on the same bus from Erzurum, he'd gone into the Green Pastures Restaurant and had run into Osman Nuri Çolak, a friend of thirty-odd years. Çolak was an old classmate from the Kuleli Military Academy. In those days, he was the only other person in Kuleli who had heard of Pirandello and could list Sartre's plays. 'Unlike me, he couldn't get himself expelled for lack of discipline, but nor could he embrace the military wholeheartedly,' said Sunay. 'So he never became a general staff officer. And there were people who whispered that he was too short to be a general anyway. He's an angry, troubled man, but not, I think, because of professional problems – it's because his wife took their children and left him. He's tired of being alone, bored of having nothing to do here and worn out by the small-town gossip, although, of course, he's the one who does most of the gossiping. Those unlicensed butchers I raided after declaring the revolution, the disgraceful stories about the Agricultural Bank loans and the Koran courses – he was the first to tell me about them. And he was drinking too much. He was over-joyed to see me, but full of complaints about loneliness. And then, by way of apology but also with a note of boastfulness in his voice, he told me that he was the highest-ranking official in Kars that night, so, sadly, he was going to have to get up early the next morn-ing. The commander of his brigade had gone to Ankara with his wife to see doctors about her rheumatism, the deputy colonel had been called to an urgent meeting in Sarıkamış, and the governor was in Erzurum. He had all the power! And, with the snow still falling, he knew from past experience that the roads would be closed for days. I saw at once that this was the opportunity I had been awaiting all my life, so I ordered my friend another double raki.'

According to the report submitted by the major sent from Ankara, the man Ka had heard moments earlier on the walkie-talkie was indeed Colonel Osman Nuri Çolak (or Crooked Arm, as Sunay, his old friend from military school, preferred to call him). The major also reported that the colonel had initially taken this strange suggestion that he stage a military coup as nothing more than a joke, a whim of the raki table invented just for fun, but he had played along with the gag, claiming that the job could be done with two tanks. That he would later actually execute the plan owed more to his desire not to be seen as a coward in the face of Sunay's insistence, and to his belief that Ankara would be pleased with the outcome, than it did to any grudge, grievance or hope for personal glory. The major's report added, however, that he had sadly compromised his principles when in the turmoil he'd gone into the Republic district and raided the home of an Atatürk-loving dentist to settle an argument the two men had been having over a woman.

The colonel had used half a squadron to search houses and schools, and four trucks and two T-1 tanks – these had to be driven with great care because spare parts were scarce – but no other military equip-ment. If the 'unexplained deaths' ascribed to 'special teams' such as that of Z Demirkol and his friends are put to one side, most of what happened followed the usual course of a Turkish coup. In other words, the hard-working officials of MİT and at police headquarters were the major players during the revolution. After all, they had files on everyone in the city, and employed a tenth of the population as informers. These officials were so elated to hear the spreading rumour of the demonstration that the secularists were planning to make at the National Theatre that they sent out official telegrams to friends away from the city on leave advising them to return at once lest they miss the fun.

From what he could hear coming in on the walkie-talkie, Ka gathered that the skirmish in the Sukapı district had reached a new stage. Three gunshots sounded first over the radio frequency and then echoed outside the windows, albeit muffled by the snowy plain.

'Don't be cruel,' Sunay said into the walkie-talkie, 'but let them feel the power of the revolution and the state, and let them see how determined we are.' He'd raised his left hand and, clutching his chin between thumb and forefinger, assumed a pose of deep thought. The gesture was so distinctive that Ka now remembered an image from the mid-seventies of Sunay posing in this way while uttering the exact same words in a history play. He wasn't as handsome as he'd been in those days – he looked tired, pale and worn.

Sunay picked up a pair of 1940s army-issue field-glasses from the table. Then he grabbed the thick but ragged felt coat he'd worn throughout his ten-year tour of Anatolia and, putting on his fur hat, took Ka by the hand and led him outside. The cold took Ka by surprise, and made him think how weak and thin are men's dreams and desires, how insubstantial the intrigues of politics and everyday life compared with the cold winds of Kars. He noticed that Sunay's left leg was far more damaged than he'd thought. As they set off down the snow-covered pavement, he marvelled at the emptiness of the bright white streets, and when it occurred to him that they might be the only people walking outside in the whole of Kars, joy surged through him. While the beautiful snow-covered city with its old, empty mansions could lead a man to fall in love with life and find the will to love, there was more to what Ka felt than that: he was also enjoying his proximity to power.

'This is the most beautiful part of Kars,' said Sunay. 'This is my theatre company's third visit to the city in ten years. And each time this is where I come when the light fades, to sit under the poplars and the oleanders, to listen to the melancholy cries of the crows and the magpies while I gaze at the castle, the bridge and the four-hundred-year-old hamam.'

They were now standing on the bridge over the frozen River Kars. Sunay gazed out over the shanties scattered on the hill rising above the left bank and pointed at one of them. Below that house, just above the road, Ka saw a tank and, a little further on, an army truck. 'We can see you,' Sunay said into the walkie-talkie, as he peered through the field-glasses. A few moments later, they heard two gunshots – first through the walkie-talkie, then in the air above the valley into which the river flowed. Was this some manner of greeting? Up ahead, at the entrance to the bridge, two bodyguards awaited them. They gazed at the wretched shanty town – a hundred years after Russian cannon had destroyed the villas of the Ottoman pashas, the poor had come here to stake their claims – and looked at the park on the opposite bank that had once been home to Kars' bourgeoisie and the city rising behind it.

'It was Hegel who first noticed that history and theatre are made of the same materials,' said Sunay. 'Remember that, just as in the theatre, history chooses those who play the leading roles. And just as actors put their courage to the test on the stage, so, too, do the chosen few on the stage of history.'

The entire valley rattled with explosions, and Ka deduced from this that the machine-gun atop the tank was now in use. The tank's cannon had also fired shots, but these had missed their target. Later explosions were caused by hand-grenades. A black dog was barking. The shanty's door opened and two people came out, their hands in the air. Ka could see tongues of flame licking at the broken window panes. All the while, the dog continued to bark happily, darting back and forth, his tail wagging, until he went over to join the people crouching on the ground. Ka saw someone running in the distance, then heard the soldiers open fire. The man in the distance fell to the ground, and all noise stopped. Much later, someone shouted, but by then Sunay's attention was elsewhere.

Followed by the bodyguards, they made their way back to the tailor's shop. The moment Ka noticed the exquisite antique wallpaper in the old mansion, he knew that he could not contain the new poem forming within him, so he retreated to a corner.

This poem, to which he would give the title 'Suicide and Power', contains bold references to his walk with Sunay: he describes the thrill of power, the flavour of the friendship he's struck up with this man, and his guilt about the girls committing suicide. Later he would decide that in this 'sound and considered' poem the events he had witnessed in Kars had found their most powerful and authentic expression.

23

God Is Just Enough to Know That It's Not a Question of Reason or Logic but How You Live Your Life

With Sunay at Military Headquarters

When Sunay saw that Ka had completed his poem, he rose from his cluttered desk and limped across the floor to offer his congratulations. 'The poem you read at the theatre yesterday was very modern, too,' he said. 'What a shame that audiences in our country are not sophisticated enough to understand modern art. This is why my shows always include belly-dancing and the confessions of Vural the goalkeeper. I give the people what they want, and then I give them an unadulterated dose of "life theatre". I would far rather mix high and low art for the people than be in Istanbul doing bank-sponsored boulevard comedies. Now tell me, as a friend, why didn't you identify any of the suspicious Islamists they showed you at the police headquarters and the veterinary faculty?'

'Because I didn't recognise any of them.'

'When they saw how fond you were of that youth who took you to see Blue, the soldiers wanted to arrest you, too. They were already suspicious – you'd come all the way from Germany in this time of revolution, and you'd witnessed the assassination of that institute director. They wanted to put you through an interrogation – torture you a little – just to see what they could turn up. I stopped them; I'm your guarantor.'

'Thank you.'

'The thing no one can understand is why you kissed that boy who took you to Blue.'

'I don't know why,' said Ka. 'He was very honest and he spoke from the heart. I thought he was going to live for a hundred years.'

'This Necip you're so sorry about – would you like to know what kind of Necip he really was? Let me read you something.' He produced a piece of paper with the following information: one day last March, the boy had run away from school; he was associated with a group that had smashed the windows of the Joyous Beerhall for selling alcohol during Ramadan; he'd been doing odd jobs at the branch headquarters of the Prosperity Party for a while, but he'd stopped, either because his extreme views caused alarm or because he'd suffered a breakdown that frightened everyone (there was more than one informer at Prosperity Party headquarters); he was an admirer of Blue and had been making overtures to him during the eighteen months Blue had been visiting the city; he had written a story judged to be 'incomprehensible' by MİT and had it printed by a religious newspaper with a circulation of seventy-five; on a few occasions a retired pharmacist who wrote columns for the same paper had kissed him in a rather odd way, so Necip and his friend Fazıl had conspired to murder him (this was according to their dossier: the original of the letter explaining their act which they'd planned to leave at the scene of the murder had been stolen from the archives); on various occasions Necip had been seen walking down Atatürk Avenue, laughing with his friends, and on one such occasion, in October, he'd made an obscene gesture at an unmarked police car.

'MİT is doing important work here,' said Ka.

'His Excellency Sheikh Saadettin's house is bugged, so they also know that the first thing you did when you met him was to kiss his hand. They know that you confessed in tears to him that you believed in God. What they can't understand is why. There are quite a few left-wing poets who've panicked and decided that they might as well find religion before the Islamists come to power and they're forced to change sides.'

Ka felt himself flush, and when he saw that Sunay viewed his behaviour with the sheikh as a sign of weakness, his shame only increased.

'I know the things you saw this morning upset you deeply,' continued Sunay. 'The police treat our young very badly. We have in our midst a number of animals who beat up young boys just for the fun of it. But let's leave that matter to one side for now . . .' He offered Ka a cigarette. 'Like you, I spent the years of my youth roaming the streets of Nişantaş and Beyoğlu. I was mad about films from the West – I couldn't see enough of them. I read everything Sartre and Zola had ever written, and I believed that our future lay with Europe. To see that whole world destroyed, to see my sister forced to wear a headscarf, to see poems banned for being anti-religious, as we've seen already in Iran – this is one spectacle I don't think you would be prepared to take lying down. Because you're from my world, and there's no one else in Kars who's read the poetry of T. S. Eliot.'

'Muhtar, the candidate for the Prosperity Party, has,' said Ka. 'He has a great interest in poetry.'

'We don't even have to keep him locked up any more,' said Sunay with a smile. 'He's signed a statement declaring his withdrawal from the race. He gave it to the first soldier who knocked on his door.'

They heard an explosion. The window panes rattled and the frames shook. Turning in the direction of the noise, the two men looked through the windows towards the River Kars, but all they could see were snow-covered poplars and the icy eaves of the undistinguished, abandoned building opposite. Apart from the guard outside their door, there was no one on the street. Even this late in the morning, Kars was heavy with gloom.

'A good actor', said Sunay in a light, theatrical tone, 'is a man who represents the sediment, the unexplored and unexplained powers that have drifted down through the centuries. He takes the lessons he has gleaned and hides them deep inside himself. His self-mastery is awesome; never does he bare his heart; no one may know how powerful he is until he strides on to the stage. All his life, he travels down unfamiliar roads, to perform at the most out-of-the-way theatres in the most godforsaken towns, and everywhere he goes, he searches for a voice that will grant him genuine freedom. If he is so fortunate as to find that voice, he must embrace it fearlessly and follow it to the end.'

'In three days, when the snow melts and the roads reopen, Ankara is going to come down hard on the people responsible for this carnage,' said Ka. 'But not because they can't bear bloodshed. They'll be angry because this time they weren't the perpetrators. The people of Kars will hate you, and they'll feel the same about this strange production of yours. What will you do then?'

'You saw the doctor. I have a weak and diseased heart, I've come to the end of my allotted time, they can do what they want with me, I don't care,' said Sunay. 'Listen: they're saying that if we caught someone important, say the man who shot the director of the Education Institute, and hanged him right away, and broadcast the hanging on live TV, we'd have everyone in the city sitting as still as candles.'

'They're already as still as candles,' said Ka.

'We've heard that they're about to use suicide bombers.'

'If you hang someone, all you'll do is increase the terror.'

'Are you afraid of the shame you'll feel when the Europeans see what we've done here? Do you know how many men they hanged to establish that modern world you admire so much? Atatürk had no time for bird-brained fantasists – he had people like you swinging from the rope from the very first day. Get this into your head, too,' said Sunay: 'those religious high-school boys you saw in the cells today have your face permanently etched on their memories. They'll throw bombs at anyone and anything – they don't care as long as they are heard. And furthermore, since you read a poem during the performance, they'll assume you were in on the plot. No one who's even slightly Westernised can breathe freely in this country unless they have a secular army protecting them, and no one needs this protection more than intellectuals who think they're better than everyone else and look down on the people – if it weren't for the army, the fanatics would be turning their rusty knives on the lot of them and their painted women, chopping them all into little pieces. But what do these upstarts do in return? They cling to their little European ways and turn up their affected little noses at the very soldiers who guarantee their freedom. When we go the way of Iran, do you really think anyone is going to remember how a porridge-hearted liberal like you shed a few tears for the boys from the religious high school? When that day comes, they'll kill you just for being a little Westernised; for being frightened and forgetting the Arabic words of a simple prayer; even for wearing a tie, or that coat of yours. Where did you buy this beautiful coat, by the way? May I wear it for the play?'

'Of course.'

'Just to keep you from getting any holes in your nice coat, I'll give you a bodyguard. In a little while I'm going to make an announcement on television. The curfew ends at midday, so stay off the streets.'

'I can't believe that there's an Islamist here in Kars who's so dangerous I can't go outside.'

'What's done is done,' said Sunay. 'Above all, they know that the only way they'd ever get to run this country is by terrorising us. Over time, our fears will turn out to have been well founded. If we don't let the army and the state deal with these dangerous fanatics, we'll end up back in the Middle Ages, sliding into anarchy, travelling the doomed path already well travelled by so many tribal nations in Asia and the Middle East.'

His perfect posture, his commanding voice, his long and frequent gazes at an imaginary point high above the heads of his audience – Ka remembered seeing Sunay striking these same poses on stage twenty years earlier. But it didn't make him laugh – he felt as if he, too, were an actor in the same dated play.

'What do you want from me?' asked Ka. 'Spell it out.'

'If it weren't for me, you'd have a hard time keeping your head above water in this city. No matter how much you toady to the Islamists, you'll still get holes in your coat. I'm the only friend you have here; I'm the only person in Kars who can protect you. And don't forget, without my friendship, you'd soon be trembling in one of those cells beneath police headquarters, waiting to be tortured. As for your friends at the *Republican*, it's not you they put their faith in; it's the army. Know where you stand.'

'I do know.'

'Then confess to me what you hid from the police this morning. Tell me of the guilt you hide deep in your heart.'

'I think I may be starting to believe in God here,' said Ka with a smile. 'It's something I may be hiding even from myself.'

'You're deceiving yourself! Even if you did believe in God, it would make no sense to believe alone. You'd have to believe in Him as the poor do; you'd have to become one of them. It's only by eating what they eat, living where they live, laughing at the same jokes and getting angry whenever they do that you can believe in their God. If you're leading an utterly different life, you can't be worshipping the same God they are. God is just enough to know that it's not a question of reason or logic but how you live your life. But that's not what I was asking you about just now. In half an hour I'm going on television to address the people of Kars. I want to bring them good tidings. I'm going to say that we've caught the assassin who shot the director of the Education Institute. There's a high probability that the same man shot the mayor. May I say that you identified this person for us this morning? Then you can go on television and tell the whole story.'

'But I didn't identify anyone.'

With an anger that owed nothing to theatricality, Sunay grabbed Ka's arm and marched him out of the room, down a wide corridor, and into a bright white room with a view on to the inner courtyard. One look at this room was enough to repel him: it wasn't the filth, but the sordid atmosphere. There were stockings hanging on a line strung between the window latch and a nail in the wall. Ka saw in the corner an open suitcase containing a hairdryer, a pair of gloves, shirts and a huge bra that might just have fitted Funda Eser. She was sitting in a chair beside the suitcase; the table in front of her was piled high with paper and cosmetics she'd pushed aside to make room for a bowl. Stewed fruit? Ka wondered. Or was it soup? She was reading as she ate.

'We're here in the name of modern art . . . We're as attached to each other as a fingernail is to flesh,' said Sunay as he squeezed Ka's arm even harder.

Ka wasn't sure what Sunay was trying to say – and Sunay didn't seem to know whether this was life or a play.

'Vural the goalkeeper has gone missing,' said Funda Eser. 'He went out this morning and hasn't come back.'

'He's passed out somewhere,' said Sunay.

'But where?' said his wife. 'Everything's closed. No one's allowed out in the street. The soldiers have started a search. I'm afraid he's been kidnapped.'

'I hope to God he has been kidnapped,' said Sunay. 'If they would skin him alive and cut out his tongue, we'd all be better off.'

For all their coarse manners and rough language, there was something refined about the couple's convivial banter, something stemming from the depth of their mutual understanding, and Ka could not help feeling a certain respect for them – even a little envy. The moment he came eye to eye with Funda Eser, he instinctively bowed so low that he almost touched the floor.

'Madam, you were a veritable sensation last night,' he said in an affected voice that nevertheless contained traces of heartfelt admiration.

'Shame on you,' she said with faint embarrassment. 'In our company, it's not the players who make the masterpiece; it's the audience.'

She turned to her husband, and they began to converse, flitting from one subject to the next, as a king and queen pressed by many important matters of state might. Ka listened with a mixture of appreciation and amazement as husband and wife fretted over which costume was right for his impending TV appearance. (Civilian clothes?

Military uniform? Black tie?) They went on to discuss the script for his speech (Funda Eser had written part of it) and the statement taken from the owner of the hotel where they'd stayed during previous visits (nervous about the soldiers continually coming by for another search, and anxious to curry favour, the hotel-owner had formally denounced two young guests who looked suspicious). Finally, they pulled out a pack of cigarettes on which someone had scribbled the afternoon schedule for Border City Television (five reruns of the gala at the National Theatre, three of Sunay's speech, folk songs about heroism and the borderlands, a travelogue about the beauties of Kars, and a Turkish film, *Gülizar*). They read it through, and it met with their approval.

'And now,' said Sunay, 'what are we to do with this poet of ours, whose intellect belongs to Europe, whose heart belongs to the religious high-school militants, and whose head is all mixed up?'

'It's clear from his face,' said Funda Eser, smiling sweetly. 'He's a good boy. He's going to help us.'

'But he's been shedding tears for the Islamists.'

'He's in love, that's why,' said Funda Eser. 'Our poet has been awash in emotions these last few days.'

'Ahhhh, is our poet in love?' asked Sunay, gesturing wildly. 'Only the purest poets allow love into their hearts in times of revolution.'

'He's not pure poet, he's pure lover,' said Funda Eser.

As husband and wife carried the scene forward with their usual flawless technique, Ka grew both furious and stupefied.

Afterwards, they returned to the atelier and drank tea together at the big table.

'I'm telling you this so you'll see why helping us is the wisest thing to do,' said Sunay. 'Kadife is Blue's mistress. You see, it's not politics that draws Blue to Kars but love. They didn't arrest him because they wanted to know which young Islamists were his associates. Now they're sorry, because last night, just before the raid on the religious high-school dormitory, he vanished like smoke. All the young Islamists in Kars are in his thrall, and in his clutches. He's somewhere in the city, and he will definitely want to see you again. It could be difficult for you to tip us off. I suggest that we plant one or two microphones on you and perhaps a transmitter in your coat – you'd then have the same protection as the late director of the Education Institute had, so you'd have little worry for your safety. After you leave the meeting, we can go in and capture him.'

By the look on Ka's face, Sunay could tell he had not warmed to this proposal.

'I'm not going to insist,' he said. 'You don't look it, but your behaviour today has shown you to be a cautious person. Of course, you are a man who can look after himself, but I'm still telling you that you need to be very careful around Kadife. We suspect that she tells Blue everything she hears, and this must include her father's conversations with his guests at their supper table every evening. It's partly the thrill of betraying her father. But it's also because she's bound by love to Blue. How do you explain the strength of this passion?'

'Do you mean Kadife's?' asked Ka.

'No,' said Sunay impatiently. 'I mean this passion for Blue. What does this murderer have that makes everyone fall for him? Why is his name legend throughout Anatolia? You've spoken to him – can you solve this mystery for me?'

Funda Eser had picked up a plastic comb and was passing it through her husband's sandy hair with such tender care that Ka, distracted, fell silent.

'I'd like you to hear the speech I'm going to make on television,' said Sunay. 'Come with me in the army truck and we can drop you off at the hotel along the way.'

The curfew was due to end in forty-five minutes. Ka politely declined the offer and asked whether he might have permission to walk back to the hotel. It was granted.

It was a relief to walk down the wide, empty pavements of Atatürk Avenue – to feel the silence of the snow-packed side-streets, to gaze once again at the beautiful snow-covered Russian houses and the oleanders – but he soon realised he was being followed. He crossed over to Halitpaşa Avenue, and then turned left on Little Kâzımbey. The detective behind him was huffing and puffing as he hurried through the snow to catch up. Running after him was the same friendly black dog that Ka had seen hanging around the station when he'd met Necip and his two friends. Ka hid in the doorway of one of the workshops in the Yusufpaşa district, hoping to give the detective the slip, but suddenly he found himself face-to-face with his pursuer.

'Are you following me for intelligence purposes or for my protection?'

'God only knows, sir. Whichever sounds better to you is fine by me.'

But the man looked so exhausted that Ka doubted he could even protect himself. He must have been at least sixty-five years old, his face was lined and wrinkled, his voice thin, and the light had gone from his eyes. He gazed at Ka timidly, as fearfully as most people gaze at the police. Like all the plainclothes agents in Turkey, he was wearing Sümerbank shoes, and when Ka saw the soles were coming away from the uppers, he took pity on him.

'You're a policeman, aren't you? If you have your identity card on you, let's get them to open up the Green Pastures Restaurant and sit down for a while.'

They did not have to knock on the restaurant's door for long before it opened. Ka and the detective, whose name was Saffet, entered and then sat drinking raki and sharing cheese pastries with the black dog as they listened to Sunay's speech on the TV. It was identical to the speeches of leaders of military coups during Ka's childhood. In fact, by the time Sunay had explained how Kurdish and Islamist militants in the pay of 'our enemies abroad' and degenerate politicians who would stop at nothing to win votes had pushed Kars to the brink of destruction, Ka had become a little bored.

While Ka was drinking his second raki, Saffet, pointing respectfully at Sunay, directed his attention back to the television. His face had changed somehow: it was no longer that of a third-rate detective. He had assumed the air of a long-suffering citizen submitting a petition. 'You know this man; and, what's more, he respects you,' said Saffet plaintively. 'I hope you will be able to help me with my humble request. If you would present it to him, you could rescue me from this hellish life. Please, ask him to remove me from this poison investigation and reassign me.'

He then went over to bolt the restaurant door. Returning to the table, he started to tell Ka the tale of the 'poison investigation'. But the wretched detective had difficulty expressing himself, and the raki had gone straight to Ka's already addled head, so he was having a hard time following the story. It began at the Modern Buffet, a snack bar in the city centre not far from the military and intelligence headquarters. Many soldiers went there for sandwiches and cigarettes. Lately, however, suspicions had arisen that the cinnamon sherbet sold there had been laced with poison.

The first victim had been an infantry officer trainee from Istanbul. Two years earlier, on the morning of a much-dreaded, exceptionally arduous manoeuvre, this officer had come down with a fever that made his whole body shiver so wildly that he couldn't even stay on his feet. He was carted off to the infirmary, where they soon established that he had been poisoned, whereupon the officer, thinking he was about to die, blamed the spicy sherbet he had drunk at the snack bar on the corner of Little Kâzımbey and Kâzım Karabekir avenues – just because, he had added angrily, he had felt like trying something new.

At first this seemed like a simple case of accidental food poisoning, so it was soon forgotten. But not long after, two other officers with similar symptoms turned up at the same infirmary. Like the first, they were shaking so much they could barely talk and couldn't stand up for long before falling to the ground. Both blamed the same hot cinnamon sherbet that they'd drunk out of simple curiosity. It then emerged that a Kurdish granny was producing this refreshment in her home in the Atatürk district; everyone loved it, so her grandsons had decided to sell it at their snack bar. This information came to light during the secret interrogation conducted at Kars' military headquarters immediately after the second and third cases. But when samples of the granny's sherbet were tested at the veterinary faculty, no trace of poison could be found.

The investigation took an unexpected turn when the general happened to mention it to his wife. To his alarm and dismay, he discovered that she'd been drinking several cups of the sherbet every day, hoping that it might be good for her rheumatism. It turned out that quite a few other officers' wives, and several officers, too, had been knocking back huge quantities of this sherbet – all claiming it was for health reasons, though really it was out of simple boredom. Further investigation revealed the officers and their wives were not alone in succumbing to this fad. Soldiers on leave were indulging too, as were their visiting families, partly because the snack bar was convenient, being right in the centre of town, but mostly because the sherbet was the only new thing in Kars. When the general added his new findings to the investigation, he was so concerned about the possible implications that he handed the matter over to MİT and the army inspectorate.

As the army pressed home its advantage in its savage conflict with the Kurdish PKK guerrillas, the morale of the weak, despairing and unemployed Kurdish youths who'd fallen in with them plummeted further. This situation had led some of these youths to nurture strange and frightful dreams of revenge, as was reported by quite a few of the detectives who spent their days dozing in the city's coffee-houses. They'd overheard youths discussing bomb and kidnap plots, possible attacks on the statue of Atatürk, a scheme to poison the city's water supply and another to blow up its bridges. This was why the officials had taken the cinnamon sherbet scare so seriously, but, owing to the acute sensitivity of the issue, they'd been unable to interrogate or torture the snack bar's owners. So, instead, they assigned a number of detectives attached to the governor's office to infiltrate not just the Modern Buffet but the kitchen of the granny, who by now was over the moon about all the business she was doing.

The detective assigned to the snack bar subjected the granny's cin-namon confection to yet another test, and he also examined the glasses, the heat-resistant handles of the ladles, the change box, a number of rusty holes and the employees' hands for any sign of a strange powder. A week later, he, too, had all the symptoms of a poisoning: he was shaking and coughing so much that he had to leave work.

The detective who'd been planted in the granny's kitchen was even more industrious. Every night, he would sit down and write a full report listing not just the people who'd passed through the kitchen that day, but every item of food she purchased (carrots, apples, plums, dried mulberries, pomegranate flowers, dog roses and marshmallows). His reports soon revealed the recipe for this much-praised and appetising sherbet. The detective, who was drink-ing five or six jugs of the stuff a day, suffered no ill effects whatsoever: indeed, he even claimed it was a bona fide tonic, a genuine 'moun-tain' sherbet as mentioned in the Kurdish epic *Mem u Zin*.

Experts drafted in from Ankara quickly lost faith in this detective because he was himself a Kurd. Furthermore, they were able to deduce from his reports that the sherbet was poisonous to Turks but not to Kurds. However, because of the official state position that Kurds and Turks are indistinguishable from one another, they kept this conclusion to themselves.

At this point, a group of doctors brought in from Istanbul set up a special clinic at the Social Insurance Hospital. But soon it was overrun by perfectly healthy Kars inhabitants just looking for free treatment, not to mention some so-called invalids complaining of hair loss, rashes, hernias and even stammers. This stampede cast a long shadow over the seriousness of the investigation.

So it fell once again to the Kars intelligence services to unravel the sherbet plot that was slowly incapacitating the city and had already endangered the health of thousands of soldiers. MİT had to capture the perpetrators before the whole city's spirit was broken, and Saffet was just one of several diligent agents assigned to the case. Most were simply ordered to follow the people who drank the sherbet the granny produced with such relish. So the investigation was no longer into the source of the poison, but rather a vain attempt to discover who was being poisoned by the sherbet and who was not. To discover this, the detectives were following all the military and plainclothes police consumers of the granny's cinnamon drink, sometimes all the way home.

When Ka heard that this exhausting, painstaking mission had worn out not just the detective's shoes but his spirit, he promised to raise the subject with Sunay, who had yet to reach the end of his televised speech.

The detective was so elated to hear this promise that he gratefully threw his arms around Ka and kissed him on both cheeks, and unbolted the door with his own two hands.

24

'I, Ka'

The Six-Sided Snowflake

With the black dog following close behind, Ka walked back to the hotel, savouring again the empty beauty of the snow-covered streets. He dashed off a note – 'Come at once' – to İpek, and asked Cavit, the receptionist, to deliver it to her right away. He went upstairs and threw himself down on the bed. As he waited, he thought first of his mother, but soon his thoughts turned to İpek, who had still not arrived. He was quickly racked with such pain as to make him decide he had been a fool to fall in love with her, to come to Kars at all. More time passed and still there was no sign of İpek.

Thirty-eight minutes after Ka had returned to the hotel, İpek walked into his room. 'I had to go to the coal merchant,' she said. 'I knew there would be a line once the curfew ended, so I went out at a quarter to twelve through the back courtyard. After twelve I spent some time wandering around the market. If I'd known, I would have come straight back.'

İpek brought such life into the room, and Ka's mood soared to such dizzy heights that he was terrified of doing something to destroy this moment of bliss. He gazed at İpek's long, shiny hair. Her hands never stopped moving. (In no time at all, her left hand travelled from her hair to her nose, to her belt, to the edge of the door, and on to her beautiful long neck, before it was back straightening her hair again, only to be found a moment later caressing her jade necklace – she must have just put it on. Only now had Ka noticed it.)

'I'm terribly in love with you and I'm in pain,' said Ka.

'Don't worry – love that blooms this fast is just as fast to wither.'

Ka threw his arms around her and kissed her. İpek kissed him back, but she was as calm as he was frenzied. He felt her small hands on his shoulders, and the sweetness of her kiss sent his head spinning. He knew from the easy way she moved her body that she was ready to make love with him now, and he was so happy that his eyes, his mind and his memory opened up fully to the moment and to the world.

'I want to make love to you, too,' said İpek. For a moment she looked straight ahead. Then she lifted her eyes with swift determination and met Ka's gaze. 'But, as I've already said, it can't happen under my father's nose.'

'So when is your father going out?'

'He never goes out. I have to go,' she said as she pulled herself away.

Ka stood in the doorway watching İpek until she had disappeared down the stairs at the end of the dimly lit corridor. Then he closed the door, sat down on the edge of the bed, whipped his notebook out of his pocket, and, turning to a clean page, began writing the poem he would call 'What the Helpless Must Endure'.

After finishing the poem, Ka stayed on the edge of the bed and realised, for the first time since his arrival in Kars, that – apart from chasing İpek and writing poems – there was nothing for him to do in this city. This insight made him feel deprived and liberated in equal measure. He knew now that if he could trick İpek into leaving Kars with him, he would find lifelong happiness with her. Knowing that the moment was fast approaching when he would persuade her, after finding the place that would make the job easier, he felt grateful for the snow.

He threw on his coat and went outside, unnoticed by anyone. Instead of heading towards the city hall, he turned left on National Independence Avenue and walked down the hill. He went into the Pharmacy of Knowledge to buy some vitamin C tablets and then turned left off Faikbey Avenue, keeping straight, pausing now and then to look in restaurant windows, and then turning into Kâzım Karabekir Avenue. The campaign banners he'd seen fluttering above the avenue the day before had all been taken down, and all the shops were now open. One stationery and cassette vendor was playing loud music. The pavements were crowded with people who'd come out just to mark the end of the curfew; they walked down as far as the market and then up the hill again, pausing now and then to shiver in front of a shop window. Those who usually travelled in by minibuses serving the outlying areas, the men who frequented the city centre to doze in the tea-houses and perhaps stop off at the barber's for a shave, had not shown up today, and Ka was pleased to see so many tea-houses and barber shops empty. The children in the streets made him forget the fear inside them. He watched them sledging on the bridges, throwing snowballs, fighting and cursing in the vacant lots, the snow-covered squares, the school playgrounds and the gardens surrounding the government offices. Only a few wore coats; most were in their school jackets, scarves and skullcaps. They were happy about the coup because it had given them a day off school. Whenever the cold got too much for him, Ka went to join Saffet at the nearest tea-house. He'd go straight to the detective's table, have a glass of tea, and then return outside.

Now used to Saffet following him, he no longer found the man frightening. He knew that if they really wanted to find out everything he did, they'd use a man he couldn't see. That's why Ka panicked when, at one point in his walk, he lost sight of Saffet, and why he went in search of him. He found Saffet panting, a plastic bag in his hand, on the corner of Faikbey Avenue – the same spot where he'd seen the tank the night before.

'The oranges were very cheap, I couldn't help myself,' said the detective. He thanked Ka for waiting, adding that he had proved himself to be 'well intentioned' by choosing not to give him the slip. 'From now on, why don't you just tell me where you're going – that would save us both a lot of effort.'

Ka didn't know where he was going, but after two more glasses of raki in yet another empty tea-house, he realised that he wanted to pay a visit to His Excellency Sheikh Saadettin. There was no chance of his seeing İpek again in the near future, and he dreaded the torment of letting himself think about her, preferring to bare his soul to the sheikh. He'd begin by telling him about the love of God in his heart and then they could have a civilised conversation about God's intentions and the meaning of life. But then he remembered that the sheikh's lodge was bugged: the police would hear what he said and they'd never stop laughing.

Still, when he passed His Excellency's modest residence on Baytarhane Street, Ka stopped for a moment; he looked up at the windows.

Later, he noticed that the doors of the local library were open. He went inside and walked up the muddy stairs. On the landing was a bulletin board on to which someone had carefully tacked the seven local newspapers. Since, like the *Border City Gazette*, they had all been printed the day before, there was no mention of the revolution but a great deal about the splendid performance at the National Theatre and the continuing blizzard.

Although the city's schools were closed, he saw five or six students in the reading room, along with a handful of retired government officials. Like the students, they had probably come here to escape the cold in their houses. In a corner, among the dog-eared dictionaries and tattered children's encyclopedias, Ka found several old volumes of *The Encyclopedia of Life*, which had given him so many hours of pleasure as a child. Inside the back cover of every volume was a series of coloured transparencies, which, as you leafed through them, revealed the inner workings of a car, a ship, or a man. Ka went straight for the fourth volume, hoping to find the series featuring the baby nestled like a chick inside an egg within its mother's distended tummy, only to find that the pictures had been torn out. All that remained were frayed edges attached to the back cover.

On page 324 of the same volume (PE–TA) he found an entry that he read with care:

> SNOW. The solid form taken by water when falling, crossing, or rising through the atmosphere. Beautiful crystal starlets, usually forming a hexagon. Each crystal snowflake forms its own unique hexagon. Since ancient times mankind has been awed and mystified by the secrets of snow. In 1555, when a priest named Olaus Magnus in Uppsala, Sweden, discovered that each snowflake, as indicated in the diagram, had six corners . . .

How many times Ka may have read this entry during his stay in Kars, to what degree he internalised its illustration of a snow crystal, is impossible for me to say. Years later, when I went to visit his family home in Nişantaş, to spend long hours discussing him with his tearful and – as always – troubled and suspicious father, I asked whether I could look at the old man's library. Memory told me that what I was looking for would not be in Ka's room with all the other books from his childhood but in a dark corner of the sitting room on the shelves where his father kept his own collection. Here, among the handsome spines of his father's law books, the collection of novels from the forties – some in Turkish, others in translation – and the row of telephone directories, I found the beautifully bound volumes of *The Encylopedia of Life*. The first thing I did was turn to the back of the fourth volume to glance at the anatomical illustration of the pregnant woman. Then I directed my attention to the book as an object. I was still admiring its perfect condition when there, before my eyes, was page 324. It was almost as if the book had opened of its own accord on that page. There, right by the entry on snow, I found a thirty-two-year-old piece of blotting paper.

After Ka had finished looking at the encyclopedia he reached into his pocket and, like a student sitting down to do his homework, took out his notebook. He began to write a poem – the tenth to have come to him since his arrival in Kars. In the opening lines, he extolled the singularity of snowflakes, then went on to describe his childhood memories of the mother-and-child he had just failed to find at the back of the fourth volume of *The Encyclopedia of Life*. In the final lines he mapped out a vision of himself and his place in the world, his special fears, his distinctive attributes, his uniqueness. The title he gave this poem was 'I, Ka'.

Ka was still writing the poem when he noticed someone else sitting at his table. Lifting his eyes from the page, he gasped: it was Necip. He felt no terror at this apparition, and nor was he amazed. Instead he felt ashamed – here was someone who didn't die so easily and yet Ka had been willing to believe he was dead.

'Necip,' he said. He wanted to throw his arms around the boy and kiss him.

'I'm Fazıl,' said the youth. 'I saw you in the street and followed you.' He glanced over at the table where Saffet was sitting. 'Tell me quickly – is it true that Necip's dead?'

'It's true. I saw him with my own eyes.'

'Then why did you call me Necip? You're still not sure, are you?'

'No, I'm not.'

For a moment Fazıl's face crumpled, and then he pulled himself together.

'He wants me to take revenge. That's why I am convinced he's dead. But when school opens all I want to do is study, I don't want to take revenge, I don't want to get involved in politics.'

'Anyway, revenge is a terrible thing.'

'Even so, I would take revenge if I thought he really wanted me to,' said Fazıl. 'I've been told that you discussed this with him. Did you give those letters to Hicran . . . I mean Kadife?'

'I did.'

Fazıl's gaze made him uncomfortable. Should I correct that? he asked himself. Say, 'I meant to,' instead? But it was already too late. For some reason, his lie made him feel more secure.

The pain on Fazıl's face was hard to bear. The boy covered his face with his hands and cried a little. But he was so angry that the tears wouldn't come. 'If Necip is dead, who is the person I should be taking revenge on?' When Ka said nothing Fazıl looked him straight in the eye. 'You know who it is,' he said sternly.

'I was told that sometimes the two of you thought the same thing at the same time,' said Ka. 'If you can still do that, then you know who it is.'

'But what he thinks, what he wants me to think, causes me terrible pain,' said Fazıl.

Now, for the first time, Ka saw in his eyes the same light he'd seen in Necip's. It was like sitting across from a ghost.

'So what is it that he's forcing you to think?'

'Revenge,' said Fazıl. He cried some more.

Ka could tell immediately that Fazıl's own thoughts were of something other than revenge. And Fazıl said so himself when he saw Saffet rise from his table to join them.

'Please may I see your identity card,' said the detective, giving Fazıl a fierce look.

'They have my school identity card at the lending desk.'

Ka watched the fear that swept over Fazıl as he realised he was talking to a plainclothes policeman. They all walked over to the lending desk. The detective snatched the identity card from the hand of the terrified woman on duty, and when he saw that Fazıl was a student at the religious high school, he shot a look that said, 'I might have known,' and, like an old man confiscating a child's toy, he put the card into his pocket.

'If you want this ID of yours back, you'll have to come to police headquarters and ask for it.'

'With all due respect,' said Ka, 'this boy has gone to great lengths to stay out of trouble, and he's only just heard that his best friend is dead, so couldn't you just give him his card back now?'

Having tried so hard to ingratiate himself earlier in the day so that Ka might put in a good word for him, Saffet now refused to budge. But, hoping he might persuade Saffet to entrust the card to him later, when no one was watching, Ka arranged to meet Fazıl at five o'clock at the iron bridge. The boy left the library at once.

By now, everyone in the reading room was on tenterhooks, thinking that they, too, were going to have their identity cards checked. But Saffet ignored them, returning to his table and a 1960s volume of *Life* magazine to read about the sad Princess Sureyya, who had been spurned by her husband the Shah after failing to give him a child, and to look at the last picture taken of Adnan Menderes, the former prime minister, before he was hanged.

Calculating now that he would not be able to get his hands on Fazıl's identity card, Ka too left the library. When he returned to the enchanted white street to see swarms of joyous children throwing snowballs, all his fears vanished. He felt like running. But in Government Square he saw a line of gloomy, shivering men clutching burlap sacks and packages wrapped in newspaper, tied up with string. These were the cautious citizens of Kars who'd decided to take the coup seriously and were now turning over all of their weapons to the state. The authorities didn't trust them and had refused to let them inside the provincial headquarters, but they were still queuing like cold little lambs at the main entrance. When it had first been announced that all weapons were to be handed in, most Kars residents had gone straight out into the snow in the dead of night to bury theirs in the frozen ground where no one would think to look.

While he was walking down Faikbey Avenue, Ka ran into Kadife and felt himself blushing. He'd just been thinking of İpek, and because he associated Kadife with her sister he now thought Kadife extraordinarily beautiful, too. He had to exercise great self-control to refrain from embracing her.

'I must have a very quick word with you,' said Kadife. 'But there's a man following you, so I can't say anything while he's looking. Could you go back to the hotel and come to Room 217 at two o'clock? It's the last room at the end of your corridor.'

'Are you sure we can speak openly there?'

'If you don't tell anyone we've spoken' – Kadife opened her eyes wide – 'and I mean not even İpek, then no one will ever know.' She gave him a stern and businesslike handshake. 'Now look behind you as casually as you can and tell me if I have one or maybe even two detectives following me.'

Nodding with a slight smile, Ka was surprised at his own duplicity.

Although the thought of meeting Kadife secretly in a room confused him, he had no trouble putting it out of his mind. He knew at once that he didn't want to see İpek again before his meeting with Kadife, not even by chance, so he decided to continue his walk to kill time. No one seemed to be complaining about the coup; instead, the mood was much as he remembered from the coups of his youth. There was a sense of a new beginning, of a change from the vexing routines of everyday life. The women had gathered up their handbags and their children and gone out to pick through the fruit in the stalls and at the greengrocer's in search of a bargain. Men with thick moustaches stood on street corners smoking filterless cigarettes, gossiping as they watched the crowds go by. The beggar he'd seen feigning blindness twice the day before was no longer in position under the eaves of an empty building between the garages and the market. The vendors who had been selling oranges and apples out of pick-up trucks they'd parked right in the middle of the street were also absent. The traffic, normally light, was now almost non-existent, but it was hard to say whether this was due more to the coup or to the snow. There were more plainclothes policemen out on the streets (one had been recruited as a goalkeeper by the boys playing football at the bottom of Halitpaşa Avenue). The two hotels next to the garages that served as brothels (the Pan and the Freedom) were, like the cock-fight ring and the unlicensed butchers, were to be barred from pursing their black arts 'indefinitely'. As for the explosions they'd heard coming from the shanty areas, especially at night, the people of Kars were already accustomed to these, so their calm was generally undisturbed.

Ka found the general lack of interest liberating, which was why he went into the snack bar on the corner of Little Kâzımbey and Kâzım Karabekir avenues and ordered himself a hot cinnamon sherbet. He drank it with relish.

25

This Is the Only Time We'll Ever Be Free in Kars

Ka with Kadife in the Hotel Room

When he stepped into Room 217 sixteen minutes later, Ka was so worried someone might have seen him that he tried to joke with Kadife about the cinnamon sherbet, its sour taste still in his mouth.

'For a while there were rumours of angry Kurds poisoning that sherbet to kill military personnel,' said Kadife. 'It's even said that they sent in secret investigators to solve the mystery.'

'Do you believe these stories?' asked Ka.

'When educated, Westernised outsiders come to Kars and hear these conspiracy theories,' said Kadife, 'they immediately try to disprove them by going to the snack bar and ordering a sherbet, and then the fools end up poisoning themselves. Because the rumours are true. Some Kurds are so unhappy that they know no God.'

'Then why, after all this time, hasn't the state stepped in?'

'Like all Westernised intellectuals, you put all your trust in the state, without even realising it. MİT knows everything that goes on in Kars, and they know about the sherbet, too, but they don't stop it.'

'So does MİT know we're here together in this room?'

'Don't worry. Right now they don't,' said Kadife with a smile. 'One day they'll find out, but until that day comes, we're free here. This is the only time we'll ever be free in Kars. Appreciate it, and take off your coat.'

'This coat protects me from evil,' said Ka. Seeing fear in Kadife's face, he added, 'And it's cold in here.'

The room in which they were meeting was half of an old storage room. One narrow window looked on to the inner courtyard, and there was room only for the single bed on which they were now sitting, Ka perched uncertainly on one end and Kadife on the other. The room had that stifling, dusty smell that you find only in unaired hotel rooms. Kadife leaned over to fiddle with the dial on the radiator, but when it refused to budge, she gave up. When she saw Ka had jumped nervously to his feet, she tried to conjure a smile.

For a moment it seemed to Ka that Kadife was taking great pleasure from this assignation. After so many years of solitude, he, too, was pleased to be alone in a room with a beautiful woman, but he sensed she had no time for such fripperies: the light shining in her eyes spoke of something darker and more destructive.

'Don't worry – right now the only agent they have following you is that poor man with the bag of oranges. You can take this to mean that the state isn't afraid of you; it just wants to frighten you a little. Who was following me?'

'I forgot to look,' said Ka with embarrassment.

'What?' Kadife shot him a poisonous look. 'You're in love, aren't you? You're madly in love,' she cried. But she quickly pulled herself together. 'I'm sorry, it's just that we're all so scared,' she said, and once again the expression on her face changed abruptly. 'You must make my sister happy; she's a very good person.'

'Do you think she'll love me back?' asked Ka in a near whisper.

'Of course she will – she must. You're a very charming man,' said Kadife. When she saw how much she'd shocked him, she added, 'What's more, you're a Gemini, like İpek.' She then explained that while Gemini men are best suited to Virgo women, the double personality of Geminis, which makes them light and shallow, can either delight or disgust a Gemini woman. 'But you both deserve to be happy,' she added consolingly.

'When you've discussed me with your sister, has the question of her coming back with me to Germany ever come up?'

'She thinks you're very handsome,' said Kadife, 'but she doesn't trust you. Trust takes time. Impatient men like you don't fall in love with a woman, they take possession of her.'

'Did she tell you that?' asked Ka, raising his eyebrows. 'Time is a scarce commodity in this city.'

Kadife glanced at her watch. 'First, let me thank you for coming here. I've summoned you to discuss something very important. Blue has a message he wants to give you.'

'If we meet again, they'll follow me and arrest him on the spot,' said Ka. 'Then they'll torture us all. They've been in his house. The police hear everything he says.'

'Blue knew they were listening,' said Kadife. 'He sent you this message before the coup, and he also sent a message for you to pass on to the West. He sent it to make a philosophical point: stop sticking your noses into this suicide business. That's what he wanted to tell them. But now everything's changed, so he wants to cancel that message. And there's something more important: now he has a new message.'

The more Kadife talked, the more uncertain Ka became. 'It's not possible to go anywhere in this city without someone seeing you,' he said finally.

'There's a horse-drawn carriage. Twice a day it stops just outside the kitchen door to drop off gas canisters, coal and bottled water. It then goes on to make deliveries all over the city, and it's draped in canvas to protect its goods from the snow and the rain. The driver can be trusted.'

'Am I going to hide under the canvas like a thief?'

'I've done it plenty of times myself,' said Kadife. 'And it's lots of fun to go right across the city without anyone knowing. If you agree to this meeting, then I promise I'll do everything in my power to help you with İpek. Because I want you to marry her.'

'Why?'

'What woman wouldn't want her older sister to be happy?'

Not once in his life had Ka come across a pair of siblings who didn't feel deep hatred for each another. Even if they seemed to get along, there was always something oppressive about their solidarity, something that betrayed they were just going through the motions. But that wasn't why Ka dismissed Kadife's claim. He doubted her because of the way her left eyebrow shot up almost of its own accord, and because she pouted like a child about to cry – or rather, like a Turkish film actress simulating innocence. Nevertheless, when Kadife looked at her watch again and said that the carriage would be arriving in seventeen minutes, and that if he accompanied her to see Blue she would tell him everything, Ka immediately agreed. 'But first you have to tell me why you're willing to put this much trust in me,' he said.

'You're a dervish, Blue says. He believes that God has graced you with lifelong innocence.'

'OK then,' said Ka hurriedly. 'Is İpek also aware of this special gift?'

'Why should she be? This is Blue's view.'

'Please tell me everything İpek thinks of me.'

'Actually, I've already told you everything we've discussed,' said Kadife. But, seeing that she was breaking Ka's heart, she thought for a few moments, or else pretended to do so – Ka was too upset by now to tell the difference – and said, 'She thinks you're fun. You've just arrived from Germany and so on. You have so much to talk about!'

'What do I have to do to convince her?'

'It might not happen in the first instant, but within ten minutes of meeting a man, a woman has a clear idea of who he is, or at least who he might be, and her heart has already told her whether she's going to fall in love with him. But her head needs time to understand what her heart has decided. If you ask me, there's very little a man can do at that point except wait for time to take its course. If you really love her, all you have to do is tell her all the beautiful things you feel about her. Why you love her. Why you want to marry her.'

Ka said nothing. When Kadife saw him gazing out of the window like a dejected child, she told him how she could already imagine Ka and İpek living happily together in Frankfurt – and how happy İpek was to put Kars behind her. She could even see the two of them smiling on some Frankfurt street as they walked to the cinema of an evening. 'Just give me the name of a cinema you might go to if you were in Frankfurt,' she said. 'Any cinema.'

'Filmforum Hochts,' said Ka.

'Don't they have cinemas with names like the Alhambra, the House of Dreams and the Majestic in Germany?'

'They do. The Eldorado!'

As they watched snowflakes swirling aimlessly above the courtyard, Kadife told him about a part she'd been offered when she had been in the university drama society. It was a German-Turkish production in which the cousin of a classmate had some involvement. They'd wanted someone to play a covered girl, but Kadife had refused. Now she was hoping that İpek would find happiness with Ka in that same German-Turkish world, because her sister was meant to be happy. The problem was that she didn't realise it, so until now she'd been unhappy. Her failure to produce a child had destroyed her, but her main source of anguish came from not understanding why – being so beautiful, so refined, so thoughtful and so straightforward – she should be so unhappy. Sometimes she even wondered whether her unhappiness was due precisely to her having so many fine qualities. Here Kadife's voice began to crack. She went on to say that throughout her childhood, she had looked up to her sister, tried to be as good and as beautiful as she was. Her voice cracked again. But when she compared herself to İpek, she felt evil and ugly. Her sister was aware of this, so had tried to hide her beauty, hoping to make things easier for Kadife. By now, Kadife was crying. Between tearful gasps, she told Ka in a trembling voice about when she'd been in middle school 'We were in Istanbul at this time, and not so poor,' she said, whereupon Ka took the opportunity to point out that they 'weren't so poor now, either,' but Kadife promptly silenced him by saying, 'We live in Kars'. One morning, when she arrived late for her first class, Mesrure Hanım, her biology teacher, asked, 'Is your brilliant sister late, too?' and then added, 'I'll let you off this time because I'm so fond of your older sister.' Of course, İpek wasn't late.

The horse-drawn carriage entered the courtyard. It was a typical old rig, with red roses, white daisies and green leaves painted on its wooden sides. The tired, old horse stood behind a cloud of misty breath, and the edges of its nostrils were covered with ice. The driver was broad-shouldered and slightly hump-backed; a light blanket of snow covered his hat and coat. When Ka saw another blanket of snow on the tarpaulin, his heart began to beat faster.

'Please, don't be afraid,' said Kadife. 'I'm not going to kill you.'

Ka saw a gun in her hand, but he didn't register that she was pointing it at him.

'I'm not having a nervous breakdown, if that's what you're thinking,' said Kadife. 'But if you try anything funny, believe me, I will shoot you . . . We don't trust journalists who go to Blue looking for quotes, or anyone else for that matter . . .'

'But you invited me,' said Ka.

'You're right, but even if you don't think so, MİT could have guessed we were planning this visit and might be listening in. I'm suspicious that you wouldn't take off your beloved coat just a moment ago. Now, take it off and leave it on the bed – quick!'

Ka did as she asked. Kadife passed her delicate hands, which were as small as her sister's, over every corner of the coat. Finding nothing, she said, 'Please don't take this the wrong way, but now you have to take off your jacket, your shirt and your vest. Because these people strap microphones to people's backs and chests. There are probably about a hundred people wandering around Kars with these microphones on them any time of the day or night.'

After Ka had removed his jacket, he lifted up his shirt and vest, like a child showing his stomach to a doctor.

'Now turn around,' said Kadife. Ka obeyed her silently. 'That's fine then. My apologies . . . But when people are wearing a wire, they won't let us do a search, they won't keep still at all . . .' She still hadn't put down the gun. 'Now, listen to me,' she said menacingly. 'You are to tell Blue nothing about our conversation or our friendship.' She sounded like a doctor scolding a patient after an examination. 'You are not to mention İpek or let him know you're in love with her. Blue doesn't take kindly to filth like that . . . If you insist on talking about it, and he doesn't burn you for it, then rest assured, I will. He reads minds better than a genie – he might try to coax you into saying something. If he does, you're to act as if you've seen İpek once or twice, but that's it. Understood?'

'Understood.'

'Make sure you show Blue respect. Whatever you do, don't try to belittle him by playing the conceited, foreign-educated, European sophisticate. If you let this sort of foolishness slip out by accident, don't even think of smiling . . . And don't forget, the Europeans you admire and imitate so slavishly couldn't care less about you . . . and they're scared to death of people like Blue.'

'I know.'

'I'm your friend, be frank with me,' said Kadife, assuming a pose from a second-rate Turkish film.

'The driver's removed the tarpaulin,' said Ka, looking out of the window.

'You can trust this driver. His son died last year in a clash with the police. Enjoy the journey.'

Kadife went downstairs first. When she reached the kitchen, Ka saw the horse-drawn carriage move under the arch that divided the old Russian courtyard from the street, then he went downstairs as he'd been instructed. Seeing no one in the kitchen, he had a moment of panic, but then he saw the driver standing in the doorway that led into the courtyard. Without a word, he lay down next to Kadife among the empty propane canisters.

The journey, which he knew at once he would never forget, lasted only eight minutes, but to Ka it seemed much longer. As he wondered where in the city they were, he listened to the people of Kars commenting on the creaking carriage moving past them, and he listened to Kadife's steady breathing as she lay quietly next to him. A gang of boys caught the tail of the carriage and were pulled along with them for a while. He liked the sweet smile Kadife gave him; it made him as happy as those boys.

26

It Is Not Poverty That Brings People Like Us so Close to God

Blue's Statement to the West

As the wheels of the horse-drawn carriage rolled over the snow, rocking Ka like a baby, the first lines of a new poem came to him. But when the carriage mounted a pavement he was jolted back to reality. They creaked to a stop and there followed a silence that lasted long enough for Ka to receive a few more lines of the poem. Then the driver lifted the tarpaulin and Ka saw they were in an empty, snow-covered courtyard ringed by car-repair and welding shops and containing a broken tractor. In one corner was a black dog on a chain; when they emerged from under the tarpaulin, the dog greeted them with a few barks.

They went through one walnut door, then another, and Ka saw Blue gazing down at the snow-covered courtyard. Once again, Ka was struck by the red highlights in Blue's brown hair, the freckles on his face, and his midnight-blue eyes. Walking into yet another threadbare room filled with a number of familiar items (the same hairdryer as yesterday, the same open suitcase and the same plastic 'Ersin Electric' ashtray with Ottoman figures running along the edges), it didn't take Ka long to guess that Blue had moved house the night before. But from his icy smile Ka could tell that he'd already adjusted to the new situation and was even rather pleased with himself for having eluded the authorities.

'One thing's for sure,' said Blue, 'you can't write anything about the suicide girls now.'

'Why not?'

'Because the military doesn't want anything written about them any more than I do.'

'I'm not a spokesman for the military,' said Ka carefully.

'I know that.'

For a long, tense moment, the two men stared at each other.

'Yesterday you told me that you had every intention of writing about the suicide girls in the Western press,' said Blue.

Remembering his little lie, Ka felt embarrassed.

'Which Western newspaper did you have in mind?' asked Blue now. 'In which of the German papers do you have contacts?'

'The *Frankfurter Rundschau*,' said Ka.

'Who?'

'It's a liberal German newspaper.'

'What's your contact's name?'

'Hans Hansen,' said Ka, hugging his coat.

'I have a statement for Hans Hansen. I intend to speak out against the coup,' said Blue. 'We don't have much time; I want you to write it down this instant.'

Ka went to the back page of his poetry notebook and began to take notes.

Blue said that at least eighty people had been killed so far (the actual death toll, including those shot at the theatre, was seventeen). Numerous schools and houses had been raided and tanks had destroyed nine shanties (the real figure was four). After claiming that a number of students had died under torture, Blue alluded to a number of street skirmishes that Ka had not heard anyone else mention. Glossing rather quickly over the sufferings of the Kurds, he slightly exaggerated those visited on the Islamists. He said that the state had arranged for the mayor and the director of the Education Institute to be assassinated to provide a pretext for the coup. And the coup itself was designed to prevent the Islamists winning the election. The banning of all political parties and associations proved his point, he said.

As Blue went into more detail, Ka looked straight into Kadife's eyes – she was hanging on his every word. In the margins of these pages that he would later tear out of his notebook, he made a number of drawings and doodles that proved he was thinking about İpek: a slender neck, a head of hair, a child's house with a child's smoke rising out of a child's chimney. Many years earlier, Ka had explained to me that when a good poet was confronted with difficult facts that he knew to be true but that were also inimical to poetry, he had no choice but to flee to the margins. It was, he said, this very retreat that allowed him to hear the hidden music that was the source of all art.

Ka appreciated some of Blue's pronouncements enough to record them in his notebook verbatim. 'Contrary to what the West seems to think, it is not poverty that brings people like us so close to God. It's the fact that no one is more curious than we are to learn why we are here on earth and what will happen to us in the next world.'

But rather than explaining the source of this curiosity and revealing mankind's purpose on earth, Blue's final words posed a challenge: 'Will the West, which takes its great invention, democracy, more seriously than the Word of God, come out against this coup that has brought an end to democracy in Kars?' He paused to make a grand gesture. 'Or are we to conclude that democracy, freedom and human rights don't matter, that all the West wants is for the rest of the world to imitate it like monkeys? Can the West endure any democracy achieved by enemies who in no way resemble them? And I have something to say to all the other nations that the West has left behind. Brothers, you're not alone . . .' He paused again. 'But can you be sure that your friend at the *Frankfurter Rundschau* is going to print all this?'

'He takes offence when people discuss the West as if it's a single person with a single point of view,' Ka said, still choosing his words with care.

'But that's how it is,' said Blue after another pause. 'There is, after all, only one West and only one Western point of view. And we take the opposite point of view.'

'The fact remains that they don't live that way in the West,' said Ka. 'It's not as it is here – they don't like everyone thinking the same way. Everyone, even the most ordinary grocer, feels compelled to boast of having his own personal views. So if we said "Western democrats" instead of "the West", you'd have a better chance of pricking people's consciences.'

'Fine, do what you think best. Do we need to make any more corrections to get this published?'

'Although it began as a news item, it's become something more interesting; more like a proclamation,' said Ka. 'They might even want to put your name to it . . . and maybe include a few biographical details . . .'

'I've prepared those already,' said Blue. 'All they need to say is that I'm one of the most prominent Islamists in Turkey, and perhaps the entire Middle East.'

'Hans Hansen is not going to print this as it stands.'

'What?'

'If the social-democratic *Frankfurter Rundschau* were to print a statement from a single Turkish Islamist, it would seem as if they were taking sides,' said Ka.

'I see. When it doesn't serve Herr Hans Hansen's interests, he has a way of slithering away,' said Blue. 'What do we need to do to convince him?'

'Even if the German democrats come out against a military coup in Turkey – and it has to be a real coup, not a theatrical one – they'll still be very uneasy if the people they're defending are Islamists.'

'Yes, these people are all terrified of us,' said Blue.

Ka could not tell if he was boasting or merely feeling misunderstood. 'So,' he said, 'if you also included the signatures of an ex-communist, a liberal and a Kurdish nationalist, you'd have no trouble getting this announcement into the *Frankfurter Rundschau*.'

'Come again?'

'If we could find two other people in this city to come in on this, then we could get started on a joint announcement immediately,' said Ka.

'I'm not going to drink wine just to make Westerners like me,' said Blue. 'I'm not going to flutter around imitating them just so that they can stop fearing me long enough to understand what I'm doing. And I'm not going to abase myself at the door of this Westerner, this Herr Hans Hansen, just to make the godless atheists of the world feel pity for us. Who is this Herr Hans Hansen anyway? Why is he laying down so many conditions? Is he a Jew?'

Ka did not answer.

Sensing that Ka thought he'd misspoken, Blue glared at him with hatred. 'The Jews are the most oppressed people of our century,' he said, by way of recovery. 'Before I change a word of my statement, I want to know more about this Hans Hansen. How did you meet him?'

'Through a Turkish friend who told me that the *Frankfurter Rundschau* was going to publish a feature on Turkey and that the commentator wanted to speak to someone familiar with the background.'

'So why didn't Hans Hansen take his questions to this friend of yours? Why did he need to speak to you?'

'That particular Turkish friend didn't have as much background knowledge of these things as I did.'

'Let me guess what these things might be,' said Blue. 'Torture, brutality, prison conditions, and various other things that make us look even worse.'

'Perhaps, around that time, some religious high-school students in Malatya had killed an atheist,' said Ka.

'I don't remember hearing about any such event,' said Blue. He was watching Ka carefully. 'It is deplorable when Islamists go on television to boast about killing just one poor atheist, but it is just as appalling when secularist-orientalists seek to vilify the Islamists by running news reports that augment the death toll to ten or fifteen. If Herr Hans Hansen is one of these people, let's forget him.'

'All Hans Hansen did was to ask me a few questions about the EU and Turkey. I answered his questions. A week later he called me again. He invited me to his house for supper.'

'Just like that – without giving any reason?'

'Yes.'

'That's very suspicious. What did you see while you were in his house? Did he introduce you to his wife?'

Ka looked at Kadife, seated beside the fully drawn curtains and staring at him intensely.

'Hans Hansen has a lovely, happy family,' said Ka. 'One evening, after the paper was put to bed, Herr Hansen picked me up from the *Bahnhof*. A half-hour later, we arrived at a beautiful, bright house set inside a garden. They were very kind to me. We ate roast chicken and potatoes. His wife boiled the potatoes first and then roasted them in the oven.'

'What was his wife like?'

Ka brought to mind the image of Hans Hansen the Kaufhof sales clerk who had sold him his precious coat. 'Hans Hansen is blond, handsome and broad-shouldered; his wife Ingeborg and his children have the same blond beauty.'

'Did you see a cross on the wall?'

'I don't remember. I don't think so.'

'There was a cross, but you probably didn't notice,' said Blue. 'Contrary to what our own Europe-admiring atheists assume, all European intellectuals take their religion, and their crosses, very seriously. But when our guys return to Turkey, they never mention this, because all they want to do is use the technological supremacy of the West to prove the superiority of atheism . . . Tell me what you saw, what you spoke about.'

'Although he works on the foreign news desk of the *Frankfurter Rundschau*, Herr Hans Hansen is a lover of literature. The conversation soon turned to poetry. We talked about poems, countries, stories. I lost all sense of time.'

'Did they pity you? Did their hearts go out to you because you were a miserable Turk, a lonely, destitute political exile, the sort of Turkish nobody that drunken German youths beat up just for the fun of it?'

'I don't know. No one was putting pressure on me.'

'Even if they did not put pressure on you and told you how they pitied you, it's human nature to seek pity. There are thousands of Turkish-Kurdish intellectuals in Germany who've turned that pity into a livelihood.'

'Hans Hansen's family – his children – they're all good people. They were refined, gentle. It's possible that they were too refined to let me know how much they pitied me. I liked them a lot. Even if they did pity me, I wouldn't hold it against them.'

'In other words, this situation didn't crush your pride.'

'It's possible that it did hurt my pride, but I still had a lovely evening. The lamps on the side-tables cast an orange glow that I found very comforting. The knives and forks were a make I'd never seen before, but they weren't so unusual that you felt uneasy using them . . . The television was on all evening, and from time to time they'd glance in its direction, and this, too, made me feel at home. Sometimes, when they saw I was having a hard time understanding their German, they'd switch to English. After we finished eating, the children asked their father for help with their homework; when they put the children to bed, they kissed them. By the time the meal was over, they had made me feel so welcome that I helped myself to a second slice of cake. And no one noticed – or, if they did notice, they acted as if it were the most natural thing in the world. I thought about all this a great deal afterwards.'

'What sort of cake was it?' asked Kadife.

'It was a Viennese torte with figs and chocolate.'

After a pause, Kadife asked, 'What colour were the curtains? What sort of design did they have?'

'They were off-white or cream-coloured,' said Ka. He tried to look as if he were struggling to recall a distant memory. 'I seem to remember their having little fishes on them, and flowers, and moons, and fruits of every colour.'

'In other words, the sort of material you buy for children?'

'Not really – the atmosphere in this house was very serious. Let me say this: they were a happy family, but that didn't mean they were flashing smiles every other minute, as we do here even when there's nothing to smile about. Maybe this is why they were happy. For them, life was a serious business to be dealt with responsibly. It wasn't a dead-end struggle or a painful ordeal the way it is here. But their gravity of purpose permeated every aspect of their lives. Just as the moons and fishes and suchlike on their curtains helped lift their spirits.'

'What colour was the tablecloth?' asked Kadife.

'I can't remember,' said Ka, pretending to dredge his memory for more details.

'And how many times did you go there?' asked Blue with faint annoyance.

'I had such a lovely time that night that I was very much hoping for a second visit. But Hans Hansen never invited me again.'

The dog on the chain in the courtyard was barking louder now. Ka saw melancholy in Kadife's face as Blue glared at him with angry contempt.

'There were many times when I thought I should call them,' Ka continued obstinately. 'Sometimes I wondered whether Hans Hansen might have called some time I wasn't home to invite me to supper again, and whenever I had this thought it was hard to stop myself leaving the library and running home. I so longed for another look at that beautiful dresser with the mirror behind the shelves, and those chairs – I've forgotten what colour they were, they must have been lemon yellow. I dreamed of sitting at their table again as they cut bread on the wooden board and they would turn to ask me, "Is this how you like it?" (As you know, the Europeans don't eat as much bread as we do.) There were no crosses on their walls, just big, beautiful scenes from the Alps. I would have given anything to see all of it again.'

Ka saw that Blue was now eyeing him with open revulsion.

'Three months later a friend brought me news from Turkey,' said Ka. 'It concerned a horrifying new wave of torture, brutality and destruction, and I used this as an excuse to call Hans Hansen. He listened to me carefully and again he was very refined and courteous. A small item appeared in the paper. I didn't care about the torture and death that were reported. All I wanted was for Hans Hansen to call me. But he never called me again. From time to time I toyed with the idea of writing him a letter, to find out what I had done wrong, to ask him why he'd never invited me back to his house.'

Ka allowed himself a smile, even as Blue grew more visibly tense.

'Well, now you have a new excuse to call him,' he said contemptuously.

'But if you want your statement to appear in his newspaper, you're going to have to meet German standards and prepare a joint document,' said Ka.

'Who is this Kurdish nationalist who's going to help me with this joint document, and where am I going to find a liberal communist?'

'If you're worried they might turn out to be working for the police, you can suggest the names yourself,' said Ka.

'Without a doubt, for the Western journalist, an atheist Kurdish nationalist is worth more than an Islamic Kurdish nationalist. There are many Kurdish youths up in arms over what's happened to the religious high-school boys. A young student might just as well represent the Kurds in our statement.'

'Fine. If you can arrange for a young student,' said Ka, 'I can guarantee that the *Frankfurter Rundschau* will accept him.'

'Yes, of course,' said Blue sarcastically. 'You're our ambassador to the West.'

Ka did not rise to the bait. 'As for the communist-turned-new-democrat, your best man is Turgut Bey.'

'My father?' said Kadife with alarm.

When Ka nodded, Kadife warned him that her father never went outside the hotel. They all began to talk at once. Blue insisted that, like all old communists, Turgut Bey was not really a democrat, that he was probably quite pleased about the coup because it was hammering the Islamists, but he didn't want to give the left a bad name, so he was pretending the coup was wrong.

'My father's not the only pretender!' said Kadife.

From the tremble in her voice and the way Blue's eyes flashed with anger, Ka could tell that they had arrived at the threshold of an argument these two had had many times before, like so many couples worn down by constant quarrelling, with hardly the strength to hide their differences from outsiders. Kadife had that determined look of

a mistreated woman who's decided she's going to fight back, no matter what the cost, while Blue's expression was a mixture of pride and extraordinary tenderness. But then, in the space of a moment, everything changed: now all he saw in Blue's eyes was resolve.

'Like all atheist poseurs and Europe-loving leftist intellectuals, your father is a pretender with a contempt for the people.'

Kadife picked up the 'Ersin Electric' ashtray and hurled it at Blue. She may have missed on purpose: the ashtray hit the picture of Venice hanging on the wall behind him before falling to the floor.

'And furthermore,' said Blue, 'your father likes to pretend that his daughter is not the secret mistress of a radical Islamist.'

Kadife beat her two hands lightly against Blue's chest and then burst into tears. Blue sat her down on the chair in the corner, but now they were carrying on in such a contrived way that Ka became convinced it was all so much theatre staged expressly for his benefit.

'Take back what you said,' sobbed Kadife.

'I take back what I said,' replied Blue. It was the voice you'd use to comfort a crying child. 'And, to prove this to you, I'm prepared to ignore the impious jokes your father makes morning, noon and night, and sign a joint declaration with him. But since it's just possible that this representative of Hans Hansen we have here' – he paused to smile at Ka – 'since it's just possible he might be trying to lure us into a trap, I'm not going to come to your hotel. Do you understand, darling?'

'But my father never leaves the hotel,' said Kadife. To Ka's dismay, she was talking like a spoiled little girl. 'The poverty of Kars ruins his mood.'

'Then you must convince your father for once to go out, Kadife,' said Ka, in a commanding tone he had never used with her before. 'The city won't depress him now – it's covered with snow.' He looked straight into her eyes.

This time Kadife read his meaning. 'All right,' she said. 'But, before he leaves the hotel, someone has to convince him to put his name to the same document with an Islamist and a Kurdish nationalist. Who's going to do that?'

'I will,' said Ka. 'And you can help me.'

'Where are they going to meet?' asked Kadife. 'What if this nonsense ends with my poor father getting arrested? What if he has to spend the rest of his life in prison?'

'This isn't nonsense,' said Blue. 'If there are one or two news items in the European press, Ankara will whisper into a few ears and stop them.'

'This is not about planting a news item in the European press. It's about getting your name in the Turkish press, isn't it?' asked Kadife.

When Blue met this question with a sweetly tolerant smile, Ka felt a certain respect for him. It was only now that he realised the little Islamist papers in Istanbul would seize upon any mention in the *Frankfurter Rundschau* and proudly exaggerate it. This would make Blue famous throughout Turkey.

There was a long silence. Kadife took out a handkerchief and wiped her eyes. Ka imagined that as soon as he left, these lovers would quarrel and then make love. Did they want him to leave? High in the sky, a plane was passing. They all raised their eyes to the upper panes of the window, staring at the sky, and listening.

'Planes never fly over here,' said Kadife.

'Something very strange is going on, something extraordinary,' said Blue, chuckling at his own paranoia. But he took offence when Ka joined in.

'They say that even when the temperature is way below minus twenty, the government will never admit it,' said Ka.

Blue glared at Ka defiantly.

'All I ever wanted was a normal life,' said Kadife.

'You've thrown away your chance for a normal, bourgeois life,' said Blue. 'This is what makes you such an exceptional person.'

'But I don't want to be exceptional. I want to be like everyone else. If it weren't for the coup, who knows? I might even decide to be like everyone else and take off my scarf.'

'All the women here wear scarves,' said Blue.

'That's not true. Most educated women of my background and education don't cover their heads. If it's a question of being ordinary and fitting in, I've certainly distanced myself from my peers by wearing a headscarf. There's an element of pride in this that I'm not at all happy about.'

'Then go ahead and uncover your head tomorrow,' said Blue. 'People will see it as a triumph for the junta.'

'Everyone knows that, unlike you, I don't live my life wondering what people think,' said Kadife. Her face was pink with excitement.

Blue responded with another sweet smile, but this time Ka could

see that it took every bit of strength he had to produce it. And Blue saw that Ka had noticed this. It created an awkward intimacy between the two men and made Ka feel as if he had invaded the couple's privacy. As he listened to Kadife harangue her lover, and as he caught the undertones of desire, it seemed to him that she was dragging out their dirty laundry deliberately – and not just to vex Blue, but to embarrass Ka for having witnessed it. And, one might well ask, why did he choose this moment to remember the love letters from Necip to Kadife that he had been carrying around in his pocket since the night before?

'As for girls who've been roughed up and thrown out of school for wearing headscarves, we can be sure there'll be no mention of them in these articles.' Her tone matched the blind fury in her eyes. 'They'll pass right over the women whose lives have been ruined and instead we'll get pictures of the cautious provincial Islamist simpletons who presume to speak in their name. Whenever you do see a picture of a Muslim woman, it's because her husband is a mayor or something and she happens to be standing next to him during a religious festival. For this reason, I'd be more upset to appear in those papers than not to appear. I pity these men who waste so much effort to gain exposure themselves while we endure so much to protect our privacy. That's why I think it's important to mention the girls who've committed suicide. Come to think of it, I think I have the right to tell Hans Hansen a thing or two myself.'

'That would be excellent,' said Ka, without thinking. 'You could sign as the representative of the Muslim feminists.'

'I have no wish to represent anyone,' said Kadife. 'If I'm going to stand up to the Europeans, it will be on my own, to tell my own story – my whole story, with all my sins and my foibles. You know how sometimes you'll meet someone you've never met before, someone you're sure you'll never see again, and you're tempted to tell him everything, your whole life story – the way it seemed the heroes told their stories to the authors of the European novels I read when I was a girl? I wouldn't mind telling my story like that to four or five Europeans.'

There was an explosion that sounded very close; the whole house shook and the windows clattered in their frames. A second or two later, both Blue and Ka rose to their feet.

'Let me take a look,' said Kadife finally, seeming the coolest of the three.

Ka peeked timidly through the curtains. 'The carriage isn't there,' he said.

'It's dangerous for him to stand too long in this courtyard,' said Blue. 'When you leave, you'll be going through the side entrance.'

Ka took that to mean, 'Why don't you leave now?', yet he returned to his seat and waited, and exchanged hateful looks with Blue. Ka remembered the fear he'd felt at university whenever he'd crossed paths in dark, empty hallways with armed students of the extreme nationalist variety, but at least in those days there'd been no sexual undercurrent to the exchange.

'I can be a little paranoid sometimes,' said Blue. 'But that doesn't mean you're *not* a spy for the West. You may know you're not a spy, and you may have no desire to be one, but it doesn't change the situation. You're the stranger in our midst. You've sown doubt in this lovely and devout girl, and the strange things going on around her are the proof. And now you've aired all your smug Western views, probably even having a few laughs deep down inside at our expense. I don't mind, and nor does Kadife, but by inflicting your own naïve ideas on us, by rhapsodising about the Western pursuit of happiness and justice, you've clouded our thinking. But I'm not angry with you, because, like all good people, you are not aware of the evil inside you. However, having now heard it from me, you can't claim to be an innocent from this point on.'

27

Be Strong, My Girl, Help Is on Its Way from Kars

Ka Tries to Convince Turgut to Sign the Statement

Ka left the house unseen by anyone in the courtyard or the car-repair shops and walked straight to the market. He went into the same little stocking–stationery–cassette shop where he'd heard Peppino di Capri singing 'Roberta' the day before. Taking out Necip's letters to Kadife, he handed them, page by page, to the pale, beetle-browed, teenage assistant in charge of the photocopier. But to do this Ka had first opened the envelopes. So, once the letters were copied, he put each of the originals into a new envelope made from the same cheap, faded paper as the letters, and, imitating as best he could Necip's hand, addressed them to Kadife Yıldız.

Ever ready to fight for his happiness, to tell any lie, play any trick to make his dream come true, he hurried back to the hotel, musing upon a vision of İpek he had conjured in his mind. It was snowing again – the same huge snowflakes as before. Everyone in the streets seemed as tired and tense as they would be on any ordinary evening. At the corner of Palace Path Road and Halitpaşa Avenue, a mud-splattered coal wagon drawn by a tired horse was stuck between the snowbanks. The wipers on the truck standing behind it were barely able to keep the windscreen clear. He looked at the passers-by clutching their plastic bags and imagined them all running home to happy safety. Although he sensed in the air a melancholy that called to mind the grey winter evenings of his childhood, he remained full of resolve, determined to start life anew.

He went straight up to his room, hid the photocopies of Necip's letters in the bottom of his suitcase before he'd even removed his coat and hung it up, and washed his hands with care, almost too much. Then, without quite knowing why, he brushed his teeth (something he usually did in the evening). Sensing that a new poem was on its way, he spent a long while looking out of the window, enjoying the heat rising from the radiator. But in the place of a poem came a stream of childhood memories: the fine spring morning he had accompanied his mother to Beyoğlu to buy buttons when a 'dirty man' had followed them; the day his mother left with his father for a tour of Europe when he had watched the taxi taking them from Nişantaş to the airport disappearing around the corner; the hours spent dancing with a tall, long-haired, green-eyed girl at a party on Büyükada (his neck had been so stiff for days afterwards that he could barely move) – he'd fallen for her but had no idea how to get in touch with her . . . These memories were not in any way related to one another, except that they all shared the commonality of love. Ka knew very well that life was a meaningless string of random incidents.

He bounded downstairs as eagerly as a man who had just arrived somewhere he'd been planning to visit for years. Then, with a sangfroid he was shocked to discover in himself, he knocked on the white door that divided the lobby from the owner's office. The Kurdish maid answered, and her expression, half conspiratorial, half respectful, was straight out of Turgenev. Ka entered the room where they'd eaten supper the night before to find Turgut Bey and İpek sitting side by side on the long divan facing the back door; they were watching television.

'Kadife, where have you been? It's about to begin,' said Turgut Bey.

The pale light pouring through the windows of the Russian house gave this spacious, high-ceilinged room a very different ambience than it had possessed the night before.

When father and daughter saw it was Ka who had joined them, they bristled for a moment, like a couple whose privacy has just been invaded by a stranger. But then Ka was cheered to see the light in İpek's eyes. He sat down on a chair that faced both father and daughter and the television, and noticed once again how much more beautiful İpek was in reality than in his memories. This intensified his fear, though, before long, he had convinced himself that they were destined to live happily ever after.

'Every afternoon at four my daughters and I sit down on this divan and watch *Marianna*,' said Turgut Bey. There was a note of embarrassment in his voice, but also something else, which said, 'But don't expect me to make any apology for it.'

Marianna, a Mexican soap opera, went out five times a week on one of the big Istanbul channels, to the delight of the entire country. The eponymous heroine was a small, bubbly, charming girl with large green eyes and skin so fair as to suggest an affluence; she was, however, from the very lowest class. The innocent, long-haired Marianna had been orphaned early in childhood and had spent most of her life in impoverished solitude. Hardly a day passed without a new setback; and whenever she fell in love with someone who refused to love her back or was the victim of some misunderstanding or false accusation, Turgut Bey and his daughters would nestle up against one another like cats. With the two girls' heads propped against their father's chest and shoulders, they would all shed a few tears. Perhaps out of embarrassment at being so enraptured by a silly soap opera, Turgut Bey offered a running commentary on the underlying reasons for Marianna's and Mexico's persistent poverty. He applauded Marianna for her own war against the capitalists, and from time to time even addressed the screen: 'Be strong, my girl, help is on its way from Kars.' When he did this, his teary-eyed daughters would smile faintly.

As the show began, Ka's lips curled into a smile, too, but then he came eye to eye with İpek, and, sensing that she didn't welcome this smile, he assumed a more serious expression.

During the first commercial break, Ka quickly and confidently broached the subject of the joint statement. In no time at all, he had aroused the interest of Turgut Bey, who seemed flattered to be taken so seriously. He asked whose idea this was, and how his name had come to be suggested.

Ka said it was a decision he'd reached himself after consulting with the liberal press in Germany. Turgut Bey asked for the circulation of the *Frankfurter Rundschau* and wondered whether Hans Hansen called himself a 'humanist'. To prepare Turgut Bey for Blue, Ka described him as a dangerous religious fanatic who had nevertheless learned the importance of democracy. But Turgut Bey seemed unperturbed. People gave themselves to religion because they were poor, he said; he went on to reiterate that even if he didn't believe in what his daughter and her friends were doing, he respected it. In much the way, he respected the Kurdish nationalist – whoever he might be; were he himself to be a Kurdish youth living in Kars today, he'd be a fierce nationalist, too. Turgut Bey said all this in the same jocular tone with which he offered his support to Marianna. 'It's wrong to say this in public, but

I am against military coups,' he declared. Ka calmed him down by reminding him that this statement was not going to be printed in Turkey, and went on to say that the only place where the meeting with Blue could safely take place was in the shed at the top of the Hotel Asia. Turgut Bey could get there via the back door of an adjacent shop giving on to the same courtyard – and no one would be any the wiser.

'We must show the world that there are true democrats in Turkey,' said Turgut Bey. He spoke fast because the soap opera was about to resume. Just before *Marianna* reappeared, he looked at his watch and said, 'Where's Kadife?'

Then the three of them returned to watching *Marianna* in silence.

At one point Marianna climbed a flight of stairs with her lover; once she was sure no one could see them, she wrapped her arms around him. They didn't kiss, but Ka found what they did even more moving: they embraced each other with all their might. During the long silence that followed, it occurred to Ka that the whole city was watching this same scene; throughout Kars housewives just returning from the market were tuning in with their husbands; girls in middle school were watching with their ageing relatives. With everyone watching, Ka realised, it wasn't just the wretched streets of Kars that were empty, but every street in the country. At that moment, he also understood that his intellectual pretensions, political activities and cultural snobbery had brought him to an arid existence that had cut him off from the feelings this soap opera was now provoking in him. And, worst of all, it was his own stupid fault. Ka was sure that, after they'd finished making love, Blue and Kadife had curled up in a corner and wrapped their arms around each other to watch *Marianna*, too.

When Marianna turned to her lover and said, 'I've waited all my life for this day,' Ka saw it as no coincidence that she was echoing his own thoughts. He tried to catch İpek's eye. She was resting her head on her father's chest, and her large, sad, lovelorn eyes were glued to the set, lost in the desires the soap opera had awakened.

'But I'm still so worried,' said Marianna's handsome, clean-shaven lover. 'My family won't allow us to be together.'

'As long as we love each other, we have nothing to fear,' said the good-hearted Marianna.

'Watch out, my girl, this man is your worst enemy!' Turgut Bey shouted at the screen.

'I want you to love me without fear,' said Marianna.

Looking deep into İpek's mysterious eyes, Ka now succeeded in getting her attention – but she quickly averted her gaze. At the next commercial break, she turned to her father and said, 'Daddy dear, if you ask me, it's too dangerous for you to go to the Hotel Asia.'

'Don't worry,' said Turgut Bey.

'You're the one who's been telling me for years that it brings you bad luck to go out into the streets of Kars.'

'Yes, but if I don't attend this meeting, it has to be through principle, not because I'm scared,' said Turgut Bey. He turned to Ka. 'The question is, speaking as the communist, modernising, secular, democratic patriot I now am, what should I put first – the Enlightenment or the will of the people? If I believe first and foremost in the European Enlightenment, then I am obliged to see the Islamists as my enemies and should support this military coup. If, however, my first commitment is to the will of the people – if, in other words, I've become an unadulterated democrat – then I have no choice but to go and sign that statement. Which of the things I've said is true?'

'Take the side of the oppressed and go and sign that statement,' said Ka.

'It's not enough to be oppressed, you must also be in the right, because most oppressed people are in the wrong to an almost ridiculous degree. What shall I believe in?'

'He doesn't believe in anything,' said İpek.

'Everyone believes in something,' said Turgut Bey. 'Please, tell me what you think.'

Ka did his best to convince Turgut Bey that if he signed the statement, he would be doing his bit to help Kars move towards democracy. Sensing a strong possibility that İpek might not want to go to Frankfurt with him, he started to worry that he might fail to convince Turgut Bey even to leave the hotel. To express beliefs without conviction was liberating. As he nattered on about the statement, about issues of democracy, human rights and many other things, he saw a light shining in İpek's eyes that told him she didn't believe a word he was saying. But it wasn't a shaming, moralistic light he saw. Quite the contrary: it was the gleam of sexual provocation. Her eyes said, 'I know you're spouting all these lies because you want me.'

So it was, just minutes after discovering the importance of melodramatic sensibilities, that Ka decided he'd learned a second great truth that had eluded him all his life: there are women who can't resist a man who believes in nothing but love. Overcome with excitement at this new discovery, he launched into a further monologue about human rights, freedom of thought, democracy and related subjects. As he mouthed the wild simplifications of so many well-intentioned but shameless and slightly addled Western intellectuals, and the platitudes repeated verbatim by their Turkish imitators, he thrilled at the knowledge that he might soon be making love to İpek, and all the while stared straight into her eyes to see the reflection of his own passion.

'You're right,' said Turgut Bey when the commercials finished. 'Where's Kadife?'

As the show resumed, Turgut Bey grew nervous – part of him wanted to go to the Hotel Asia and part of him didn't. Like a sad old man lost in a sea of dreams and ghosts, he talked about the political memories that came to him when he was watching *Marianna*, and about his fear of winding up back in prison, and about man's responsibilities. Ka could see perfectly well that İpek was annoyed at him for drawing her father into this anxious state, but she also admired the speed with which he had convinced the old man to leave the hotel. He didn't mind that she kept averting her eyes. And when at the end of the soap opera she turned to her father, wrapped her arms around him, and said, 'Don't go if you don't want to, you've already suffered enough to help others, Father,' Ka was not offended.

He saw a cloud pass over İpek's face, but now a new, joyful poem had come into his head. In the chair next to the kitchen, where, only moments earlier, Zahide Hanım had sat with tears streaming down her face as she watched *Marianna*, Ka now sat, beaming silently with optimism, and he began to write. It was only much later that he decided to call this poem 'I Am Going to Be Happy', perhaps choosing this title to torment himself. Ka had just completed it without a single missing word when Kadife came rushing into the room.

Turgut Bey jumped to his feet, threw his arms around her and kissed her, and asked her where she'd been, and why her hands were so cold. A single tear rolled down his cheek. Kadife said she'd been to see Hande. She'd stayed later than expected, and as she'd been reluctant to miss any of *Marianna*, she'd decided to stay there until it had finished. 'So how's our girl doing?' asked Turgut Bey (he was referring to Marianna). But he did not wait for Kadife's answer before turning to the other subject. A great cloud of apprehension descended over him as he quickly summarised what he'd heard from Ka.

It was not enough for Kadife to pretend she was hearing all of this for the first time; when she caught sight of Ka at the other end of the room, she pretended to be surprised to see him. 'I'm so happy you're here,' she cried, as she hastened to cover her hair, but her scarf was not yet back in place when she sat down in front of the television to advise her father. Kadife was so convincing in her feigned surprise at seeing him that when she went on to encourage her father to attend the meeting and sign the joint statement, Ka thought that this too must be an act. And since Blue wanted to produce a statement that the foreign press would be willing to print, his suspicion may have been correct, but Ka could tell from the fear in İpek's expression that there was something else going on here, too.

'Let me come with you to the Hotel Asia,' said Kadife.

'I'm not about to let you get into trouble on my account,' said Turgut Bey, affecting a gallant air straight out of the soap operas they watched together, and the novels they had read together once upon a time.

'Please, Daddy, if you get involved in this business, you could be exposing yourself to unnecessary risks,' said İpek.

While İpek spoke to her father, Ka took stock. It seemed that – as with everyone else in the room – everything she said had a double meaning. As for this game she was playing with her eyes – averting her gaze one moment, staring at him intensely the next – he could assume only that this was just another way of transmitting the same mixed message. Only much later would he realise that – apart from Necip – everyone he met in Kars spoke in the same code, and so harmoniously that they seemed almost to comprise a single chorus. He would go on to ask himself whether it was poverty that brought it out in them, or fear, solitude or the very simplicity of their lives. Even as İpek said, 'Daddy, please don't go,' she was teasing Ka; even as Kadife spoke of the statement and her bonds to her father, Ka could see that she was revealing her bonds to Blue.

With all this in mind, Ka entered into what he would later call 'the most profoundly duplicitous conversation of my life'. He had a strong feeling that if he could not get Turgut Bey to leave the hotel now, he would never have a chance to sleep with İpek; and, since the challenge he saw in İpek's eyes only confirmed this notion, he told himself that this was his last chance in life for happiness. When he began to speak, he used the same words and ideas that had ruined his life. But, as he tried to convince Turgut Bey to leave the hotel – because it was important to act for the common good, to take responsibility for his country's poor and to share in their struggles; because he was on the side of the civilisers and so obliged to stand up against the forces of darkness, even if the gesture itself seemed insignificant – he found that even he believed some of what he was saying. He remembered how he had felt as a young leftist, when he'd been so determined not to join the Turkish bourgeoisie, when all he'd wanted was to sit in a room reading great books and entertaining great thoughts. So it was with the elation of a twenty-year-old that he repeated those thoughts and ideals that had so upset his mother, who had been right to wish that he would never become a poet, which had, after all, condemned him to exile in a rat hole in Frankfurt. Meanwhile, he was well aware what the force of his words conveyed to İpek: 'This is how passionately I want to make love to you.' He was thinking that at last those fine words of youth that had ruined his life would serve a purpose: thanks to them, he would be making love to the object of his desires. At the same moment, though, he'd lost faith in them. He now knew that the greatest happiness in life was to embrace a beautiful, intelligent woman and sit in a corner writing poetry.

Turgut Bey announced that he was leaving 'at once' for the meeting at the Hotel Asia. He went to his room to change, accompanied by Kadife.

Ka walked over to İpek, still in the spot where she'd been watching television with her father. She looked almost as if she were still leaning on the old man. 'I'll be waiting for you in my room,' whispered Ka.

'Do you love me?' asked İpek.

'I love you very much.'

'Is that true?'

'It's very true.'

For a while, neither spoke. İpek turned to gaze out of the window, and then Ka followed suit. It had started to snow again. The street-lamps in front of the hotel had come on, but darkness had not yet descended, so even as they illuminated the frenzy of the giant snowflakes, they seemed superfluous.

'Go to your room,' said İpek. 'As soon as they leave, I'll come up.'

28

The Difference between Love and the Agony of Waiting

Ka with İpek in the Hotel Room

But İpek did not come straight up. And the waiting was torture – the worst Ka had ever known. It was this pain, this deadly wait, he now remembered, that had made him afraid to fall in love. Upon arriving in the room, he'd thrown himself on the bed, only to stand up again at once to straighten his clothes. He washed his hands, felt the blood draining from his arms, his fingers, his lips. With trembling hands, he combed his hair; then, seeing his reflection in the window, he messed it up again. This all took very little time, and he then directed his anxious attention to the scene through the window.

He'd hoped to see Turgut Bey leaving the hotel with Kadife. Perhaps they'd gone past while he was in the bathroom. But if this were the case, İpek should have come up by now. Perhaps she was back in the room he'd seen the night before, painting her face and dabbing her neck with perfume. What a waste of the little time they had together! Didn't she understand how much he loved her? Whatever she was doing, it couldn't justify the pain he felt at this moment; he was going to tell her so when she finally arrived. But would she come at all? With every passing moment, he became more convinced that İpek had changed her mind.

He saw a horse-drawn carriage approach the hotel; aided by Zahide Hanım and Cavit the receptionist, Turgut Bey and Kadife climbed in, and the carriage's oilskin drapes closed around them. But the carriage remained motionless. Ka watched the blanket of snow on the awning growing thicker and thicker; in the light from the streetlamps each snowflake looked bigger than the previous one. It was as if time had stopped, Ka thought; it was driving him mad. Just then, Zahide came running out of the doorway and passed something

Ka couldn't see into the carriage. The carriage began to move, and Ka's heart began to beat faster.

But still İpek didn't come.

What was the difference between love and the agony of waiting? Like love, the agony of waiting began in the muscles somewhere around the upper belly, but soon it spread to the chest, the thighs and the forehead, to invade the entire body with numbing force. As he listened to sounds from other parts of the house, he tried to guess what İpek was doing. He saw a woman in the street, and, even though she didn't resemble İpek at all, he thought it must be her. How beautiful the snow looked as it fell from the sky!

As a child, when he and his classmates had been sent down to the school cafeteria for their injections, while the cooking fumes tinged with iodine had swirled around his head, his stomach had ached like this and he had wanted to die. He'd yearned for home, for his own room. Now he wanted to be in his own miserable room in Frankfurt. What a huge mistake he'd made by coming here! Even the poems had stopped coming now. He was in such pain. And yet he took some comfort from standing at this warm window, watching the snow; this was at least better than dying. But if İpek didn't come soon, he would die anyway.

The lights went out.

This was a sign, he thought, sent specially to him. Perhaps İpek hadn't come because she knew there was about to be a power cut. He looked down at the dark street for a sign of life, something that might explain İpek's absence. He caught sight of a truck – was it an army truck? No, just his mind playing tricks on him. As were the footsteps he thought he heard on the stairs. No one was coming. He left the window and lay supine on the bed. The pain that had begun in his belly had now spread to his soul; he was alone in the world with no one to blame but himself. His life had come to nothing; he was going to die here, of misery and loneliness. This time he wouldn't even find the strength to scurry like a rat into that hole in Frankfurt. His terrible unhappiness grieved and distressed him, but worse was knowing that, had he acted more intelligently, his life might have been much happier. And worst of all was knowing that no one even noticed his fear, his misery, his loneliness. If İpek had known this, she'd have come right up without delay! If his mother had seen him in this state . . . She was the only one in the world who might have understood; she would have run her fingers through his hair and consoled him.

The ice on the windows glowed orange with the light from the streetlamps and the surrounding houses. Let the snow keep falling, he thought. Let it fall for days and months on end. Let it cover the city of Kars so completely that no one will ever find it again. He wanted to fall asleep on this bed and not wake up until it was a sunny morning and he was a child again, with his mother.

There was a knock on the door. By now, Ka told himself, it could only be someone from the kitchen. But he flew to the door and the moment he opened it he could feel İpek's presence.

'Where have you been?'

'Am I late?'

But it was as if Ka hadn't even heard her. He was already embracing her with all his strength; he'd put his head against her neck and buried his face in her hair; and there he stayed, not moving a muscle. He felt such joy that the agony of waiting now seemed absurd. But the agony had worn him out all the same; that, he thought, was why he could not fully relish her presence. And why he demanded that İpek explain her delay: even knowing he had no right to do so, he kept complaining. But İpek insisted that she had come up as soon as her father had left. OK, she had stopped off in the kitchen to give Zahide one or two instructions about supper, but that couldn't have taken more than a minute. So Ka showed himself to be the more ardent and fragile of the two. Even at the very beginning of their relationship, he had let İpek have the upper hand. And even if his fear of seeming weak had moved him to conceal the agony she'd put him through, he would still have to grapple with his insecurity. Besides, didn't love mean sharing everything? What was it if not the desire to share your every thought? He related this chain of thought to İpek as breathlessly as if revealing a terrible secret.

'Now put it all out of your head,' said İpek. 'I came here to make love to you.'

They kissed, and with a softness that brought Ka comfort, they fell on to the bed. For Ka, who had not made love in four years, it felt like a miracle. So, even as he succumbed to the pleasures of the flesh, his conscious mind was reminding him what a beautiful moment this was. Just as with his first sexual experiences, it was not so much the act as the thought of making love that occupied him. For a while, this protected him from overexcitement. Details from the pornographic films to which he'd become addicted in Frankfurt rushed through his head, creating a poetic aura that seemed beyond logic. But he wasn't imagining these scenes to arouse himself; he was celebrating the fact that he could at last enact such fantasies as had played incessantly in his mind. So it was not İpek herself who was arousing Ka but pornographic imagery; and the miracle was less her presence than the fact that he could imagine his fantasy here in bed with him.

It was only when he began to pull off her clothes with an almost savage clumsiness that he began to look at the real İpek. Her breasts were enormous, the skin of her neck and shoulders wonderfully soft, its scent strange and foreign. He watched the white light playing on her. Occasionally something sparkled in her eyes that frightened him. Those eyes were very sure of themselves: Ka worried that İpek was not as fragile as he wanted her to be. That was why he pulled her hair to cause her pain, why he took such pleasure from her pain that he yanked it again, why he subjected her to a few other acts also inspired by the pornographic film still playing in his head, and why he treated her so roughly – to the accompaniment of an internal musical soundtrack as deep as it was primitive. When he saw that she enjoyed his roughness, his triumph gave way to brotherly affection. He wrapped his arms around her; no longer wishing to save just himself from the miseries of Kars, he wanted to save İpek, too. But when he decided her reaction was commensurate with his ardour, he pulled away. In a corner of his mind he was able to control and coordinate these sexual acrobatics with surprising finesse. But when his mind was somewhere distant he could seize the woman with a passion verging on violence; at such a moment he wanted to hurt her.

According to the notes Ka made about his lovemaking – notes that I feel I must share with my readers – his passion was finally reciprocated, and they fell upon each other with such intensity as to leave the rest of the world behind. The same notes also reveal that İpek let out a mournful cry when it was over.

Ka's paranoia came rushing back now as he wondered whether this was why they'd given him a room in the most remote corner of the hotel. The pleasure they'd taken in causing each other pain now gave way to the old loneliness. It seemed to him that this remote room on this remote corridor had freed itself from the rest of the hotel and floated off to the most remote corner of this empty city. And the city was so silent that it seemed as if the world had come to an end. And it was snowing.

For a long time they lay side by side in bed gazing silently at the snow. From time to time, Ka turned his head to watch the snow falling in İpek's eyes.

29

It's Not Just You I've Lost

In Frankfurt

It was four years after Ka's visit to Kars and forty-two days after his death that I went to see the small Frankfurt apartment in which he spent the last eight years of his life. It was a sleety, windy February day. When I arrived in Frankfurt on the morning flight from Istanbul, the city looked even drearier than in the postcards Ka had been sending me for sixteen years. Except for the dark cars rushing past in the streets, the trams that appeared out of nowhere like ghosts only to vanish a moment later, and the umbrella-wielding housewives hurrying along the pavements, the streets were empty. It was the middle of the day, but, looking into the dark, dense mist, I could still see the deathly yellow glow of streetlamps.

Still, it cheered me to see – in the streets surrounding the central train station, along the pavements lined with döner-kebab restaurants and travel agencies and ice-cream parlours and sex shops – signs of the energy that sustains all big cities. After I had checked into my hotel and phoned the young Turkish-German literature enthusiast who had (at my request) arranged for me to give a talk at the city hall, I went to the Italian café at the station to meet with Tarkut Ölçün. In Istanbul, Ka's sister had given me his number. This tired, well-meaning man in his sixties was Ka's closest acquaintance during his years in Frankfurt. He had given a statement to the police during the inquiry into Ka's death. He was the one who had contacted Ka's family in Istanbul and helped to arrange for the body to be flown back to Turkey. At the time, I was still hoping to find the typescript of the poetry collection on which Ka said he had been labouring ever since returning from Kars four years earlier and had only just completed, so I asked his father and sister what had happened to his belongings.

They'd not been strong enough to make the trip to Germany, so they'd asked me to collect Ka's things and clear out his apartment.

Tarkut Ölçün had come to Germany in the first wave of immigration in the early sixties. For years he'd worked as a teacher and a social worker serving a number of Turkish associations and charities. When he brought out pictures of his German-born son and daughter, he told me proudly that he'd sent them both through university. Although Tarkut was a figure of some standing in Frankfurt's Turkish community, in his face I still saw the loneliness and defeat so commonly visible in first-generation immigrants and political exiles.

The first thing Tarkut Ölçün gave me was the small satchel Ka had been carrying when he was shot. The police had made Tarkut sign for it before they handed it over. I opened it at once and frantically rummaged through it. Inside, I found the pyjamas Ka had bought in Nişantaş eighteen years earlier, a green pullover, shaving stuff, a toothbrush, a pair of socks, a change of underwear and a number of literary magazines I had sent him from Istanbul, but there was no sign of his green poetry notebook.

Later, as we sat drinking our coffees and gazing into the crowded station, where two ageing Turks were laughing and talking as they mopped the floor, Tarkut said, 'Orhan Bey, your friend Ka Bey was a solitary man. No one in Frankfurt apart from me knew much about what he was doing.' He promised to tell me everything he knew.

We walked around to the back of the station, wending our way past the old army barracks and the hundred-year-old factory buildings to the apartment block near Gutleustrasse where Ka had spent his last eight years. But when we arrived the landlord was not there to open the old front door with flaking paint to let us in. As we stood waiting in the sleet, I recognised many of the things Ka had described to me in his letters and his far less frequent phone calls. (Prone as he was to paranoia, Ka suspected someone was listening in on all of his calls to Turkey, so he didn't like using the phone.) His apartment overlooked a little square with a playground, a small, neglected park and a grocery store. As my eyes wandered beyond them to the dark windows of the shops that sold alcohol and newspapers, I felt I was looking at my own memories. The swings and seesaws in the playground, like the benches where Ka had spent summer evenings drinking beer with the Italian and Yugoslavian workmen who were his neighbours, were now covered with a light blanket of wet snow.

We gave up waiting and returned to Station Square, following the route to the city library Ka had taken every morning during his last years. He had enjoyed walking through crowds of people rushing to work, so we followed in his footsteps into the station and down to an underground arcade. Then we emerged above ground again to follow the tram route past the sex shops, souvenir stores, patisseries and pharmacies of Kaiserstrasse as far as Hauptwache Square. Tarkut Ölçün saw many Turks and Kurds he knew in the döner shops, kebab restaurants and greengrocers' we passed along the way, and, as he waved to them, he told me that when these same people had seen Ka walking to the city library every morning at exactly the same time, they'd all cried out, 'Good morning, Professor!' When we arrived in Hauptwache Square, he pointed out the big store on the opposite side of the square – the Kaufhof. I told him that it was here that Ka had bought the coat he had worn in Kars, but I declined his offer to take me inside.

Ka's final destination each day, the city library, was a modern, anonymous building. Inside were the types you always find in such libraries: housewives, old people with time to kill, unemployed men, one or two Turks and Arabs, students giggling over their homework assignments, and various stalwarts from the ranks of the obese, the lame, the insane and the mentally handicapped. One drooling young man raised his head from his picture-book to stick out his tongue at me. My guide was not particularly interested in books, so I left him in the coffee-shop downstairs and went to look at the shelves where they kept their collection of English poetry. Here I searched the check-out slips on the inside back covers for my friend's name. Whenever I opened a copy of Auden, Browning or Coleridge to find his signature, I shed tears for him, for the years he'd wasted in this library.

I cut short my search, which had plunged me into melancholy. My friendly guide and I then walked back along the same avenues without saying a word. We turned left somewhere in the middle of Kaiserstrasse – just before a place that was called the World Sex Centre, or something equally absurd – and from there we walked down one street to Munchenerstrasse, where I saw more Turkish-owned greengrocers' and kebab restaurants, as well as an empty hairdresser's. By now I had guessed what I was about to be shown, so my heart was pounding. As my eyes moved from the leeks and oranges displayed outside the greengrocer's to the one-legged man begging near by, and on to the headlights flashing across the condensation-streaked windows of the Hotel

Eden, I looked into the charcoal twilight, and there, shining in bright, pink, solitary splendour, I saw the neon letter 'K'.

'This is where it happened,' said Tarkut Ölçün. 'Yes it is, I'm afraid. They found Ka's body right here.'

I stared helplessly at the ground. Two boys came flying out of the greengrocer's, pushing and shoving each other. As they ran off, one of them stepped on the patch of wet pavement where Ka had lain dying with three bullets in his body. The red lights of a truck parked just ahead were reflected in the tarmac. Ka had spent several minutes writhing on this very pavement, but he'd died before the ambulance had arrived. For a moment, I lifted my head to find the patch of sky he'd seen as he was dying: between the old dark buildings that housed the Turkish döner shops, travel agencies, barbers', beerhalls, the streetlamps and the power lines, there was a sliver of sky.

Ka had been shot at around midnight. Tarkut Ölçün told me that there would still have been a smattering of prostitutes walking up and down the street. The actual red-light district was one street up, along the Kaiserstrasse, but on busy nights and weekends, or during one of the trade fairs, the ladies would spread out along this street, too. 'They didn't find anything,' he said, when he saw me looking left and right, as if in search of a clue. 'And the German police aren't like our Turkish police – they do their job well.'

But when I started canvassing the occupants of the shops in the immediate vicinity, this good-natured man decided to help. The girls at the hairdresser's recognised him, and, after exchanging a few niceties, he asked whether they'd seen anything. But, of course, they had not been in the shop at the time of the murder, and had not even heard anything about the incident. 'The only thing Turkish families teach their daughters here is how to be hairdressers,' he told me when we were outside again. 'There are hundreds of Turkish hairdressers in Frankfurt.'

The Kurds in the greengrocer's, by contrast, were only too well aware of the murder and the police inquiry that had followed. This could explain their evident displeasure at meeting us.

The good-hearted waiter in the Holiday Kebab House had been wiping off the Formica tabletops at around twelve on the night in question when he'd heard the gunshots. He'd been using the same dirty cloth he was holding now. On the night of the shooting he'd waited a short time before going outside, to become the last person Ka would see.

After leaving the kebab restaurant, I walked swiftly into the first passageway I could find and ended up in the rear courtyard of a dark building. I followed Tarkut Bey down two flights of stairs, through a door, into a forbidding space the size of a hangar, which had once served as a warehouse. This underworld was as wide as the street above. It now served as a mosque, where between fifty and sixty worshippers were saying their evening prayers on the carpeted area in the middle. It was lined with shops as dark and dirty as the ones you'd find in any underground arcade in Istanbul. I saw a dreary jeweller's and a greengrocer almost small enough to qualify as a dwarf. The butcher's next door was crowded, but the man in the grocery store sat idly watching the television in the coffee-house, surrounded by coils of garlic sausage. In that corner stood cases of Turkish fruit juice, Turkish macaroni, Turkish canned goods and religious literature, and it was obvious that the café was even more popular than the mosque. The air was thick with cigarette smoke; the men at the tables looked tired; most had their eyes glued to the Turkish film on the TV, but now and then someone shuffled over to the makeshift fountain. After filling it with water from a plastic bucket, he would perform his ablutions before joining the worshippers outside. 'On Fridays and holidays, you can see two thousand people here,' Tarkut Bey told me. 'The overflow goes all the way up the stairs to the back courtyard.' I went over to the stall selling books and magazines, and – for no particular reason – I bought a copy of *Communication*.

Afterwards, we repaired to the old Munich-style beer parlour directly overhead. 'That mosque belongs to the Süleymanians,' Tarkut Ölçün said, pointing at the ground below us. 'They're theocrats, but they won't have anything to do with terrorism. They're not like the National Advocates or the Cemalettin Tigers – they don't want to take up arms against the Turkish state, either.' Perhaps troubled by the suspicions he could read in my face and the attention with which I was poring over *Communication*, as if looking for clues, he now told me everything he knew about Ka's murder, and what he had later discovered from the police and the press.

At half-past eleven, exactly forty-two days before my visit, Ka had returned from Hamburg, where he had taken part in a poetry evening. The journey had taken six hours, but when he arrived at the station he did not take the south exit straight back to his apartment in Gutleustrasse. Instead, he took the north exit on to Kaiserstrasse and spent the next twenty-five minutes wandering among the tourists, the drunks, the solitary men and the prostitutes who were waiting for customers. He'd been walking around for half an hour when he turned right at the World Sex Centre. He was shot crossing Munchenerstrasse.

He was probably on his way to the Big Antalya Greengrocer to buy some recently arrived tangerines. This was the only greengrocer's in the area still open at this hour and the shop assistant recalled that Ka had often stopped there to buy tangerines. Faced with his claim of total ignorance about Ka's murder, the police were suspicious enough to take the shop assistant in for questioning, but they released him the next day, having discovered nothing.

The police had been unable to find anyone who'd seen Ka's assailant. The waiter from the Holiday Kebab House had heard the gunshots, but with the television and the customers making so much noise, he couldn't even say how many there had been. And it was impossible to see through the fogged-up windows of the beer parlour that was situated directly above the mosque. A prostitute on the next street down who'd been smoking a cigarette between tricks reported having seen a short, dark, 'Turkish-looking' man in a black coat running in the direction of Kaiserstrasse at around midnight, but she was unable to provide the police with a more detailed description. A German who happened to be standing on the balcony of his apartment when Ka fell to the ground had called the ambulance, but he'd not seen the assailant, either.

The first bullet had gone into the back of Ka's head and out of his left eye. The other two had shattered major blood vessels around his heart and his liver, piercing both the front and the back of his charcoal-coloured coat, which was drenched in blood.

'He was shot from the back, so it was probably premeditated,' concluded the garrulous old detective with a hacking cough who was in charge. The murderer may even have followed Ka all the way from Hamburg. The police considered a variety of motives: everything from sexual jealousy to the sort of political vendetta carried out so frequently in the Turkish community. Ka had had no connection with the underworld that operated in the neighbourhoods around the station. When the police showed his photo to people who worked in the immediate vicinity, some remembered seeing him in the sex shops from time to time and others even recalled that he had used the small cubicles in the back for viewing porno films. But there was no eyewitness testimony, true or false; and there was no pressure from on high to find the killer; nor any outcry in the press.

When he interviewed Ka's acquaintances, the garrulous detective sometimes seemed to have lost sight of the point of the investigation; and he wound up doing most of the talking. It was from this paternal Turkophile that Tarkut Ölçün first heard about the two women who had entered Ka's life eight years before his visit to Kars. One was German and the other Turkish (I carefully recorded their names in my notebook). In the four years since his return from Kars, Ka had had no relations with any women at all.

With their inquiries going nowhere, the police eventually suspended the investigation.

Tarkut and I went back out into the snow. As we made our way back to Ka's house, neither of us spoke. This time we were able to see the large and affable, if also irritable, landlord. He let us into the building, which was cool and smelled of soot, and took us up to the penthouse apartment, which, he told us querulously, he was about to rent out again. Any of this filth we didn't clear out, he was going to throw away. Having said that, he left. Tears came to my eyes the moment I stepped into the small, dark, low-ceilinged rooms in which Ka had spent his last eight years: the distinct smell took me back to our childhood years. It was the smell I associated with his school satchel and his room at home and the pullovers his mother had knitted. I thought it must be a Turkish brand of soap I'd never known by name, and never thought to ask about.

During Ka's early years in Germany, he had worked as a porter, a removal man and a house painter, and he'd given English lessons to Turks. But once he was officially declared a 'political exile' and granted asylum benefits, he cut his links with the Turkish communists who ran the neighbourhood centres and who had, until then, made sure he was gainfully employed. His fellow exiles had found Ka too remote, and too bourgeois. During his last twelve years, Ka supplemented his income by doing poetry readings in city libraries, cultural foundations and Turkish associations. Only Turks attended, and the audiences rarely exceeded twenty. Even so, if he could do three of them each month, that was an extra five hundred marks, which, combined with his asylum benefit, would have allowed him to live comfortably.

But it was clear now that such months had been few and far between. The chairs in his apartment were broken, the ashtrays chipped and the electric stove covered with rust. Still affronted by the landlord's threat when he'd let us in, I wanted to stuff all Ka's belongings into an old suitcase and a couple of plastic bags and leave. I wanted to take everything: the pillow on the bed that still smelled of his hair; the belt and the tie I remembered him wearing in high school; the Bally shoes that (according to his letters) he had continued using as 'house slippers' once his toes had poked through the leather; the dirty glass in which he kept his toothbrush and toothpaste; his collection of about three hundred and fifty books; the television; the video recorder he'd never mentioned to me; his threadbare jacket and worn-out shirts; and the pyjamas he'd brought with him from Turkey eighteen years earlier. But when I looked at the worktable and failed to find what I coveted most, what I now realised I had flown to Frankfurt to retrieve, I found my zeal had dissipated.

In his last letter from Frankfurt, Ka had happily announced that, after four years of hard work, he had finally completed a new book of poetry. The title was *Snow*, he wrote. Most of the poems were based on childhood memories that had come to him in flashes during his visit to Kars, and he had duly recorded these inspirations in a green notebook. In an earlier letter written almost immediately upon leaving Kars, he had told me he had come to believe that the emerging book had a 'deep and mysterious' underlying structure. He had spent his last four years in Frankfurt 'filling in the blanks' in this hidden design. For this gruelling purpose, he'd withdrawn from the world, abstained from its pleasures like a dervish. In Kars, he had felt like a medium, as if someone were whispering the poems into his ear; but back in Frankfurt, he could hardly hear them at all.

Still he laboured to reveal what he had become convinced was the hidden logic of this testament to the visions and inspirations he'd had in Kars. In his last letter, he said that with the arduous task now complete, he was going to test the poems at readings in several German cities. He had no copy of the longhand version he kept in the green notebook, he told me, but would have one typed up and duplicated once he was sure everything was in its rightful place. He was planning to send one copy to me and one to his Istanbul publisher. Would I mind writing a few words for the back cover, and sending them on to the publisher – our mutual friend, Fahir?

The view from Ka's desk of the snow-capped rooftops of Frankfurt was now darkening as night fell over the city. The desk itself, covered with a green tablecloth, was surprisingly tidy for that of a poet. On the right were the diaries in which Ka described his visit to Kars and the poems that had come to him there; on the left a pile of books and magazines that he'd been in the process of reading. Equidistant from the centre of the table stood a bronze lamp and a telephone. I searched the desk drawers for the notebook; I fanned through the books, the diaries and the collection of newspaper clippings without which no political exile's room seems complete. With rising panic, I went on to search his wardrobes, his bed, the cabinets in his kitchen, his refrigerator, his bathroom, his little laundry basket, and every other corner of the apartment where a man might think to hide a notebook. Refusing to accept that it might be lost, I then checked all the same places again, while Tarkut Ölçün stood smoking a cigarette and watching the snow fall over Frankfurt. If the notebook wasn't in the suitcase he'd taken with him to Hamburg, then it had to be here, in this apartment. Ka had always refused to make copies of his poetry until every last word was in place – he thought it was bad luck. But he'd told me himself that the book was finished and ready to go, so where was it?

Two hours later, still refusing to accept the loss of the green notebook in which Ka had recorded his Kars poems, I had convinced myself that it was here, somewhere, right under my nose, and that it was only on account of having let myself become so upset that I could have missed it. When the landlord knocked impatiently again, I scooped up all the notebooks in Ka's drawers and threw them into a plastic bag, along with every handwritten note I could find. I then gathered up the porno tapes piled higgledy-piggledy around the VCR – proof he'd never received visitors here – and threw these into a shopping bag from the Kaufhof. Then, like a man about to set out on a long journey who takes along some everyday memento of the life he's left behind, I searched the room for a simple keepsake by which to remember my friend. But I couldn't make up my mind, and before I knew it I was stuffing a plastic bag with the ashtray and the cigarettes sitting on his desk, the knife he'd used as a letter opener, the clock on his bedside table, the threadbare waistcoat that had been worn over his pyjamas for twenty-five years and so still smelled of him, and the photograph of him and his sister standing on Dolmabahçe wharf. By now I had become the curator of my own passion. Recognising my last chance, I gathered up almost everything else; and almost everything had value, from his dirty socks to his never-used handkerchiefs, from the kitchen spoons to the empty cigarette packets in the waste-paper basket. During one of our last meetings in Istanbul, Ka had asked about my plans for a new novel, and I had told him about *The Museum of Innocence*, an idea that up to that point I'd kept from everyone.

The moment I returned to my hotel room, having parted from my guide, I resumed my analysis of Ka's belongings. By now, I had decided to be clinical and put memories of my friend to rest for the night, before despair could destroy me. The first task I set myself was to review the porn tapes. My room didn't have a VCR, but from the notes in Ka's own hand on the cassette sleeves, it was clear that he had a special affection for an American star called Melinda.

I proceeded next to read the notebooks in which Ka had written about the poems that had come to him in Kars. Why had he never mentioned this love affair, the terrors he had witnessed? I was to find the answer in a file retrieved from one of Ka's drawers. When I opened it, almost forty love letters fell into my lap; all were addressed to İpek; none had been sent. Every one began exactly the same way – 'My darling, I have thought long and hard about whether I should write to tell you this . . .' – but then each went on to describe a different experience of his in Kars, each time adding a heart-wrenching new detail to my understanding of his love affair with İpek. There were also scattered insights into his everyday life in Frankfurt (the lame dog he'd seen in Von-Bethmann Park and the zinc tables in the Jewish Museum, both of which sources of distress he'd also mentioned in letters to me). He'd not folded any of these love letters, which revealed to me a degree of indecision about sending them that would not admit even the commitment of an envelope.

'Just say the word and I'll come to you,' he has written in one letter; though, in another, he declares he would 'never return to Kars, because I would never allow you to misunderstand me again'. One letter refers to a poem (not enclosed), and another invites one to imagine a preceding letter from İpek: 'I'm so sorry you took my letter amiss.'

That evening, I laid out all Ka's belongings on the bed and on every other surface in the room, and examined every item with a forensic eye. And it is with certainty that I can say Ka never received a single letter from İpek. So why did Ka pretend to answer one, even knowing that he would never send her a single letter, either?

Here, perhaps, we have arrived at the heart of our story. How much can we ever know about the love and pain in another's heart? How much can we hope to understand those who have suffered deeper anguish, greater deprivation and more crushing disappointments than we ourselves have known? Even if the world's rich and powerful should ever try to put themselves in the shoes of the rest, how much would they really understand the wretched millions suffering around them? So it is when Orhan the novelist peers into the dark corners of his poet friend's difficult and painful life: how much can he really see?

'All my life, I've felt as lost and lonely as a wounded animal,' wrote Ka. 'Perhaps if I hadn't embraced you with such violence, I wouldn't have angered you so much, and I might not have undone the work of twelve years, ending up exactly where I started. But here I am, abandoned and wasting away. I carry the scars of my unbearable suffering on every inch of my body. Sometimes I believe it's not just you I've lost, but everything in the world.' Now, could the mere act of my reading these words ensure that I understood them?

Late that night, made pleasantly tipsy by the whiskeys I'd taken from the minibar, I went back to the Kaiserstrasse to investigate Melinda.

She had enormous, olive-coloured eyes with a slight cast to them. Her skin was fair, her legs were long, her lips, which an Ottoman court poet might have likened to cherries, were small but full. She was also quite well known: it took me only twenty minutes to locate six films bearing her name in the video section of the World Sex Centre. I smuggled these videos back to Istanbul, and only once I'd watched them did I begin to have some sense of what Ka might have been feeling. Whatever sort of man she was kneeling before – he could be the coarsest, ugliest fellow in the world – Melinda always responded to his moans of ecstasy in the same way: her pale face softened with a compassion unique to mothers. No matter how provocative when in costume (whether as an impatient businesswoman, a frivolous stewardess or a housewife tired of her ineffectual husband), she was always fragile and vulnerable when naked. As I would later discover on my own visit to Kars, there was something of İpek in her manner, her large eyes and her curvaceous body.

I know I risk offending those poor souls who insist on seeing poets as saintly or metaphysical when I suggest that my friend spent the last four years of his life engrossed by this sort of adult entertainment. But as I wandered around the World Sex Centre hunting for videos of Melinda, it seemed to me that Ka had just one thing in common with the hordes of miserable men, lonely as ghosts, who were my fellow customers. They all answered their guilt by retreating into the shadows to watch these films. In the cinemas around New York's 42nd Street, Frankfurt's Kaiserstrasse and the backstreets of Beyoğlu, the lonely, lost men who watch the films with shame and self-loathing, struggling to avoid one another's eye at the intermissions, and in defiance of all national stereotypes and anthropological distinctions, all look exactly the same. I left the World Sex Centre with my black plastic bag full of Melinda videos, and walked down the empty streets, through the giant snowflakes, to my hotel.

I had two more whiskeys at the makeshift bar in the lobby, and while I waited for them to take effect I looked outside at the falling snow. I decided that if I did manage to get tipsy again, I'd take a break from Melinda and Ka's notebooks. But as soon as I reached my room, I picked out one of Ka's notebooks at random. Without pausing to undress, I lay down on the bed and began to read. On the third page I found the snowflake reproduced below.

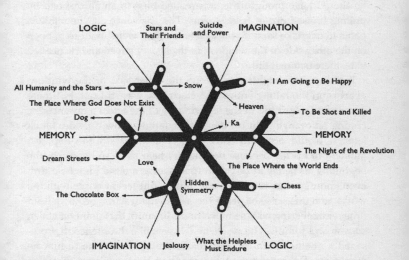

267

30

When Can We Meet Again?

A Short Spell of Happiness

After Ka and İpek had made love, they stayed in bed with their arms wrapped around each other; for a time, neither moved. The world was shrouded in silence, and Ka's happiness was so great that the embrace seemed to last for an age. This alone explains why he was seized with a sudden impatience and sprang from the bed to go and look out of the window. Later, he would come to see their long-shared silence as his happiest memory, so he would ask himself why he should have brought this unequalled bliss to an abrupt end by pulling himself out of İpek's arms. The answer is that he allowed panic to overtake him: it was as if something were about to happen on the other side of the window, in the snowy street, and he needed to be there before it did.

But there was nothing to see on the other side of the window, apart from the falling snow. The electricity was still out, but there was a candle burning in the icy window of the kitchen downstairs, casting an orange light on the thickly falling snow outside. Much later, it would occur to Ka that he had cut short the happiest moment of his life because he couldn't bear to be so happy. In the beginning, as he lay in bed with İpek's arms around him, he didn't even know he was totally happy. But he did feel at peace with the world, and this sense of peace seemed so natural that he had a hard time remembering why so much of his life until that point had been sorrow and tumult. The peace he felt was like the silence that presaged a poem, but in those times before a poem came to him he would see the meaning of life stripped bare, a vision that also brought him joy. There was no such moment of enlightenment in this happy memory of İpek. It had about it a simple, childish purity

268

– like that of a child with the words that explained the meaning of life on the very tip of his tongue.

One by one, he recalled the facts about snowflakes he had read in the library that afternoon. He had gone there to prepare himself, just in case another poem came to him on the subject of snow. But now his head was empty of poetry. Although his poems had come to him individually, he now saw that they all fitted together as neatly as the childish six-pointed snowflake in the encyclopedia. At this moment he had the first intimation that his poems were all part of a grand design.

'What are you doing over there?' asked İpek.

'I'm looking at the snow, darling.'

It seemed to him that İpek somehow knew he could see more than just beauty in the geometry of snowflakes, but at the same time he knew this could not be so. Part of him knew that İpek was not altogether happy to see his attention drawn elsewhere. Until then, he had been the pursuer, and his evident desire had made him feel uncomfortably vulnerable, so Ka was pleased to see the tables turned: from this, he deduced that making love had given him a slight advantage.

'What are you thinking?' asked İpek.

'I'm thinking about my mother,' said Ka, at first not knowing why: for, though she had just died, his mother had actually been far from his thoughts. But later, when returning to this moment, he would explain it by saying, 'My mother was on my mind throughout my visit to Kars.'

'So what are you remembering about your mother?'

'I'm remembering how we were standing at the window one winter night, looking out at the snow, and she ran her hands through my hair.'

'Were you happy as a child?'

'People don't know when they're happy, at least not while it's going on. It was only years later that I decided I'd been happy as a child; but, the truth is, I wasn't. On the other hand, I was not unhappy in the way I was during the years that followed. I just wasn't interested in happiness when I was a child.'

'So when did you start to become interested?'

Ka longed to say 'never', but he didn't, partly because it wasn't true, and partly because it seemed too aggressive. He was still tempted, if only because it might impress İpek, but there were weightier things on his mind now than the desire to make an impression on her.

'A moment arrived when I was so unhappy I could barely move, and that's when I began to think about happiness,' Ka told her.

Was this the right thing for him to say? Her silence made him uneasy. If he told her how unhappy he'd been in Frankfurt, how in the world would he convince her to return there with him? As a wild wind scattered the snowflakes outside, the nervous panic that had seized Ka earlier now returned with a vengeance, and his stomach ached more fiercely than ever with love and the agony of waiting. The happiness he'd felt only moments before now gave way to the awful certainty that he was going to lose it. In the place of happiness, doubts mounted. He wanted to ask İpek, 'Are you coming with me to Frankfurt?' but he was already too afraid of not receiving the answer he desired.

He returned to bed, pressed himself up against İpek's back and embraced her with all his strength. 'There's a store in the market,' he said. 'It was playing a very old song called "Roberta", by Peppino di Capri. Where do you think they found it?'

'There are still a few old families hanging on in Kars,' said İpek. 'Eventually the parents die and the children sell off their belongings and leave. So all sorts of things turn up in the market that seem very out of place in the poor city we see today. There used to be a junk dealer who'd come from Istanbul every spring and buy everything cheap and cart it off. But now even he's stopped coming.'

For a moment, Ka thought he had recaptured his earlier unequalled bliss, but it just wasn't the same as before. Once again, he succumbed to the fear that it might be lost to him for ever. Everything before his eyes increased his panic. He was never going to convince İpek to come to Frankfurt with him, that much was clear.

'So, darling, I think it's time for me to get up.'

Even when she used the word 'darling', even when she kissed him sweetly, Ka still could find no peace.

'When can we meet again?'

'I'm worried about my father. The police might have followed him.'

'I'm worried about them, too,' said Ka. 'But first I'd like to know when we can meet again.'

'I'm not coming to this room if my father's in the hotel.'

'But everything's changed now,' said Ka. However, as he watched the silent ease with which İpek dressed in the dark, he was hit by the fear that nothing had changed. 'Why don't I move to another hotel, then we could see each other right away,' he said.

There was a devastating silence. Now a new wave of panic overtook him. A helpless jealousy ran him through. He allowed himself to wonder whether İpek might have another lover. Part of him was still sane enough to remember that this sort of jealousy was common in the early stages of an untested love affair, but a stronger internal voice told him to wrap his arms around her with all the strength he could muster, and devote all his energy to overcoming the obstacles still standing between them. He knew it was a matter of urgency, but he also knew that if he acted too hastily he might put himself in an awkward situation, so he stayed uncertainly silent.

31

We're not Stupid! We're Just Poor!

The Secret Meeting at the Hotel Asia

When Zahide rushed out to the horse-drawn carriage that was to take Turgut Bey and Kadife to the secret meeting at the Hotel Asia, the light was failing, so Ka, watching from the window, could not quite make out what the loyal servant had in her hands. It was an old pair of woollen gloves. Uncertain as to what he should wear to the meeting, Turgut Bey had taken out the two jackets he had from his teaching days – one black, one grey – and spread them out on the bed with the felt hat he saved for national holidays and inspection visits and the checked tie he had not worn for years, except to amuse Zahide's son. He would spend a good deal more time poring over the other elements of his wardrobe and the contents of his drawers; but, seeing him acting like a dreamy girl unsure what her father would let her wear to the ball, Kadife stepped in to make the final selection. After buttoning his shirt for him, she helped him on with his jacket and his coat; then came the pair of white dog-leather gloves that she struggled to pull on to his small hands. At this moment Turgut Bey remembered his old woollen gloves; and, stubbornly insisting these were the ones he had to wear, he sent İpek and Kadife rushing around the house frantically to search every wardrobe and every chest from top to bottom. When they finally found them and saw how many holes the moths had made, they threw the gloves aside. But once he was ensconced in the horse-drawn carriage, Turgut Bey again insisted that he refused to leave without them. Years ago, he explained, when his left-wing activities had landed him in prison, his dear, departed wife had brought him these gloves, which she had knitted. Kadife, who knew her father better than he knew himself, saw the matter for what it was: if the old man was insisting on these gloves as talismans, then he must be very scared indeed.

After the gloves had arrived and the horse-drawn carriage set off into the snow, Kadife asked her father to tell her more about his prison days. She listened to his stories (how he'd cried whenever he received letters from his wife; how he'd taught himself French; how he'd worn these very gloves to bed on winter nights) as intently as if she were hearing them for the first time, occasionally interrupting him to say, 'What a brave man you are, Father!' Then he did what he always did when he heard his daughters utter these words (which, over the last few years, was hardly ever): fighting back tears, Turgut Bey enfolded Kadife in his arms, and, shuddering, kissed her cheeks.

As he stepped out of the carriage, Turgut Bey said, 'Look at all these new shops. Stop, let's see what they have in their windows.'

Kadife knew that he was dragging his feet out of fear, so she was careful not to hurry him. Turgut Bey proposed they stop off for a cup of linden tea – if a detective was following them, he said, they might as well give him a run for his money. So they made their way into a tea-house, where they sat silently watching a race on the TV. Just as they were leaving, Turgut Bey spotted his old barber at a nearby table, and insisted they turn around and re-enter the tea-house. He didn't want anyone who recognised him to see him going to the meeting with Blue.

'Do you think we're too late now?' Turgut Bey asked Kadife. 'Do you think we'll offend them if we don't go at all?'

The fat barber seemed to be eavesdropping, so Turgut Bey spoke to Kadife in whispers. He took her arm, but instead of heading straight for the rear courtyard, he now went into a stationery store, where he picked out a navy-blue pen. When they finally reached the rear courtyard of Ersin Electric and Plumbing Supplies and turned towards the dark door that was the back entrance to the Hotel Asia, Kadife saw the blood drain from her father's face. Nothing was stirring, but still they stuck close together to steel their nerves. No one was following them. They took a few steps inside, but it was so dark that Kadife had to grope her way to the stairs that led to the lobby. 'Don't let go of my arm,' said Turgut Bey.

The lobby was in shadow, its high windows hidden behind heavy curtains. But there was a weak, dirty lamp on the desk that gave off just enough light for them to see the face of the unshaven, unkempt receptionist standing behind it. In the darkness beyond the desk they could make out a few silhouetted figures wandering about the lobby and gliding up and down the stairs. These were either plainclothes policemen, black-marketeers who dealt in livestock or lumber, or undocumented workers who had been smuggled across the border.

Eighty years earlier, this hotel had been popular with Russian businessmen. After the revolution, most of its custom came from Istanbul Turks and aristocratic English double agents heading into Armenia to spy on the Soviet Union. Now it was full of women who'd come over from Georgia and the Ukraine to work as prostitutes and petty smugglers. By and large, men from the villages around Kars rented rooms for these women. They'd live with them here during the day, almost like married couples, then return to their villages on the last minibus of the day. Once they'd gone, the women would come downstairs to drink coffee and cognac in the dark recesses of the hotel bar.

As Turgut Bey and Kadife made their way among the wooden chairs that had once been upholstered in red tapestry, they came face to face with one of these tatty blondes. Turgut Bey turned to Kadife and whispered, 'The Grand Hotel, where Ismet Pasha stayed when he was negotiating the Treaty of Lausanne, was just as cosmopolitan as this,' and, with that, he took the pen he had just bought out of his pocket. 'And I'm going to do just what Ismet Pasha did in Lausanne – I'm going to sign the statement with a brand-new pen.'

For the longest time, he wouldn't move. It wasn't clear to Kadife if he was stalling or listening for noise on the stairs. But eventually he set off up the stairway. When they arrived at Room 307, Turgut Bey said, 'Let's just sign this thing and leave.'

It was so crowded inside that Kadife at first thought they'd come to the wrong room. Seeing Blue sitting glumly near the window with two other Islamist militants, she took her father across the room and sat him beside them. A naked lightbulb hung from the ceiling; on the table was a lamp in the shape of a fish; but the room was still dark. The fish was made of Bakelite; propped on its tailfins, it held the lightbulb in its mouth. A state-owned microphone was hidden in one of its eyes.

Fazıl was in the room, too. The moment he saw Kadife, he jumped to his feet, before the others also rose to pay their respects to Turgut Bey. Fazıl looked stunned, as if someone had cast a spell on him. A few people in the room thought he was about to speak. But Kadife didn't even notice him. Her eyes were on Blue and Turgut Bey, whose eyes were on each other. The atmosphere was tense.

Blue had decided that the West would take the statement more seriously if the Kurdish nationalist who signed it was also an atheist. But the thin, pale teenager who'd reluctantly agreed to sign now disagreed with his two Kurdish nationalist associates over the wording. The three of them were waiting sullenly for their turn to speak. Since the associations of angry, hopeless, jobless youths known to admire the Kurdish guerrillas from the mountains tended to convene in the houses of individual members, and since association leaders were often arrested, beaten and tortured following frequent raids on meetings, it was hard to find these youngsters after the coup. But the three young Kurds who were present had an even more pressing problem: the mountain warriors might find their very presence in this room suspicious. They might decide that these young men had it too easy in these warm city rooms and accuse them of collaboration with the Turkish Republic. In fact, the charge that the associations were not sending their fair share of guerrilla recruits up to the mountains had already demoralised the handful of members who had not yet been arrested.

Also at the meeting were two old-style 'socialists', both in their thirties. The possibility of a joint statement to the German press had been conveyed to them by the Kurdish youths, who'd gone to the socialists to brag a little but also to ask for advice. Socialist militancy had once cast a long shadow over Kars, but it was now a spent force; these days, no socialist would dare set an ambush, kill a policeman or embark on a mail-bomb campaign without first seeking the blessing of the Kurdish guerrillas and enlisting their support. As a result, the socialists' once-formidable ranks were beset by stagnation and widespread depression. These two old-style militants had come uninvited to the meeting, having heard that Marxism was still thriving in Europe. The elder of the two, at the far end of the room, had adopted an attitude of boredom. Next to him was his relaxed, clean-faced comrade, who was in high spirits as he gathered the details he would relay to the local branch of MİT. His intentions weren't malign: he did this to help the associations avoid police harassment. He would inform the state of any activities he didn't like – most of which in retrospect seemed unnecessary anyway – but, in his heart of hearts, he was proud that there were rebels out there fighting for the cause; so proud, in fact, that he bragged about the shootings, the kidnappings, the beatings, the bombings and the assassinations to anyone who would listen.

At first no one spoke, so sure were they that the room was bugged and that there were several informers in the crowd. And when the silence was finally broken, it was only with a nod in the direction of the window to note that it was still snowing, or to admonish someone about stubbing out cigarettes on the floor. This continued until a Kurdish granny who had sat unnoticed in the room until that moment stood up and told the story of her son's disappearance. (They had knocked on the door in the middle of the night and taken him away.)

Although he was only half listening to this disappearance story, Turgut Bey felt uneasy. He was as appalled to hear of the abduction and murder of Kurdish teenagers in the middle of the night as he was angry to hear them described as 'innocents'. Holding her father's hand, Kadife tried to make sense of the disgust and contempt she could see in Blue's face. Blue felt that he had walked into a trap, but, fearing what people would say about him if he left, he remained, against his better judgement. And then:

1 The Islamist youth who was sitting next to Fazıl, and whose connection to the murder of the director of the Education Institute would be proved months later, began to argue that the director had been assassinated by a government agent.

2 The revolutionaries in the room made a long announcement about the hunger strike begun by their comrades in prison.

3 The three youths from the Kurdish association read out an even longer statement, in which they threatened to withdraw their signatures from the joint declaration unless the *Frankfurter Rundschau* published it, thus restoring Kurdish culture and literature to its proper place in world history.

When the granny, who had come to submit a petition on behalf of her missing son, asked where the 'German journalist' was, Kadife rose to explain in a reassuring voice that Ka was still in Kars, but had stayed away from the meeting lest his presence cast any doubt on the 'impartiality' of the statement. The others were unaccustomed to seeing a woman address a political meeting with such confidence, and she quickly gained their respect. The granny with the missing son threw her arms around Kadife and began to cry, and, hearing that Kadife would do everything in her power to get her story published in the German press, she then gave her a piece of paper on which someone had written her son's name.

The well-meaning leftist-militant informer chose this moment to present the first draft of the statement, which he had written in long-hand in a notebook. As he read it, he did his best to look inscrutable.

The title was 'An Announcement to the People of Europe about the Events in Kars'. Almost everyone warmed to it at once. Remembering how he felt at that moment, Fazıl would later smile and tell Ka that 'This was the first time it ever occurred to me that our small city might one day have a role to play in world history.' Ka would later use these very words in his poem 'All Humanity and the Stars'.

Only Blue adamantly opposed the title. 'We're not speaking to Europe,' he said. 'We're speaking to all humanity. Our friends should not be surprised to learn we have been unable to publish our statement – not just in Kars and Istanbul, but also in Frankfurt. The people of Europe are not our friends but our enemies. And it's not because we are *their* enemies – it's because they instinctively despise us.'

The leftist in charge of the first draft interrupted here to say that it wasn't all humanity who despised them, just the European bourgeoisie. The poor and unemployed were their brothers, he reminded them, but no one aside from his fellow socialist was persuaded.

'No one in Europe is as poor as we are,' said one of the three Kurdish youths in a shrill voice.

'My son, have you ever been to Europe?' asked Turgut Bey.

'I haven't had the opportunity yet, but my uncle is a worker in Germany.'

This provoked a smattering of laughter.

Turgut Bey straightened his chair. 'Although the word means so much to me, I have never been to Europe either,' he said. 'This is not a laughing matter. Please would all those in the room who have been to Europe raise their hands.'

Apart from Blue, who had spent many years in Germany, no one raised their hand.

'But we all know what Europe has come to mean,' Turgut Bey continued. 'Europe is our future, and the future of our humanity. So if this gentleman here' – he pointed at Blue – 'thinks we should say "all humanity" instead of "Europe", we might as well change our statement accordingly.'

'Europe is not *my* future,' said Blue with a smile. 'As long as I live I shall not imitate them or hate myself for being different to them.'

'It's not just Islamists who take pride in this country. Republicans feel the same way,' said Turgut Bey. 'If we say "all humanity" instead of "Europe", what do we have?'

'"Announcement to All Humanity on the Events in Kars",' said the man in charge of the statement. 'That might be too bold.'

There followed a discussion in which they considered replacing 'all humanity' with 'the West', but the freckled man beside Blue objected to this. The Kurdish youth with the shrill voice then suggested simply 'An Announcement', and this met with everyone's approval.

Contrary to everyone's expectations, the draft statement was very short. It declared that a coup had been 'staged' at the very moment when it had become clear that Islamist and Kurdish candidates would prevail in the upcoming elections. Turgut Bey alone objected, saying that their whole argument was therefore based on opinion polls, and this would be unconvincing to European readers, who knew that on the eve of elections, or even on their way to the polls, people could change their minds on a whim and give their vote to the party that stood for everything they'd claimed to oppose the day before. For this reason, Turgut Bey thought it would be better not to imply that the result of the election was a foregone conclusion.

In response, the leftist-militant informer in charge of the draft said, 'Everyone knows that this coup happened in advance of the elections in order to prevent certain people from winning those elections.'

'You have to remember that we're dealing with a theatre troupe,' said Turgut Bey. 'The only reason they've succeeded is that the roads are blocked. Everything will be back to normal in a matter of days.'

'If you're not against the coup, then why are you here?' asked a young man with a flushed face who was sitting next to Blue.

Turgut Bey offered no answer, but Kadife immediately rose to her feet (she was the only one in the room who stood when she was speaking, though no one, certainly not she, saw how strange this was). Her eyes burning with anger, she told the room that her father had spent many years in prison for his political beliefs and remained categorically opposed to all forms of state-sponsored oppression.

Turgut Bey quickly removed his jacket and indicated that she should sit down. 'My answer to your question is this,' he said: 'I have come to this meeting because I wish to prove to the Europeans that in Turkey, too, we have people who believe in common sense and democracy.'

'If a big German paper gave me two lines of space, this would not be the first thing I'd be aiming to prove,' said the red-faced man contemptuously. He would have said more, but Blue placed a warning hand on his arm.

It was enough to make Turgut Bey regret having come. He overcame his disappointment by telling himself he'd just stopped by on his way to somewhere else. Assuming the air of someone preoccupied with matters far away from this room, he rose and took a few steps towards the door; but then, noticing the snow accumulating on Karadağ Avenue, he walked over to the window. Kadife took his arm in such a way as to suggest that her father might be unable to walk any further without assistance. For a long time, father and daughter stood there like mournful children trying to forget their troubles, as a horse-drawn carriage made its way down the street.

One of the three Kurdish boys – the one with the shrill voice – succumbed to curiosity and joined them at the window. The others watched with a mixture of respect and apprehension. As they wondered whether there was about to be a raid, the room grew tense. The various factions were soon so worried that in no time they reached an agreement about the rest of the statement.

It made clear that the military coup had been led by a handful of adventurers. Blue had suggested this. When others proposed a broader definition, he pointed out the error of giving Westerners the impression that the military had taken over all of Turkey. In the end, they agreed to describe it as a 'local coup supported by Ankara'. A brief reference was made to the Kurds who'd been shot or taken from their homes and killed, and to the torture and intimidation suffered by the boys from the religious high school. 'A wholesale assault on the people' was amended to read 'An assault on the people, the spirit and religion'. And they changed the last line, calling not just on the people of Europe but on the whole world to unite in protest against the Turkish Republic. As he was reading out this line, Turgut Bey caught Blue's eyes for a moment and saw contentment in them. Again, the old man was sorry he had come.

'If there are no more objections, let's sign this at once,' said Blue, 'because there could be a raid at any moment.'

By now the statement was a tangle of crossed-out words, arrows and circled emendations, but this deterred no one from rushing to the middle of the room, where they all jostled for position with the same objective: to sign and then make themselves scarce. A few were already heading for the door when Kadife cried: 'Stop! My father has something to say to you!'

This only heightened the panic, but Blue ordered the red-faced boy to guard the door. 'No one's allowed to leave,' he said. 'Let Turgut Bey make his objection.'

'I don't have an objection,' said the old man. 'But before I put my name to this statement, there's something I want from that teenager over there.' He paused to think. 'And not just from him – from everyone in the room.' He pointed at the red-faced boy who'd been arguing with him earlier and now was standing guard at the door. 'I'm going to ask a question, and I want an answer first from that teenager and then from the rest of you. If I don't get it, I won't be signing this statement.' He turned to Blue to gauge the effect of his remark.

'Please, be my guest, ask your question,' said Blue. 'If it's in our power to answer it, we'll be only too pleased to do so.'

'Just a moment ago, you laughed at me. So now I want you all to answer me this. If a big German newspaper gave each of you personally two lines of space, what would you say to the West? I want that boy over there to go first.'

The red-faced teenager was strong and powerful, with an opinion on everything, but this question caught him unprepared. Clutching the door handle tightly, he looked to Blue for help.

'Just say whatever you think you'd say if you had two lines to fill. Then we can leave,' said Blue, forcing a smile. 'If you don't, the police will raid us.'

The teenager searched the air as he racked his brain like a boy struggling with an exam question he'd known the answer to the day before.

Hearing nothing, Blue said, 'Fine, then let me answer first. I couldn't care less about your European masters. Where they're concerned, all I want to do is step out of their shadow. But the truth is, we all live under a shadow.'

'Don't try to help him, let him speak from his own heart,' said Turgut Bey. 'You can go last.' He smiled at the red-faced teenager, still squirming with indecision. 'It's a difficult decision. It's a complicated business. It's not the sort of dilemma you can resolve on your way out of the door.'

'He's looking for excuses!' someone shouted from the back of the room. 'He doesn't want to sign the statement!'

They all retreated, each into his own thoughts. A few moved to the window, to watch a horse-drawn carriage swaying back and forth as it made its way down the street. Later that same night, when describing the 'enchanted silence' that had fallen over the room, Fazıl would tell Ka that it 'was as if we were all brothers suddenly, as if we were closer to one another than we'd ever been before'. The first sound to break the silence came from a plane passing far above them in the night sky. Everyone heard it.

'That's the second plane that's passed today,' Blue whispered.

'I'm leaving!' someone shouted.

The speaker, a pallid man in his thirties, was wearing a pale jacket. No one had noticed him until that moment. He was one of the three working men in the room, a cook in the Social Insurance Hospital, and he couldn't stop looking at his watch. He'd come in with the families of the disappeared. According to later reports, his older brother, a political activist, had been carted off to the police station for questioning, never to return. It was said that the pale cook had wanted to secure a death certificate from the state so that he could marry his missing brother's beautiful wife. He'd made a formal request a year after his brother's disappearance, but the police, MİT, the public prosecutor's office and the army garrison all gave him the brush-off. He'd joined the families of the disappeared two months earlier, not out of any desire for revenge, but simply because they were the only people willing to listen to him.

'You'll call me a coward behind my back. But you're the cowards. And these Europeans of yours, they're the biggest cowards of all. You can go ahead and quote me.' He kicked open the door and walked out.

It was at this point that someone asked just who was this 'Hans Hansen Bey'. Kadife panicked, but, to her great surprise, Blue courteously explained that he was a well-intentioned German journalist who took a deep interest in Turkey's problems.

'Beware of Germans with good intentions!' cried someone.

A man in a black jacket standing by the window asked if the paper planned to supplement the joint statement with extra quotes.

'My friends, let's not hang back like frightened little schoolchildren, waiting for the other kid to speak first,' said someone.

'I'm at the lycée,' piped up one of the Kurdish boys. 'I knew what I would say before I got here.'

'Are you telling me you already knew a day would come when you would be called upon to give a quote to a German newspaper?'

'Yes, exactly,' said the teenager. His voice couldn't have been calmer, but his face burned with passion. 'I've always dreamed of the day when I'd have a chance to share my ideas with the world – and so has everyone else in this room.'

'I've never thought about things like that . . .'

'What I would say is very simple,' said the passionate youth. 'All I'd want them to print in that Frankfurt paper is this: "We're not stupid! We're just poor! And we have a right to insist on this distinction."'

'Such humble words!'

'Who do you mean, my son, when you say "we"?' asked another man. 'Do you mean the Turks? The Kurds? The Circassians? The people of Kars? To whom exactly are you referring?'

'Because mankind's greatest error,' continued the passionate youth, ignoring the question, 'the biggest deception of the past thousand years, is this: to confuse poverty with stupidity.'

'What exactly does he mean by "stupidity"? He should explain his terms,' said someone.

'Throughout history, religious leaders and other honourable men of conscience have always warned against this shaming confusion. They remind us that the poor have hearts, minds, humanity and wisdom, just like everyone else. When Hans Hansen sees a poor man, he feels sorry for him. He would not necessarily assume that the man's a fool who's blown his chances, or a drunk who's lost his will.'

'I can't speak for Hans Hansen, but that's what everyone thinks when they see a poor man.'

'Please listen to what I have to say,' said the passionate Kurdish youth. 'I won't speak long. People might feel sorry for a man who's fallen on hard times, but when an entire nation is poor, the rest of the world assumes at once that all the people of that nation must be brainless, lazy, dirty, clumsy fools. Instead of pity, the people provoke laughter. It's all a joke – their culture, their customs, their practices. As time goes by, some of the rest of the world begins to feel ashamed for having thought this way, and when they look around and see immigrants from that poor country mopping their floors and doing all the other lowest-paying jobs, naturally they worry about what might happen if these workers one day rose up against them. So, to keep things sweet, they start taking an interest in the immigrants' culture, and sometimes even pretend to think of them as equals.'

'It's about time he tells us what nation he's talking about.'

'Let me add this,' said the shrill-voiced Kurd before his friend could respond. 'Mankind refuses to laugh any longer at those who kill and murder and oppress one another. This is what I learned from my uncle when he came to Kars from Germany last summer. The world has lost patience with oppressive countries.'

'Are we to assume then that you're making a threat on behalf of the West?'

'As I was saying,' the passionate Kurd continued, 'when a Westerner meets someone from a poor country, the first thing he feels is deep contempt. He thinks it must be because the fellow comes from a country of fools that he's as poor as he is. And the next thing this Westerner thinks is that the poor man's head must be full of all the nonsense that plunged his country into poverty and despair.'

'And if he did, he wouldn't be far off the mark, would he?'

'If you're like that conceited poet and think we're stupid, stand up and state your case. That godless atheist will end up in Hell, but at least he showed some courage. He went on live TV, looked the entire country in the eye and told us to our faces we are stupid.'

'Excuse me, but people on live TV can't look the audience in the eye.'

'The gentleman didn't say he "saw" their eyes. He said he "looked".'

'Friends! Please! Let's not be a debating society,' pleaded the leftist who was taking minutes. 'And please don't speak so fast.'

'If he's not brave enough to say what nation he's talking about, then I refuse to be quiet. Let's be clear that it's treason to give a German paper a quote that debases our nation.'

'I'm no traitor. I agree with you,' the passionate Kurd said, rising to his feet. 'That's why I want to tell this German paper that even if I get a chance to go to Germany one day, even if they give me a visa, I'm not going to go.'

'They'd never give a European visa to a feeble, unemployed nobody like you.'

'Forget the visa. Our own state wouldn't even give him a passport.'

'You're right, they wouldn't,' admitted the passionate but humble youth. 'But say they did and I went, and the first Western man I met in the street turned out to be a good person who didn't despise me. I'd still mistrust him, just for being a Westerner. I'd still worry that this man was looking down on me. Because, in Germany, they can spot people from Turkey just by the way they look. There's no avoiding humiliation except by proving at the first opportunity that you think exactly as they do. But this is impossible, and it can break a man's pride to try.'

'You started badly, my son, but you've ended up in the right place,' said an old Azeri journalist. 'But I still think we shouldn't say this to the German press, because it will lay us open to ridicule.' He paused for a moment, and then cunningly asked, 'So what nation was it you were talking about?'

When the Kurdish teenager sat down without responding, the old journalist's son, seated at his father's side, cried out, 'He's afraid!'

'He's right to be afraid,' someone muttered, while others whispered, 'He's not on the government payroll like you.'

Neither the journalist nor his son took offence at this comment. Everyone was talking at once, but not in frustration: all the joking and teasing and keeping score had made the atmosphere festive and had brought them all closer together. Later, on hearing Fazıl's account of the proceedings, Ka would observe in his notebook that this sort of political meeting could go on for hours, and that the beetle-browed, mustachioed, cigarette-smoking men who attended them did so precisely to enjoy the pleasure of the crowd, even though they didn't realise they were having a good time.

'We can never be Europeans!' cried one of the proud young Islamists. 'They might try to roll over us with their tanks and spray us with bullets and kill us all. But they can't change our souls.'

'You can take possession of my body but never my soul,' said the Kurd with the shrill voice. He made his contempt clear by reciting the line in the style of a Turkish melodrama.

Everyone laughed, including the boy who'd just spoken.

'Now I'm going to say something,' said one of the youths sitting near Blue. 'No matter how hard our friends here try to draw a line between themselves and the lowlifes who ape the ways of the West, I still sense a certain note of apology. It's as if they're saying, "I'm so sorry I'm not a Westerner."' He turned to the man in the leather jacket who was taking minutes. 'Please, dear sir, ignore these preliminary remarks!' He had assumed the air of a polite thug. 'Here's what I'd like you to write: I'm proud of the part of me that isn't European. I'm proud of the things in me that the Europeans find childish, cruel and primitive. If the Europeans are beautiful, I want to be ugly; if they're intelligent, I prefer to be stupid; if they're modern, let me stay simple.'

No one in the room would sign on to that sentiment. But the ensuing laughter preserved the new spirit of the gathering, with everything now said giving way to a joke. However, someone then went too far: 'But you're stupid already!' Luckily, at that moment, the two leftists both had coughing fits, so no one was sure who had uttered these insulting words.

The red-faced teenager guarding the door rattled off a poem. The first lines went:

> Europe, O Europe
> Let's stop and take a look
> When we're together in our dreams
> Let's not let the devil have his way . . .

Fazıl had a hard time hearing the rest over all the coughing, taunting and sniggering. But, though he missed the poem itself, he recounted in detail the objections to it. Jotted down on the same sheet that bore his record of the various two-line statements for the West were snippets of reaction that ultimately appeared in 'All Humanity and the Stars', the poem Ka was to write shortly afterwards:

1 'Let's not be afraid of them; there's nothing there to be afraid of,' shouted one of the leftist militants.

2 The old Azeri journalist – who could not stop asking, 'To what nation are you referring?' – said, 'Let's not sacrifice our Turkishness or forsake our religion.' Then, in the course of his long speech about the Crusades, the Holocaust, the American massacre of the Indians and the French massacre of the Algerian Muslims, a defeatist in the crowd slyly asked, 'And whatever happened to

the millions of Armenians who once lived all across Anatolia, including Kars?' Feeling pity for this man, the informer–secretary did not write down his name.

3 'No one in his right mind would ever want to translate such a long and idiotic poem, and Hans Hansen would never let it be published in his newspaper.' This came from one of the poets in the room (of whom there were three). They took their chance to bemoan the luckless isolation of Turkish poets on the international stage.

On finishing his recitation of the poem that all those present denounced as idiotic and primitive, the red-faced youth was drenched in sweat. He received scattered and rather contemptuous applause. Most seemed to agree that it would be unwise to let this poem be published in Germany, as it would open 'us' to more ridicule.

The Kurdish youth whose uncle lived in Germany was the most outspoken on this point: 'When they write poems or sing songs in the West, they speak for all humanity. They're human beings – but we're just Muslims. When *we* write something, it's just ethnic poetry.'

'My message is this. Write this down,' said the man in the black jacket. 'If the Europeans are right, and our only future, and only hope, is to be more like them, then it's foolish to waste time talking about what makes us who we are.'

'Ah, of all the things said so far, that's the one that will most effectively convince the Europeans that we're idiots.'

'Please, once and for all, state clearly which nation it is that's going to look idiotic.'

'And here we are, acting as if we're so much smarter and worthier than Westerners, but, gentlemen, I put it to you that if Germany opened a consulate in Kars today and started handing out free visas, the city would be empty within a week.'

'That's a lie. After all, our friend over there just told us he wouldn't go if they gave him the chance. I wouldn't, either. I'd do the honourable thing and stay here.'

'And many others would stay, too, gentlemen – make no mistake. All those who wouldn't go, raise your hands so we can see you.'

A few gravely raised their hands. A handful of youths saw them but remained undecided. 'And why is it that he thinks those who would go are being dishonourable?' asked the man in the black jacket.

'This is hard to explain to people who don't already understand,' said one mysterious fellow.

Fazıl noticed that Kadife had turned away and was looking mournfully out of the window. His heart began to thump wildly. Please God, he thought, help me preserve my purity; protect my mind from confusion. It occurred to him that Kadife might like these words. It occurred to him to make this his quote for the West. But with so many people speaking, there was no chance of his being heard.

The only one who managed to be audible above all the noise was the shrill-voiced Kurd. He proposed to tell the German newspaper about a dream he'd had. Pausing from time to time with a shiver, he explained how in this dream he'd been sitting all alone in the National Theatre watching a film. It was a European film, so everyone in it was speaking a foreign language, but this didn't make him uncomfortable: he somehow understood everything they said. And then, in the blink of an eye, he entered the film himself. He was suddenly in the sitting room of a Christian family. There, before his eyes, was a table laden with food. He longed to fill his stomach, but, fearful of doing something wrong, he held back. His heart began to race: there, before him, was a beautiful blonde woman, and the moment he saw her he remembered that he'd been in love with her for years. The woman was warmer and more gentle than he could ever have imagined. She complimented him on his clothes and his manners, kissed his cheeks, ran her fingers through his hair. He was deliriously happy. Before he knew it, she sat him on her lap and pointed to the food on the table. It was only then that he realised he was still a child. Tears now welled in the Kurdish youth's eyes. It was only because he was still a child that the woman had found him so charming.

This dream seemed to issue from a deep-seated fear.

The old journalist broke the silence. 'No one could dream a dream like that,' he said. 'This Kurdish boy made it up just to mock us to the Germans.'

To prove the authenticity of his dream, the teenager offered a detail he'd omitted from his account: every time he'd woken up since having the dream, he'd remembered this same blonde woman. He'd first seen her five years ago, stepping out of a bus, one of a group of tourists who'd come to see the Armenian churches. She was wearing a blue dress that revealed her shoulders. She wore the same dress in his dreams.

This produced more laughter. 'We've all seen European women like that,' said someone, 'and we've all been tempted by the Devil.'

Others took the opportunity to tell a few mischievous anecdotes, make some off-colour jokes or launch into angry diatribes against Western women. A tall, thin and rather handsome youth who had stayed in the shadows until that moment began the following story: A Westerner and a Muslim met at a train station. Sadly, the train didn't arrive. At the end of the same platform they saw a beautiful Frenchwoman waiting for the same train . . .

Anyone who'd ever attended a boys' school or done his military service would have already recognised this for a story that would link sexual prowess with national culture. It contained no rude words, its coarseness hidden under a veil of insinuation. But in no time at all there had fallen over the room a mood that was perfectly evoked in a line from Fazıl's report: 'My heart is heavy with shame!'

Turgut Bey rose to his feet. 'All right, my boy, that's enough,' he said. 'Bring me this statement so that I can sign it.'

He fished out his new pen, and it was done. The noise and the cigarette smoke had worn him out, and he needed Kadife's help to stand.

'Now listen to me for a minute,' she said. 'You seem to feel no shame, but my face is red from what I've just heard. I cover my head with this scarf so you won't see my hair, and maybe you think this causes me undue hardship, but –'

'You don't do it for us!' someone said in a respectful whisper. 'You do it for God, to proclaim your spirituality!'

'I have a few things to say to the German paper, too. Please write them down.' She was enough of an actress to know that her audience half hated and half admired her. '"A young woman of Kars" – no, don't write that, say, "A Muslim girl who lives in Kars" – "has covered her head for personal religious reasons but also wears the scarf as an emblem of her faith. One day this girl is overcome by a sudden revulsion and pulls the scarf off her head." The Westerners would greet this as good news. If we did that, Hans Hansen would certainly want to print our views. "When she pulled off her scarf, this girl said,

'Please God, forgive me, because I have to be alone. This world is so loathsome, and I am so powerless and so full of woe that your –'"'

'Kadife,' whispered Fazıl. 'Please, I beg you, don't bare your head. We're all here right now, all of us. Including me and Necip. It would kill us, kill us all.'

Everyone in the room seemed confused by these words. 'Stop talking nonsense,' said someone, and then someone else added, 'But of course she shouldn't bare her head.' The rest looked at her expectantly, half hoping that she was about to do something shocking and newsworthy, and half wondering who had staged this melodrama, and who was playing games with whom.

'The two lines I want to give the German paper are as follows,' said Fazıl. The buzzing in the room grew louder. '"I speak not only for myself, but for my friend Necip, who was so cruelly martyred on the night of the revolution: Kadife, we love you very much. If you bare your head, I'll kill myself, so please, please don't."'

According to some reports, Fazıl didn't say 'we love you' but 'I love you', though it's possible that these witnesses' memories were influenced by what Fazıl would do later.

'No one in this city is allowed to talk about suicide!' bellowed Blue, and he stormed out of the room without even pausing to look at Kadife. This brought the meeting to an immediate close and, although they were not particularly quiet about it, they cleared the room in a matter of seconds.

32

That's Not Going to Be Possible While I Have Two Souls Inside My Body

On Love, Insignificance and Blue's Disappearance

At a quarter to five, Ka stepped out of the Snow Palace Hotel. Turgut Bey and Kadife had not yet returned from the meeting at the Hotel Asia, and Ka still had fifteen minutes to go before he was due to meet Fazıl, but he was too happy to sit still. He turned left off Atatürk Avenue and walked as far as the Kars River, slowing down from time to time to gaze into the windows of grocers', photographers' studios and tea-houses crowded with men watching television. When he reached the iron bridge, he smoked two Marlboros in quick succession. His head was full of visions of living happily ever after with İpek in Frankfurt, and he didn't feel the cold at all. Across the river was the park where the rich families of Kars used to go to watch the ice-skaters. It was now ominously dark.

Fazıl was late arriving at the iron-bridge rendezvous, and when he emerged from the shadows Ka for a moment again mistook him for Necip. Together they went into the Lucky Brothers Tea-house, where Fazıl reported everything he could remember about the meeting at the Hotel Asia. When he reached the part where he declared that the history of his small city had become one with the history of the world, Ka silenced him, as one might hush someone in order to catch something being said on the radio. He then proceeded to write the poem entitled 'All Humanity and the Stars'.

In the notes he made afterwards, Ka described its subject as the sadness of a city forgotten by the outside world and banished from history. The first lines followed a sequence recalling the opening scenes of the Hollywood films he had so loved as a child. As the titles rolled past, there was an image from space of the earth turning slowly. As the camera zoomed in, more detail became visible, until you could see a single country. Of course – just as in the imaginary films that had rolled in Ka's head since childhood – this country was Turkey. Zooming closer still, the blue waters of the Sea of Marmara, the Bosphorus and the Black Sea came into view; then Istanbul, and the Nişantaş of Ka's childhood, with the traffic policeman on Teşvikiye Avenue, Nigâr the Poetess Street, and trees and rooftops (how lovely they looked from above!). Then came a slow pan across laundry hanging on a line, a billboard advertising Tamek canned goods, rusty gutters and pitch-covered pavements, before the pause at Ka's bedroom window. Through the window began a long tracking shot of rooms packed with books, dusty furniture and carpets, and then Ka at a desk facing the opposite window. From over his shoulder the camera revealed a piece of paper on the desk, and came finally to rest on the last letters of the message he was writing, thus inviting us to read: 'ADDRESS ON THE DAY OF MY ENTRANCE INTO THE HISTORY OF POETRY: POET Ka, 16/8 NIGÂR THE POETESS STREET, NİŞANTAŞ, ISTANBUL, TURKEY'. As discerning readers will already have realised, this poem, while located on the 'Logic' axis, is positioned close enough to 'Imagination' to acknowledge its influence, too.

Fazıl's main preoccupation was clear by the end of his story: he was now very uneasy about having threatened to kill himself if Kadife were to bare her head. 'And it's not just because committing suicide is tantamount to losing your faith. It's also because I didn't mean it. Why did I say something I didn't believe?' Fazıl claimed that right after his vow he had said, 'God forgive me, I'll never say that again!' But then, coming eye to eye with Kadife at the door, he had trembled like a leaf. 'Do you think Kadife thought I was in love with her?' he asked Ka.

'Are you in love with her?'

'You know the truth already. I was in love with Teslime, may she rest in peace. My friend Necip, may he also rest in peace, was the one who was in love with Kadife. I feel so ashamed of myself for falling in love with the same girl not a day after his death. And I know that there can be only one explanation. This scares me, too. Tell me why you're so sure that Necip is dead!'

'I had looked at the place where the bullet entered his forehead before I laid my hands on his shoulders and kissed him.'

'It's possible that Necip's soul is now living inside my body,' said Fazıl. 'Listen, I stayed away from the gala last night. I didn't even watch it on television. I went to bed early and fell asleep immediately. Only later did I hear about the terrible things that had happened to Necip while I was sleeping. Then the soldiers raided our dormitory, and I had no doubt that what I'd heard was true. By the time I saw you at the library, I knew that Necip was dead, because his soul had been in my body since early morning. The soldiers who came to empty the dormitory passed me by, so I spent the night on Market Street, at the home of one of my father's friends from his army days – he's from Varto. As I lay in his guest bed, my head suddenly started spinning, and a deep, rich feeling came over me: my friend was at my side again; he was *inside* me. It's just as they say in the old books – the soul leaves the body six hours after death. According to Suyuti, at that instant the soul is a playful, mercurial thing, and it has to sit in Berzah till the Day of Judgement. But Necip's soul decided to enter my body instead. I'm sure of this. I'm also very afraid, because this is never mentioned in the Koran. But there's no other way to explain how I fell in love with Kadife so quickly. So the idea of committing suicide over her wasn't mine, either. Do you think it could be true that Necip's soul has taken refuge in my body?'

'If that's what you believe,' said Ka carefully.

'You're the only one I'm telling. Necip told you secrets he never told anyone else. He never once told me that the doubts of atheism had taken root in him. But he could have mentioned it to you. I beg you, tell me the truth. Did Necip ever tell you that he – God forbid – doubted God's existence?'

'It wasn't the sort of doubt you imagine. What he told me was different. It was more like the tears that come from imagining your parents might die one day, and taking pleasure from that sadness. It was about the thoughts that came to him unbidden about what might happen if his beloved God did not exist.'

'Now the same thing's happening to me,' said Fazıl. 'I've no doubt that Necip's soul has planted these thoughts in me.'

'But these uncertainties don't equal atheism.'

'But I'm already siding with the suicide girls,' said Fazıl sadly. 'Just a few minutes ago, I said I was ready to commit suicide myself. I don't want to believe that my dear, departed friend was an atheist. But now I hear the voice of an atheist inside me and this makes me very scared. I don't know if it's the same for you. But you've been to Europe, you've met all the intellectuals and all those alcoholic sleeping-pill addicts who live there. So, please, tell me again, what does it feel like to be an atheist?'

'Well, they certainly don't fantasise endlessly about suicide.'

'I don't fantasise endlessly, but sometimes I do think about it.'

'Why?'

'Because of Kadife. I can't get her out of my mind! I close my eyes and there she is, shimmering before me. When I'm studying, watching television, waiting for evening to fall, everything reminds me of Kadife, even if it has nothing to do with her, and it causes me great pain. This started happening before Necip died. To tell you the truth, it was not Teslime really; it was always Kadife I loved. But, because my friend loved her, I hid my feelings. It was actually Necip who provoked it, by talking endlessly about Kadife. When the soldiers raided our dormitory I knew there was a chance they had already killed him, and, yes, this thought made me glad. And it wasn't because I saw a chance to make my feelings plain but because I thought it served him right for provoking this love in me. Necip is dead now, and I am free, but that only means I love Kadife more than ever. I've been thinking of her since I woke up this morning, and she's consuming my thoughts more and more. It's got so that I can't think about anything else and – dear God – I just don't know what to do.'

Fazıl buried his face in his hands and began to sob. Ka lit a Marlboro as a wave of selfish indifference passed through him. But he still reached out to comfort the boy and, for the longest time, stroked his head.

Saffet, the detective assigned to follow them, had been sitting at the other end of the tea-house, watching them with one eye and the television with the other. Now he rose and walked over to their table. 'Tell this boy to stop crying. I didn't take his identity card to headquarters, I still have it here with me.' When this failed to stem Fazıl's tears, he put his hand in his pocket and produced the ID; Ka reached out and took it. 'Why is he crying?' asked Saffet, half out of professional curiosity and half out of compassion.

'He's in love,' said Ka.

The detective immediately relaxed. Ka watched him leave the tea-house and vanish into the night.

Later, Fazıl asked what he had to do to get Kadife's attention. This was when he mentioned that all of Kars knew Ka was in love with

Kadife's sister İpek. Fazıl's passion seemed so plainly hopeless and impossible that Ka was soon asking himself whether his own love for İpek might not be similarly doomed. As Fazıl's sobs faded away, Ka dolefully repeated the advice İpek had given him: 'Just be yourself.'

'That's not going to be possible while I have two souls inside my body,' said Fazıl. 'Especially with Necip's atheist soul slowly taking over. For years and years I've thought my friends and classmates were wrong to get mixed up in politics, and now suddenly I want to join the Islamists and do something to protest against this military coup. But even there my motivation, I think, is to make Kadife notice me. It scares me to have nothing but Kadife inside my head. It's not just because I don't know her. It's because this proves I'm a typical atheist: I don't care about anything except love and happiness.'

When Fazıl broke into sobs again, Ka wondered if he should tell him that he would be wise to keep his infatuation with Kadife to himself, as he would be in serious trouble if Blue found out about it. If everyone knew about his own relationship with İpek, he reasoned, then it followed that everyone also knew about Kadife's relationship with Blue. And if that were common knowledge, Fazıl's professed ardour would be a direct challenge to the Kars Islamist hierarchy.

'We're poor and insignificant,' said Fazıl, with a strange fury in his voice. 'Our wretched lives have no place in human history. One day all of us living here in Kars today will be dead and gone. No one will remember us; no one will care what happened to us. We'll spend the rest of our days here arguing about what sort of scarf women should wrap around their heads, and no one will care in the slightest as we're eaten up by our own petty, idiotic quarrels. When I see so many people around me leading such stupid lives and then vanishing without a trace, an anger runs through me because I know then nothing really matters in life more than love. And when I think that, my feelings for Kadife become even more unbearable – it hurts to know that my only consolation would be to spend the rest of my life with my arms around Kadife.'

'Yes,' said Ka ruthlessly. 'These are the thoughts of an atheist.'

Fazıl started crying again. Ka either couldn't remember what they discussed after that or else he chose not to write it down, as the notebooks show no record of the end of their conversation. On the television screen a horde of little American children were clowning for the camera, knocking over chairs, then an aquarium was smashed, and finally they were all crouching on the ground to the sound of canned laughter. Like everyone else in the tea-house, Fazıl and Ka forgot their troubles and sat laughing at the antics of the American children.

When Zahide entered the tea-house, Ka and Fazıl were watching a truck weaving stealthily through a forest. Zahide gave Ka a yellow envelope in which Fazıl showed no interest. Ka opened it and read the note inside: it was from İpek. She and Kadife proposed to meet him in twenty minutes at the New Life Pastry Shop. Fortunately, Zahide had learned from Saffet the detective that Ka was in the Lucky Brothers Tea-house.

As Zahide was leaving, Fazıl said, 'Her grandson is in our class. He's mad about gambling. If there's a cock-fight or a dog-fight going on, he'll have a bet on it.'

Ka handed him the student identity card that he'd retrieved from Saffet. 'They want me back at the hotel for supper,' he said as he rose to his feet.

'Are you going to see Kadife?' asked Fazıl, hopelessly. The pity and annoyance he could see on Ka's face made him blush with shame. As the latter left the tea-house, Fazıl shouted, 'I want to kill myself. If you see her, tell her, if she bares her head, I'm going to kill myself. But it won't be because she's bared her head. I'll do it just for the pleasure of killing myself in her honour.'

Having some time to kill before his next appointment, Ka decided to take the back streets. Walking down Canal Street, he saw the tea-house where he'd written 'Dream Streets' that morning. Only when he went inside did he realise that he was not destined to write his next poem in the same smoky, half-empty tea-house, so he strode straight across the room and out of the back door. He walked into the snow-covered courtyard, stepped over the low wall he could hardly see now that it was dark, and passed the same barking dog on his way down the three steps into the basement.

A weak lamp illuminated the interior. Mixed with the smell of coal and the stench of old bedding there were now also raki fumes. He could see several silhouettes huddled around the humming stove. When he saw that it was the hook-nosed MİT agent drinking raki with the tubercular Georgian woman and her husband, he wasn't at all surprised. Nor did they seem surprised to see Ka. He noticed that the woman was wearing a fashionable red hat. She offered him hard-boiled eggs with pitta bread, and her husband poured him a glass of raki. While Ka was still peeling his egg, the hook-nosed MİT agent told him that this furnace room was not merely the warmest place in Kars – it was Heaven itself.

The poem Ka wrote during the ensuing silence, without a single pause or missing word, he would later call 'Heaven'. If he placed it on the 'Imagination' axis of the snowflake, far from the centre, right at the top, this was not to suggest that Heaven was the future of which we dream: for Ka, Heaven was the place where you kept alive the dreams of your memories. Recalling this poem years later, he would summon, one by one, a string of recollections: the summer holidays of his childhood, the days he'd stayed home from school, the times he and his sister had gone into their parents' bed, various drawings he'd done as a child, and the time he went on a date with a girl he'd met at a school party and dared to kiss her.

As he walked to the New Life Pastry Shop, his mind was full of İpek. When he arrived, she and Kadife were already there. İpek looked so beautiful, and Ka felt such happiness at the sight of her that tears came to his eyes (although it's possible that his reaction might have had something to do with the raki he'd just drunk on an empty stomach). To sit at a table with two lovely women didn't just make him happy. It made him proud: he thought of those worn-out Turkish shopkeepers in Frankfurt who smiled and waved at him every morning and evening, and imagined what they would think if they saw him now with these two women. Today he had no audience; no one else was here apart from the old waiter who'd been working when the director of the Education Institute had been assassinated. But even as he sat in the New Life Pastry Shop with İpek and Kadife, Ka thought of this scene like a photograph, taken from outside. It showed him sitting at a table with two beautiful women – never mind that one of them had her head hidden inside a scarf.

Those two women were as agitated as Ka was calm. After he had explained that Fazıl had given him a full report of the meeting at the Hotel Asia, İpek came right to the point.

'Blue left the meeting in a fury. And Kadife now regrets what she said there. We sent Zahide to his hiding-place, but he wasn't there. We can't find Blue anywhere.' She had the tone of an eldest daughter trying to help a sister in trouble, but soon it was clear that she, too, was distressed.

'If you find him, what are you going to ask of him?'

'We want to be sure they haven't caught him; above all, we need to know he's still alive,' said İpek. She glanced at Kadife, who looked as if she were about to burst into tears. 'So find him and ask him if he has anything he wants to say to us. Tell him that Kadife's ready to do whatever he asks.'

'You know Kars a lot better than I do.'

'It's dark now and we're just two women,' said İpek. 'You've learned your way around the city by now. See what you can find out at the Man in the Moon and the Divine Light tea-houses – that's where the religious high-school boys and the Islamist students go. They're both swarming with undercover police right now, and they're terrible gossips. If something bad's happened to Blue, they're sure to be talking about it.'

Kadife had taken out her handkerchief and was now blowing her nose. Ka thought she was still on the verge of tears.

'Bring us news of Blue,' said İpek. 'If we stay here any longer, our father will begin to worry. He's expecting you for supper.'

'Don't forget to check out the tea-houses on Bayrampaşa Avenue!' said Kadife as she rose from her chair. Her voice was about to crack.

It seemed to Ka that both women were scared witless and fast losing hope. He was uneasy leaving them in this state, so he walked them halfway back to the Snow Palace Hotel. Fearful as he was of losing İpek, the knowledge of being their accomplice, helping them do something behind their father's back, bound him to them both. As they walked, he imagined one day when he and İpek would be in Frankfurt and Kadife would come to visit, and the three of them would weave in and out of the cafés on Berliner Avenue, stopping from time to time to gaze at a shop window.

But soon he began to doubt he'd be able to accomplish the mission they had set him. He had no trouble finding the Man in the Moon Tea-house, a place so ordinary and uninspiring that Ka soon forgot why he was there. For the longest time he sat alone watching television. There were a few men there who seemed young enough to be students, but, although he tried to initiate a conversation with a few remarks about the football match on the screen, none of them responded. Ka's next move was to take out his cigarettes, ready to offer them to anyone who might approach him; he even went so far as to put his lighter on the table. However, when he realised that no one, not even the cross-eyed man at the counter, was going to talk to him, he went next door to the Divine Light, where he found a handful of youths watching the same football match in black and white. Had he not gone over to the wall to look at the newspaper clippings and the schedule of all Karsspor matches to be played that season, he would not have remembered that this was the tea-house where, only yesterday, he and Necip had discussed God's existence and the meaning of life. Looking again at the doggerel someone had scribbled on the Karsspor poster, and seeing that another poet had added a few more lines since yesterday, he took out his notebook and began to transcribe them:

> So it's settled: our mother's not coming back from Heaven,
> Never again will we know her embrace,
> But no matter how many beatings she suffers at our father's hand,
> She'll still keep warming our hearts and breathing life into
>   our souls,
> Because that's our fate,
> And the shit we're sinking into smells so bad it makes even
>   the city of Kars look like Heaven.

'Are you writing a poem?' asked the boy at the counter.

'Congratulations,' said Ka. 'Tell me, do you know how to read writing upside down?'

'No, brother, I can't even read when it's the right way up. I ran away from school. So I never managed to crack the code. But that's all in the past now.'

'Who wrote this new poem on the wall here?'

'Half the boys who used to come here are poets.'

'Why aren't they here today?'

'The soldiers rounded them all up. Some are locked up now, and the rest are in hiding. Ask those people over there if you want. They're undercover agents, so they should know.' The boy pointed towards two young men in the corner who were feverishly debating the football match.

But, rather than approaching them to ask about the missing poets, Ka headed for the door. He was glad to see that the snow had started falling again. He was sure he'd find no clues to Blue's whereabouts in the tea-houses of Bayrampaşa Avenue. Immersed as he was in the dusky melancholy that had started to descend over the city, he still felt happy. A long procession of images paraded before his eyes as he awaited his next poem: a waking dream of ugly, unadorned concrete buildings, car parks buried in snow, tea-houses, barbers' and grocers', all hidden behind their icy windows, the courtyards in which dogs had been barking in unison since the days of the Russians, the shops selling spare parts for tractors alongside horse-drawn-carriage supplies and cheese. He was seized by the certainty that every last little detail he saw – the banners for the Motherland Party, the tightly drawn curtains behind tiny windows, the slip of paper someone had taped to the icy shopfront of the Knowledge Pharmacy months earlier to announce that the 'shot for Japanese influenza' had finally arrived, the yellow anti-suicide poster – would stay with him for the rest of his life. There arose from these minor items a vision of extraordinary power: convinced that 'everything on earth was interconnected, that I, too, am inextricably linked to this deep and beautiful world', he concluded that another poem was on its way, so he stepped into one of the tea-houses on Atatürk Avenue. But the poem never arrived.

33

A Godless Man in Kars

The Fear of Being Shot

No sooner had Ka left the tea-house for the snow-covered pavement than he came face to face with Muhtar. The latter had the absent-minded look of a man on a mission. When he first saw Ka through the swarm of giant snowflakes, he didn't seem to recognise him, and for a moment Ka was tempted to run away. Then they both rushed forward at once to embrace like long-lost friends.

'Did you pass my message on to İpek?'

'Yes.'

'What did she say? Come, let's sit down in that tea-house over there and you can tell me.' In spite of the coup, the beating at the police station and the cancelled election, Muhtar did not seem at all downcast. 'So why do you suppose they didn't arrest me? Because when the snow melts, and the roads open, and the soldiers are sent back to their barracks, they'll set a new date for the elections – that's why! Make sure you tell İpek,' he said once they were seated.

Ka assured him that he would pass on the message. Then he asked if there was any news of Blue.

'I'm the one who first summoned him to Kars. In the beginning, he always stayed with me,' Muhtar told him proudly. 'But after the Istanbul press branded him a terrorist, he didn't want to put the party in a difficult position, so now when he comes here, he never gets in touch. I'm always the last to know what he's up to. What did İpek say when you passed on my message?'

Ka told Muhtar that İpek had not seemed particularly impressed by his proposal that they remarry.

But Muhtar replied that his ex-wife was an especially sensitive, refined and understanding woman; he made the point as though disclosing precious information. He went on to reiterate his regret for having treated her so poorly during a difficult crisis in his life. 'When you get back to Istanbul, you'll take the poems I gave you and deliver them by hand to Fahir, won't you?' he then asked.

When Ka had given his word, he rearranged his expression to take on the air of a sad and tender-hearted uncle. Ka's embarrassment was already giving way to something halfway between pity and revulsion when Muhtar produced a newspaper from his pocket.

'If I were you, I wouldn't be wandering the streets so casually,' Muhtar said pleasantly.

Ka grabbed the next day's edition of the *Border City Gazette*, on which the ink wasn't yet dry. He scanned the headlines: 'Theatrical Revolutionaries Take the City by Storm', 'Happy Days Return to Kars', 'Elections Postponed', 'Citizens Applaud the Revolution' . . . Then he turned his attention to the article that Muhtar indicated:

A GODLESS MAN IN KARS
QUESTIONS ASKED ABOUT Ka,
THE SO-CALLED POET

WHY DID HE CHOOSE TO VISIT OUR CITY
IN SUCH TROUBLED TIMES?

Yesterday we introduced the so-called poet to the people of Kars. Today we report the suspicions he has aroused in our readers.

We have been hearing many rumours about the so-called poet who came close to ruining yesterday's joyous performance by the Sunay Zaim Players when he strode on to the stage halfway through the celebrations of Atatürk and the Republic and robbed the audience of their happiness and their peace of mind by bombarding their ears with a joyless, meaningless poem. Although the people of Kars once lived side by side in happy harmony, in recent years outside forces have turned brother against brother, with disputes between the Islamists and the secularists, the Kurds, the Turks and the Azeris driving us asunder for specious reasons and reawakening old accusations about the Armenian massacre that should have been buried long ago. So it is only natural that the people of Kars wonder whether this suspicious character, who fled Turkey many years ago and now lives in Germany, has chosen to grace us with his company because he is some sort of spy. Can it be true that his efforts to provoke an incident at our religious high school resulted in his making the following statement to the youths who engaged him in a conversation two days ago: 'I am an atheist. I don't believe in God, but that doesn't mean I'd commit suicide, because after all God – *God forbid* – doesn't exist.' Can these be his exact words? And when he said that 'an intellectual's job is to speak against holiness', was he denying God's existence, and, if so, was he expressing European views on freedom of thought? Just because Germany is bankrolling you, that doesn't mean you have the right to trample on our beliefs! Is it because you are ashamed of being a Turk that you hide your true name behind the fake, foreign, counterfeit name of Ka? Many readers have telephoned our offices to express their regret about this godless imitation European's decision to stir up dissent in our city in these troubled times, and they have voiced particular concern about the way in which he has wandered through the shanty towns, knocking on the doors of the most wretched dwellings to incite rebellion against our state, and indeed even in our own presence vainly attempted to stick out his tongue at our country, and even at the great Atatürk, father of our Republic. The youth of Kars knows how to deal with blasphemers who deny God and the Prophet Mohammed! (SAS)

'When I passed by their office twenty minutes ago, Serdar's two sons had only just started printing this edition,' said Muhtar, who, far from commiserating with Ka, seemed cheerful, as if having just introduced a fun new topic.

Reading the article more carefully a second time, Ka felt very much alone.

Long ago, when he'd first dreamed of a glittering literary future, he had foreseen that the modernist innovations he would bring to Turkish poetry (the very concept now seemed excessively nationalist) would provoke harsh criticism and personal attacks. Still, he'd assumed that notoriety would at least confer a certain aura. Although his fame in the years since had been modest, he had never been subject to harsh criticism, and it hurt him now to be referred to as a 'so-called' poet.

After warning him not to wander the streets 'like a moving target', Muhtar left him alone, and Ka was overtaken by the fear that he could be shot at any moment. He left the tea-house and wandered through the snow, lost in thought; the giant snowflakes that floated down from the heavens were moving so fast they looked bewitched. In his youth, Ka had firmly believed that there could be no higher honour than to die for an intellectual, political cause, or for what he had written. By his thirties, he'd seen too many of his friends and ex-classmates tortured for the sake of foolish, even malign principles; and then there were those shot dead in attempts to rob a bank, or those who'd made bombs that had exploded in their hands. Seeing the havoc of his lofty ideas put into action, Ka deliberately distanced himself from them. And his years of exile in Germany for political beliefs he no longer held had finally severed the connection between politics and self-sacrifice. Whenever he picked up a Turkish paper in Germany and read that this or that columnist had been shot for polit-ical reasons, 'most probably' by political Islamists, he felt some respect for the victim as a dead man, but no particular admiration for him as a murdered writer.

On the corner of Halitpaşa Avenue and Kâzım Karabekir Avenue, Ka saw a pipe protruding from an icy hole in a windowless wall and imagined it was the barrel of a gun aimed straight at him. In his mind's eye he saw himself dying on the snow-covered pavement. What would they say about him in the Istanbul papers? Most likely the governor's office or the local branch of MİT would want to downplay the political dimension; and if the Istanbul press didn't pick up on his having been a poet, they might not cover the incident at all. Even if his friends in the poetry world and at the *Republican* did everything in their power to publicise the political angle (and who would write that article? Fahir? Orhan?), it would serve only to diminish his literary significance. Similarly, if someone succeeded in placing a piece that established him as an important poet, his death would be reported on the arts pages, where no one would read of it. Had there really been a German journalist called Hans Hansen, and had Ka really been his friend, the *Frankfurter Rundschau* might have run a story about his murder, but still it would have been the only Western newspaper to do so. Ka took some consolation in imagining that his poems might be translated into German and published in *Akzent*, but it was still perfectly clear to him that, should this article in the *Border City Gazette* prove to be the death of him, the published translations would mean nothing. Finally, what frightened him most was the thought of dying just at the dawn of hope that he might live happily ever after in Frankfurt with İpek.

The many writers killed in recent years by Islamist bullets paraded before his eyes: first the old imam-turned-atheist who had tried to point out 'inconsistencies' in the Koran (they'd shot him from behind, in the head); then the righteous columnist whose love of positivism had led him to refer in a number of articles to girls wearing headscarves as 'cockroaches' (they strafed him and his chauffeur one morning as they drove to work); and finally there was the determined investigative journalist who had tenaciously sought to uncover the links between the Turkish Islamist movement and Iran (when he turned the key, he and his car were blown into the sky). Even as he recalled these victims with tender sorrow, he knew they'd been naïve. As a rule, the Istanbul press, like the Western press, had little interest in these fervent columnists, and even less in journalists who got shot in the head for similar reasons in a back street of some remote Anatolian city. But Ka reserved his bile for a society that so easily forgot its writers and poets: for this reason, he thought the smartest thing to do was to retreat into a corner and try to find some happiness.

Arriving at the offices of the *Border City Gazette* on Faikbey Avenue, Ka looked up to see the next day's edition taped to the back of the recently de-iced window. He read the article about himself again and then went inside. The elder of Serdar Bey's two busy sons was bundling a pile of freshly printed papers with nylon twine. Ka took off his hat so that they could see who he was and brushed off the snow sticking to the shoulders of his coat.

'My father's not here!' This was the younger son, who had just entered from the other room with the cloth he'd been using to polish the press. 'Would you like some tea?'

'Who wrote the article about me in tomorrow's edition?'

'Is there an article about you in there?' said the younger son, raising his eyebrows.

'Yes, there is,' said the elder son, giving him a warm and happy smile. He had the same thick lips as his brother. 'My father wrote the whole edition today.'

'If you distribute this paper tomorrow morning . . .' said Ka. He paused to think. 'It will be bad for me.'

'Why?' asked the elder son. He had a soft, kind face and pure, innocent eyes.

By now, Ka had seen that if he talked to them in a gentle, friendly voice and kept his questions short, the way you do with children, he could find out quite a bit from them. So the brothers had soon informed him that only three people had purchased the paper so far: Muhtar Bey, a child who'd been sent from the branch headquarters of the Motherland Party, and the retired literature teacher Nuriye Hanım, who made a habit of stopping by every evening. Normally they would have dispatched a bundle of papers to Istanbul and Ankara, but because the roads were closed these would have to wait with today's edition until the snow began to melt. The sons would be distributing the rest of the papers tomorrow morning and, if their father wished it, of course, they could print a new edition for that day. Their father, they told Ka, had only just left the office, telling them not to expect him back in time for supper. Ka told them he wouldn't stay for tea; he bought a copy of the paper and went out into the murderous Kars night.

The boys' untroubled innocence had calmed him somewhat. As he walked among the slowly falling snowflakes, he began to feel ashamed – had he been wrong to take such fright? But in another corner of his mind, he knew he would share the fate of so many other luckless writers who had died of multiple gunshot wounds after facing similar dilemmas and choosing, either out of pride or courage, to do nothing, or the many who, assuming that any package from a stranger had to be an ardent fan's gift of Turkish delight, had died eagerly tearing open what would turn out to be a mail bomb. For example, the poet Nurettin, had admired all things European but took little interest in politics until the day a radical Islamist newspaper unearthed something he'd written years earlier – an essay on art and religion – and distorted it to charge that he'd 'insulted our faith'. Afraid of being branded a coward, Nurettin dusted off his old ideas and passionately reasserted them; the army-backed secular press warmed to his fine Kemalist words and inflated their importance to make him seem their lifelong hero. Then, one morning, a device in a plastic bag hanging from the front tyre of his car blew him into so many pieces that his ostentatious throng of mourners had to march behind an empty coffin. There was the small-town version, too – the materialist doctors, and the old leftist journalists of the regional papers who, when faced with similar indictments, responded with fiery anti-religious rhetoric, just so 'no one can say we are scared'. Some perhaps even entertained vain hopes of attracting world-wide attention, 'like Salman Rushdie'; but the only ones listening were the angry young fanatics in their own neighbourhoods, and they had no time for the fancy bomb plots of their colleagues in the cities, or even for guns. As Ka knew only too well from the small, lifeless news items he'd seen when poring over the back pages of the Turkish newspapers in Frankfurt's city library, they preferred to knife the godless in dark alleyways or strangle them with their bare hands.

Ka was still trying to figure out how to save both his skin and his pride if the *Border City Gazette* gave him a chance to reply ('I'm an atheist but I've never insulted the Prophet'? 'I'm not a believer but I'd never dream of disrespecting the faith'?) when suddenly he heard someone tramping through the snow behind him. A chill went down his spine as he turned around to see it was the bus company manager he'd met the day before at the same hour at His Excellency Sheikh Saadettin's lodge. It occurred to him that this man could testify that he wasn't an atheist; immediately the thought embarrassed him.

He continued dragging his feet down Atatürk Avenue, slowing to negotiate the icy street corners and pausing from time to time to admire the huge snowflakes, the endless repetition of an ordinary miracle. In later years, he would often think back to the beautiful scenes he had witnessed while wandering the city's snow-covered streets (as three children pulled a sledge up a narrow street, the windows of the Palace of Light Photographer's Shop reflected the green light of Kars' only traffic signal) and wondered why it was that he carried these sad postcard memories with him wherever he went.

He saw an army patrol truck and two soldiers guarding the door to the old tailor's shop that Sunay was using as his base of operations. Ka told the soldiers huddled at the threshold trying to dodge the snow that he wanted to contact Sunay, but they treated him like a lowly peasant who'd come in from the outlying villages to make a petition to the chief of staff. Ka had been hoping that Sunay might be able to prevent the newspaper from being distributed.

If we are to make sense of the fury that was soon to overtake him, it's important to understand the sting of this rebuff. His first thought was to run off into the snow and seek refuge in the hotel, but before even reaching the corner he turned left into the Unity Café. Here he took a table between the wall and the stove and wrote the poem he would call 'To Be Shot and Killed'. As he would later relate in his notes, it was an expression of 'pure fear', so he placed it between the axes of 'Memory' and 'Imagination' on the six-pronged snowflake and humbly turned his back on its prophecy.

As soon as the poem was finished, Ka left the Unity Café. It was twenty past seven when he reached the Snow Palace Hotel. Stretched out on his bed, he watched the snowflakes floating through the haloes of the streetlamp and the pink letter 'K' pulsating in the window across the way, and he tried to quell his growing panic by conjuring happy visions of life with İpek in Frankfurt. Ten minutes later, he was overcome by a desire to see her. He went downstairs to find the entire family seated around the supper table with that evening's guest, and his heart leaped to see İpek's hair shimmering in the haze of heat above the bowl of soup that Zahide had just set before her. When İpek beckoned him to take the place next to her, Ka was proud to see that everyone at the table knew they were in love. Across the table he saw Serdar Bey, the proprietor of the *Border City Gazette*.

As Serdar Bey extended his hand, his smile was so friendly that Ka began to doubt what his own eyes had read in the newspaper folded in his pocket. After serving himself soup, he reached under the table and put his hand on İpek's lap; he brought his head closer to hers, smelling her scent and savouring her presence, and then whispered that he was sorry to have no news of Blue for her. He had hardly finished speaking when he came eye to eye with Kadife, sitting next to Serdar Bey. It amazed and infuriated him to realise that İpek had already silently communicated his news to her.

Although his mind was full of Serdar Bey, Ka managed to contain his feelings and give his attention to Turgut Bey, who was complaining that the meeting at the Hotel Asia had succeeded only in stirring things up. He then added that the police knew all about it. 'But I'm not at all sorry to have taken part in this historic occasion,' he said. 'I'm glad I got to see with my own eyes how low the level of political understanding has sunk – young and old alike, they're hopeless. I went to this meeting to protest against the coup, but now I think the army is right to want to keep them out of politics. They're the dregs of society, the most wretched, muddled, brainless people in the city. I'm glad the army couldn't stand by and let us abandon our future to these shameless looters. I'll say this again, Kadife, before meddling with national politics, consider your actions carefully.'

When Ka took out his copy of the *Border City Gazette*, they'd been sitting at the table for twenty minutes, and, even with the television blaring in the background, the room seemed quiet.

'I was going to mention it myself,' said Serdar Bey. 'But I couldn't make up my mind; I thought you might take it the wrong way.'

'Serdar, Serdar, who gave you the order this time?' said Turgut Bey. 'Ka, you're not being fair to our guest. Give it to him so he can read it and see what a bad thing he has done.'

'First, let me make it clear that I don't believe a single word I wrote,' said Serdar Bey as he took the newspaper from Ka. 'If you thought I believed it, you'd break my heart. Please realise that it's nothing personal. Please, Turgut Bey, help me explain why it is that a journalist in Kars might be commanded to write such things.'

'Serdar's always under orders to sling mud at someone,' Turgut Bey explained. 'So, let's hear this article.'

'I don't believe a single word,' Serdar Bey repeated proudly. 'Our readers won't believe it, either. That's why you have nothing to fear.' He read out his article in a sarcastic voice, pausing here and there for dramatic effect. 'As you see, there's nothing to fear!' he said with a smile.

'Are you an atheist?' Turgut Bey asked Ka.

'That's not the point, Father,' said İpek with annoyance. 'If this paper gets distributed, they'll shoot him in the street tomorrow.'

'Nonsense,' said Serdar Bey. 'Madam, I assure you, you have nothing to fear. The soldiers have rounded up all the radical Islamists and reactionaries in town.' He turned to Ka. 'I can see in your eyes that you haven't taken offence, and you know how much I respect your work – and the esteem in which I hold you as a human being. Please don't do me the injustice of holding me to European standards that were never designed for us. Let me tell you what happens to fools who wander around Kars pretending to be Europeans – and Turgut Bey knows this as well as I do. Three days, that's all it takes, three days and they're dead, gone, shot, forgotten. The Eastern Anatolian press is in desperate trouble. Our average Kars citizen doesn't bother to read the paper. Almost all our subscribers are government offices. So, of course, we're going to run the sort of news our subscribers want to read. All over the world – even in America – newspapers tailor the news to their readers' tastes. And if your readers want nothing but lies from you, who in the world is going to sell papers that tell the truth? If the truth could raise my paper's circulation, why wouldn't I write the truth? Anyway, the police don't let me print the truth, either. In Istanbul and Ankara we have a hundred and fifty readers with Kars connections. To please them, we're always bragging about how rich and successful they've become there; we exaggerate everything, because, if we don't, they won't renew their subscriptions. And you know what, they even come to believe the lies we print about them. But that's another matter.' He let out a laugh.

'And who ordered you to print this article? Go on, tell him,' said Turgut Bey.

'My dear sir! As you know only too well, the first principle of Western journalism is to protect your sources.'

'My girls have grown very fond of our guest here,' said Turgut Bey. 'If you distribute this paper tomorrow, they'll never forgive you. If some crazed fundamentalist shoots him, won't you feel responsible?'

'Are you that afraid?' Serdar smiled as he turned to Ka. 'If you're that afraid, then stay off the streets tomorrow.'

'It would be better that the paper rather than Ka remains unseen,' said Turgut Bey. 'Just don't circulate this edition.'

'That would offend my subscribers.'

'All right then,' said Turgut Bey. He'd had an inspiration. 'Whoever's ordered a copy, let him have it. As for the others, I suggest you remove the offending article and print a new edition.'

İpek and Kadife agreed this was the best solution.

'I'm thrilled to see my paper taken so seriously,' said Serdar Bey. 'But who's going to pay for this new print run? That's the next thing you need to tell me.'

'My father will take you and your sons out to dinner at the Green Pastures Restaurant,' said İpek.

'I accept, if you come, too,' said Serdar Bey. 'But let's wait until the roads open and we can be rid of this bunch of actors! Kadife must come as well. Kadife Hanım, I wonder if you could help me with the new article to replace the one we're taking out. If you could give me a quote about this coup, this *coup de théâtre*, I'm sure our readers would be very pleased.'

'No, she can't. That's out of the question,' said Turgut Bey. 'Don't you know my daughter at all?'

'Kadife Hanım, could you tell me if you think the Kars suicide rate is likely to decline in the wake of our theatre coup? I'm sure our readers would like your views on this – especially as they know you were opposed to these Muslim girl suicides.'

'I'm not against these suicides any more!'

'But doesn't that make you an atheist?' asked Serdar Bey. Though he may have hoped this would set them off on a fresh discussion, he was sober enough to see that everyone at the table was glaring at him, and so he relented. 'All right, then, I promise. I won't circulate this edition.'

'Are you going to print a new one?'

'As soon as I leave this table, before I go home.'

'We'd like to thank you, then,' said İpek.

A long, strange silence followed. Ka found it very soothing: for the first time in years, he felt part of a family. In spite of the trials and responsibilities of what was called 'family', he saw now the joys of its unyielding togetherness, and was sorry not to have known more of it in his life. Could he find lasting happiness with İpek? But it wasn't happiness he was after – this was very clear to him following his third glass of raki; he would even go so far as to say that he preferred to be unhappy. The important thing was to share the hopelessness, to create a little nest in which two people could live together, keeping the rest of the world at bay. He now thought that he and İpek could create such a space, just by making love for months on end. To sit at a table with these two women, knowing that he'd made love to one of them only that afternoon, to see the softness of their complexions, to know that he would not be lonely tonight . . . As sexual bliss beckoned, he allowed himself to believe the paper would not be circulated, and his spirits soared.

His happiness took the edge off the stories and rumours he then heard. They lacked the thud of bad news; it was more like listening to the chilling lines of an ancient epic. One of the children working in the kitchen had told Zahide that many detainees had been taken to the football stadium. With the goalposts only half visible, half buried in snow, most had been kept outside all day in the hope that they would fall ill or perhaps even die; it was said a few of them had been taken into the changing rooms and pumped full of bullets as an example to the others. There were also eyewitness reports, perhaps exaggerated, about the terror Z Demirkol and his friends had been visiting on the city throughout the day. They'd raided the Mesopotamia Association, founded by a number of Kurdish nationalist youths to promote 'folklore and literature'. None of the members happened to be there at the time, so instead they'd taken the old man who made the tea in the office – someone who was utterly indifferent to politics – and beaten him severely. Then there were the three men – two of them were barbers, the third unemployed – who'd been implicated in an incident six months earlier in which parties unknown had poured coloured sewer water over the statue of Atatürk that stood outside the Atatürk Work Plant. Although these men had been investigated over the crime, they'd never been put behind bars. But, after taking beatings that had gone on all night, they'd admitted responsibility for a number of other anti-Atatürk incidents in the city: taking a hammer to the nose of the statue that stood in the garden of the Trade and Industry Lycée, writing ugly remarks on the poster hanging on the wall at the Gang of Fifteen Café, entering into a conspiracy to use a hatchet to destroy the statue standing outside the government offices. Just after the coup had started, Z Demirkol and his cohorts had shot and killed one of the two Kurdish boys they'd caught writing slogans on the walls of Halitpaşa Avenue. After seizing another boy, they'd beaten him until he'd fainted. Then there was the young unemployed boy they'd taken to the religious high school so that he could clean the graffiti off its walls. When he'd tried to escape, they'd shot him in the legs. Thanks to various informers, all those who'd been saying derogatory things about the soldiers and the actors and spreading groundless rumours about them in the city's tea-houses had been rounded up. But, as was always the case in murderous times like these, there were still plenty of rumours and exaggerations doing the rounds, from the Kurdish youths who'd died when bombs had exploded in their hands, to the headscarf girls who'd killed themselves to protest against the coup, to the truck laden with dynamite that they'd stopped as it approached İnönü Police Station.

Although Ka suddenly started paying attention when they mentioned the truck carrying explosives (he'd heard someone else discussing this suicide-bomb attack earlier), he did little else that night but enjoy every moment he spent sitting peacefully at İpek's side.

Much later, when Serdar Bey rose to leave, and Turgut Bey and his daughters stood to bid him farewell before going to their rooms, it crossed Ka's mind to ask İpek to join him in his room. But he was afraid of the shadow that might fall over his happiness if she refused, so he went upstairs without even hinting at what he desired.

34

Kadife Would Never Agree to It

The Mediator

Ka stood at his window smoking a cigarette. It had stopped snowing, and finally, as the pale streetlamps cast their ghostly glow over the empty, snow-covered courtyard, the stillness of the scene brought him peace. But the peace he felt had more to do with love than with the beauty of the snow. He was so happy that he could also admit that his peace derived in part from the easy sense of superiority he possessed from knowing he was from Istanbul and Frankfurt.

There was a knock at the door. When he opened it, Ka was astonished to see it was İpek.

'I can't stop thinking about you. I can't sleep,' she said as she stepped inside.

Ka knew at once that they would make love till morning, even as Turgut Bey slept under the same roof. It was the most sublime surprise to wrap his arms around İpek without first enduring the agony of waiting. Their long night of lovemaking took Ka to a place beyond the outer reaches of happiness, or at least of what he had thought happiness to be. He was outside time, impervious to passion; his only regret was that it had taken him a lifetime to discover this paradise. He was more at peace than he ever had been before. He forgot the sexual fantasies that were stored at the back of his mind, the pornographic images from magazines. As he and İpek made love, he heard music playing inside him, music he'd never heard before, never even imagined, and by obeying its harmonies he found his way forward. From time to time he fell asleep and dreamed of summer holidays bathed in heavenly light; he was running free, he was immortal; his plane was about to fall out of the sky but he was eating an apple, an apple he would never finish, an apple that would last for all time. Then he would awake to the warm apple aroma of İpek's skin. Guided by moonlight and the faint yellow glow of the streetlamps, he would press his eyes against İpek's and try to see into them. When he saw that she was awake and silently watching him, it seemed to him that they were like two whales basking side by side in shallow water. It was only then that he realised they were holding hands.

At just such a moment, when they had awoken to find themselves gazing into each other's eyes, İpek said, 'I'm going to speak to my father. I'm going with you to Germany.'

Ka couldn't sleep for a long time after that. Instead, he watched his life play before him like a happy film.

Somewhere in the city, there was an explosion. It was strong enough to shake the bed, the room and the hotel. They heard distant machine-gun fire. It was muffled by the snow that still covered Kars. They embraced each other and waited in silence.

The next time they awoke, the gun-battle was over. Twice Ka rose from the warm bed and smoked a cigarette as the icy air coming through the open window cooled his perspiring body. No poems came to his mind. He was happier than he'd ever been.

When he was awoken in the morning by a knock at the door, İpek was no longer lying beside him in bed. He had no idea what time it was, or what he and İpek had talked about, or what time the gun-shots had ended.

It was Cavit, the receptionist. He'd come to tell Ka that an officer had appeared at the front desk with an invitation from Sunay Zaim: Ka was to report to the actor's headquarters at once; the officer was downstairs, waiting to escort him. Ka took his time shaving.

The empty streets of Kars looked more beautiful, more enchanted, than they had the previous morning. On Atatürk Avenue, he saw a house with broken windows, a shattered door and a front wall riddled with bullet holes.

At the tailor's shop, Sunay told him there'd been an attempted suicide-bomb attack. 'The poor man got his houses mixed up, and instead of coming here he attacked a building farther up the hill,' he explained. 'He blew himself into so many pieces we don't even know yet whether he died for Islam or the PKK.'

Ka was struck by the childish gravity of a famous actor taking himself so seriously. Freshly shaved, he looked clean, pure-hearted, bursting with energy.

'We've captured Blue,' he said. He looked straight into Ka's eyes.

Ka made a valiant effort to conceal his joy at this news, but Sunay wasn't fooled.

'He's an evil man,' he said. 'He's definitely the mastermind behind the assassination of the director of the Education Institute. He goes around telling everyone that he's against suicide while he's busy turning poor, brainless teenagers into suicide bombers. MİT is not in any doubt that he's come here with enough explosives to send the entire city of Kars up in smoke. On the night of the revolution, he managed to lose the men we'd put on his tail. No one had any idea where he was hiding. Of course, you know all about that ridiculous meeting yesterday evening at the Hotel Asia.'

It was as if they were on stage, playing a scene together, so Ka gave Sunay an affected, theatrical nod.

'My aim in life is not to punish these heinous creatures, these reactionaries and terrorists in our midst,' said Sunay. 'There's a play I've been longing to do for years; that's the real reason I'm here. There's an English writer who goes by the name of Thomas Kyd. They say Shakespeare stole *Hamlet* from him. I've discovered another injustice, too, a forgotten play by Kyd called *The Spanish Tragedy*. It's a blood feud, a tragedy that ends in suicide. Funda and I have been waiting for an opportunity like this for fifteen years.'

When Funda Eser entered the room, brandishing a long, elegant cigarette-holder, Ka greeted her with an exaggerated bow which obviously pleased her. With no encouragement from Ka, the two actors now launched into a discussion of the play.

'We want our people to enjoy this play, to be uplifted by it, and, towards this end, I've simplified the plot,' said Sunay. 'We plan to perform it tomorrow at the National Theatre, in front of a live audience, and, of course, it will go out on television at the same time so that the whole city can see it.'

'I'd love to see it, too,' said Ka.

'We want Kadife to be in it. Funda will play her evil-hearted rival. Kadife will appear on stage wearing a headscarf. Then, in defiance of the ludicrous customs that have given rise to the blood feud, she'll bare her head for all to see.' With a broad, theatrical flourish, Sunay took hold of an imaginary scarf around his head and made as if to rip it off.

'This is bound to cause more trouble!' said Ka.

'Don't worry – there won't be any trouble. Don't forget, the army's in charge now.'

'And anyway, Kadife would never agree to it,' continued Ka.

'We know that Kadife is in love with Blue,' said Sunay. 'If Kadife bares her head, I can have her Blue released at once. They can run off together to some foreign land and live happily ever after.'

Funda Eser's face radiated the compassion of a good-hearted aunt from a nice Turkish melodrama who smiles as she watches the two lovers departing to find happiness in the great beyond. For a moment, Ka imagined his own love affair with İpek bringing the same smile to her lips.

'I still don't think Kadife would agree to bare her head on live TV,' said Ka.

'The situation is such that you would seem to us to be the only one who might be able to talk her into it,' said Sunay. 'To bargain with us is to bargain with the biggest devil in creation. She knows that you have a great deal of time for the headscarf girls. And you're in love with her elder sister.'

'It's not just Kadife. You'd also have to persuade Blue. But Kadife must be approached first,' said Ka, still smarting from the brutal directness of Sunay's last remark.

'You can do it any which way you like,' said Sunay. 'I'll give you whatever authorisation proves necessary, and your very own army truck. You have permission to negotiate in my name.'

There was silence, and Sunay picked up on Ka's reluctance.

'I don't want to get involved in this,' said Ka eventually.

'And why not?'

'Well, it could be because I'm scared. I'm very happy right now. I don't want to turn myself into a target for the Islamists. When they see her bare her head, those students will think I'm the atheist who arranged the performance. And even if I can manage to escape to Germany, they'll track me down – I'll be walking down a street late one night and someone will shoot me.'

'They'll shoot me first,' said Sunay proudly. 'But I admire your courage in admitting you're afraid. I'm the coward to end all cowards – please believe that. Only the cowards survive in this country. But there's not a coward in the world who doesn't dream of the day when he might find himself capable of great courage – don't you agree?'

'I'm very happy right now,' repeated Ka. 'I have no desire to play the hero. Heroic dreams are the consolation of the unhappy. After all, when people like us say we're being heroic, it usually means we're about to kill each other – or ourselves.'

'Yes,' insisted Sunay, 'but isn't there a small voice somewhere inside reminding you that this happiness of yours is not destined to last very long?'

'Why do you want to scare our guest?' said Funda Eser.

'No happiness lasts very long, that much I know,' said Ka cautiously. 'But I have no desire to do something heroic that will get me killed just because I know how likely it is that I'll be unhappy again at some point in the future.'

'If you don't get involved, they're not going to wait until you're back in Germany to kill you. They'll kill you right here. Have you seen today's paper?'

'Does it say I'm going to die today?' asked Ka with a smile.

Sunay took out the *Border City Gazette*, turned to the back page, and pointed to the article Ka had read the previous evening.

'A godless man in Kars!' read Funda Eser in a booming voice.

'That's from yesterday's first print run,' said Ka evenly. 'In the evening, Serdar Bey decided to correct the inaccuracies in this article and printed up a new edition.'

'No, he was unable to do so. This is the edition that went out this morning. Never take a journalist's promise at face value. But we'll protect you. Those fundamentalists can't do anything against the military, so naturally they'll want to vent their spleen by taking a pot shot at a Western spy.'

'Are you the one who told Serdar to write this piece?' asked Ka.

Raising his eyebrows, pursing his lips, Sunay glared at Ka and played the affronted man of honour, but Ka still recognised him as a politician pulling a fast one.

'If you agree to protect me all the way, I'll be your mediator,' said Ka.

Sunay gave his word and, still in revolutionary mode, threw his arms around Ka, congratulated him and assured him that his two men would never leave his side.

'If necessary, they'll even protect you from yourself!' he boomed.

They sat down to work out the details of Ka's mission, with two fragrant cups of tea to help them along. Funda Eser was all smiles, as

316

if a brilliant, famous actress had just joined the company. She spoke for a time about the power of *The Spanish Tragedy*, but Ka's mind was elsewhere: he was looking at the wondrous white light pouring through the high windows of the tailor's shop.

His dream ended abruptly when, after leaving the shop, he met the two burly, armed guards who'd be protecting him. He'd hoped at least one of them would be an officer or a plainclothes detective with a modicum of sartorial sense. Years before, a famous writer had gone on television to say that Turks were fools and that he didn't believe in Islam. Ka had once seen him with the two bodyguards the government had given him towards the end of his life: they had excellent manners and wore stylish clothes. They insisted on the sort of exaggerated servility Ka thought appropriate towards famous radical writers: not only did they carry the man's bag, they even held the door open for him, and locked arms with him on staircases, to protect him from any fan or enemy who might pass. The soldiers sitting next to Ka in the army truck could not have been more different: they acted like jailers, not protectors.

When Ka walked into the hotel, he felt as happy as he had in the early hours of the morning. However, although he longed to see İpek at once, he dreaded having to keep something from her. He feared she might take it as a betrayal, and, even though it might be small in the scheme of things, he was still worried that it could diminish their love. It would be better all round, he thought, if he could find a way to see Kadife alone first. But then he ran into İpek in the lobby.

'You're even more beautiful than I remembered!' he told her, awestruck. 'Sunay summoned me for a meeting. He wants me to be his mediator.'

'For what?'

'They've caught Blue. It happened yesterday evening,' said Ka. 'Why do you look like that? We're not in any danger. Yes, Kadife will be upset, but in my view it's a relief, believe me.' Very quickly, he repeated what Sunay had told him, explaining the noises they'd heard during the night, the gun-battle, everything. 'Don't worry, I'll take care of everything, no one will come out of this with so much as a bloody nose. We're going to Frankfurt, we're going to be happy. Have you spoken to your father?' She didn't reply, but he carried on regardless, telling her that he was charged to negotiate a deal, and would soon be speaking to Blue. First, though, he had to talk to Kadife.

He registered the extreme concern in İpek's eyes as a sign that she was worried for him, which gladdened his heart.

'I'll send Kadife up to your room in a few minutes,' she said, and drifted away.

When he reached his room, he saw that someone had made the bed. The room in which he had spent the happiest night of his life had changed: the glare from the snow outside gave a new aspect to the bed, the table and the pale curtains; even the silence in the room seemed different. But the smell of their lovemaking lingered, and he could still breathe it in. He lay down on the bed and, gazing up at the ceiling, thought of all the trouble ahead if he couldn't manage to win Kadife's and Blue's cooperation with the plan.

Kadife burst into the room. 'Tell me everything you know about Blue's capture,' she demanded. 'Did they treat him roughly?'

'If they'd roughed him up, they wouldn't be letting me see him,' said Ka. 'They're going to take me over there in a few minutes. They captured him after the hotel meeting; that's all I know.'

Kadife gazed out of the window at the snow-covered avenue below. 'So now you're the one who's happy, and I'm the one who's sad. How things have changed since our meeting in the box room.'

Ka thought back to their meeting in Room 217, where Kadife had pointed a gun at him and made him strip before they left. It was now a sweet, distant memory, and it bound them together.

'That's not the whole story, Kadife,' said Ka. 'Sunay's associates are convinced that Blue had a hand in the assassination of the director of the Education Institute. What's more, it seems that the dossier connecting him to that TV host has also reached Kars.'

'Who are these "associates"?'

'A handful of people from the Kars MİT . . . Plus one or two soldiers who have links to Sunay. But don't think he's completely in their pocket. He has artistic ambitions of his own, too. He's got a proposal for you. This evening he plans to perform a play at the National Theatre, and he wants you to be in it. Don't make a face – listen! There's going to be a live broadcast, too, and all of Kars is going to watch it again. If you're willing to play this part, and if Blue can convince the religious high-school boys to come and watch the play and sit quietly, to be polite and clap at all the right moments, Sunay will have Blue released. Then this whole thing can be forgotten, and we'll all come out of it without so much as a bloody nose. They've asked me to be the go-between.'

'What's the play?'

Ka told her everything he knew about Thomas Kyd and *The Spanish Tragedy*, explaining as well that Sunay had amended the play to make it more relevant. 'In the same way, during their long years of touring Anatolia, they've made Corneille, Shakespeare and Brecht more relevant by adding belly-dances and bawdy songs.'

'And I suppose that I'm the one who gets the blood feud started by being raped on live television.'

'No. You're a proper Spanish lady with a covered head, but then you tire of the blood feud and in a burst of anger you pull off your scarf to become the rebel heroine.'

'To play the rebel heroine in Turkey, you don't pull off your scarf. You put it on.'

'This is just a play, Kadife. And, because it's just a play, it shouldn't be a problem to take off your scarf.'

'I see now what they want from me. But even if it's just a play, I'm still not baring my head.'

'Look, Kadife, the snow's going to melt in two days' time, the roads will open, and the people sitting in jail will pass into the hands of men who know no pity. If that happens, you won't see your Blue again in this lifetime. Have you really thought this through?'

'I'm afraid that if I did think about it, I'd agree to it.'

'Don't forget: you could wear a wig underneath your scarf. Then no one would see your real hair.'

'If I'd wanted to wear a wig, I would have done it a long time ago, like a lot of other women I know. And I'd be back at the institute.'

'This is not a question of sitting outside the institute and trying to save your honour. You'll be doing this to save Blue.'

'Well, let's see if Blue will want me to save him by pulling off my scarf.'

'Of course he will,' said Ka. 'You won't hurt his honour by baring your head. After all, no one even knows you two are involved.'

Ka could tell at once from the fury in her eyes that he had found her weak spot, but then she gave him a strange smile that filled him with fear . . . and jealousy. He was afraid that Kadife was about to tell him something damning about İpek. 'We don't have much time, Kadife,' he said. He could hear that strange note of dread in his own voice. 'I know you're bright enough and sensitive enough to get through all of this with grace. I'm saying this to you as someone

319

who's spent years as a political exile. Listen to me: life's not about principles; it's about happiness.'

'But if you don't have any principles, and if you don't have faith, you can't be happy at all,' said Kadife.

'That's true. But in a brutal country like ours, where human life is "cheap", it's stupid to destroy yourself for the sake of your beliefs. Beliefs? High ideals? Only people in rich countries can enjoy such luxuries.'

'Actually, it's the other way round. In a poor country, people's sole consolation comes from their beliefs.'

Ka wanted to say, 'But the things they believe aren't true,' but he managed to hold his tongue. Instead, he said, 'But you're not one of the poor, Kadife. You're from Istanbul.'

'That's why I do what I believe in. I don't fake things. If I decide to bare my head, I won't go halfway. I'll really do it.'

'All right, then, what would you say to this? What if they give up on the idea of a live audience? What if they just televise it, and that's the only performance that the people of Kars ever see? So, when they get to your moment of fury, all they show is your hand pulling off the scarf. Then they can cut to another woman who looks like you, and we'll simply show her hair swinging free, from the back.'

'That's even more dishonest than wearing a wig,' said Kadife. 'And in the end, when the coup is over, everyone will think I really did bare my head.'

'What's more important – honouring the law of God or worrying what people might say about you? The important thing is, if we do it like that, you won't really have bared your head. But if you are so worried what people will think, it's still not a problem, because once all this nonsense is over, we can make sure everyone knows about the last-minute switch. When it gets around that you were prepared to do all this to save Blue, those boys at the religious high school will be even more in awe of you than they are now.'

'Has it ever occurred to you that when you're trying with all your might to talk someone into something,' said Kadife, her tone suddenly changed, 'you say things you don't believe at all?'

'That can happen. But it's not that way now.'

'But if it were, and you finally managed to convince this person, wouldn't you feel some remorse for having fooled her? I mean, for having left her out on a limb.'

'This is not about leaving you out on a limb, Kadife. It's about your using your head and seeing that this is the only option. Sunay's people are ruthless. If they decide to hang Blue, they won't hesitate. But you're not prepared to let them do that, are you?'

'So let's just say I bared my head in front of everyone – that would be admitting defeat. And what guarantee is there that they'd release Blue after I did it? Why should I believe any promise that comes from the Turkish state?'

'You're right. I'm going to have to discuss that with them.'

'With whom? And when?'

'First I'll meet with Blue. Then I'm going back to speak to Sunay.'

In the long silence that followed, it became clear that Kadife was more or less prepared to go along with the plan. But Ka still needed to be sure, so he made a show of looking at his watch.

'Who has Blue?' asked Kadife. 'MİT or the army?'

'I don't know. It probably doesn't make much difference.'

'If it's the army, he may not have been tortured,' said Kadife. She paused. 'I want you to give these to him.' She handed Ka an old-fashioned bejewelled lighter coated with mother-of-pearl and a pack of red Marlboros. 'The lighter belongs to my father. Blue will enjoy lighting his cigarettes with it.'

Ka took the cigarettes but handed back the lighter. 'If I give him the lighter, Blue will know that I came here to talk to you first.'

'So what? Why shouldn't he?'

'Because then he'll know what we've been talking about and he'll want to know what your decision was. I wasn't planning to tell him I'd seen you first, or that you were ready to bare your head, so to speak, in order to save him.'

'Is that because you know he'd never agree to it?'

'No. He's an intelligent, rational man, and he'd certainly agree to your doing something like baring your head if it would save him from the gallows. You know that as well as I do. The thing he would never accept is my having asked you first instead of going straight to him.'

'But this is not just a matter of politics; it's also personal, something between him and me. Blue would understand this.'

'That may be, Kadife, but you know that he wants the first word. He's a Turkish man. And a political Islamist. I can't go to him and say, "Listen, Kadife's decided to bare her head to win your freedom." He must believe it's his decision. I'm going to ask him what he thinks of the various options – whether you should wear a wig or if it's better to do that montage with another woman's hair. He must convince himself that this will save your honour and solve the problem. Please believe me, it's *his* idea of honour that counts now, not yours. If you are to bare your head, he'll certainly want everyone to know that he sanctioned it.'

'You're jealous of Blue. You hate him,' said Kadife. 'You don't even want to see him as a human being. You're like all republican secularists: anyone who isn't Westernised is dismissed by you as a primitive, underclass reprobate. You tell yourself a good beating is bound to make a man of him. Do you enjoy seeing me bow to the army to save Blue's skin? It's immoral to take pleasure from something like that, but you're not even trying to hide it.' Her eyes glittered with hatred. 'And anyway, if it had to be Blue's decision, and if you are an enlightened Turkish man, why is it that you did not go straight to him after you left Sunay? I'll tell you why: you wanted to watch me deciding to bow my own head. This was to make you feel superior to Blue – the man who terrifies you.'

'Yes, you're right, he does terrify me. But everything else you said is unfair, Kadife. Say I'd gone to Blue first and then come to you with his decision that you had to bare your head. You would have taken it as an order, and you'd have refused.'

'You're not a mediator, you're cooperating with the tyrants.'

'My only ambition is to get out of this city in one piece. You shouldn't take this coup any more seriously than I do. You've already done more than enough to prove to the people of Kars what a brave, clever, righteous woman you are. After we get out of this, your sister and I are going to Frankfurt. We hope to find happiness there. I would advise you to do the same – do whatever you have to do to find happiness. If you and Blue can manage to escape, I promise you could live happily ever after as political exiles in any number of European cities. And I've no doubt your father would want to join you. But, before any of this can happen, you've got to put your trust in me.'

All this talk of happiness had caused a large tear to roll down Kadife's cheek. Smiling in an odd way that Ka found alarming, she quickly wiped it away with the palm of her hand. 'Are you sure my sister is ready to leave Kars?'

'I'm positive,' said Ka, though his uncertainty was evident in his voice.

'I'm not going to insist that you give Blue the lighter or tell him that you came to see me first,' said Kadife. She was speaking now like a haughty but patient princess. 'But, before I bare my head in front of anyone, I must be absolutely sure they'll set him free. I need more than the guarantee of Sunay or one of his henchmen. We all know what the word of the Turkish state is worth.'

'You're a very intelligent woman, Kadife. No one in Kars deserves happiness as much as you do,' said Ka. He was tempted to add, 'Except for Necip,' but no sooner had he thought this than he forgot it. 'If you give me the lighter right now, I can take that to Blue, too. But please, try to trust me.'

Kadife bent forward to pass him the lighter, then they embraced with a warmth that neither expected. For a fleeting moment, Ka enjoyed the thrill of touching Kadife's body, which was much lighter and slimmer than her sister's, but he stopped himself from kissing her. A moment later, when there was a loud knock on the door, he thought, It's a good thing I stopped myself.

It was İpek, who'd come to tell Ka that an army truck was waiting for him. She stood there and gazed softly, searchingly, into their eyes, as if trying to understand what Ka and Kadife had decided. Ka left the room without kissing her, but he felt he didn't need to: she was his now. At the end of the corridor, he turned around to savour the power he felt he now possessed over both sisters, only to see them locked in a silent embrace.

I'm Not Anyone's Agent

Ka with Blue in His Cell

The image of Kadife and İpek embracing in the corridor lingered in Ka's mind. Sitting beside the driver in the army truck, at the Atatürk and Halitpaşa Avenue intersection, waiting for the only set of traffic lights in the city to change, he was high enough off the road to see into the second-floor window of an old Armenian house; someone had opened it to let in some fresh air. As a light wind swayed the shutters and ruffled the curtains, Ka could tell at once that he was witnessing a secret political meeting. So penetrating was his awareness of what was going on inside that he felt like a doctor looking at an X-ray. Therefore, though a pale and frightened woman soon dashed forward to draw the curtains, he had already guessed with extraordinary accuracy what had transpired in that bright room: two of Kars' most seasoned Kurdish militants were talking to an apprentice tea-man whose elder brother had been killed in a raid on the night of the coup. The apprentice was now hunched, sweating, by the stove, wrapping his brother's body in bandages, while the militants assured him how easy it would be to enter the police headquarters on Faikbey Avenue and set off a bomb.

Ka had not, however, guessed his own destination. Instead of taking him to those same police headquarters or turning into the grand old square dating from the early years of the republic, where MİT had its headquarters, the army truck went straight through the Faikbey Avenue intersection, continued along Atatürk Avenue, and turned finally into the military compound in the centre of the city. In the 1960s there'd been a plan to convert this space into a park, but after the military coup in the early seventies they'd built a wall around it, and before long it had become a garrison comprising barracks, new

324

command headquarters and training grounds. Bored children rode bicycles among the stunted poplars. According to *Free Nation*, the pro-army newspaper, it was thanks to the new occupants that the house in which Pushkin had stayed during his visit to Kars, as well as the Cossacks' stables built by the Tsar forty years later, had been saved from demolition.

The cell in which they were holding Blue was right next door to these stables. The army truck dropped Ka outside a pleasant old stone building that stood under an old oleander tree; its branches, he noticed, were bowing under the weight of the snow. Inside were two gracious men whom Ka correctly took to be MİT operatives. They picked up a roll of bandages and a tape-recorder (which was awfully primitive-looking, considering it was the nineties), and after they had used the former to secure the latter to Ka's chest, they showed him how to operate the on/off button. When they spoke about the prisoner downstairs, it was as if they were sorry he'd been caught and wanted to help him. At the same time, they made it clear that they expected Ka to extract Blue's confession, in particular concerning the murders he had committed or had ordered others to commit. It didn't occur to Ka that they might not know his real reason for being there.

In the days of the Tsar, when the Russian cavalry had this little building as its headquarters, you would go down a cold stone staircase to reach the large, windowless room in which soldiers were punished for poor discipline. After the founding of the Turkish Republic, the same cell had for a time served as a depot, and then, during the nuclear panics of the Cold War, it was turned into a model fallout shelter. It was far cleaner and more comfortable than Ka had expected.

The room was well heated by an Arçelik furnace (donated several years earlier by Muhtar, the area's main distributor, in an effort to ingratiate himself), but Blue, who was in bed reading a book, had still found it necessary to cover himself with a clean army blanket. He rose the moment he saw Ka and stepped into his shoes, from which the laces had been removed. Assuming an official air but still managing a smile, he shook Ka's hand, and, with the decisiveness of one ready to talk business, pointed to a Formica table pushed up against the wall. When they had claimed their seats at opposite ends of the table, Ka looked across to see an ashtray filled with cigarette butts, so he took the pack of Marlboros out of his pocket and passed them to Blue, commenting as he did so on the comforts of the surroundings. Blue told him that he'd not been tortured; he then struck a match and lit Ka's cigarette before lighting his own. 'So tell me, sir, for whom are you spying today?'

'I've given up spying,' said Ka. 'These days I'm a mediator.'

'That's even worse. Spies traffic in snippets of information that aren't much use to anyone, and mostly they do it for the money. Mediators, on the other hand – well, they're just smart alecs who think they can stick their noses into your private business on the pretext of being "impartial". So what's your game here? What are you trying to get out of all this?'

'To get out of this dreadful city in one piece.'

'As things stand today, only one person in this city is in any position to protect an atheist flown in from the West to spy on us, and that's Sunay.'

Thus Ka learned that Blue had seen the back page of the *Border City Gazette*. How he hated that smile forming underneath Blue's moustache! How could this militant Islamist who'd spent half his life railing against the merciless Turkish state, and who was now sitting in a prison cell because he was implicated in two separate murder inquiries, be so calm and cheerful? Now, more than ever, Ka could see why Kadife was so madly in love with him. Blue never looked more handsome than he did that day.

'So, what are you here to mediate?'

'I've come to try to arrange your release,' said Ka, and in a very calm voice he relayed Sunay's proposal. He didn't mention the possibility of Kadife's wearing a wig, nor did he discuss the various tricks they might resort to during the live transmission – he kept these in reserve in case he might need some bargaining chips later. While he was explaining the gravity of the situation, and the pressure certain merciless parties were putting on Sunay to hang Blue at the first opportunity, he felt a certain joy, but as guilt followed fast on its heels, he went on to denounce Sunay as the crackpot to end all crackpots, and to assure Blue that as soon as the snow melted everything would return to normal. Later, he would ask himself if he'd said this just to please the MİT operatives upstairs.

'What all this means is that my only chance for freedom is to take part in Sunay's latest crackpot scheme, then,' said Blue.

'Yes, that's right.'

'So tell him this: I reject his proposal. I thank you for taking the trouble to come all this way.'

Ka expected that Blue would now rise, shake his hand and see him to the door, but instead he remained seated in silence. Tipped back on the hind legs of his chair, Blue was now rocking happily back and forth.

'But if your mediation efforts come to nothing, and you don't escape this dreadful city in one piece, it won't be because of me,' he said finally. 'It will be because of your loose-lipped, atheist boasting. The only time people in this country brag about atheism is when they know the army is behind them.'

'I'm not the sort of person who takes pride in being an atheist.'

'I'm glad to hear it.'

Both men fell silent again, smoking their cigarettes. Searching for an alternative to getting up and leaving, Ka asked, 'Aren't you afraid of dying?'

'If that's a threat, then the answer is no, I'm not afraid of dying. If you're asking me as a concerned friend, the answer is yes, I'm very afraid. But whatever I do now, these tyrants will still want to hang me. There's nothing I can do to change that.'

Blue flashed a damningly sweet smile. The message Ka took from it was 'Look, I'm in a far worse fix than you are, but I'm still taking it better than you!' Shame forced Ka to admit to himself that his panic and discomfort stemmed from the sweet, aching hope for happiness that he'd been carrying around since falling in love with İpek. Was Blue immune to that sort of hope? 'I'll count to nine and then I'll get up and leave,' he told himself. 'One, two . . .' By the time he'd reached five, he'd decided that if he failed to dupe Blue, he'd never be able to take İpek back with him to Germany.

Suddenly inspired, he began to talk, saying whatever came into his head. He started by describing a luckless mediator he remembered from a black-and-white American film he'd seen as a child. He went on to remind Blue that – once things were straightened out – he was sure he'd be able to get their Hotel Asia statement printed in Germany. Then he commented that those who go through life making bad decisions out of some stubborn intellectual passion sometimes live to regret it. He recounted as an example when, in a fit of pique, he'd quit a basketball team, never to return. The time he would have spent on the court, he'd idled away at the Bosphorus, watching the sea for hours on end. Once on this train of thought, he couldn't stop himself from telling Blue how much he loved Istanbul, and how beautiful the little Bosphorus town of Bebek could be on a fine spring evening. All the while he struggled to keep Blue's cold-blooded stare from crushing him into silence. It was like the final visit before an execution.

'Even if we broke all precedents and did everything they asked, they'd never keep their word,' said Blue. He pointed to the paper and pens sitting on the table. 'They want me to write down my whole life story – every crime I've ever committed. If I do, and they decide I'm sincere, they could pardon me under the Remorse Law. I've always pitied the fools who fell for such lies only to spend their last days on trial having betrayed themselves. But since I'm going to die anyway, I want to make sure those who follow get to hear a few things about me that are true.' On the table there were several sheets already covered with handwriting, and now Blue picked up one of them. With the same grave and rather ludicrous expression he'd assumed for giving a 'quote' to the German press, he began to read:

'"On the subject of my execution, I would like to make clear that I have no regrets about anything I have done for political reasons at any time in the past, including today, 20 February. My father is a retired clerk, formerly of the Istanbul Regional Treasury Office, and I am his second child. During my childhood and early youth, my father maintained secret links with a Cerrahi lodge and I grew up inside his humble, silent world. In my youth I rebelled against him by becoming a godless leftist, and when I was at university I tagged along with the other young militants and stoned the sailors coming off the American aircraft carriers. Around the same time I married; then we split up and I managed to survive the crisis. For years no one noticed me. I was an electronic engineer. Because of the hatred I felt for the West, I admired the revolution in Iran. I returned to Islam. When the Ayatollah Khomeini said that 'The most important thing today is not to pray or fast but to protect the Islamic faith,' I believed him. I took inspiration from Frantz Fanton's work on violence, from the pilgrimages Seyyid Kutub has made in protest against oppression, from the same man's ideas on changing places, and from Ali Sheriyat. I escaped to Germany after the military coup. Then I returned to Turkey. I was wounded while fighting in Grozny with the

Chechens against the Russians, and, as a result of that wound, I have a limp in my right leg. When I was in Bosnia during the Serbian siege, I married a Bosnian girl named Merzuka and took her back to Istanbul with me. Because my political obligations and my ideas on pilgrimage meant that I was hardly ever in any given city longer than two weeks, my second wife and I eventually separated. After cutting off relations with the Islamist groups that sent me to Chechnya and Bosnia, I set out to explore all four corners of Turkey. In spite of the fact that I believe it is sometimes necessary to kill the enemies of Islam, I have never killed anyone; nor have I ever ordered anyone's death. The man who assassinated the former mayor of Kars was a deranged Kurdish driver who was angry because he was threatening to take all the horse-drawn carriages off the streets. I came to Kars for the girls who were committing suicide. Suicide is the greatest sin of all. I leave behind my poems as my testament, and I would like them to be published. Merzuka has them all. That's all I have to say."'

Silence followed.

'You don't have to die,' said Ka eventually. 'That's why I'm here.'

'Then let me tell you something else,' said Blue.

Once he was sure he had Ka's full attention, he lit another cigarette. Did he know about the tape-recorder whirring silently on Ka's chest, working as unobtrusively as a dutiful housewife?

'When I was living in Munich, there was this cinema I went to a lot. They had discount double-features after midnight,' said Blue. 'And you know that Italian who did *The Battle of Algiers*, about the French oppression of Algeria – one day they showed his latest film *Queimada!* It's set on an island in the Atlantic where they produce sugar cane, and it's about the tricks the colonialists played and the revolutions they staged. First they find a black leader and get him to rise up against the French, and then they sail in and take over. After failing the first time, the blacks rise up again, this time against the English, but the English defeat them by setting the entire island on fire. The leader of both rebellions is arrested and soon it is the morning of his execution. Then, who should arrive but the man who first discovered him, the man who talked him into the first rebellion and went on to crush the second for the English. Before you know it, Marlon Brando has gone into the tent in which they're keeping the black captive. He cuts his ropes and sets him free.'

'Why?'

Blue bridled at the question. 'Why do you think? So he wouldn't hang, of course! Marlon knew very well that if they hanged this man, they'd turn him into a legend, and then the local people would use his name as a battle cry for years to come. But the black leader, knowing exactly why Marlon has cut his ropes, rejects his chance for freedom and refuses to run away.'

'Did they hang him?' asked Ka.

'Yes, but they didn't show the hanging in the film,' said Blue. 'Instead, they showed what happened to Marlon Brando, the agent who, like you, tried to tempt the condemned man with his freedom. Just as he was about to leave the island, one of the locals stabbed him to death.'

'I'm not an agent!' said Ka, unable to hide his annoyance.

'Don't be so sensitive about the word "agent". After all, I see myself as an agent of Islam.'

'I'm not anyone's agent,' insisted Ka, still perturbed.

'Do you mean to tell me that no one even bothered to put some amazing drug into this cigarette to make me dizzy and sap my will-power? Ah, the best thing America ever gave the world were these red Marlboros. I could smoke these Marlboros for the rest of my life.'

'If you use your head, you can smoke your Marlboros for another forty years.'

'This is just what I meant by the word "agent",' said Blue. 'An agent's main job is to talk people into changing their minds.'

'All I mean is that it's stupid to let yourself be killed by these crazed, bloodthirsty fascists. Don't count on becoming a revolutionary icon, either – it's not going to happen. These meek lambs here – they might have strong religious beliefs, but at the end of the day they obey the state's decrees. And all those rebel sheikhs, all those who rise up because they fear our religion is slipping away, all those militants trained in Iran, even those like Saidi Nursi who enjoyed long-lasting fame – they can't even count on having graves in the first place, let alone resting in peace in them. As for all those religious leaders in this country who dream of the day their names turn to emblems of faith – the soldiers load their bodies on to military planes and dump them in the sea. But you know all this. Those Hezbollah cemeteries in Batman to which so many came on pilgrimage – one night was all it took to raze them. Where are they now, those cemeteries?'

'In the people's hearts.'

'Empty words. Only twenty per cent of the people give their votes to the Islamists. And a moderate Islamist party at that.'

'If it's so moderate, then why do they panic and send in the military? Please explain that! So much for your impartial mediating.'

'I *am* an impartial mediator,' said Ka, raising his voice.

'No, you're not. You're a Western agent. You're the slave of the ruthless Europeans and, like all true slaves, you don't even know you're a slave. You're just a typical little European from Nişantaş: not only were you brought up to look down on your own traditions, you think you live on a higher plane than ordinary people. According to your kind, the road to a good, moral life is not through God or religion, or through taking part in the life of the common people. No, it's just a matter of imitating the West. Perhaps from time to time you say a word or two reproaching the tyrannies visited on the Islamists and the Kurds, but in your heart of hearts you don't mind at all when the military takes charge.'

'What if I did this for you: Kadife could wear a wig under her headscarf. That way, when she bares her head, no one will see her real hair.'

'You can't make me drink wine!' said Blue. He'd raised his voice, too. 'I refuse to be a European, and I won't ape their ways. I'm going to live out my own history and be no one but myself. I, for one, believe it's possible to be happy without becoming a mock-European, without becoming their slave. There's a word Europhiles very commonly use when they denigrate our people: to be a true Westerner, a person must first become an *individual*, and then they go on to say that, in Turkey, there are no individuals! Well, that's how I see my execution. I'm standing up against the Westerners as an individual. It's because I'm an individual that I refuse to imitate them.'

'Sunay believes so deeply in this play that I can even do this for you. The National Theatre will be empty. The live TV camera will show Kadife's hand pulling off the scarf first. Then we can do some tricky editing and the hair we show will really belong to someone else.'

'I find it rather suspicious that you are prepared to go through such contortions just to save me.'

'I'm very happy right now,' said Ka, and just saying this made him feel as guilty as if he'd been lying. 'I've never been so happy in my entire life. I want to preserve that happiness.'

'What is it that's made you so happy?'

Ka did not give the answer that later occurred to him as wise: 'Because I'm writing poems.' Nor did he say, 'Because I believe in God.' Instead, he blurted out, 'Because I'm in love!' He added, 'I'm taking my love back to Frankfurt with me.' For a moment, he was glad just to be speaking so openly about his love with a virtual stranger.

'And who is this love of yours?'

'Kadife's sister, İpek.' Ka could see confusion in Blue's face, and he immediately regretted his joyous outburst.

Blue lit another Marlboro, and after a long silence said, 'When a man is so happy that he is willing to share his happiness with someone about to be executed, it is a gift from God. Let's imagine I agreed to your proposals and fled the city to save your happiness, and if Kadife found a way to take part in the play using some trickery that saved her honour, and also secured her sister's hope for happiness, what guarantee do I have that these people will keep their word and let me go?'

'I knew you would ask that!' cried Ka. He paused for a moment, brought his finger to his lips and signalled to Blue to keep quiet and vigilant. He undid the buttons of his jacket, and made a great show of turning off the tape-recorder taped to his chest. 'I'll be your guarantor, and they can release you first,' he said. 'Kadife can wait before going on stage until she hears of your release and that you have gone back into hiding. But to get Kadife to agree, you will need to write her a letter saying you've approved the plan. I must deliver it to her personally.' He was making all this up as he went along. 'And if you would tell me how this release should happen and where they should leave you,' he whispered, 'I'll make sure they do as you ask. And then you can stay underground until the roads have reopened. You can trust me on this. You have my guarantee.'

Blue handed Ka a piece of paper. 'Put in writing: in securing my consent for Kadife to go on stage and bare her head without staining her honour, and to ensure that I am able to leave Kars in one piece, you, Ka, have undertaken to act as mediator and guarantor. If you don't keep your word, if this turns out to be a trap, what sort of punishment should the guarantor expect?'

'Whatever they do to you they must also do to me,' said Ka.

'OK, write that down.'

Now Ka gave Blue a sheet of paper. 'I'd like you to write that you have agreed to my plan, that I have your permission to relay the plan to Kadife, and that the final decision is up to her. If Kadife agrees, she must make a written statement to this effect and sign it with the understanding that she must not bare her head until you have been freed in a suitable way. Write all that down. But when it comes to the time and place of your release, I'd rather not be involved – it would be better if you chose someone you trusted. I'd recommend Fazıl – the blood brother of the dead boy, Necip.'

'Is that the boy who was sending love letters to Kadife?'

'That was Necip, the one who died. He was a very special person, a gift from God,' said Ka. 'But Fazıl's just as good-hearted.'

'If you say so, I'll believe you,' said Blue, and, turning to the sheet before him, he began to write.

Blue finished first. When Ka then completed his own guarantee, he detected a contemptuous half smile flashing across Blue's face – but it didn't concern him. He'd set things in motion, he'd removed all the obstacles, so he and İpek were now free to leave the city. He could hardly contain his joy. They exchanged their papers in silence. When Blue folded Ka's statement and put it in his pocket without bothering to read it, Ka followed suit. Then, making sure Blue could see what he was doing, he switched the tape-recorder back on.

After a brief silence, Ka went back to the last thing he had said before turning off the recorder. 'But unless the two sides can establish some sort of trust, no agreement is possible. You'll just have to trust the state to keep its word.'

They looked into each other's eyes and smiled. He would return to this moment many times over the years that followed, and each time he would feel great remorse. Happiness had blinded him to the fury in Blue's eyes. Looking back, he often thought that if he'd sensed this fury, he might never have asked the question:

'Will Kadife agree to this plan?'

'She'll agree to it,' whispered Blue, his eyes still bright with rage, and paused for a moment. 'Seeing that you aim to make a contract with me that binds me to life, you might as well tell me more about this great happiness of yours.'

'I've never loved anyone like this in my whole life,' said Ka. He knew his words sounded credulous and clumsy, but he ploughed on. 'For me, there's only one chance for happiness, and that's İpek.'

'And how do you define happiness?'

'Happiness is finding another world to live in, a world where you can forget all this poverty and tyranny. Happiness is holding someone in your arms and knowing you hold the whole world –' He would have said more but now Blue jumped to his feet.

At this moment, the poem Ka would later call 'Chess' came rushing into his head. He cast a quick glance at Blue, then took the notebook from his pocket and began to write. As he jotted down the lines of the poem – which was about happiness and power, wisdom and greed – Blue peered over his shoulder, curious to know what was going on. Ka could sense Blue's eyes on him, and that image too found its way into his poem. It was as if the hand that was writing belonged to someone else. Ka knew that Blue wouldn't be able to see it, but that did not stop his wishing Blue could know that Ka's hand was in thrall to a higher power. It was not to be: Blue sat on the edge of the bed, gloomily smoking in the manner of condemned men the world over.

On an impulse he would spend much time trying (and failing) to understand afterwards, Ka found himself opening his heart to Blue yet again. 'Before I got here, I hadn't written a poem in years,' he said. 'But since coming to Kars, all the roads on which poetry travels have reopened. I attribute this to the love of God I've felt here.'

'I don't want to destroy your illusions, but your love for God comes out of Western romantic novels,' said Blue. 'In a place like this, if you worship God as a European, you're bound to be a laughing stock. Then you cannot even believe you believe. You don't belong to this country; you're not even a Turk any more. First try to be like everyone else, then try to believe in God.'

Ka could feel Blue's hatred. He gathered up a few of the sheets from the table, announced that he had to go and see Sunay and Kadife without any further delay, and pounded on the cell door. When it opened, he turned back to Blue and asked him if he had a special message for Kadife.

Blue smiled. 'Be careful,' he said. 'Don't let anyone kill you.'

36

You're Not Really Going to Die, Sir, Are You?

*Several Rounds of Bargaining in Which Life Vies
with the Theatre, and Art with Politics*

As the MİT agents upstairs cut through the tape and slowly
unwound the bandage with which they had attached the recorder to
his chest, Ka tried to ingratiate himself by assuming their scornful air
of efficiency and making fun of Blue. This may explain why he was
not preoccupied with Blue's show of aggression downstairs.

He sent the driver of the army truck back to the hotel with instructions to wait. Then, flanked by military guards, he walked from one
end of the garrison to the other. The officers' quarters overlooked a
large, snow-covered courtyard where a number of boys were throwing snowballs among the poplars. Waiting there was a girl in a red
and white woollen coat that reminded Ka of the one he'd worn in the
third year of primary school, and, a little farther, two of her friends
were making a snowman. The air was crystalline, the gruelling storm
was over, and it was just beginning to feel a little warmer.

He walked on to the hotel, and when he arrived went straight to
see İpek. She was in the kitchen, dressed in a smock, the one all lycée
girls in Turkey had worn once upon a time, and over it an apron. As
he gazed happily at her, he longed to throw his arms around her, but
there were other people in the room, so he held himself back and
instead told her of the morning's developments: things were going
well, he said, for them, and for Kadife. He said that while the newspaper had been circulated without amendment, he was no longer
worried about being shot. There was much more to say, but now
Zahide came into the kitchen to make a plea on behalf of the two
soldiers guarding the door. She asked İpek to invite them inside and
give them some tea. In the few moments left to them, İpek arranged
to continue the conversation in Ka's room.

Upstairs, Ka hung up his coat and stared at the ceiling as he waited for İpek. With so much to discuss, he knew she would be there soon, but still it wasn't long before he fell prey to a dark pessimism. First, he imagined that İpek had been delayed because she'd run into her father; then he began to worry that she didn't want to be with him. That old ache returned, spreading from his stomach like a poison. If this was what others called love pangs, they held no promise of happiness. As his love for İpek deepened, these dark panics seemed to descend on him ever faster. He was well aware of this, but was he right to assume that these attacks, these fearsome fantasies of deception and heartbreak, had anything to do with what others called 'love'? He seemed alone in describing the experience in terms of misery and defeat. Being unable even to imagine bragging about it, as everyone else bragged of love, he could only suppose that his own brand of it was abnormal, and this bothered him more than anything else.

Even in the torment of these paranoid theories (İpek was not coming, İpek didn't really want to come, all of them – Kadife, Turgut Bey and İpek – were having a secret meeting, discussing Ka as an enemy outsider and plotting to be rid of him), a part of him knew these fantasies were pathological. So, for example, as his stomach began to ache at the terrible visions before his eyes of İpek as another man's lover, another region of his brain would repeat assurances that these were only symptoms of his sickness. Sometimes, to relieve the pain, to erase the evil scenes intruding on his thoughts (in one, İpek refused even to see Ka, much less come to Frankfurt), he would by sheer force of will take refuge in logic, the one part of his mind that love had not thrown off balance. Of course she loves me, he would tell himself – if she didn't, why would she be looking so ecstatic? With such thoughtful focus, his evil anxieties would float away, but before long a new worry would inevitably come flying in to undo his precarious inner peace.

He heard footsteps in the corridor. It couldn't be İpek, he told himself: someone else was coming to tell him that İpek wasn't. And when he opened the door to see İpek, his face radiated hostility as much as joy. He'd been waiting for exactly twelve minutes and had grown tired of it. His consolation was to see that İpek had made herself up and was wearing lipstick.

'I've spoken to my father, and I've told him I'm going to Germany,' she said.

Ka was still so much in thrall to the dark images in his head that his first response was disappointment. He couldn't give İpek his full attention, and his failure to show any pleasure at her news planted some doubts in her mind – or, more to the point, a disillusionment. But she still knew that Ka was madly in love, and already bound to her like a hapless five-year-old who can't bear to be apart from his mother. She also knew that he wanted to take her to Germany not merely so she could share his happy home in Frankfurt. His greater hope was that, when they were far away from all these eyes, he would know for sure that he possessed her absolutely.

'Darling, is something bothering you?'

In later years, when racked with pangs of love, Ka would recall a thousand times over how softly and sweetly İpek had asked this question. For now, he replied by telling İpek about the terrible thoughts that had been running through his mind. One by one, he recounted them for her – the dreaded abandonment, the worst scenes of horror that had played before his eyes.

'If love pangs cause you such dread, I can't help thinking there was a woman earlier in your life who hurt you very badly.'

'I've known some suffering in my life – but already I'm terrified of how much you could hurt me.'

'I'm not going to hurt you at all,' said İpek. 'I'm in love with you, I'm coming back to Germany with you, everything's going to be fine.'

She threw her arms around Ka, embracing him with all her strength, and they made love with such ease that Ka could hardly believe it. Now he felt no urge to be rough with her; instead, he took pleasure in the strong but tender embrace, glorying in the whiteness of her delicate skin. But they were both aware that their lovemaking was neither as deep nor as intense as it had been the night before.

Ka's mind was on his mediation plans. He believed that if, for once in his life, he could be happy, and if, by using his head, he could manage to get out of Kars not just in one piece but with his lover on his arm, his happiness might last for ever. He had been thinking this for some time as he was smiling and gazing out of the window, when to his great surprise he realised another poem was beckoning. He wrote it down very fast, just as it came, as İpek watched in loving admiration. He would recite this poem, called 'Love', at six readings in Germany. Those who heard it told me that, although apparently concerned with the familiar tension between peace and isolation, or security and fear, and special relations with a woman (though only one listener thought to ask afterwards who this woman might be), the poem in fact emanated from the darkest, most incomprehensible part of Ka's being. As for the notes Ka later made, these were mostly explicit remembrances of İpek, how he missed her, and scattered remarks about how she dressed and moved. It may be because I'd read these notes so many times that İpek made such a strong impression on me during our first meeting.

İpek dressed quickly and left – she had to say goodbye to her sister. But a moment later, Kadife was at the door. Seeing her eyes larger than ever, and her evident anxiety, Ka assured her she had nothing to fear and in particular that no one had laid a hand on Blue. He told her he now knew what a very brave man Blue was because he'd had such difficulty persuading him to agree to the plan. Then, suddenly, a lie he had sketched out in advance occurred to him in glorious detail. He began by saying that the hardest part had been convincing Blue that Kadife would agree to the plan. Ka said that Blue had been worried that Kadife might be offended by this plan, and that he'd insisted he couldn't agree to it before talking it over with her. At this point, little Kadife raised an eyebrow, so Ka retreated a little, giving his lie a more truthful ring by expressing doubt that Blue had spoken with absolute sincerity. Then, not merely to keep the lie afloat, but also to help Kadife save face, he added that Blue's reluctance (in other words, the respect he showed for a woman's feelings) was a positive thing. It cheered Ka to be spinning lies for these luckless people who'd allowed themselves to be swept into the asinine political feuds of this stupid city, the city that had taught him so late in life that the only important thing was happiness. But a part of him knew that he needed to spin them because Kadife was so much braver, so much readier to make sacrifice, than he was, and, as he sensed how much unhappiness lay before him, his mood darkened. That's why, before cutting his story short, he told one more white lie: just as he was leaving, Blue had asked him in a whisper to give Kadife his best, he claimed. Ka then proceeded to set out the plan. When he had finished, he asked her what she thought.

'I'll bare my head, and I'll be the one to decide how,' said Kadife.

Ka tried to convince her that Blue didn't mind her wearing a wig or something along those lines, but he paused when he saw he'd angered her.

The plan now went like this: first they were to release Blue, then Blue was to go into hiding, somewhere he felt safe, and only after that would Kadife bare her head (in a manner of her own choosing). Could Kadife write out the plan as she understood it on a sheet of paper and sign it at once? Ka handed her the statement Blue had given him, hoping that she would use it as a model for her own. But, seeing the emotion on Kadife's face at the mere sight of Blue's hand-writing, Ka felt an unexpected wave of affection for her. As she read, Kadife did her best to keep Ka from looking on, and at one point she even sniffed the paper. Then, sensing some hesitation, Ka told her he would use the statement to persuade Sunay and his associates that they should set Blue free. The army was probably angry with Kadife, and certainly the headscarf affair had not won her any friends in high places, but everyone in Kars respected her courage and honesty. Ka handed Kadife a fresh sheet of paper and watched her as she threw herself into the assignment. He thought about the Kadife he'd met for the first time a couple of days earlier, the woman with whom he'd discussed astrology while walking down Butcher Street. The Kadife sitting before him now looked so much older.

As he put her statement into his pocket, Ka said that, assuming Sunay could be persuaded to go along with the plan, their next task would be to find a haven for Blue after his release. Would Kadife help with this?

She gave her assent with a grave nod.

'Don't worry,' said Ka. 'At the end of this we'll all be happy.'

'Doing the right thing doesn't always end in happiness,' replied Kadife.

'The right thing makes us happy,' said Ka. He imagined a day not far off when Kadife would come to Frankfurt and see the happy life he and her big sister had made for themselves. İpek would take Kadife to the Kaufhof and buy her a chic new raincoat; the three of them would go to the cinema together; afterwards, they would stop off at one of those restaurants on the Kaiserstrasse for beer and sausages.

They put on their coats, and Kadife followed Ka downstairs to the army truck waiting in the courtyard. The two bodyguards took the back seat. Ka wondered whether he'd been right to worry about being attacked walking the streets alone. From the front seat of an army truck, the streets of Kars didn't look at all frightening. He watched the women clutching string bags on their way to the market, children throwing snowballs and elderly men and women clinging to one another to keep from slipping on the ice, and then imagined himself with İpek at a cinema in Frankfurt, holding hands.

Sunay was with Colonel Osman Nuri Çolak, the coup's other mastermind. What Ka told them was coloured by the optimism engendered by his happy daydreams. He said that everything had been arranged: Kadife would take part in the play and bare her head at the appointed moment, and Blue was only too eager to allow this condition of his release. He sensed a quiet understanding between these two men – the sort one found only between two people who spent their youths reading the same books. In a careful but confident voice, Ka explained how delicate the mediation had been. 'First I had to flatter Kadife, then I had to flatter Blue,' he said, presenting Sunay with their statements. As Sunay read them, he could sense that the actor had already been drinking, though it wasn't even noon. Catching a whiff of Sunay's breath a moment later, he was sure of it.

'This guy wants us to release him before Kadife goes on stage to bare her head,' said Sunay. 'He has his eyes open, this one. He's no fool.'

'And Kadife wants the same thing,' said Ka. 'I tried really hard, but this was the best deal I could make.'

'But we represent the state. Why should we believe either of them?' asked Colonel Osman Nuri Çolak.

'They don't trust the state any more than you trust them,' said Ka. 'If we don't accept some mutual assurances, we won't get anywhere.'

'He could be hanged as an example to others, then, when the authorities hear what a drunken actor and a broken-down colonel have done in the name of a military coup, they could use this to destroy us. Hasn't any of this occurred to Blue?' asked the colonel.

'He's very good at pretending nonchalance at his own death. I can't tell you what's really going on in his head. But he did insinuate that hanging him would make him a saint, an icon.'

'OK, let's say we released Blue first,' said Sunay. 'How can we be sure that Kadife will keep her word about appearing in the play?'

'If you bear in mind that Turgut Bey once endured a bitter trial and terrible suffering to preserve his honour, and that Kadife is this man's daughter, then it should be clear that, at the very least, we can trust her to keep her word – far more than we can trust Blue. Still, if you told her now that Blue was certain to be released, it's possible that she wouldn't yet know her own mind as to appearing on stage this evening. She does have a temper, and she is given to snap decisions.'

'So what do you suggest?'

'I know that you staged this coup not just for the sake of politics but also as a thing of beauty and in the name of art,' said Ka. 'Just to look at his career is to see that Sunay Bey's every political action has been for the sake of art. If you want to see this now as an ordinary political matter, then you don't have to set Blue free and put yourself in considerable danger. But at the same time, you know only too well that a play in which Kadife bares her head for all in Kars to see will be no mere artistic triumph; it will also have profound political consequences.'

'If she's really going to bare her head, then we'll let Blue go,' said Osman Nuri Çolak. 'But we must make sure everyone in the city sees the play.'

Sunay wrapped his arms around his old army comrade and kissed him. When the colonel had left the room, the actor took Ka's hand and led him deeper into the house, saying, 'And now I'd like to tell my wife all about this!' They approached an unfurnished room, still cold, despite the electric heater burning in the corner, and there was Funda Eser, posing dramatically as she read a script. She saw Sunay and Ka looking at her through the open doorway, but continued to read without losing her composure. Dazzled by the dark rings of kohl around her eyes, her thick, rouged lips, the great breasts swelling out of her low-cut dress, and her exaggerated gestures, Ka found it impossible to listen to what she was saying.

'Thomas Kyd's *The Spanish Tragedy* – the rebellious rape victim's tragic speech!' Sunay said proudly. 'With some alterations inspired by Brecht's *The Good Woman of Szechuan*, though most of the changes are the fruits of my own imagination. When Funda reads this speech tonight, Kadife will not yet have found the courage to bare her head, but she will be using the edge of her scarf to wipe the tears from her eyes.'

'If Kadife Hanım is ready, let's start rehearsals at once.'

The desire in Funda's voice not only made clear to Ka how much she loved the theatre, but reminded him of the oft-repeated claim of those who'd wanted to deny Sunay the chance to play Atatürk – that his wife was a lesbian. Looking less the soldier of the revolution than the proud theatre producer, Sunay was just explaining to Funda that

Kadife had not yet resolved all the questions concerning her decision to 'accept the role' when an orderly came to report they had just brought in Serdar Bey, the owner of the *Border City Gazette*.

Standing face to face with the man, Ka felt himself succumbing to an impulse unknown to him since the time when he had still lived in Turkey. For a moment, he was tempted to punch Serdar Bey in the face. But now, as they welcomed this man to a carefully laid meal, with the white cheese, he was sure, soon to be accompanied by raki, it was clear to Ka that such urges had no place at the table of revolutionary leaders. They sat down with an easy confidence known only to those for whom it has become second nature to decide other people's fates; and, as they ate and drank, they discussed the affairs of the world with merciless assurance.

At Sunay's request, Ka told Funda Eser what he'd just been saying about art and politics. When he saw how much Ka's words excited her, the newspaperman said he wanted to write them down for use in a future article, but Sunay roughly put him in his place. First, he had to correct the lies he'd printed about Ka in today's edition. And so it wasn't long before Serdar Bey had promised to print a new and very positive front-page article that he hoped would encourage his already absent-minded readers to forget that they had recently been prompted to think ill of Ka.

'But the headline must mention the play we're putting on this evening,' said Funda Eser.

Serdar Bey assured them they'd get the article they wanted: they could dictate every detail, down to the point size of the headlines. But, as he wasn't very knowledgeable about classical or modern theatre, it might be better, he said, if Sunay could describe this evening's play in his own words, just to ensure that tomorrow's front page was 100 per cent accurate. He reminded everyone that he'd been writing about events before they had happened for most of his working life: this, it could be said, was his forte. But there were still four hours to work with: they were operating on a special schedule in accordance with martial law, so the edition would not be put to bed until four that afternoon.

'It won't take me much time to give you a rundown of the performance,' said Sunay.

They hadn't been sitting at the table for long, but he'd already finished a glass of raki, Ka noticed. As Sunay knocked back a second, Ka could see pain and passion flicker in his eyes.

'Write this down, Mr Journalist!' bellowed Sunay, glaring at Serdar Bey as if delivering a threat. 'The headline is as follows: "Death on stage".' He paused to think. 'And then another headline right below, in smaller print: "Illustrious actor Sunay Zaim shot dead during yesterday's performance".'

He was speaking with an intensity Ka could not help but admire. He listened, unsmiling and utterly respectful, as Sunay continued, speaking only when Serdar Bey needed help to make sense of the actor's words. From time to time, Sunay paused to ponder what he'd said and clear his head with another raki, so it took him about an hour to complete the article that followed the headlines.

I was to acquire the final version from Serdar Bey during my visit to Kars many years later:

DEATH ON STAGE

ILLUSTRIOUS ACTOR SUNAY ZAIM
SHOT DEAD DURING YESTERDAY'S
PERFORMANCE

Yesterday, while appearing in an historic play at the National Theatre, Kadife the headscarf girl shocked audiences first by baring her head in a moment of enlightened fervour, and then by pointing a weapon at Sunay Zaim, the actor playing the villain, and firing. Her performance, broadcast live, has left the people of Kars trembling in horror.

Three days ago, the Sunay Zaim Theatre Company stunned the people of Kars with an evening of original revolutionary plays that gave way to a real-life revolution before their very eyes, and last night, during their second gala, the Sunay Zaim Players shocked us yet again. The vehicle on this occasion was an adaptation of a drama penned by Thomas Kyd, a wrongfully neglected English playwright who nevertheless is said to have influenced the work of Shakespeare. Sunay Zaim, who has spent the last twenty years touring the forgotten towns of Anatolia, pacing its empty stages and bringing culture to its tea-houses, brought his love of the theatre to an ultimate climax in the play's closing scenes. In a moment of excitement induced by this daring modern drama, which pays homage to both French Jacobin and English Jacobean drama, Kadife, the stubborn leader of the head-scarf girls, brashly bared her head for all to see, and as all of Kars watched in amazement, she then produced a gun, the contents of which she proceeded to empty into Sunay

Zaim, the illustrious actor who was playing the villain, and whose name, like Kyd's, has languished in the shadows for too long.

This real-life drama reminded the people of Kars of the performance two days earlier in which the bullets flying across the stage had turned out to be real, so it was in the horrified knowledge that these were real bullets too that the people of Kars watched Sunay fall.

So it was that the death of great Turkish actor Sunay Zaim was for the audience more shattering than life itself. Although the Kars audience was fully aware that the play was about a person liberating herself from tradition and religious oppression, they were still unable to accept that Sunay Zaim was really dying, even as the bullets pierced his body and blood gushed from his wounds. But they had no trouble understanding the actor's last words, and they will never forget that he sacrificed his life for art.

When Sunay had made his last corrections, Serdar read out the final draft to the assembled guests. 'If this meets with your approval, I shall print it verbatim in tomorrow's edition,' he said. 'But in all my years of writing news before it's happened, this is the first time I'll be praying that an article doesn't come true. You're not really going to die, sir, are you?'

'What I am trying to do is push the truths of art to their outer limits, to become one with myth,' said Sunay. 'Anyway, once the snow melts tomorrow and the roads open again, my death will cease to have the slightest importance for the people of Kars.'

For a moment Sunay's eye caught Funda's. Seeing how deeply these two understood each other, Ka felt a pang of jealousy. Would he and İpek ever learn to share their souls like this, or enjoy such deep happiness?

'Mr Newspaperman, the time has come for you to leave, dear sir. Our work is done, so please prepare the presses,' said Sunay. 'In view of the historical importance of this edition, I shall see to it that my orderly provides you with a negative of my photograph.' As soon as Serdar Bey had left, Sunay dropped the mocking tone that Ka had attributed to too much raki. 'I accept Blue's and Kadife's conditions,' he said. He then turned to Funda Eser, whose eyebrows rose as he explained that Kadife was willing to bare her head on stage only if they would release Blue first.

'Kadife Hanım is a very brave woman. I am sure we'll come to an understanding once we start rehearsals,' said Funda.

'You can go to her together,' said Sunay. 'But first Kadife must be convinced that Blue has been released, and that no one has followed him to his hiding-place. This will take time.'

Making it clear he would ignore Funda Eser's desire to launch immediately into rehearsals with Kadife, Sunay turned to Ka to discuss how best to organise Blue's release.

My sense from studying his notes of this meeting is that Ka was still taking Sunay's promises at face value. In other words, Ka did not think that Sunay would have Blue followed to the hiding-place after his release, and recaptured once Kadife had bared her head on stage. It is likely that this concealed plan emerged slowly, and that its masterminds were in fact MİT, still planting microphones everywhere and struggling to decipher the intelligence furnished by their double agents in the hope of staying one step ahead of everyone, perhaps even manipulating Colonel Osman Nuri Çolak to their own advantage. The secret police knew they were outnumbered – as long as Sunay, the disgruntled colonel and his small gang of like-minded officers were in control of the army, there was no chance of MİT taking charge of the revolution – but nevertheless they had men everywhere doing everything in their power to keep Sunay's 'artistic' lunacies in check. Before the article he'd written out at the raki table went to be typeset, Serdar Bey had used his walkie-talkie to read it out to his friends at the Kars branch of MİT, causing great consternation, and not a little concern about Sunay's mental health and stability. As for Sunay's plan to release Blue, until the very last moment it was generally unknown how much MİT knew. But today I would say that these details have little bearing on the end of our story, so I shall not dwell overmuch on the minutiae of the plan to release Blue. Suffice it to say that Sunay and Ka decided to leave the job to Fazıl and Sunay's orderly.

Sunay dispatched an army truck the moment he learned Fazıl's address from MİT. Ten minutes later, they'd brought him in. This time there was fear in his face and he no longer reminded Ka of Necip. It was quickly decided that he and the orderly should head for the army garrison in the city centre. Immediately they left the tailor's shop by the back door and shook off the detectives who'd been following them. For, while MİT by now had grave doubts about Sunay and were keen to keep him from doing any mischief, they were caught so unprepared by the speed of events that they hadn't posted a guard at every exit.

So the plan progressed, and Sunay's assurances that there would be no double-cross held firm. Blue was removed from his cell and put into an army truck, which the orderly drove straight to the iron bridge over the Kars River. With the truck parked on the near bank, Blue faithfully followed the instructions he'd been given: he made straight for a grocer's, its windows plastered with posters featuring special deals on garlic sausages, and plastic balls and boxes of detergent piled high behind them. He then slipped out the back, where a horse-drawn carriage was waiting. Taking cover under the tarpaulin and making himself comfortable among the gas canisters, he was whisked off to a safe house. Ka would hear of all this after the fact. At the time, only Fazıl knew where the horse-drawn carriage had taken Blue.

It was an hour and a half before this business was concluded. At about half-past three, as the oleander and chestnut trees were losing their shadows, disappearing like ghosts, giving way to the first shades of darkness to descend on the empty streets of Kars, Fazıl came to tell Kadife that Blue had reached his hiding-place. From the door leading from the courtyard to the kitchen, he stared at Kadife as if having just landed from outer space, but Kadife – just as she'd always failed to notice Necip – took no heed of Fazıl. Instead, she sprung with joy up to her room.

İpek was just leaving Ka's room, where she'd been for over an hour. It had been an hour of undiluted bliss, and my dear friend's heart was soaring as never before at the prospect of his future happiness, as I shall undertake to explain in the opening pages of the next chapter.

37

The Only Script We Have This Evening is Kadife's Hair

Preparations for the Play to End All Plays

As I have already mentioned, Ka was one of those who shy away from happiness for fear of the pain that might follow. So we already know that his most intense emotions came not when he was happy but when he was beset by the certainty that this happiness would soon be lost to him. When he rose from Sunay's raki table and returned to the Snow Palace Hotel with his two bodyguards, Ka still believed that everything was going according to plan, and the prospect of seeing İpek again filled his heart with joy, even as the fear of loss was fast overtaking him. When my friend later alluded to the poem he wrote on Thursday afternoon around three o'clock, he made it clear that his soul was vacillating between these two poles, so I now feel it my duty to pass on what he said. The poem, to which Ka gave the title 'Dog', seems to have been inspired by another chance encounter with the charcoal-coloured station dog, this time on his way back to the hotel from the tailor's shop. Four minutes later, he was back in his room, writing out this poem, and great as his hopes for happiness might have been at the time, the fear of loss was now spreading through his body like poison: love equalled pain. The poem refers to his great fear of dogs as a child, to the strays that would bark at him in Maçka Park when he was six, and to a cruel neighbour who was always allowing his dog to chase passers-by. Later in life, Ka had come to see his fear of dogs as punishment for his many hours of childhood bliss. But underlying all of this he felt there was a paradox: Heaven and Hell were in the same place. Because in those same streets he had played football, gathered mulberries, collected those football-player cards you got with chewing gum, and it was precisely because the dogs turned the scene of these childish joys into a living hell that he felt the joys so keenly.

Seven or eight minutes after hearing of his return to the hotel, İpek went up to his room. Considering that İpek could not have been certain of his return, and bearing in mind that Ka had sent her no message, this was a very modest delay. For the first time, they'd managed to meet without Ka having the time to read any dark motives into her tardiness, much less being able to conclude that she'd abandoned him. This achievement made Ka even happier. What's more, İpek's face was also radiating happiness, and something in her expression implied she couldn't be talked out of it. Ka confirmed that everything was going to plan, and she did likewise. She asked about Blue, and Ka told her that his release was imminent. İpek glowed at this news, just as she had when he'd told her everything else. It was not enough to be convinced that their own fortunes were still on course; they had to believe all the unhappiness around them had been extinguished to keep a shadow from falling over their own bliss. Despite incessant embraces and impatient kisses, they refrained from getting into bed to make love. Ka told İpek that once they were in Istanbul he'd be able to get her a German visa in a day: he had a friend at the consulate. They'd need to marry right away to qualify, but they could always have a proper ceremony and celebration later if they wished. They discussed the possibility of Kadife and Turgut Bey joining them in Frankfurt once their own affairs in Kars were settled; Ka even mentioned the names of some hotels where they might stay. Their heads were so dizzy with wild dreams that they were even a bit ashamed of themselves. İpek changed the tone to tell Ka about her father's anxieties, particularly his fear of suicide bombers, and she warned him that on no account was he to go out into the street again. Then, promising each other that they would leave the city on the first bus, they spent a long time standing at the window, hand in hand, gazing at the snowy mountain roads.

İpek said that she'd already started packing. Ka told her not to bring anything, but İpek had quite a few things she'd been carrying around with her since childhood, items so much a part of her that she couldn't imagine life without them. Still in front of the window, they saw the dog that had inspired Ka's poem dash in and out of sight, and Ka took stock of those articles İpek insisted she couldn't leave behind: a wristwatch that her mother had given her when İpek was still a child in Istanbul, all the more precious now that Kadife had lost the one given to her on the same day; an ice-blue angora sweater that her late uncle had brought her from Germany, a garment of high quality but so tight-fitting that she'd never been able to wear it in Kars; a tablecloth from her trousseau, embroidered by her mother with silver filigree, which Muhtar had stained with marmalade on the very first use – which explained why there hadn't been a second; seventeen miniature perfume and alcohol bottles holding the collection of evil eyes that she'd started for no particular reason many years earlier and now saw as bringing her *good* luck; the photographs of herself as a child on her parents' laps (the moment she mentioned these, Ka wanted to see them); the beautiful black velvet evening dress Muhtar had bought for her in Istanbul, its back so low that he had only ever allowed her to wear it at home; the embroidered silk satin shawl that she'd bought to conceal the almost equally low-cut front, in the hope of one day inducing Muhtar to change his mind; the suede shoes never worn for fear the Kars mud would ruin them; the jade necklace that she was able to show him because she happened to have it with her.

If I say now that I saw the same impressive jade stone hanging on a black silk cord around İpek's neck exactly four years later, as she sat across from me at a dinner hosted by the mayor of Kars, I hope my readers won't accuse me of having strayed too far from the subject. To the contrary, we are now approaching the heart of the matter. For, until that moment, I could have said I had seen nothing for which I had been prepared so utterly, and so it must be for all of you following the story I have related in this book: İpek was more beautiful than anyone could have imagined. At this dinner, where I had my first glimpse of her, I must confess to finding myself stunned, bedazzled and deeply jealous. And as this passion overtook me, my dear friend's lost poetry collection, which mystery I'd been trying to unravel, turned into a story of a very different order. It was at this astounding moment that I must have decided to write the book now in your hands. But at the time my soul remained entirely unaware of this decision. I was beset by all manner of feelings that women of exceptional beauty never fail to inspire: gazing at this paragon before me, I felt myself crumbling; I felt possessed. When I think back now to the transparent manoeuvres of the other Kars residents at that same table – ploys I'd foolishly ascribed to the aim of exchanging a few words with this novelist who had come to town, or of collecting a few titbits for the next day's gossip – it is clear to me that all their activity served a single purpose: to draw a veil over İpek's beauty, concealing it not just from me but from themselves. A terrible jealousy was gnawing at me that I feared might turn to love: for a while, just like my dear friend Ka, I too dreamed that I might enjoy the affections of a woman this beautiful. For a moment, I let myself forget my sadness at how Ka's life had ultimately come to nothing, and I found myself thinking admiringly: Only a man with a soul as deep as Ka's could have won the heart of a woman like this! Did I myself have the slightest chance of beguiling İpek and whisking her off with me to Istanbul? I would have proposed to her on the spot, or, if she wished, kept her as my secret mistress until the day it all fell apart, but by whatever path I wanted to end up beside her. She had a wide, commanding forehead, moist eyes, elegant lips so much like the film star Melinda's I could hardly trust myself to look at them . . . What, I wondered, did she think of me? Had I ever come up in conversation between her and Ka? Without another sip of raki, my head was swimming, my heart pounding. Then I noticed Kadife, sitting just a few places away, and lancing me with a fierce glare. I must return to my story . . .

As they stood before the window, Ka picked up the jade necklace, draped it around İpek's neck, and, giving her a tender kiss, carelessly recited the words fast becoming an incantation: they would be happy in Germany. Just then, İpek saw Fazıl dart into the courtyard; she waited for a moment and went downstairs, where she found Kadife standing at the kitchen door. It was here that she must have heard the good news about Blue's release. The two women bounded up to Kadife's room. Ka remained in his own room. His heart was so full of his new poems and his new faith in love that, for the first time, the part of his mind that had kept track – sometimes meticulously, sometimes fancifully – of their every movement through the Snow Palace Hotel was now at rest, and he let them go.

At about this time the weather bureau announced the first clear signs of a thaw. The sun had been shining all day long and now the icicles dangling from the trees and eaves began to drip and then drop, and the rumours started to spread throughout the city: the roads were sure to open tonight and this theatre coup would come to an end. Those who remembered the evening's events in detail told me that Kars Border Television ran the first announcement of the new play that the Sunay Zaim Players would be performing that evening at the National Theatre immediately after the weather report. It was Hakan Özge, the city's favourite young announcer, who advised the people of Kars that the bloody events of two days earlier were no cause for concern, and in any case no excuse for non-attendance. Security forces would be flanking the stage, and as the event was free to the general public, the people of Kars should feel welcome to bring the entire family. The effect of these assurances was to fan popular fears and empty the streets earlier than usual. Everyone was convinced there would be another evening of violence and madness at the National Theatre. So, apart from the usual assortment of wild-eyed ne'er-do-wells prepared to attend virtually anything just to say that they had (their sizeable ranks comprising aimless, unemployed youths, bored leftists with a penchant for violence, elderly denture-wearers so desperate for entertainment it mattered little to them if anyone was killed in the process, and staunch Kemalists who'd seen Sunay on TV and admired his republican views), most Kars residents decided they would stay at home to watch the live broadcast on television.

Meanwhile, Sunay and Colonel Osman Nuri Çolak met again. Fearing that the National Theatre would be empty, they sent out the army trucks to gather up all the religious high-school boys, and let it be known that all lycée students, all resident teachers and all government officials in the city were required to report to the performance in coat and tie.

After the meeting, a number of people saw Sunay passed out in the back of the tailor's shop on a small, dusty floormat, surrounded by scraps of cloth, paper wrappers and empty boxes. This wasn't a case of drunken expedience. For years, Sunay had been convinced that soft beds would make his body go soft, so he was in the habit of napping on a hard, coarse mattress before any great performance of huge importance to him. Before he could lie down, however, he'd had a row with his wife about the script, which had yet to be finalised, so he put her into an army truck and sent her over to join Kadife at the Snow Palace Hotel and begin rehearsals.

Funda Eser sauntered into the hotel like a woman to whom all doors are open. She went straight up to Kadife's room, and the dulcet tones by which she so effortlessly created an atmosphere of female intimacy offered off stage a more compelling proof of her greatness than the play that night would ever allow her. Certainly, her eyes must have noticed İpek's crystalline beauty, but her mind was on the role Kadife was to play that evening. Her own estimation of this role must have derived from the importance her husband gave it. Because, in the twenty years she'd been touring Anatolia playing wronged and raped women, the only goal she'd ever had when presenting the victim was to arouse the men in the audience. Marriages, divorces, the covering of heads or the baring of them – these were all means to the same ordinary end: to reduce the heroine to such a state of helplessness that no man could resist her. However, although it is impossible to say whether she fully understood her roles in dramas celebrating the republican enlightenment, it must be allowed that the male dramatists who invented these stereotypes could not see a heroine expressing a notion any deeper or more refined than eroticism or social duty. Funda Eser used these roles to splendid effect in her life off stage, and to a degree the male dramatists could not have anticipated.

Not long after entering the room, she suggested to Kadife that they rehearse the scene in which she was to bare her head and reveal her beautiful hair. Kadife feigned reluctance, but not for long, and when she loosened her mane, Funda let out a loud cry, remarking how healthy and shiny it was, and that she couldn't take her eyes off it. Sitting Kadife in front of the mirror, Funda picked up an imitation-ivory comb and, running it slowly through Kadife's hair, explained that the essence of theatre was to be found not in the words but in the images. 'Let your hair speak for itself, and let the men go mad!' she said.

By now, she had Kadife's head spinning, so she kissed the young woman's hair to calm her down. She was clever enough to see that this kiss awakened the dormant evil that Kadife kept hidden, and experienced enough to draw İpek into the game, too. Providing a flask from her bag, she began to pour cognac into the tea glasses Zahide had set for them. When Kadife objected, she mocked her, saying, 'But tonight you're going to bare your head!'

Kadife burst into tears, and Funda planted insistent little kisses on her cheeks, her neck and her hands. Then, to amuse the sisters, she recited 'Sunay's unknown masterpiece', 'The Innocent Air Hostess Protests'. But, far from diverting İpek and Kadife, this only made them more anxious.

When Kadife said, 'I would like to study the script,' Funda pro-claimed that the only script that counted that night would be the moment when all the men of Kars gazed, dumbfounded, at her long, beautiful, radiant hair. The women in the audience would be so moved by love and jealousy that they would want to reach out and touch it. As she said this, she kept refilling their glasses with cognac. She said that when she looked into İpek's face, she saw happiness; and when she looked into Kadife's, she saw courage and fury. But she couldn't decide which sister was the more beautiful. Funda Eser continued in this amusing vein until a purple-faced Turgut Bey burst into the room.

'They've just announced on television that Kadife, the leader of the headscarf girls, is going to bare her head during this evening's per-formance,' he said. 'Tell me – is this true?'

'Let's see this on TV!' said İpek.

'Please allow me to introduce myself, sir,' said Funda Eser. 'I am the life partner of the illustrious actor and newly anointed statesman Sunay Zaim. My name is Funda Eser. I would like to congratulate you on having raised two such marvellous and outstanding daugh-ters. Thanks to Kadife's heroic decision, I can advise you that you have nothing to fear.'

'If my daughter does this, the religious fanatics in this city will never forgive her,' said Turgut Bey.

They moved to the dining room so they could all watch the televi-sion. Funda Eser took Turgut Bey by the hand and said something to the effect that she could promise, in the name of her husband, the city's supreme ruler, that everything would go according to plan. Then, hearing noise in the dining room, Ka came in to join them, whereupon a happy Kadife informed him that Blue had been released. Without waiting for Ka to ask, she declared that she was planning to keep the promise she had made to him that morning, and that she and Funda Hanım were now preparing to rehearse the play.

As everyone watched the television, talking over one another, Funda Eser applied herself to charming Turgut Bey lest he should stand in the way of his daughter's appearance. Ka would often think back to this ten-minute interlude as one of the happiest of his life. He was now utterly free of doubt about his destiny of lifelong happiness and was dreamily imagining life as part of this jovial family. It was not yet four o'clock, but the dark old wallpaper in the high-ceilinged dining room was already as comforting as a childhood memory. Looking into İpek's eyes, Ka could not help but smile.

Seeing Fazıl standing at the door to the kitchen, Ka hastened to push him back inside, and, before the boy could ruin the mood, pump him for information. But Fazıl resisted: he stood fast in the doorway, pretending to stare at the TV screen, but in fact his angry eyes fixed in astonishment on the animated crowd around it. Seeing that Ka was trying to manoeuvre the boy into the kitchen, İpek walked over to them.

'Blue wants to talk to you one more time,' said Fazıl, and it was clear from the tone of his voice that he was happy to be ruining the party. 'He's changed his mind about something.'

'About what?'

'He'll tell you himself. The carriage will pick you up in the courtyard in ten minutes,' he said, leaving the kitchen to return to the courtyard himself.

Ka's heart began to pound: it wasn't just reluctance to set foot outside the hotel again today; he was also afraid that his cowardice would betray him.

'Please, whatever you do, don't go!' cried İpek, giving voice to Ka's own thoughts. 'After all, they know all about the carriage by now. No good can come of this.'

'No, I'm going,' said Ka.

Why, given his reluctance, did he decide to go? It was an old habit. In school, whenever a teacher asked a question he knew he couldn't answer, he'd always raise his hand. He was the sort who went into a shop and, finding the perfect sweater, perversely bought something else not nearly as suitable for the same money, knowing all the while it made no sense. It may have been a form of anxiety that made him do this, or perhaps it was his fear of happiness.

They went up to his room, taking care that Kadife didn't notice. How Ka wished that İpek had found a little ingenuity, contrived something imaginative to let her linger in the room with peace of mind, but as they stood looking out of the window, İpek could voice only the same impotent words, adding: 'Don't go, darling, don't leave the hotel at all today. Don't put our happiness at risk,' and so on.

Ka listened dreamily, like a sacrificial lamb. Soon the horse-drawn carriage appeared in the courtyard: he was shocked to see how quickly his luck had turned and it broke his heart. Without pausing to give İpek a kiss, but remembering to embrace her and say his farewells, he went downstairs. His two bodyguards were in the lobby reading papers, but he managed to slip past them into the kitchen, and then out through the back door and into the hated horse-drawn carriage, to lie down once again underneath the tarpaulin.

It is tempting to read too much into this moment. We are, after all, fast approaching the point of no return, and the mission on which Ka was now embarked would change his life for ever. So I feel obliged to caution readers against viewing Ka's decision to accept Blue's invitation as the pivotal moment in this story. Certainly, I am not of this view myself: Ka had not yet run out of chances. He still had time to make a success of his visit to Kars, and he would have other opportunities to put right his fortunes and find 'happiness' – whatever it was he meant by that word. But, with all his bridges burned, when the events in this story had reached their conclusion, it was this moment that Ka himself would look back to with stinging regret and undying curiosity as to how things might have turned out if only İpek had managed to keep him in his room. She might have said something to talk him out of going to see Blue, but, even after he'd racked his brain hundreds of times over the following years, he'd still had no idea what the right words might have been.

As we turn back to the image of Ka under the tarpaulin, we are right to see him as a man who has surrendered to his fate. He was sorry to be there; he was angry with himself and with the world. He was cold; he was afraid of falling ill; and he knew no good could come of this appointment. He paid careful attention to the noises of the street and to what people said as the carriage passed by, just as he had done during his first journey in this carriage, but this time he was not in the least interested to know where in Kars the carriage was taking him.

When the carriage came to a halt, the driver prodded him, and Ka emerged from underneath the tarpaulin. Before he could discern where he was, he saw in front of him a decrepit building that, like so many others in Kars, was lurching to one side and half-covered in flaking paint. Inside, he made his way up a narrow, crooked staircase to the landing two floors up. (In a happier moment, he would remember seeing a door with shoes at the threshold and a child's bright eyes staring at him through the gap in the wood.) The door opened and he found himself face to face with Hande.

'I've made up my mind,' said Hande with a smile. 'I'm refusing to cut myself off from the girl I really am.'

'It's important for you to be happy.'

'What makes me happy is being here and doing what I want,' said Hande. 'It doesn't scare me any more if I'm someone else in my dreams.'

'Isn't it a little dangerous for you to be here at all?'

'Yes, but it's only in times of danger that a person can really concentrate on life,' she said. 'What I understand now is that I will never be able to concentrate on things I don't believe in, things like baring my head. Right now I'm happy to share a cause with Blue. Could you write poems here?'

Although only two days had passed since their first meeting, Ka's memories of their dinner conversation were now so distant that for a moment he stood there gaping like an amnesiac. How much did Hande wish to draw attention to her intimacy with Blue? The girl opened the door to the next room for Ka to find Blue watching a black-and-white television.

'I knew you'd come,' said Blue. He seemed pleased.

'I have no idea why I'm here,' said Ka.

'You're here because of the turmoil inside you,' said Blue. Now he looked very knowing.

They eyed each other hatefully. It didn't escape either of them that Blue was delighted about something, and that Ka was full of sorrow. Hande left the room and closed the door.

'I want you to tell Kadife not to have anything to do with that disaster they plan to stage this evening,' said Blue.

'Couldn't you have sent this news with Fazıl?' said Ka. He could tell from the expression on his face that Blue had no idea who Fazıl was, so he added, 'He's the religious high-school boy you sent to fetch me.'

'Ha!' said Blue. 'Kadife wouldn't have taken him seriously. You're the only one she's going to take seriously. And it's only when she hears this from you that she'll understand how serious I am about my decision. And she'll understand why after she's seen the loathsome way they're promoting this on television.'

'When I left the hotel, Kadife was already starting to rehearse,' said Ka with pleasure.

'Then you can tell her that I couldn't be more opposed to this performance. Kadife didn't decide of her own free will to bare her head

– she did it to free *me*. She was negotiating with a state that takes political prisoners as hostages, so she's under no obligation to keep her word.'

'I can tell her all this,' said Ka. 'But I can't predict what she'll do.'

'In other words, if Kadife decides to play this her way, you're not responsible – that's what you're trying to tell me, is it?'

Ka said nothing.

'Then let me make it clear. If Kadife goes on stage this evening and bares her head, you, too, *will* be to blame. You've been involved in this deal every step of the way.'

For the first time since his arrival in Kars, Ka felt the peace of righteousness: at long last, the villain was talking like a villain, and saying all the vicious things that all villains say. His head cleared with this realisation. 'You're right to think you are a hostage,' he said in the hope of calming Blue, as he considered how he might get out of this place without angering him further.

'Give her this letter,' said Blue. He handed Ka an envelope. 'Kadife may refuse to believe my spoken message.' Ka took the envelope. 'And one day, when you've found your way back to Frankfurt, I trust you'll also find a way to make Hans Hansen publish that statement which so many people risked so much to sign.'

'Of course.'

There was something in Blue's face that hinted at frustration. He'd been far more relaxed that morning as he sat in his cell awaiting execution. Now he'd managed to save himself, but he was already looking ahead with anger, aggrieved to know he'd never manage to do anything in life but generate more wrath. Ka was slow to realise that Blue also saw what Ka could see.

'It doesn't matter where you live – here, or in your beloved Europe – you'll always be imitating them; you'll always be grovelling.'

'If I'm happy, that's all I care about.'

'You can go now,' shouted Blue. 'And know this: people who seek only happiness never find it.'

38

I Didn't Bring You Here to Upset You

An Enforced Visit

Ka was glad to get away from Blue, but at the same time he knew there was now a bond, however damning, between them. It was not a simple bond – there was more to it than fear and hatred – for as Ka shut the door behind him, he realised with some remorse that he was going to miss this man.

Hande appeared, all good intentions and deep thoughts, and, though Ka tried to dismiss her as utterly guileless and even rather simple, he soon found himself ceding to her the higher ground. Eyes opened wide, Hande asked him to send her best to Kadife and tell her it didn't matter what she decided about baring her head on television (no, she didn't say on *stage*; she said *television*) – Hande's heart would be with her no matter what she did. She then told Ka what he needed to do by way of leaving the building without attracting the attention of the plainclothes police.

Ka fled from the apartment in a panic, but on the first-floor landing he felt a poem coming, so he sat down in front of the shoes lined up beside the door, took out his notebook and began to write.

It was the eighteenth poem Ka had written since his arrival in Kars. Its subject was the link between love and hate, but if he hadn't explained the allusion in the notes he later wrote, no one could have guessed it. When he was at the Advanced Şişli Middle School, there'd been a boy whose family owned a prosperous construction company. This boy, who had won a Balkan equestrian championship, was very spoiled, but Ka was fascinated by his air of independence. Then there was another boy, whose mother, a White Russian, had been a lycée classmate of Ka's mother. He'd grown up without a father, without any siblings, and while he was still a student, he had started using drugs. Although this enigmatic, pallid boy had never seemed to pay anyone any mind, it turned out he always knew everything to be known about those around him. Finally, during Ka's military training in Tuzla, there'd been a handsome, laconic, rather aloof wise guy in the neighbouring regiment who had tirelessly taunted him with small acts of cruelty, such as hiding his cap. Ka had been bound to all of these fellows by an unveiled contempt and a secret adoration. The title of the poem, 'Jealousy', referred to the feeling that bound together these two conflicting emotions and that also bound Ka to the task of resolving the contradiction in his mind. But the poem itself revealed an even deeper problem: after a time, these boys' souls and voices had taken up residence in Ka's own body.

On leaving the apartment building, Ka still had no idea where he was, but after following a narrow lane he saw that he had reached Halitpaşa Avenue, and something inside him made him turn around and cast a final glance at Blue's hiding-place.

As he made his way back to the hotel, he missed his bodyguards; he felt unsafe without them. Walking past the city hall, he noticed an unmarked police car drawing up alongside him. When he saw the rear door had opened, Ka stopped.

'Ka Bey, please don't be afraid, we're from police headquarters. Why don't you get in? We'll drive you back to the hotel.'

As he was trying to figure out which option was the more danger-ous – returning to the hotel without a police escort or being spotted getting into a police car in the middle of the city – the passenger door swung open. Suddenly a huge brute of a man stood before him. (He seemed so familiar. Who did he look like? It was someone in Istanbul . . . a distant uncle . . . Uncle Mahmut!) Departing from the polite tone of the previous exchange, the giant pushed Ka roughly into the car. Once they were under way he delivered two punches to Ka's head. (Or had he punched him as he was pushing him into the car?) Ka was deeply scared, and inside it was eerily dark. One of the men in the front – not Uncle Mahmut, the driver – was muttering terrible curses. When he was a child, there had been a man on Nigâr the Poetess Street who had cursed that way whenever a ball had landed in his garden.

Now Ka kept calm by telling himself he was a child. The car itself helped in this (the unmarked police cars in Kars were little Renaults, not big, flashy '56 Chevrolets like this one). They took him on a long and winding tour of the dark, mean streets of Kars, as though he were a disobedient child they hoped to frighten; it seemed a very long while before the car finally pulled into a courtyard.

'Face front,' the driver said after they'd pulled him out of the car.

They took him by the arm and led him up two steps. Ka was certain that these men – there were three of them – were not Islamists (where could Islamists have got their hands on a car like this?). And they couldn't be MİT either, because some of those guys were in league with Sunay. A door opened, another door closed, and Ka found himself in another old Armenian house with very high ceilings; the window beside him overlooked Atatürk Avenue. As he scanned the room, he saw a television in the corner and a table covered with dirty plates, orange peel and newspapers. He also saw a Magneto that he later realised must have been used in electric-shock torture. Finally, there were a couple of walkie-talkies, a few guns, a vase, and a mirror in which he saw himself framed . . . When he realised he'd fallen into the hands of a special operations team, he thought he was finished. But when he came eye to eye with Z Demirkol, he relaxed. The man was a murderer, to be sure, but a familiar face at least.

Z Demirkol was playing good cop. He told Ka how sorry he was that they'd had to bring him in like this. Ka guessed that Uncle Mahmut was playing bad cop, so he decided to give his full attention to Z Demirkol and his questions.

'What is Sunay planning?'

Ka sweetly surrendered every scrap of information he possessed, including all there was to know about Kyd's *The Spanish Tragedy*.

'Why did they release that crackpot Blue?'

Ka explained that they'd let him go in exchange for Kadife's promise to bare her head on live television. In a moment of inspiration, he used a pedantic chess term: maybe this was an overambitious 'sacrifice' in need of an exclamation mark. But the fact remained that the political Islamists would see this as a demoralising 'move'.

'How likely is it that the girl will keep her word?'

Ka said that Kadife had agreed to go on stage, but that no one was sure whether she would go through with the unveiling.

'Where is Blue's new hiding-place?' asked Z Demirkol.

Ka said he had no idea.

They then asked why Ka had had no bodyguards when they'd picked him up, and where had he just been?

'I was taking an evening stroll,' said Ka.

When he stuck to this answer, Z Demirkol did exactly what Ka had expected: he quietly left the room, leaving Uncle Mahmut to sit down across from Ka with an evil glare. Like the driver of the car, he had a large repertoire of exotic curses with which he adorned every statement and question. It didn't matter what he was saying: he could be making a threat, or pontificating about national interests, or expounding his highly unoriginal political views. He was like a child who can't eat his supper unless it's swimming in ketchup.

'What do you think you've achieved by concealing the whereabouts of an Islamist terrorist with blood on his hands who is in the pay of Iran?' asked Uncle Mahmut. 'You know what these people will do when they come to power, don't you? What they have planned for porridge-hearted wannabe European liberals like you?'

Ka was quick to confirm that he did know, but Uncle Mahmut was not deterred from describing vividly and at length what the Iranian mullahs had done to their former democratic and communist allies: they'd stuck dynamite up their asses and blown them sky high, lined up all the prostitutes and homosexuals and gunned them down, banned all non-religious books, and when they got their hands on intellectual poseurs like Ka, they would immediately shave their heads, and as for their ludicrous books of poetry . . .

As he launched into another well-rehearsed string of unsavoury anecdotes, by now looking very bored, he paused to ask again where Blue was hiding, and where Ka had been that evening, before they'd picked him up. When Ka offered the same bland answers, Uncle Mahmut, still looking bored, slapped on the handcuffs. 'Watch what I do to you now,' he said before launching into a perfunctory beating: a few aimless slaps around the head, a few half-hearted punches.

Reviewing Ka's notes after the fact, I've been able to identify five reasons why he did not find this beating unbearable. I hope my readers won't judge me too harshly if I make them explicit:

1 Ka believed happiness comprised good and evil in equal measure, so he could readily see the beating as the suffering he was due for the right to take İpek back to Frankfurt.

2 Ka belonged to the ruling elite, and this, he guessed, afforded him a degree of protection. This special operations team surely had one standard for his kind and quite another for the miserable,

guilty hordes of Kars. So, not wishing to leave too many traces of their frustration upon him, they would take care to beat him with restraint, and certainly wouldn't subject him to serious torture.

3 He thought, rightly, that the beating would only heighten İpek's affection for him.

4 During his visit to police headquarters two days earlier, the look on Muhtar's bloody face had been that of a man so guilt-ridden over his country's wretchedness that he could see that in all fairness he had a beating coming to him. Infected by this attitude himself, Ka now stupidly hoped that a good beating would cleanse his own guilt, too.

5 Whatever the discomforts of the beating, they could scarcely equal the pride he felt for being a real political prisoner, standing up to his tormentors, and refusing to divulge the whereabouts of a fugitive.

This last pleasure would have meant far more to him twenty years earlier, but as it now seemed somewhat dated, Ka could not help but feel a little embarrassed. The salty taste of blood gushing from his nose took him back to childhood again. When was the last time he'd had a bloody nose? As Uncle Mahmut and the others turned their attentions to the television, leaving him to languish in a half-lit corner of the room, Ka thought back to the windows that had snapped shut in his face, and all the footballs that had bounced against his nose, and then he remembered the blows to his nose in a scuffle during his military service. As Z Demirkol and his friends tuned in to that night's episode of *Marianna*, Ka, cradling his bloody nose and his swollen head, was perfectly content to be sitting like a child in the corner. It occurred to him that they might search him and find Blue's note. Fear washed over him as he silently watched *Marianna* with his captors and mused that Turgut Bey and his daughters were at the hotel watching the same programme.

During a commercial break, Z Demirkol rose to his feet, pointed to the Magneto on the table, and asked Ka whether he knew what it was for. When Ka said nothing, Z Demirkol answered the question himself, then, like a father menacingly brandishing his belt, he waited in silence.

'Do you want me to tell you why I love Marianna?' he said when the soap opera resumed. 'Because she knows what she wants. But intellectuals like you, you never have the faintest idea, and that makes me sick. You say you want democracy, and then you enter into alliances with Islamic fundamentalists. You say you want human rights, and then you make deals with terrorist murderers . . . You say Europe is the answer, but you go around buttering up Islamists who hate everything Europe stands for . . . You say feminism, and then you help these men wrap their women's heads in scarves. You don't follow your own conscience; you just guess what a European would do in the same situation and act accordingly. But you can't even be a proper European. Do you know what a European would do here? Let's just imagine that your Hans Hansen printed that idiotic statement of yours, and let's say Europe took it seriously and sent a delegation to Kars, the first thing that delegation would do would be to congratulate the army on refusing to surrender the country to the political Islamists. But, of course, the moment those faggots got back to their Europe they'd start complaining about how there was no democracy in Kars. As for people like you, you love to trash the army even while you depend on it to keep the Islamists from cutting you up into little pieces. But you know all this already, and that's why I'm not going to torture you.'

Ka took all of this to signify that the good cop was back in charge; he hoped this meant his release was near and that he'd be able to catch the end of *Marianna* with Turgut Bey and his daughters.

'Before we let you go back to your lover at the hotel, we'd like to disabuse you of a few illusions. We'd like you to know a thing or two about that terrorist you've been making deals with, that murderer whose life you've just saved,' said Z Demirkol. 'But first, get this into your head: you were never in this office. We'll be out of here within an hour. Our new operations centre is the top floor of the religious high school. We'll wait for you there. I'm telling you this because, should you suddenly remember where Blue is hiding or where you went on that "evening stroll" of yours, you may wish to know where to find us. You're already aware that this handsome hero with the midnight-blue eyes is wanted for the barbarous murder of a bird-brained television host who stuck out his tongue at the Prophet Mohammed, and that he was also behind the assassination of the director of the Education Institute. As we all know, you had the pleasure of witnessing first hand this brutal killing, and you know the rest of it, too – you heard it all from Sunay while he was still compos mentis. But there's something else that the diligent agents of MİT have been able to document in some detail, and maybe no one wanted to break your heart by mentioning it. But we think it would be good for you to know.'

We have now arrived at another point to which Ka would return repeatedly over the next four years of his life, like a sentimental projectionist who vainly expects a different ending each time he screens the same sad film.

'This İpek Hanım with whom you hope to return to Frankfurt to live happily ever after – she was, once upon a time, Blue's mistress,' said Z Demirkol softly. 'According to the file I have before me, their relationship dates back four years. At the time, İpek was still married to Muhtar Bey, who, as you know, is no longer running for mayor, having withdrawn from the race of his own free will just the other day. And it seems that this half-witted old leftist – pardon the expression – poet welcomed Blue into his home as an honoured guest. Of course, he was hoping Blue would help him organise the city's Islamist youth, but don't you think it's a shame no one ever told him what a passionate relationship the firebrand was enjoying with his wife while he was sitting in his warehouse trying to sell electric cookers?'

This is a prepared speech. He's lying, thought Ka.

'The first person to become aware of the illicit affair – not counting the surveillance staff, of course – was Kadife Hanım. By then, İpek Hanım's marital relations were troubled, so when her sister came home to attend university, İpek used this as an excuse to move with her sister to another house. Blue was still visiting Kars at every opportunity, to "organise Islamist youth", and naturally he would always stay with his great admirer, Muhtar. So, whenever Kadife had classes, the two wild-eyed lovers conducted their assignations in the new house. This continued until Turgut Bey returned to Kars, at which point he and his two daughters took up residence in the Snow Palace Hotel. That was when Kadife, the leader of the headscarf girls, began *her* relationship with Blue. Our young Casanova managed to string along both women for some time after that. We have proof.'

Ka forced himself to avoid Z Demirkol's gaze, turning his now streaming eyes to the flickering, snow-covered streetlamps of Atatürk Avenue.

'I'm telling you all this only because I want you to see that a soft heart gets you nowhere, and you have no reason to conceal the whereabouts of this murderous monster,' said Z Demirkol, who, like all special operations agents, grew increasingly vituperative the more he talked. 'I didn't bring you here to upset you. It occurs to me that you might doubt whether what I've just told you has been fully documented by the surveillance teams who have been skilfully bugging the city for forty years now. Perhaps you think I just made up a load of nonsense. Maybe İpek Hanım, in her determination to keep your dream of Frankfurt happiness untainted, will manage to convince you it's all lies. Your heart is fragile and may not be strong enough to accept what I'm telling you, but allow me to chase away any doubts you might have. I shall, with your permission, read out a few excerpts of phone conversations. As I do, I ask you to bear in mind the expense lavished on this long surveillance operation, and the time it must have taken the poor secretaries to transcribe these conversations.'

'"My darling, my dearest, the days I spend without you I'm hardly alive!" That, for example, is what İpek Hanım said on a hot summer day four years ago – 16 August, to be precise – and this probably alluded to one of their first separations. Two months later, when Blue was in town to speak at a conference on "Islam and the Private Sphere of Women", he rang her from various grocers' and tea-houses all over the city – eight times in all – and they talked of nothing but how much they loved each other. Two months after that, when İpek was still entertaining the idea of eloping with him, she said, and I quote, "Everyone has only one true love in life, and you are that love in mine." Another time, out of jealousy over Merzuka, the wife he kept in Istanbul, İpek made clear to Blue that she wouldn't make love to him while her father was under the same roof. But here's the punchline: in the past two days alone, she's phoned him three times. She may have made more calls today. We don't yet have the transcripts of these last conversations, but that doesn't matter. When you see İpek Hanım, you can ask her yourself.

'I'm so sorry to upset you. I can see I've said enough. Please stop crying. Let me ask my friends to remove those handcuffs so you can wash your face. And then, if you want, my associates will take you back to the hotel.'

39

The Joys of Crying Together

Ka and İpek Meet at the Hotel

Ka declined the escort. After wiping the blood from his nose and mouth, he splashed some water over his face and, turning to the murderous villains who'd been holding him captive, bade them good evening, timidly, like an uninvited guest who had nevertheless stayed for supper. He staggered down the ill-lit Atatürk Avenue in the manner of a common drunk, turning for no particular reason into Halitpaşa Avenue. Only when he passed the little shop where he'd heard Peppino di Capri singing "Roberta" did he begin to sob again. Here, too, he ran into the slim and handsome villager who'd been his travelling companion on the bus from Erzurum to Kars, and who'd been so gracious and uncomplaining when Ka had fallen asleep and his head had rested in the man's lap. It seemed almost all of Kars was inside watching *Marianna*, but, as Ka continued down Halitpaşa, he also bumped into the lawyer Muzaffer Bey; and later, turning into Kâzım Karabekir Avenue, the bus company manager and his elderly friend, both of whom he'd first met in the lodge of His Excellency Sheikh Saadettin. He could tell from the looks that all of these men gave him that tears were still streaming down his cheeks. All those times he'd walked up and down these streets, past icy shop windows, teeming tea-houses, photography shops exhibiting their pictures of Kars in better days, flickering streetlamps, great wheels of cheese in grocers' windows, he knew – even though he didn't see them on the corner of Kâzım Karabekir and Karadağ avenues – that his plainclothes shadows were there.

Before entering the hotel, he paused to assure the bodyguards at the door that everything was on track. He did his best to steal up to his room without being noticed, threw himself on to the bed and immediately broke down. When he had managed to calm himself, he settled in to wait; and, though it was only a couple of minutes, it seemed longer than any time he'd ever spent waiting as a child, lying in bed, listening to the sounds of the city streets. There was a knock on the door. It was İpek. The boy at reception had told her something strange seemed to have happened to Ka, and she had come straight up. When she saw Ka's face, she gasped and fell silent. Neither spoke for some time.

'I've found out about your relationship with Blue,' whispered Ka.

'Did he tell you himself?'

Ka turned off the lamp. 'Z Demirkol and his friends hauled me in,' he said, still very softly. 'They've been taping your phone conversations for four years.' He lay down again, weeping silently. 'I want to die,' he said.

When İpek reached out to run her fingers through his hair, he cried even harder. Despite the loss they were suffering, they'd both relaxed – as people do when they realise they've lost their chance for happiness. İpek stretched out on the bed and wrapped her arms around him. For a while, they cried together, and this drew them closer.

As they lay in the dark, İpek answered Ka's questions and told her story. She said it was all Muhtar's fault: not only had he invited Blue into their home; he had wanted his Islamist hero to marvel at what a wondrous creature his wife was. Muhtar was treating İpek very badly at the time, and blaming her for their childlessness. And, as Ka knew only too well, Blue has a way with words, so he knew just how to turn the head of an unhappy woman. No sooner had she succumbed than she frantically started to act to avert disaster. Her first concern was to keep Muhtar in the dark – she still cared a great deal for him and didn't want to hurt him. But when the love affair started to peter out, her main worry was how to extricate herself.

In the beginning, Blue had been so attractive because of his obvious superiority to Muhtar: her husband would make a fool of himself by talking ignorantly about politics, and İpek would feel ashamed for him. This was exacerbated after she and Blue had found each other, and poor Muhtar would continue to sing his praises, always urging him to visit Kars more often, and chiding İpek for not treating him with enough hospitality and tolerance. Even when she moved to the new house to live with Kadife, Muhtar still had no clue; and, unless Z Demirkol and his friends set him straight, he would never know.

Sharp-eyed Kadife, on the other hand, had worked it all out by the end of her first day in the city, and her real motivation for associating with the headscarf girls was to get closer to Blue. İpek, who'd been living with Kadife's jealousy since childhood, was not blind to her sister's interest in Blue; on seeing Blue's fickle reciprocation of Kadife's affection, İpek's own feelings for her lover cooled. And she saw that if Kadife became involved with him, she'd have the opportunity to free herself. Once her father moved to Kars, she was able to keep her faithless lover at bay.

Her account effectively reduced the affair with Blue to a mistake that was already buried in the past, and Ka might have believed her, until she suddenly succumbed to some childish impulse and blurted out, 'The truth is, Blue doesn't really love Kadife. He loves me!' This was not what Ka wanted to hear, so he asked what İpek now thought of this 'filthy man'. Refusing to be drawn on the subject, she simply reiterated that it was all in the past, and her only wish now was to go with Ka to Frankfurt. At this point, Ka remembered Z Demirkol's final claim: that İpek had been in contact with Blue by phone several times over the last few days. İpek insisted that there'd been no such conversations, and that, anyway, Blue was too savvy to take a call that might allow his hunters to track him down.

'We're never going to be happy,' said Ka.

'No, we're going to Frankfurt, and we *are* going to be happy,' said İpek, throwing her arms around him.

According to İpek, Ka believed her for a moment, then tears returned to his eyes.

She held him tighter and tighter, and they cried together. As Ka would later write, it may have been now, as they were holding each other and crying, that İpek discovered something for the first time: to live in indecision, to waver between defeat and a new life, could offer one as much pleasure as pain. The ease with which they could hold each other and cry this way made Ka love her all the more; but, even as he embraced İpek with all his strength, part of him was already calculating his next move and remained alert to the sounds from the street. It was almost six o'clock: the next day's edition of the *Border City Gazette* was ready for circulation; the snow ploughs were already going at their furious pace to clear the road to Sarıkamış; Funda Eser, having worked her charms and spirited Kadife into the army truck, was with her at the National

Theatre, where the two women were rehearsing the play with Sunay.

It took Ka half an hour to get around to telling İpek of the message he was carrying from Blue for Kadife. Throughout this time of holding each other and crying, they'd come close to making love, but fear, indecision and jealousy had intervened to hold him back. Instead, Ka began to ask when İpek had last seen Blue; repeatedly, he accused her of speaking to him every day. Then he accused her of *seeing* him every day, too; of still being his lover. Ka would later recall that, while İpek initially baulked at his questions and accusations, angry at his refusal to believe her, subsequently, when she came to see that the emotional undercurrents were more powerful than the words themselves, she began to answer him with more compassion. She seemed to find the gentleness of her own voice soothing. There was even a part of her that embraced the hurt which Ka's questions and accusations were causing her. During his last four years, which he dedicated to remorse and regret, Ka would admit to himself that those given to verbal abuse are often obsessed by a need to know how much their lovers loved them – and so it had been with him throughout his life. Even as he taunted her in his cracked voice that she wanted Blue, that she loved him more, he was interested not so much in İpek's answers, but in how patient she would be with him.

'You're only trying to punish me for having had a relationship with him,' said İpek.

'You only want me because you're trying to forget him,' said Ka. Looking into her face, he saw with horror that he'd spoken the truth, but this time he did not lose his composure. His outburst had renewed his strength. 'Blue has sent Kadife a message from his hiding-place,' he said. 'He now says he wants Kadife to continue with her work: she must refuse to go on stage and bare her head. He's quite adamant.'

'Let's not tell Kadife any of this,' said İpek.

'Why not?'

'Because if we keep quiet we'll have Sunay's protection all the way through. And it's best for Kadife, too. I want to put some space between him and my sister.'

Ka said, 'You mean you want to break them up.' He could see from İpek's eyes that she had ceased to humour his jealousy and that he had fallen in her estimation, but he couldn't stop himself.

'I broke up with Blue a very long time ago.'

Still unconvinced by İpek's protestations, anger and jealousy now ruled Ka, and his realisation of this only inflamed his misery. 'Just how much did you love him?' With tears in his eyes, he waited to hear what İpek would say next.

'A lot,' she replied, determinedly.

'I want you to tell me just how much.' Although he had lost his cool, Ka sensed that İpek was wavering – she wanted to be honest, but she also wanted to assuage his pain by sharing it. She wanted to punish Ka, but at the same time she was sad to see him suffer.

'I loved him more than I'd ever loved anyone before,' she said finally, and averted her eyes.

'Maybe that's because the only other man you'd been with was Muhtar.'

He regretted these words even as he was saying them, not only because they were hurtful, but because he knew İpek would say something even harsher in reply.

'It's true,' she said. 'Like most Turkish girls, I've not had much opportunity to get to know a lot of men. But you probably met quite a few independent women in Europe. I'm not going to ask you about any of them, but surely they taught you that new lovers wipe out old ones.'

'I'm a Turk,' said Ka.

'Most of the time, "I'm a Turk" is either an excuse or a pretext for evil.'

'That's why I'm going back to Frankfurt,' said Ka listlessly.

'I'm coming with you and we're going to be happy there.'

'You want to come to Frankfurt because you hope you can forget him there.'

'If we go to Frankfurt together, it won't be long, I'm sure, before I love you. I'm not like you: it takes me longer than two days to fall in love with someone. If you're patient, if you don't break my heart with your Turkish jealousy, I'll love you deeply.'

'But right now you don't love me,' said Ka. 'You're still in love with Blue. What is it about this man that makes him so special?'

'I'm glad you've asked, and I believe you really do want to know, but I'm worried about how you'll take my answer.'

'Don't be afraid,' said Ka, again without conviction. 'I love you with all my heart.'

'First, let me say that the only man I could ever live with is the man who could listen to what I am about to say and still find it in him to love me.' İpek paused for a moment; she turned her eyes away from Ka to gaze at the snow-covered street. 'Blue is very compassionate, very thoughtful and generous.' Her voice was warm with love. 'He doesn't want anyone to suffer. He cried all night once, just because two little puppies had lost their mother. Believe me, he's not like anyone else.'

'Isn't he a murderer?' asked Ka hopelessly.

'Even someone who knows only a tenth of what I know about him will tell you what stupid nonsense that is. He couldn't kill anyone. He's a child. Like a child, he enjoys playing games and getting lost in his daydreams and mimicking people. He loves telling stories from the *Shehname* and *Mesnevi*. Behind that mask, he's a very interesting person. He's very strong-willed, he's decisive, he's so powerful, but also so much fun . . . Oh, I'm so sorry, darling, don't cry, please, you've cried enough.'

Ka stopped crying for a moment, long enough to tell İpek that he no longer believed they'd be able to go to Frankfurt together.

There followed a long, eerie silence, punctuated only by Ka's sobs. He lay down on the bed, his back to the window, and curled up like a child. After a time, İpek lay down next to him, her arms around his back.

Ka wanted to say, 'Leave me alone,' but instead he whispered, 'Hold me tighter.'

His tears had soaked the pillow, and he liked the way it felt against his cheek. He also liked İpek's arms around him. He fell asleep, as did İpek.

When they awoke it was seven o'clock, and at that moment they both felt that happiness was still within reach. But, unable to look each other in the eye, they were both searching for an excuse to leave.

Ka began to speak, but İpek interrupted him and said, 'Forget it, darling, just forget it.'

For a moment, he couldn't work out what she was trying to tell him: that it was all hopeless or that she knew they'd be able to put the past behind them?

He thought İpek was leaving. He knew very well that if he returned to Frankfurt alone, there would be no more solace, even in his melancholy old daily routines.

'Don't go yet, let's sit here a little longer.'

After a discomfiting silence, they embraced once again.

'Oh my God!' cried Ka. 'My God, what's to become of us?'

'Everything will turn out fine,' said İpek. 'Please believe me. Trust me. Come, let me show you the things I'm packing for Frankfurt.'

Ka was relieved just to get out of his room. Once they were in her room, İpek opened a drawer and took out the ice-blue sweater she'd never been able to wear in Kars; after unfolding it and shaking out the mothballs, she stood in front of the mirror, holding it up to her chest.

'Put it on,' said Ka.

İpek pulled off her thick woollen pullover and exchanged it for the ice-blue sweater. It was very tight and as she fitted it over her blouse Ka was once again overcome by her beauty.

'Will you love me for the rest of your life?' asked Ka.

'Yes.'

'Now put on the dress that Muhtar would let you wear only at home.'

İpek opened the wardrobe, and took the black velvet dress off its hanger; unfastening it with great care, she prepared to put it on.

'I like it when you look at me like that,' she said as their eyes met in the mirror.

He gazed at the woman's long, beautiful back, at that tender spot just below the hairline, and at the shadow of her backbone and the dimples that formed on her shoulders as she gathered up her hair to pose for him. He felt overwhelming pleasure, but jealousy, too. He felt happy, and very evil.

'Oh, what's this dress?' said Turgut Bey as he walked into the room. 'So, tell me, where's the ball?' But his face was joyless.

Ka took it for paternal jealousy, which heightened his pleasure.

'Since Kadife left for the theatre, the television announcements have become much more aggressive,' said Turgut Bey. 'If she appears in this play, she'll be making a big mistake.'

'Daddy dearest, can you please explain to me why we should be against Kadife baring her head?'

They entered the sitting room to stand in front of the TV. An announcer soon appeared, to proclaim that this evening's live performance would bring to an end a tragedy that had visited social and spiritual paralysis upon the nation, and that the people of Kars would be delivered at last from the religious prejudices that for too long had excluded them from modern life and prevented women from enjoying equality with men. Once again life and art were to merge in a bewitching historical tale of unparalleled beauty, it was promised. But this time, the people of Kars had no reason to fear for their safety, because the Central Police Station and the Martial Law Command had taken every conceivable precaution. Furthermore, admission was free.

Then Kasım Bey, the assistant chief of police, appeared on the screen. It was immediately obvious that he had been taped earlier. His hair, so dishevelled on the night of the revolution, was now neatly combed, his shirt ironed, his tie knotted neatly in place. After assuring the people of Kars that they should have no qualms about attending that evening's great artistic event, he announced that a large number of religious high-school students had already reported to the Central Police Station to promise decorous attendance and warm applause at all the appropriate moments, just as one did in Europe and other parts of the civilised world. Furthermore, he admonished, 'this time' no rowdiness would be tolerated – no one would get away with shouting or hissing or making coarse comments of any sort. But this should be no problem for the people of Kars, he continued, because, after all, they were part of a civilisation that had been prospering for a thousand years, and so knew exactly how to behave at the theatre. With that, he vanished.

The announcer returned to the screen to discuss that evening's fare, explaining how the lead actor, Sunay Zaim, had been waiting for years to perform this piece. There followed a montage of wrinkled posters from the revolutionary plays in which Sunay had so many years ago played Napoleon, Robespierre and Lenin; several black-and-white head-shots of the cast (how thin Funda Eser had been in those days!); and a variety of theatrical mementoes that Ka imagined to be just the sort of detritus a travelling theatrical couple might be carting around with them in a suitcase (old tickets and programmes, cuttings from when Sunay aspired to play Atatürk, tragic scenes staged in sundry Anatolian coffee-houses). Annoying though this promotional footage was, it was reassuring to see Sunay on screen. In one apparently very recent shot, he had an air of such ravaged determination as to appear every inch the dictator, whether from Africa, the Middle East or the Soviet Bloc.

Having by now watched a full day of this montage, the people of Kars were coming to believe that Sunay had indeed brought peace to their city. He was one of them now, a bona fide citizen, and secretly they were beginning to nurture hopes for their future. Eighty years earlier, when the Ottoman and Russian armies had abandoned the city, leaving the Turks and the Armenians to massacre one another, the Turks had devised a brand-new flag to announce the birth of a nation. Seeing this same standard now, stained and moth-eaten but defiantly displayed on the screen, Turgut Bey decided that something terrible was about to happen.

'This man is crazy. He's heading for disaster, and he wants to take us with him. On no account should Kadife go on stage.'

'You're right, she shouldn't,' said İpek. 'But if we tell her you're the one who's forbidding it, well, you know what Kadife is like, Father. She'll run straight out there and bare her head just to be obstinate.'

'What can we do, then?'

'Why not let Ka go to the theatre right now and talk her out of it?' said İpek, turning around to look at him with her eyebrows raised expectantly.

Ka, who had been gazing for the longest while not at the TV but at her, could not fathom what had led to this abrupt change of heart about their scheme, and his puzzlement made him very nervous.

'If she wants to bare her head, then it's better for her to do it at home, after all this is over,' said Turgut Bey to Ka. 'It's clear that Sunay has planned another unspeakable outrage for this evening's performance. I feel like a fool, falling for Funda's assurances and letting my girl go off with those lunatics.'

'Ka can go and talk her out of it, Father.'

Turgut said to Ka, 'Right now, you are the only person who could reason with her – and Sunay trusts you. What happened to your nose, dear boy?'

'I fell on the ice,' said Ka guiltily.

'You fell on your forehead, too, I see.'

'Ka's been walking around the city all day,' said İpek.

'Take Kadife aside when Sunay isn't watching,' said Turgut Bey. 'Don't let on that it was our idea, and make sure she says nothing to Sunay suggesting it was yours. She shouldn't even discuss it with him – better to offer some perfectly plausible excuse, something like "I'm feeling rather ill," and maybe add, "I'll bare my head tomorrow

374

at home." Yes, she should promise to do that. And please, tell Kadife how much we all love her. My child!' Tears welled in Turgut Bey's eyes.

'Father, may I speak to Ka alone for a moment?' asked İpek. She took him over to the dining table and sat him down. Zahide had set the table but not yet served the food.

'Tell Kadife that Blue is in a quandary. Say he's in trouble or else he wouldn't have her do something like this.'

'First tell me why you changed your mind,' said Ka.

'Oh, my darling, there's nothing to be jealous about, please believe me, it's just that I realised my father was right, that's all. Right now, the most important thing is to keep Kadife from this catastrophe.'

'No,' said Ka, choosing his words carefully. 'Something's happened to make you change your mind.'

'Not true: if Kadife can bare her head later, she'll do it, at home.'

'If Kadife doesn't bare her head this evening,' said Ka cautiously, 'she'll never do it in front of her father. You know that as well as I do. What are you hiding from me?'

'Darling, there's nothing. I love you very much. If you want me, I'll go back to Frankfurt with you.'

'I don't believe you,' said Ka, miserably.

'Once we've been there a while,' she continued, ignoring his doubts, 'you'll see just how securely I'm bound to you, how much I love you. You'll put these few days behind you. You'll love and trust me, too.'

She put her hand on his, which was warm and moist. In the mirror over the sideboard was İpek's beautiful reflection. He was speechless at the beauty of her back under the straps of the black velvet dress; he could hardly believe how close he was to those enormous eyes.

'I'm almost certain something terrible's about to happen.'

'Why?'

'Because I'm so happy. I can't say how or where they came from, but since coming to Kars I've written eighteen poems. One more and I'll have written an entire volume, or perhaps I should say that they'll have written themselves. I believe what you say about wanting to come back to Frankfurt with me and I can see an even greater happiness stretching out before me. It just seems dangerous to be this happy, and that's how I know something terrible is going to happen.'

'Something like what?'

375

'Like this: I go off to talk to Kadife, and you go off to meet Blue.'

'Oh, that's ridiculous,' said İpek. 'I don't even know where he is.'

'It's because I wouldn't tell them where he is that they beat me.'

'And you'd better not tell anyone else, either. I'm serious!' cried İpek, knitting her brows. 'Soon enough you'll see that you have nothing to fear.'

'So what's going on? I thought you were going to talk to Kadife,' said Turgut Bey. 'The play starts in an hour and a quarter. They've just announced on television that the roads are about to reopen.'

'I don't want to go; I don't want to leave the hotel,' whispered Ka sheepishly.

'We can't leave the city if Kadife's in distress – please understand that,' said İpek. 'Because, if we did, we wouldn't be happy. The least you can do is go over there. It will make us all feel better.'

'An hour and a half ago, when Fazıl brought that message from Blue,' said Ka, 'you were telling me not to leave the hotel at all.'

'All right. Just tell me what proof you'll accept that I haven't left the hotel while you're at the theatre – but do it quickly, we're running out of time,' said İpek.

Ka smiled. 'Come upstairs to my room. I'll lock the door. And in the half-hour I'm gone, I'll keep the key with me.'

'Fine,' said İpek cheerfully. She stood up. 'Father dear, I'm going up to my room for half an hour. You're not to worry, because Ka is going straight to the theatre to talk to Kadife. Please, don't get up, we have something to take care of upstairs first and we're in a hurry.'

'I'm so grateful,' said Turgut Bey to Ka, but he still looked very uneasy.

İpek took Ka by the hand, led him through the lobby and pulled him up the stairs.

'Cavit saw us,' said Ka. 'What must he be thinking?'

'Who cares?' said İpek blithely.

In his room, there was a faint, lingering scent of their lovemaking from the night before.

'I'll wait for you here,' said İpek. 'Be careful. Don't get drawn into an argument with Sunay.'

'So when I ask Kadife not to go on stage, should I say it's because you and her father and I don't want her to, or because Blue doesn't want her to?'

'Because Blue doesn't want her to.'

'Why?' asked Ka.

'Because Kadife's in love with him – that's why. The reason you're going there is to protect my sister from danger. You have to forget you're jealous of Blue.'

'As if I could.'

'When we get to Germany, we're going to be very happy,' said İpek, her arms hanging around Ka's neck. 'Tell me about the cinema you'll take me to.'

'There's a cinema in the Film Museum that shows undubbed American art films late on Saturday nights,' said Ka. 'That's where we'll go. We'll stop along the way at one of those restaurants around the station and have döner and sweet pickles. After we come home, we can relax in front of the television. Then we'll make love. We can live on my political-exile allowance and the money I'll make doing readings from this new poetry book of mine. We won't have to do anything more than that, except make love.'

İpek asked him what the title of his book was, and Ka told her.

'That's beautiful,' she said. 'But now you've got to go, darling. If you don't, my father will become so worried he'll go himself.'

'I'm not afraid any more,' he told her. That was a lie. 'But whatever happens, if there's some sort of mix-up, I'll be waiting for you on the first train that leaves the city.'

'I'll join you. If I can get out of this room, that is,' said İpek with a smile.

'Can you wait at the window and watch me until I've disappeared around the corner?'

'Of course.'

'I'm so afraid I won't see you again,' said Ka as he closed the door. He locked the door and dropped the key into his coat pocket.

He wanted to ensure he'd be able to turn around and take a last, leisurely look at İpek in the window, so when he reached the street he kept several paces ahead of his two bodyguards. When he turned around, there she was, like a statue, at the window of Room 203 of the Snow Palace Hotel, still wearing the black velvet evening gown, her honeyed shoulders now covered with goosebumps, from the cold. Standing there bathed in the orange light of the bedside lamp, she was his image of happiness. It was the image that Ka would hold close to him during the last four years of his life.

He never saw her again.

40

It Must Be Hard Being a Double Agent

The First Half of the Chapter

The streets Ka followed to the National Theatre were mostly empty –
here and there he could see a restaurant open for business, but all the
other shopkeepers in town had rolled down their shutters. The last
stragglers were leaving the tea-houses, exhausted by their long day
of drinking tea and smoking cigarettes, but even on their way out,
their eyes remained glued to the televisions. As he approached the
National Theatre, Ka saw three army vehicles. They all had their
lights on, and when Ka looked down the lane he saw the shadow of
a tank nestling among the oleanders. The thaw had now begun in
earnest, and the icicles that had formed on the eaves of houses were
dripping water on to the pavements below. Walking under the live
transmission cable that stretched across Atatürk Avenue, he entered
the theatre, and, taking the key from his pocket, he pressed it into the
palm of his hand.

The theatre was empty except for the soldiers and policemen
lined up in the aisles listening to the echoes of the actors' rehearsal.
Ka settled down into one of the empty seats to enjoy Sunay's deep,
rich voice and perfect diction, Kadife's weak and wavering answers,
and Funda Eser's hectoring direction ('Say it with feeling, darling
Kadife!') as she rushed about the stage moving the props (which
comprised a tree and a vanity table).

While Funda Eser was rehearsing a scene with Kadife, Sunay
noticed the light from Ka's cigarette and came to sit next to him.
'These are the happiest moments of my life,' he said. He stank of raki
but didn't seem at all drunk. 'No matter how much we rehearse,
everything depends on how we feel when we walk on stage. But it's
clear already that Kadife has a talent for improvisation.'

'I've brought her a message from her father and also an evil eye,' said Ka. 'Do you think I could have a word with her in private?'

'We know you gave your bodyguards the slip earlier. I hear the snow is melting and the railroad is about to reopen. But, before any of this happens, we're determined to put on our play,' said Sunay. 'Has Blue hidden himself well for once?' he added with a smile.

'I don't know.'

Sunay stood up and returned to the rehearsal. The spotlight came on, and, as Ka looked at the three figures framed on the stage, he could sense their deep affinity for one other. Looking at Kadife, at the scarf still draped around her head, he was alarmed by the ease with which she had entered this intimate world of the stage. And if she were to bare her head, Ka thought, what a shame that she would still be wearing one of those ugly raincoats favoured by all covered women. How much closer to her he would have felt if, like her sister, she'd been wearing a dress and showing off those long legs of hers. But when she left the stage to sit with him, there was a moment when he understood why Blue had left İpek and fallen in love with Kadife instead.

'Kadife, I've seen Blue. They released him and he's found himself a hiding-place. He doesn't want you to go on stage and bare your head tonight. He's also sent you a letter.'

Lest Sunay should see him, he passed her the letter under his arm, as one might pass the answers to a friend during an exam. But Kadife made no effort at concealment, and, as she read the letter openly, she smiled.

It was some time before Ka saw the tears in her angry eyes.

'Your father thinks the same thing, Kadife. You might be right to bare your head, but it would be insane to do so this evening, in front of all those angry religious high-school boys. There's no need for you to stay. You can tell them you're ill.'

'I don't need an excuse. Sunay's already told me I'm free to go home if I wish.'

It was clear to Ka that he was not dealing with some young girl upset at being told at the last minute that she couldn't appear in the school play: the anger and distress he read in her face ran far too deep.

'So are you planning to stay here, Kadife?'

'Yes, I'm staying here and I'm doing the play.'

'Do you know how much this will upset your father?'

'Give me the evil eye he sent me.'

'I just mentioned an evil eye so they'd let me speak to you privately.'

'It must be hard being a double agent.'

He could tell she was heartbroken, and it was with some pain that he realised her thoughts were miles away. He wanted to take Kadife by the shoulders and embrace her, but he did nothing of the sort.

'İpek has told me about her old relationship with Blue,' said Ka.

Kadife quietly took out a packet of cigarettes; slowly she raised one to her lips and lit it.

'I gave him the cigarettes and the lighter you sent with me,' said Ka clumsily. She didn't respond. 'Are you doing this because you're so in love with Blue? What is it about him that makes you love him so much, Kadife? Tell me, please.' When Ka saw that he was digging himself into a hole, he fell silent.

Funda Eser called from the stage to announce that they'd come to Kadife's next scene.

Kadife gave Ka a tearful look and stood up. At the last moment, they embraced each other. Still feeling her presence, still smelling her scent, Ka lingered for a while to watch the play, but his mind was elsewhere and he couldn't follow it. He could no longer trust his own instincts; he was missing something; jealousy and remorse were defeating his every effort to think logically. He could barely identify what was causing him such pain. And he couldn't fathom why this pain was so destructive, so violent.

Looking ahead to those years he hoped to spend with İpek in Frankfurt – assuming she did indeed come with him – he could now see that this crushing, soul-destroying pain would eat away at their happiness. With this thought on his mind, he lit a cigarette, still unable to make sense of anything. He went to the toilet where Necip had given him his letters to Kadife and walked into the same stall. Opening the window high on the wall, he looked out at the black night and stood there puffing and gazing helplessly.

At his first intimation that another poem was on the way, he could hardly believe it. Holding his breath, he pulled out his notebook to jot it down. He hoped the poem had been sent to console him, to give him hope. But when he'd finished it, he still felt the crushing pain throughout his body, so he left the National Theatre in distress.

When he reached the slushy pavement, he decided the cold air would do him good. His two bodyguards were still with him and his mind was in total disarray.

At this point, to enhance the enjoyment of my story and make it easier to understand, I must cut short this chapter and start a new one. This doesn't mean that Ka then did nothing worth narrating, but rather that I must first locate 'The Place Where the World Ends', the poem he effortlessly jotted down and which would conclude the book to which he would give the title *Snow*.

41

Every Life Is Like a Snowflake

The Missing Green Notebook

'The Place Where the World Ends', the nineteenth poem Ka wrote in Kars, was also his last. As we already know, he recorded eighteen of his poems in the green notebook he carried everywhere he went. He wrote them down just as he first 'heard' them, even if a few words here and there were missing. The only poem he did not write down was the one he read on stage on the night of the revolution. Ka alluded to it in two of the letters he wrote but never posted to İpek from Frankfurt. In both instances he called it 'The Place Where God Does Not Exist' and allowed that he'd been unable to get it out of his mind, that there was no finishing his new collection until he'd found it, and that he would be grateful if İpek could search the Border City Television archives on his behalf. When I first read one of these letters in my hotel room in Frankfurt, I sensed a certain disquiet between the lines – it was almost as if Ka was worried that İpek would think he was using the problem of the poem as an excuse to write her love letters.

In the twenty-ninth chapter, I described how, on returning to my room one evening, feeling pleasantly tipsy and still holding the Melinda tapes in my hand, I happened on Ka's diagram of a snowflake in a notebook picked up at random. While I can't possibly know Ka's exact intent, I can say that I spent a few days reading through all the notebooks, and I believed I was beginning to grasp Ka's purpose in giving each of his nineteen Kars poems a position on this snowflake.

After leaving Kars, Ka apparently read a number of books about snow. One of his discoveries was that once a six-pronged snowflake crystallises it takes between eight and ten minutes for it to fall through the sky, lose its original shape and vanish. When, with further enquiry, he discovered that the form of each snowflake is determined also by the temperature, the direction and strength of the wind, the altitude of the cloud, and any number of other mysterious forces, Ka decided that snowflakes have much in common with people. It was a snowflake that inspired 'I, Ka', the poem he wrote while sitting in Kars' public library; and later, when he was to arrange all nineteen titles for his new collection, *Snow*, he would assign 'I, Ka' to the central point of that same snowflake.

Applying the same logic to 'Heaven', 'Chess' and 'The Chocolate Box', he was able to see that each of these poems, too, had its natural and unique position on the imaginary snowflake. And soon he was certain that every poem in his new collection, and indeed everything that made him the man he was, could be indicated on the same set of crystalline axes. It was, in short, a snowflake that mapped out the spiritual course of every person who had ever lived. The three axes on to which he mapped his poems – 'Memory', 'Imagination' and 'Logic' – were, he said, inspired by the classifications in Bacon's tree of knowledge, but he wrote extensively about his own efforts to elucidate the meaning of the six-pronged snowflake's nineteen points.

Ka's three notebooks recording his thoughts about the poems he wrote in Kars are, for the most part, attempts to discover the significance of that geometry, but it should be clear by now that he was also trying to decipher the meaning of his own life. We should take care to see these objectives in the same light. For example, to read his musings on where to place the poem 'To Be Shot and Killed' is to be struck by the priority he gives to the fear that inspired that poem. He explains why it is that a poem inspired by fear belongs near the 'Imagination' axis, at the top of the right side of the 'Memory' axis, and near enough to the poem entitled 'The Place Where the World Ends' to be under its influence. Lurking throughout these commentaries was the belief that his poetry was shaped by mysterious external forces. And by the time he was recording these thoughts in the notebooks, Ka was convinced that every life is like a snowflake: individual existences might look identical from afar, but to understand one's own eternally mysterious uniqueness one had only to plot the mysteries of one's own snowflake.

Ka's exegesis of his new poetry collection, and of his personal snowflake, was vast (Why was 'The Chocolate Box' located on the axis labelled 'Imagination'? How had the poem called 'All Humanity and the Stars' shaped Ka's own snowflake? and so on), but we shall not dwell on these notes for any longer than our novel requires. As a young poet, Ka had many unkind things to say about older peers who took themselves too seriously, especially those poets who spent their later years convinced that every bit of nonsense they produced would one day inform serious literary debate, and who carved their own statues, oblivious to the fact that no one wished to look at them.

Bearing in mind the many years spent criticising poets of obscure verse, in thrall to the myths of modernism, there are but one or two excuses for Ka's extensive self-commentary. A careful reading reveals that Ka did not believe himself to be the true author of any of the poems that came to him in Kars. Rather, he believed himself to be but the medium, the amanuensis, in a manner exemplified by predecessors of his modernist *bêtes noires*. But as he wrote in several places, having written the poems, he was now determined to throw off his passivity, and it was by coming to understand them – by revealing their hidden symmetry – that he hoped to achieve this purpose. But there was a more practical urgency, too: without understanding what his Kars poems meant, he could have no hope of filling in the blanks, of completing the half-finished lines, or of recovering his lost poem, 'The Place Where God Does Not Exist' – and thus no hope of completing the book. For after Ka returned to Frankfurt, no poem ever 'came' to him again.

It's clear from his notes and letters that by the end of the fourth year, Ka had managed to divine the hidden logic of his poems and bring the book to its final form. This is why, when I returned to my Frankfurt hotel room with the papers and notebooks and other belongings rescued from his apartment, I sat there until dawn, drinking raki and sifting through the remains. I kept telling myself that his poems had to be among his personal effects. I pored over his notebooks, inspected his old pyjamas, his Melinda tapes, his ties, his books, his lighters (I realised that one of these was the lighter that Kadife had asked Ka to pass on to Blue) until finally I drifted off to sleep on a sea of nightmares and yearnings, dreams and visions. (Ka came to me in one frightening dream to say, 'You are old.')

It was noon when I awoke, to spend the rest of the day roaming the wet and snowy streets of Frankfurt, and, although I no longer had Tarkut Ölçün at my side, I did my best to gather as much information on Ka as I could. The two women with whom he had had relations during the eight years before his visit to Kars were happy to speak to me – I told them I was writing my friend's biography. His first lover, Nalan, didn't even know he was a poet, so it was hardly surprising that she knew nothing of his new collection. She was married now and with her husband ran two doner shops and a travel agency. After telling me baldly that Ka had been a contentious, peevish man, always quick to take offence, she cried a little. (The thing that grieved her most was having sacrificed her youth to her ideals.)

His second lover, Hildegard, was still single, and I guessed at once that she would know nothing of the contents of his last poems, or indeed of his having completed a collection entitled *Snow*. I may have overstated Ka's fame as a poet in Turkey, and certainly she played upon my sheepishness at having been caught out. In a rather flirtatious manner she told me that after her involvement with Ka she had stopped taking her summer holidays in Turkey. Ka, she said, was a dutiful, clever, lonesome child whose life was dominated by a restless hunger for mothering; he knew he'd never find it, but even if he did, he'd run the other way. So, while he was an easy man to love, it was impossible to live with him.

Ka had never spoken to her about me. (I've no idea why I asked her that question, nor indeed why I mention it now.) After an interview that lasted an hour and a quarter, Hildegard showed me something I had failed to notice: the top segment of the index finger on her beautiful, slender-wristed right hand was missing. She added with a smile that once, in a moment of anger, Ka had mocked her for this defect.

Ka had finished writing out his book in longhand, and as usual refrained from having it typed up or copied. Instead, just as he had done with his previous books, with manuscript in hand, he went on a reading tour, visiting Kassel, Braunshweig, Hannover, Osnabruck, Bremen and Hamburg. At the invitation of the various city councils, and with the assistance of Tarkut Ölçün, I embarked on my own lightning tour of 'literary evenings' in those same cities. Like Ka, ever the great admirer of Germany's efficient and immaculate trains, I travelled from city to city, enjoying the very Protestant comforts Ka had described in one of his poems. As he must have done, I sat by the window peacefully watching the reflections of the grassy plains, the villages with the sweet little churches nestled in the mountain foothills, and the picturesque stations full of children with their bright raincoats and backpacks. The two Turks sent by the association to greet me would listen impassively, with cigarettes hanging from their mouths, as I explained my wish to do exactly as Ka had done on his own tour seven weeks earlier. So, in every city, I checked in to a cheap little hotel like Ka's and went off with my hosts to a Turkish restaurant where, over spinach böreks and döner, we discussed politics and agreed what a shame it was that Turks had so little interest in culture. After the meal, I would wander through the cold, empty city and pretend I was Ka walking the same streets to escape the painful memories of İpek. In the evening, before a gathering of fifteen or twenty people interested in politics, literature and all things Turkish, I would half-heartedly read a page or two of my most recent novel, then, switching to the subject of poetry, I would announce that I was a close friend of the great poet Ka, who had recently been shot dead on a street in Frankfurt. Did anyone remember 'anything about his last poems, which he read here only a short time ago'?

Most of those who attended these literary evenings had been present for Ka's poetry reading, but it was clear that most had come to see him for political reasons or simply by chance. They could tell me little about his poems, in marked contrast to their detailed recollections of the charcoal-coloured coat he had never taken off, his pale complexion, his unkempt hair and his nervous mannerisms. However, although they were uninterested in Ka's life and work, they were quick to take an interest in his death. I heard quite a few conspiracy theories: he'd been assassinated by the Islamists, MİT, the Armenians, German skinheads, the Kurds, Turkish nationalists.

Fortunately, though, at every event there had been a few sensitive souls who had paid careful attention to Ka. Those keenly interested in literature confirmed that he had indeed just finished a new collection and that he had read several poems from it – 'Dream Streets', 'Dog', 'The Chocolate Box' and 'Love' – but they were unable to recall anything useful about the individual pieces, apart from their being very difficult. At several events, Ka had mentioned that he'd written the poems in Kars, sometimes implying he meant them as elegies, particularly for those longing for the towns and villages they'd left behind.

At the end of one event, a dark-haired woman in her thirties came forward, and after explaining that she was widowed with a child, she told me that she'd approached Ka in a similar manner after his reading and that they had discussed a poem called 'The Place

Where God Does Not Exist'. She believed he had read only four lines of this long poem because he didn't want to offend anyone. No matter how hard I tried to draw her out, this careful poetry lover couldn't remember any of the poem's words – only that it described 'a terrifying landscape'. But, as she'd sat in the front row during Ka's Hamburg appearance, she could at least confirm he'd been reading from a green notebook.

That evening, I took the same train that Ka had taken from Hamburg to Frankfurt. When I left the station, I took the same route that he had done – walking down Kaiserstrasse and stopping now and then to wander through a sex shop. (Although it had been only a week since my arrival in Germany, there was already a new Melinda video on the shelves.) When I arrived at the place where my friend had been shot, I stopped, and it was here that I acknowledged what I had already accepted unconsciously: when Ka fell to the ground, his assassin must have made off with the green notebook. Now I was left with but one consoling hope following this futile, week-long hunt across Germany, and all the evenings poring over Ka's notes: I might retrieve at least one of the long poems from the video archives of a television station in Kars.

Back in Istanbul, over the course of a few days I tuned in to the national channel's end-of-day news broadcasts to hear the Kars weather reports, and to judge in what sort of climate I might be received.

Like Ka, I arrived in Kars in the early evening, after a bus journey lasting a day and a half. Bag in hand, I timidly negotiated a room for myself at the Snow Palace Hotel (where there was no sign of the father or his two mysterious daughters). I then went out to explore the city, taking to those same snow-covered pavements Ka had walked four years before. While I wouldn't say the compass of my walk equalled his, I did go far enough to discover that the establishment he had known as the Green Pastures Restaurant was now a wretched beerhall. In any event, I wouldn't want my readers to imagine that I was trying to become his posthumous shadow. As Ka had so often suggested to me, I simply did not understand poetry well enough, nor the great sadness from which it issues. So there had been a wall between us; a wall that now divided me not just from the melancholy city described in his notes, but from the impoverished place I was seeing with my own eyes. There was, of course, one person who nevertheless observed a resemblance between us; it is that person who now binds us together. But let's not talk about that yet.

Whenever I remember the astonishment of first seeing İpek that evening at the dinner the mayor held in my honour, I only wish I could ascribe my stupor to too much raki; that I could say it was drink that made me lose myself and emboldened me to believe I had a chance; and that there was no other basis for the jealousy I began to feel for my dead friend. Later, at the Snow Palace Hotel, as I stood at my window watching a far less poetic snowfall than the one Ka had described – a sleet that melted on contact with the city's muddy pavements – I could not stop wondering how, having read my friend's notebooks so meticulously for so long, I had failed to grasp the extent of İpek's beauty. Without quite knowing why, I took out a notebook – you might say, 'Just like Ka' (an expression I was increasingly using myself) – and wrote down thoughts that could be called the germ of the book you are now reading. I remember trying to describe Ka's story and his love for İpek as he might have described them himself. In a smoky corner of my mind I was reminded of a truth drawn from bitter experience: immersing oneself in the problems of a book is a good way to keep from thinking of love. Contrary to popular opinion, a man can shut out love if he so desires. However, to do so, he must free himself not only from the woman who has bewitched him but from the third person in the story: the ghost who has put temptation in his way. I, however, already had an appointment with İpek the following afternoon at the New Life Pastry Shop, and the express purpose was to discuss Ka.

Or perhaps it was my desire to talk about Ka that allowed me to open up to her. We were the only customers in the shop. On that same black-and-white television in the corner two lovers were embracing before the Bosphorus Bridge. İpek confessed at the outset that she could talk about Ka only with the greatest difficulty. She could describe her pain and disillusionment only to someone who would listen patiently, so it was a comfort for her to know I was a close friend who cared enough about Ka's poetry to have come all the way to Kars. And, if she could convince me that she had not treated him unfairly, she could find release at least for a time from her sorrow. But she also warned that it would cause her great pain if I failed to accept or understand her story.

She wore the same long brown skirt in which she'd served Ka breakfast on the 'morning of the revolution', and the same wide, outdated belt (both instantly recognisable to anyone who'd read Ka's notes). There were flashes of anger in her eyes but her expression was sorrowful; it reminded me of Melinda.

She talked for a long time; I hung on her every word.

I'm Packing My Suitcase

From İpek's Point of View

When, on his way to the National Theatre with his two bodyguards in tow, Ka stopped and turned for one last glimpse of her, İpek was still hopeful, still convinced she'd learn to love him dearly. The knowledge that she could learn to love a man had always meant more to her than loving him effortlessly, more even than falling in love, and that was why she now felt that she was on the threshold of a new life, a happiness bound to endure for a very long time.

So she was not particularly disturbed to find herself locked in a room by a jealous lover for the first twenty minutes after Ka's departure. Conveniently, her mind was on her suitcase: if she could concentrate now on those things she wanted to keep with her throughout her life, she would, she thought, have an easier time parting from her father and her sister; and if she could finish packing during this unavoidable captivity, they'd have a better chance of leaving Kars at the earliest opportunity, and in one piece.

After a half-hour had passed with no sign of Ka, İpek lit a cigarette. By now, she was wondering if she'd been a fool to think everything was going to plan. Furthermore, her confinement to the room only fed her agitation; she grew as angry at herself as at Ka. Seeing Cavit the receptionist dashing across the courtyard, she was tempted to open the window and shout to him, but before she had made up her mind the teenager had scampered out of range. She was still unsure, but nevertheless still expecting Ka to return at any minute.

Forty-five minutes after Ka's departure, İpek managed to force open the icy window. She called to a youth who was passing in the street below – a bewildered religious high-school student who had somehow managed not to be carted off to the National Theatre – and asked the boy to come into the hotel and tell reception that she was locked in Room 203. The youth seemed very suspicious, but he did as she asked. Moments later, the phone in the room rang.

'What on earth are you doing in that room?' said Turgut Bey. 'If you were locked in, why didn't you just pick up the phone?'

A minute later, her father had opened the door with a skeleton key. İpek then told Turgut Bey that she'd wanted to accompany Ka to the National Theatre, but Ka had locked her in the room to keep her from danger, and, with the phone lines down throughout the city, she'd assumed the hotel phones weren't working, either.

'But the phones are working again; not just here but everywhere in the city,' said Turgut Bey.

'Ka's been gone a long time. I'm beginning to worry,' said İpek. 'Let's go to the theatre and find out what's happened to him and Kadife.'

Despite his panic, Turgut Bey dawdled in getting ready. First, he couldn't find his gloves; then, he said he was sure Sunay would take offence if he didn't put on a tie. He insisted on walking very slowly – partly because he didn't have the strength to go any faster, but also because he had much advice to give İpek and wanted her to listen carefully.

'Whatever you do, don't cross swords with Sunay,' said İpek to her father. 'Don't forget that he's a revolutionary hero who's just been endowed with special powers.'

Seeing the curious onlookers milling about at the entrance to the National Theatre, the religious high-school boys who'd been herded in on buses, and the hawkers, soldiers and policemen who'd been longing endlessly for this sort of crowd, Turgut Bey remembered his own excitement as a youth when attending political meetings. He clutched İpek's arm tighter as he looked around, part hopeful, part afraid, part listening for the conversation that might make him feel like an active participant in this event, or for the initiative to which he might lend his support. When he saw that most of the crowd were strangers, he shoved aside one of the youths standing in the entrance, but then immediately felt ashamed for what he'd done.

The auditorium wasn't yet full, but already there was a family atmosphere in the large theatre: it reminded İpek of those dreams in which you see everyone you've ever met assembled before you in a crowd. But there was no sign of Ka or Kadife, and this worried her. A sergeant then moved them into the aisle.

'I'm the father of the leading lady, Kadife Yıldız,' complained Turgut Bey. 'I must see her at once.'

He sounded every bit the father who'd come at the last minute to ban his daughter from playing the lead in an objectionable school play. The panic-stricken sergeant responded like an ethical teacher who knew that the father's concerns were more important than his own job, and he offered to help. He showed them into a room lined with pictures of Atatürk and Sunay. They'd been there a short while when Kadife appeared alone at the door.

Seeing her, İpek knew at once that, whatever they did, her sister would still be taking to the stage that evening. She asked about Ka, and Kadife revealed that they'd spoken briefly, but then she said that Ka had headed back to the hotel. İpek began to wonder at their not having run into him on the way over, but soon she dropped the subject. Turgut Bey, now in tears, was imploring his younger daughter not to go on stage.

'At this late hour, after all they've done to advertise this thing, it would be more dangerous not to go on stage, Father dear,' said Kadife.

'When you bare your head, Kadife, do you have any idea how much you'll enrage the religious high-school boys, not to mention everyone else?'

'Frankly, Father, after all these years, isn't it ironic that you're now telling me to cover my head?'

'There's nothing funny about it, little Kadife,' said Turgut Bey. 'Tell them you're feeling ill.'

'I'm not ill . . .'

Turgut Bey continued to cry. İpek felt that her father staged his tears, as he always did when he saw the opportunity to focus on the sentimental aspect of a problem. And there was something so ready and superficial about the old man's anguish which always made İpek suspect that in his heart of hearts he was in fact grieving for the opposite of what he tearfully professed. In the past, she and her sister had thought this trait was special and endearing, but now, faced with a subject they urgently needed to address, they found their father's behaviour embarrassingly trivial.

'When did Ka leave?' whispered İpek.

'He should have been back in the hotel quite some time ago,' said Kadife, with equal alarm.

They could see the fear in each other's eyes.

When I met her in the New Life Pastry Shop four years later, İpek told me that at that moment they were not worried about Ka, but about Blue. As they communicated this to each other silently with their eyes, they were paying little mind to their father. By now, I could not help seeing İpek's frankness as a sign of her affection for me, so I imagined I would be unable to see the end of this story from any other point of view but hers.

For a while, neither sister spoke.

'He told you that Blue doesn't want you to go on stage, didn't he?' asked İpek.

Kadife shot her sister a look of warning: their father had heard her. Both girls glanced at him and saw that, even through the tears still streaming from his eyes, he had been paying close attention.

'You won't mind, will you, Father dear, if we leave you for a moment to have a word alone as sisters.'

'When you two put your heads together, you always know so much more than I do,' replied Turgut Bey. He left the room without closing the door behind him.

'Have you thought this through, Kadife?' asked İpek.

'I have.'

'But do you realise that you may never see him again?'

'Maybe not,' said Kadife carefully. 'But I'm very angry with him, too.'

Kadife's affair with Blue had been full of such ups and downs – arguments giving way to peace offerings that led on to jealous fits - and now İpek thought back to the couple's long, secret history with some despair. How many years had it been? She wasn't sure, particularly as she tried not to think about how long Blue had been seeing both of them. She thought lovingly of Ka – thanks to him, she'd be able to forget Blue.

'Ka is very jealous of Blue,' said Kadife. 'And he's madly in love with you.'

'I did find it hard to believe he could be so head over heels in such a short time,' said İpek. 'But now I believe it.'

'Go with him to Germany.'

'As soon as we get home, I'm packing my suitcase,' said İpek. 'Do you really think that Ka and I can be happy in Germany?'

'Yes, I do,' said Kadife. 'But stop telling Ka about your past. He already knows too much, and he can guess a great deal more.'

İpek hated it when her younger sister spoke so condescendingly, like some seasoned woman of the world. So she said, 'You're talking as if you have no intention of coming home after this play is over.'

'Of course I'm coming back,' said Kadife. 'But I thought you were leaving right away.'

'Do you have any idea where Ka might have gone?'

As they looked into each other's eyes, İpek sensed that they both feared the same thing.

'Let's go,' said Kadife. 'It's time for me to put on my make-up.'

'The only thing that makes me happier than seeing you take off that scarf is seeing the last of that purple raincoat,' said İpek.

The raincoat in question reached all the way to the ground, and now Kadife did a defiant little two-step that sent its hem flying upwards. When they saw that Turgut Bey, who'd been watching from the door, was now finally smiling, the two sisters threw their arms around each other and exchanged kisses.

He must by now have resigned himself to Kadife's going on stage, for this time he neither cried nor offered any advice. His performance was done, and now he embraced his daughter with a kiss on both cheeks and left through the packed auditorium.

At the theatre's bustling entrance, en route back to the hotel, İpek kept her eyes peeled for Ka. Seeing no sign of him, she started to search for someone who might know his whereabouts, but there was no one who could help.

When they reached the hotel, Turgut Bey made straight for the television, and, as he sat hypnotised by the endless trailers for the live broadcast, İpek prepared her suitcase. Whenever she began to wonder where Ka was, she'd try to focus instead on the happiness awaiting them in Germany and on picking out the clothes and other things she wanted to take with her. As she would tell me later, 'Just as Ka could find any reason for pessimism, I spent the next forty-five minutes coming up with idiotic reasons for optimism.' Then she started to pack another suitcase with the things she'd previously excluded on the basis that there were 'probably things of far higher quality in Germany'. As she rummaged through her stockings and underwear, wondering whether she would be able to find the styles she preferred in Germany, something prompted her to take a look outside. Entering the courtyard was the army truck that had been ferrying Ka around the city.

She went downstairs and saw her father was at the door. A clean-shaven, hook-nosed official she'd never seen before said, 'Turgut Yıldız,' and pressed a sealed envelope into his hands.

With an ashen face and trembling hands, Turgut Bey opened the envelope to find a key. Seeing that the enclosed letter was addressed to his daughter, he handed it to İpek.

In self-defence, but also to ensure that whatever I wrote about Ka would reflect all the available facts, İpek showed me the letter when we met four years later.

Thursday, 8 p.m.

Turgut Bey – if I might ask you to use this key to let İpek out of my room, and to pass this letter on to her, it would be best for all of us, sir. I offer my apologies. Respectfully yours.

My darling. I was unable to change Kadife's mind. The soldiers have brought me to headquarters for my own protection. The road to Erzurum has reopened, and they are forcing me to leave on the first train, which leaves at half-past nine. You'll need to pack my bag as well as yours and come at once. The army truck will pick you up at quarter-past nine. On no account should you go out on the streets. Come to me! I love you very much. We are going to be happy.

The hook-nosed man said that they'd be back after nine, and left.

'Are you going?' asked Turgut Bey.

'I'm still worried about what's happened to him,' said İpek.

'The soldiers are protecting him; nothing can happen to him. So, are you going to leave us and go?'

'I think I can be happy with him,' said İpek. 'Even Kadife said so.'

In her hand was a document certifying her future happiness, and now, as she read it again, she began to cry, but she didn't know why. 'Perhaps it was because I dreaded leaving my father and my sister,' she would tell me four years later. At the time, I believed my intense interest in every detail of İpek's feelings stemmed from my need to hear her story. Then she said, 'And perhaps I was worried about the other thing on my mind.'

When İpek stopped crying, she and her father went up to her room to make a final check of what she was taking with her, and then to Ka's room to put all his belongings into his dark red suitcase. Father and daughter were both hopeful now. They were telling each other that, fingers crossed, Kadife would soon complete her course, and then she and Turgut Bey could come to visit İpek in Frankfurt.

When the bags were packed, they went downstairs, where they huddled in front of the television to watch Kadife.

'I hope it's a short play so that you can know that this business is over and done with before you get on the train,' said Turgut Bey.

They stopped talking and nestled against each other, just as they did when they watched *Marianna*, but İpek could not concentrate on what she was seeing. Years later, all she could remember of the first twenty-five minutes was Kadife coming on stage in a headscarf and a long, bright red dress and saying, 'Whatever you want, Father dear.' Sensing my sincere curiosity as to her thoughts at that moment, she added, 'Of course, my mind was elsewhere.' Repeatedly, I asked her where, particularly, that might have been, but she would allow only that her thoughts were of the journey she was about to make with Ka. Later, her mind would be gripped by fears, but she could never admit to herself what those fears were – much less manage to articulate them for me. With the windows of her mind blown open, everything but the television looked very distant. She felt like a traveller who'd returned from a long journey to find that during her absence her house had changed in mysterious ways – with every room much smaller than she remembered, and every stick of furniture much more worn. As she looked around her, everything – the cushions, the table, even folds in the curtains – surprised her. Faced with the chance to go to an utterly foreign place, she could now see her own home through the eyes of a stranger. That was her description of how she felt. And this careful account of hers, given to me at the New Life Pastry Shop, was, in her view, clear proof that she was still planning to set out for Frankfurt with Ka that evening.

When the bell rang, İpek ran to the hotel entrance. The army truck that was to take her to the station had come early. Swallowing her fear, she told the official at the door that she'd be back in a moment. She ran straight back to her father, sat down beside him and embraced him with all her strength.

'Is the truck here already?' asked Turgut Bey. 'If your bag is packed, we still have some time.'

İpek spent the next few minutes staring blankly at Sunay on the screen. But then, unable to sit still, she ran off to her room and, after packing the slippers and her little sewing kit with the mirror that she'd inadvertently left by the window, she sat for a few minutes on the edge of the bed, crying.

According to her recollection, by the time she went downstairs she was sure of her decision to leave Kars with Ka. Finally rid of the lingering hesitations that had been poisoning her mind, she was at peace, determined to spend her last minutes at home watching television with her father.

When Cavit the receptionist told her that there was someone at the door, İpek was not unduly concerned. Turgut Bey asked her to bring him a Coke from the refrigerator, and she brought in two glasses so they could share it.

İpek said that she would never forget Fazıl's face as he stood there waiting at the kitchen door. It was clear from his expression that something terrible had happened, and İpek felt something for the first time: that Fazıl was a member of their family, someone very close to her.

'They've killed Blue and Hande!' said Fazıl breathlessly. 'And only Blue could have talked Kadife out of this.'

İpek watched motionless as Fazıl cried. Then, in a dazed voice that seemed to come from deep inside him, he explained that Blue had gone into hiding with Hande, and that a group of soldiers had raided the premises and killed them. He was sure someone had tipped them off: if not, they'd never have sent so many troops. And, no, there was no chance that Fazıl had been followed: by the time he got there, everything was over and done with, and Fazıl had watched with a number of children from the surrounding houses as the army search-light had played over Blue's body.

'May I stay here?' asked Fazıl. 'I don't want to go anywhere else.'

İpek took out another glass so he, too, could share the Coke. In her distraction, she couldn't find the bottle opener; she kept looking in the wrong drawers and cupboards before finally locating it. She suddenly thought of the flowery blouse she'd been wearing the day she'd first met Blue, and then remembered having packed it in her suitcase. She took hold of Fazıl and sat him down on the chair by the kitchen where Ka, after getting so drunk on Tuesday night, had written his poem. Then, like an invalid suddenly relieved of the pain shooting through her body, she relaxed. Leaving the boy silently to watch Kadife and sip his Coke, she went to the other end of the room and gave the second glass to her father.

She went up to her room and stood there for a minute in the dark.

She stopped by Ka's room to pick up his dark red suitcase, then went out into the street. In the cold, she walked over to the official standing by the army truck and told him she had decided not to leave the city.

'We can still make the train,' said the official, trying to be helpful.

'I've changed my mind. I'm not going. But thank you. And please, give this bag to Ka Bey.'

She went back inside, and as she sat down next to her father they both heard the army truck revving its engine.

'I sent them away,' İpek told her father. 'I'm not going.'

Turgut Bey put his arms around her. For a while, they watched the play on television, but neither took in anything. The first act was just coming to an end when İpek said, 'Let's go and see Kadife. I've got something to tell her.'

Women Commit Suicide to Save Their Pride

The Final Act

It was very late in the day that Sunay decided to change the title of the drama originally inspired by Thomas Kyd's *The Spanish Tragedy* but which in its final form showed many other influences. Only during the last half-hour of the relentless promotional campaign did the television announcers begin referring to *A Tragedy in Kars*. The revision came too late for those already in the theatre. Many had been brought in by military bus; others had seen the play advertised and came to show their faith in a strong army; a fair number didn't care how catastrophic the result would be, as long as they got to see it with their own eyes (there were already rumours that the 'live broadcast' was really a tape shipped in from America). Also present were the city officials, whose attendance had been ordered (this time they'd decided not to bring their families). Hardly any of them knew of the new title, but even those who did, like the rest of the city, had a hard time following the action.

Four years after its first and last performance, a videotape of *A Tragedy in Kars* lay in the Kars Border Television archives. The first half is almost impossible to summarise. I could make out a blood feud in some 'backward, impoverished and benighted' town, but when its inhabitants started killing one another I had no notion of why; neither the murderers nor their victims offered any explanation for the copious bloodshed. Sunay raged against the backwardness of blood feuds and of people who allowed themselves to be drawn into them; he debated the matter with his wife and a younger woman who seemed to understand him better (this was Kadife.) Though a rich, enlightened member of the ruling elite, Sunay's character enjoyed dancing and joking with the poorest villagers, and indeed

399

would engage them in erudite discussions of the meaning of life, as well as regaling them with scenes from Shakespeare, Victor Hugo and Brecht, if only to furnish the promised 'play within the play'. He also offered an assortment of short soliloquies on such matters as city traffic, table manners, the special traits Turks and Muslims will never lose, the glories of the French Revolution, the virtues of cooking, condoms and raki, and the way fancy prostitutes belly-dance. But these declarations, like his subsequent exposés of adulterated brands of shampoo and cosmetics, shed little light on the bloody scenes they interrupted; and, as one outburst followed another, it became increasingly hard to believe that they conformed to any logic at all.

However, the wild improvisations were somehow still worth watching, if only for the passion of Sunay's performance. Whenever the action began to drag, whenever he sensed the people of Kars were losing interest, Sunay could always find something to bring them back under his spell. He would fly into a fury, and, borrowing a fine theatrical pose from one of the most illustrious roles of his career, rail against those who had brought down the people. He would then pace the stage with tragic abandon, recounting youthful memories and quoting Montaigne on friendship as he mused on the quintessential loneliness of Atatürk. His face was wet with perspiration.

During my visit to Kars, I was able to meet Nuriye Hanım, the teacher who loved literature and history and had been so enthralled by Sunay's performance on the night of the revolution; she told me that everyone in the front row for this second performance could smell the raki fumes. Still, she insisted Sunay wasn't drunk; she preferred 'enthusiastic'. But others in her row more than confirmed this so-called enthusiasm. It was a disparate group: many were middle-aged officials who'd risked their lives to get as close to this great man as decorum allowed. Some were widows; others perhaps best described as young admirers of Atatürk, and had already seen these images dozens of times on TV. There were also a few hungry for adventure, so to speak, or at least interested in power. But they all spoke of the light shining in Sunay's eyes, radiating in every direction; it was dangerous, they said, to stare into those eyes for more than a few seconds.

I would one day have corroborating evidence from one of the religious high-school boys who'd been herded into a military transport and frog-marched to the National Theatre. This was Mesut, the friend of Necip and Fazıl who'd been opposed to burying atheists and believers in the same cemetery. He confirmed how Sunay held them all spellbound. We can only assume that he had no more axe to grind because, after four years with a small Islamist group based in Erzurum, he had lost faith in armed struggle and returned to Kars to work in a tea-shop. He told me it was very difficult for the other religious high-school boys to speak openly about their attraction to Sunay. Perhaps this had to do with Sunay's absolute power, the thing to which they also aspired. It may be that they were relieved by the many restrictions he'd imposed on their movements, which made it impossible to take stupid risks such as inciting a riot. 'Whenever the army steps in, most people are secretly thankful,' he told me, and then confessed that his classmates had been most impressed by Sunay's courage: there he was, the most powerful man in the city, but unafraid to stride on to the stage and bare his soul to the teeming multitudes.

Watching the Kars Border Television archive videotape of the evening's performance, I was struck by the silence in the hall. It was as if the audience had left behind the struggles that defined them – the tussle of fathers and sons, the skirmishes between the guilty and the powerful – to sink into a collective terror. I myself was not immune to the power of that shimmering fiction that any citizen of an oppressive and aggressively nationalistic country will understand only too well – the magical unity conjured by the word 'we'. In Sunay's version of this, it was as if there were not a single 'outsider' in the hall: all were inextricably bound by the same hopeless story.

But Kadife threatened to break this trance, which may explain why the people of Kars couldn't quite bring themselves to accept her presence on stage. The cameraman taping the live broadcast seems to have been aware of this ambivalence: in all the happy scenes, he zoomed in on Sunay, not showing Kadife at all, so the only time the TV audience got a glimpse of her was when she was serving the great and the good, just like one of those maids in a farce. Still, everyone had seen the trailers that had been running since lunchtime, and they were all now very curious to see whether she would bare her head. There'd been the usual spate of conflicting rumours – some holding that Kadife was merely following army orders to remove her scarf, while others had it that she was planning not to go on stage at all – but an afternoon of saturation publicity had seen to it that even those only vaguely acquainted with the headscarf affair now knew all about Kadife. As a result, there was widespread disappointment at her low visibility in the early scenes – her long, red dress did not quite make up for the fact that the scarf still covered her head.

Twenty minutes into the play, an exchange between Kadife and Sunay gave the audience the first hint of what was to come. They were alone on stage, and Sunay asked if she had made up her mind, adding that he 'could not condone killing oneself just out of anger'.

Kadife gave the following reply: 'In a city where men are killing one another like animals just to make it a happier place, who has the right to stop me killing myself?' Then, seeing Funda Eser striding towards her, she made a quick exit – leaving it unclear whether this was part of the play or a hastily improvised escape.

When I'd spoken to everyone who would talk to me, I tried to reconstruct from their testimonies a minute-by-minute timeline which synchronised the performance with the action off stage. This is how I was able to establish that Blue's last glimpse of Kadife came when she delivered this line. For, according to neighbours who witnessed the raid, and various police officers still working in Kars at the time of my visit, Blue and Hande had been watching TV when the bell rang. According to the official report, Blue took one look at the soldiers and the police officers assembled outside and rushed to get his weapon; he then opened fire without warning. Several neighbours and the young Islamists who would turn him into a legend almost overnight remember that, after getting off a few rounds, he cried, 'Don't shoot!' Perhaps he was hoping to save Hande. However, Z Demirkol's special operations team had already taken up positions around the perimeter, and in less than a minute not just Blue and Hande but every wall of their safe-house was riddled with bullets. It was a fierce noise, but few other than a handful of curious neighbourhood children paid much attention. After all, the people of Kars were well accustomed to such nocturnal raids, and on that night they also didn't want to be distracted from the live broadcast from the National Theatre. All the pavements in town were empty, all the shutters closed, and, apart from the odd tea-shop with a television, no one was open for business. Sunay was well aware that all eyes in the city were on him, which lent him a feeling of both security and extraordinary power.

I would never hear Kadife's own version of events, so I cannot know precisely what she was thinking, but, realising her presence on stage was subject to Sunay's sufferance, she clearly courted his approval more than she might otherwise have done. She had to make the most of the opportunities Sunay had thrown her way if she was to have any hope of accomplishing her own ends.

Over the next forty minutes, as the audience began to grasp that Kadife was faced with two important decisions – about baring her head and about committing suicide – their admiration for her grew. As her stature increased, the play evolved into a drama more serious than had been implied by Sunay's and Funda's half-didactic, half-vaudevillian fury. Although they could not completely forget 'Kadife the headscarf girl', many were still full of sorrow for her years later, and told me that her new persona had won the hearts of the people of Kars. By the middle of the play, the audience was falling into a rapt silence whenever Kadife walked on stage; whenever she spoke, those watching in houses full of noisy children would frantically ask one another, 'What did she say? What did she say?'

With the National Theatre caught in just such a moment of silence, one could hear the whistle of the first train to leave Kars in four days. Ka was riding in the compartment into which the army had forcibly planted him. When my dear friend had seen the army transport return with his suitcase but no İpek, he desperately implored his guards to let him see her or at least talk to her. When they refused, he persuaded them to send the army transport back to the hotel. When the transport returned empty, he begged the officers to hold the train for five more minutes. When the whistle blew, there was still no sign of İpek, and even as the train began to move Ka's wet eyes were still scanning the crowds on the platform. Training his stare on the station entrance, the door that looked out on the statue of Kâzım Karabekir, he tried to conjure the image of a tall woman with a bag in her hand walking straight towards him.

As the train gathered speed, it blew its whistle once again. İpek and Turgut Bey were on their way from the Snow Palace Hotel to the National Theatre when they heard it.

'The train's on its way,' said Turgut Bey.

'Yes,' said İpek. 'And any minute now the roads will be reopened. The governor and the military chief of staff will be back in the city soon.'

They talked for a while about how this ridiculous coup would now draw to a close, about how everything would soon return to normal, but İpek would later concede that she had no particular interest in these subjects; she wanted to speak lest her father deduce from her silence that she was thinking about Ka.

But was her mind really on Ka? How much was she thinking about Blue's death? Even four years later, she wasn't sure herself, and, finding my questions and suspicions irksome, she tried to deflect them. But she did say that far stronger than any regret at missing her chance for happiness was her anger with Ka. After that night, she knew, there was no hope of ever loving him again. When she heard his train pull out of the station, she felt only heartbreak, and perhaps a little surprise. In any case, all she wanted was to share her grief with Kadife.

'It's so desolate, you'd think everyone's fled the city,' said Turgut Bey.

'It's a ghost city,' replied İpek, just for something to say.

A convoy of three army transports turned the corner to pass in front of them. Turgut Bey took this as proof that the roads had reopened. They watched the jeeps roll off into the night until only their tail-lights were visible. According to my later enquiries (but at the time unbeknown to them), the middle jeep was carrying the bodies of Blue and Hande.

A moment earlier, the lights of the last jeep had shone on the offices of the *Border City Gazette* just long enough for Turgut Bey to see that the next day's edition was hanging in the window. He stopped and read the headlines: 'Death on stage', 'Illustrious actor Sunay Zaim shot dead during yesterday's performance'.

They read the article twice and then walked as fast as they could to the National Theatre. The same police cars were parked outside the entrance. Far down the road, the same tank nestled in the shadows.

As they were searched at the entrance, Turgut Bey announced that he was the 'leading lady's father'. Once in the auditorium, they could see that the second act had begun, and, spying two empty seats in the back row, they sat down.

This act also contained a number of the stock gags on which Sunay had been relying for many years, including a modified belly-dance parody by Funda Eser. But the atmosphere had grown heavier, and the silence in the hall deeper, from the cumulative effect of Kadife and Sunay's long scenes alone on stage.

'Again I must insist that you explain to me why you wish to kill yourself,' said Sunay.

'It's not a question anyone can really answer,' said Kadife.

'What do you mean?'

'If a person knew exactly why she was committing suicide, and if she could state her reasons openly, then she wouldn't have to kill herself.'

'*No!* It's not like that at all,' said Sunay. 'Some people kill themselves for love, others kill because they can't bear their husbands' beatings any longer, or because poverty is piercing them like a knife, to the bone.'

'You have a very simple way of looking at life,' said Kadife. 'A person who wants to kill herself for love still knows that if she waits a while, her love will fade. Poverty's not a good enough reason for suicide, either. And a woman doesn't have to commit suicide to escape her husband; all she has to do is steal some of his money and leave him.'

'Very well then. What is the real reason?'

'The main reason for suicide, obviously, is pride. At least, that's why women kill themselves.'

'You mean they've been humiliated by love?'

'You don't understand a thing!' said Kadife. 'A woman doesn't commit suicide because she's *lost* her pride; she does it to *show* her pride.'

'Is that why your friends committed suicide?'

'I can't speak for them. Everyone has her own reasons. But every time I have ideas of killing myself, I can't help thinking they were thinking the same way I am. The moment of suicide is the time when they understand best how lonely it is to be a woman, and what it really means to be a woman.'

'Did you use these arguments to push your friends towards suicide?'

'They came to their own decisions; the choice to commit suicide was theirs.'

'But everyone knows that, here in Kars, there's no such thing as free choice; all people want is to escape from the next beating, to take refuge in the nearest community. Admit it, Kadife, you met secretly with these women and pushed them towards suicide.'

'But how could that be?' asked Kadife. 'All they achieved by killing themselves was an even greater loneliness. Some were disowned by their families, who in some cases refused even to arrange the funeral prayers.'

'So are you trying to tell me that you plan to kill yourself just to prove that they are not alone; just to show that you're all in this together? You're suddenly very quiet, Kadife . . . But if you kill yourself before explaining your reasons, don't you run the risk of letting your message be misinterpreted?'

'I'm not killing myself to send any message,' said Kadife.

'But still, there are so many people watching you, and they're all curious. The least you can do is say the first thing that comes into your mind.'

'Women kill themselves because they hope to gain something,' said Kadife. 'Men kill themselves because they've lost all hope of gaining anything.'

'That's true,' said Sunay, and he took his Kırıkkale gun out of his pocket. Everyone in the hall could see it gleaming. 'When you're sure that I'm utterly defeated, will you please use this to shoot me?'

'I don't want to end up in jail.'

'Why worry about that when you're planning to kill yourself, too?' asked Sunay. 'After all, if you commit suicide, you'll go to Hell, so it makes no sense to worry about the punishment you might receive for any other crime – in this world or the next.'

'But this is exactly why women commit suicide,' said Kadife: 'to escape all forms of punishment.'

'When I arrive at the moment of my defeat, I want my death to be at the hands of just such a woman!' cried Sunay, now spreading his arms theatrically and facing the audience. He paused for effect. Then he launched into a tale of Atatürk's amorous indiscretions, cutting it short just when he sensed interest flagging.

When the second act ended, Turgut Bey and İpek rushed backstage to find Kadife. Her changing room – once used by acrobats from St Petersburg and Moscow, Armenians playing Molière, and dancers and musicians who'd toured Russia – was now ice cold.

'I thought you were leaving,' said Kadife to İpek.

'I'm so proud of you, darling. You were wonderful!' said Turgut Bey, embracing Kadife. 'But if he'd handed you that gun and said, "Shoot me," I'm afraid I would have jumped up and interrupted the play, shouting, "Kadife, whatever you do, don't shoot!"'

'Why would you have done that?'

'Because the gun could be loaded,' said Turgut Bey. He told her about the story he'd read in the next day's edition of the *Border City Gazette*. 'I know that Serdar Bey is always hoping he can make things happen by writing about them first, but most of his stories turn out to be false alarms, and I wouldn't especially care about this one coming true anyway,' he said. 'But I know that Serdar would never dream of proclaiming an assassination like this unless Sunay had talked him into it – and I find that very ominous. It might just be more self-promotion, but who knows, he could be planning to have you kill him on stage. My darling girl, please don't pull that trigger unless you're sure the gun isn't loaded. And don't bare your head just because this man wants you to. İpek isn't leaving, we're going to be living in this city for some time to come, so please don't anger the Islamists over nothing.'

'Why did İpek decide not to go?'

'Because she loves her father, and you, and her family more,' said Turgut Bey, taking Kadife's hand.

'Father dear, would you mind if we spoke alone again?' asked İpek, instantly seeing her sister's face go pale with alarm.

Turgut Bey crossed to the other end of the dusty, high-ceilinged room, joining Sunay and Funda Eser.

İpek hugged Kadife tightly and sat her on her lap. Realising the gesture had only made her sister more fearful, İpek took Kadife by the hand and led her towards a corner that was separated from the rest of the room by a curtain. Just then, Funda Eser emerged with a tray of glasses and a bottle of Kanyak.

'You were excellent, Kadife,' she said. 'You two make yourselves at home.'

As Kadife's anxieties mounted with every second that passed, İpek looked into her eyes in a manner that conveyed unambiguously, 'I have some very bad news.' Then she voiced it: 'Hande and Blue were killed during a raid.'

Kadife shrank into herself. 'Were they at the same house? Who told you this?' she asked. Then, seeing İpek's stern face, she fell silent.

'Fazıl, that religious high-school boy. He's the one who told us, and I believed him, because he saw it with his own eyes.' She paused for a moment, to give Kadife a chance to take in the news. Her sister grew only paler, but İpek pressed on. 'Ka knew where he was hiding, and after his last visit to see you here, he never returned to the hotel. I think it was Ka who betrayed them to the special operations team. That's why I didn't go back to Germany with him.'

'How can you be sure?' asked Kadife. 'Maybe it wasn't him. Maybe it was someone else who told them.'

'It's possible. I've considered that myself. But I'm so sure in my heart that it was Ka that it almost doesn't matter: I know I'd never be able to convince my rational self that he didn't do it. So I didn't go to Germany because I knew I could never love him.'

Kadife was exhausted, trying to absorb the news, and, as she saw her sister's strength ebbing away, İpek knew that she had begun to accept that Blue was really dead. Kadife buried her face in her hands and began to sob. İpek folded her arms around her sister's and they cried together, though she knew they were crying for different reasons. They'd cried this way before, once or twice during those shameful days when neither of them could give up Blue and they had duelled mercilessly for his affections. Now İpek realised that this terrible vendetta was over once and for all: she wasn't going to leave Kars. She felt herself age suddenly, but also knew what she now desired: to reconcile and grow old in peace, and have the wit to want nothing from the world.

İpek could see that her sister's pain was deeper and more destructive than her own. For a moment she was thankful not to be in Kadife's place – was this the sweetness of revenge? – and guilt swept over her. In the background they were playing the familiar taped medley that the National Theatre's management always broadcast during intermissions to encourage sales of soda and dried chickpeas: the song at that moment was one she remembered from the earliest years of her youth in Istanbul: 'Baby Come Closer, Closer to Me'. In those days, both sisters had wanted to learn good English; neither would succeed. It seemed to İpek that her sister only cried harder on hearing this song. Peeking through the curtains, she could see her father and Sunay in animated conversation at the other end of the room, as Funda filled their glasses with more cognac.

'Kadife Hanım, I'm Colonel Osman Nuri Çolak.' A middle-aged soldier had yanked open the curtain, and, with a gesture evidently acquired from a film, he bowed so low he almost wiped the floor with his pate. 'With all due respect, miss – how may I ease your pain? If you do not wish to go on stage, I have some good news for you: the roads have reopened, the armed forces will be entering the city at any moment.' Later, at his court martial, Osman Nuri Çolak would adduce these words as evidence that he'd been doing all he could to save the city from the ludicrous officers who'd staged the coup.

'I'm absolutely fine, but thank you, sir, for your concern,' said Kadife.

İpek saw that Kadife had already assumed a number of Funda's affectations. At the same time she had to admire her sister's determination to pull herself together. Kadife forced herself to stand, drank a glass of water, and then quietly began to pace up and down the long backstage room like a theatre's ghost.

İpek was hoping to get away before her father could talk to Kadife, but Turgut Bey crept up to join them just as the third act had begun.

'Don't be afraid,' said Sunay, turning to his friends. 'These people are modern.'

The third act commenced with Funda Eser singing a folk song about a woman who'd been raped, an engaging number to make up for the earlier parts of the drama that the audience had found too 'intellectual' or otherwise obscure. It was Funda's usual routine: one moment she was crying and cursing the men in the audience, and the next she was showering them with whatever compliments entered her head. Following two songs and a little commercial parody only the children thought funny (she suggested that Aygaz filled their canisters not with propane but with farts), the stage grew dark, and – in an ominous reprise of the finale two days earlier – two armed soldiers marched on. The audience watched in tense silence as they erected a gallows centre stage. Sunay limped confidently across the stage with Kadife to stand right beneath the noose.

'I never expected things to happen so quickly,' he said.

'Is this your way of admitting you've failed at this thing you've set out to accomplish, or is it simply that you're old and tired now, looking for a way to go out in style?' asked Kadife.

İpek saw Kadife drawing on unsuspected reserves of strength.

'You're very intelligent, Kadife,' said Sunay.

'Does this frighten you?' asked Kadife, her voice taut and angry.

'Yes!' said Sunay, with lecherous languor.

'It's not my intelligence that frightens you. You fear me because I'm my own person,' said Kadife. 'Because, here in our city, men don't fear their women's intelligence; they fear their independence.'

409

'To the contrary,' said Sunay. 'I staged this revolution precisely so that you women could be as independent as women in Europe. That's why I'm now asking you to remove that scarf.'

'I *am* going to bare my head now,' said Kadife. 'And then, to prove that I'm motivated by neither your coercion nor by any wish to be a European, I'm going to hang myself.'

'But you do realise, don't you, Kadife, that when you act like an individual and commit suicide, the Europeans will applaud you? Don't think you haven't already turned some heads with your animated performance in the so-called secret meeting at the Hotel Asia. There are even rumours that you organised the suicide girls, just as you did the headscarf girls.'

'There was only one suicide who was involved in the headscarf protest, and her name was Teslime.'

'And now you mean to be the second.'

'No. Because, before I kill myself, I'm going to bare my head.'

'Have you thought this through?'

'Yes,' said Kadife, 'I have.'

'Then you must have thought about this, too: suicides go to Hell. And since I'm going to Hell anyway, you can kill me first with a clear conscience.'

'No,' said Kadife, 'because I don't believe I'm going to Hell after I kill myself. I'm going to kill you to rid our country of a microbe, an enemy of our nation, our religion, and our women!'

'You're a courageous woman, Kadife, and you speak with great frankness, but our religion prohibits suicide.'

'Yes, it's certainly true that the Nisa verse of the Glorious Koran proclaims that we shouldn't kill ourselves. But this would not prevent God in His greatness from finding it in His heart to pardon the suicide girls and spare them from going to Hell.'

'In other words, you've found a way to twist the Koran to suit your purposes.'

'In fact, the contrary is true,' said Kadife. 'It happens that a few young women in Kars killed themselves because they were forbidden to cover their heads as they wished. As surely as the world is God's creation, He can see their suffering. As long as I can feel the love of God in my heart, there's no place for me in Kars, so I'm going to do as they did, and end my life.'

'You're going to anger all these religious leaders who've come to

Kars through snow and ice to deliver their sermons in the hope that the helpless women of Kars might be delivered from their suicidal wishes. You do know that, Kadife, don't you? And, while we're on the subject, the Koran –'

'I am not prepared to discuss my religion with atheists or, for that matter, with those who profess belief in God out of fear.'

'Of course, you're right. Mind you, I don't bring it up to interfere with your spiritual life. It's just that I thought the fear of Hell might keep you from shooting me with a clear conscience.'

'You have nothing to worry about. I will kill you with a clear conscience.'

'That's wonderful,' said Sunay, looking a little offended at the alacrity of the reply. 'Now, let me tell you the most important thing I've learned in my twenty-five years of professional theatre: when any dialogue goes on longer than this, our audiences can't follow it without becoming bored. So, with your permission, we can stop our conversation here and turn our words to deeds.'

'Fine.'

Sunay produced the Kırıkkale gun he had brandished in the last act and showed it to Kadife and the audience. 'Now, you are going to bare your head. Then I shall place my gun in your hands and you will shoot me . . . And, as this is the first time anything like this has happened on live television, let me take this last opportunity to explain to our audience how they are to understand –'

'Let's get on with it,' said Kadife. 'I'm sick of hearing men talking about why the suicide girls commit suicide.'

'Right you are,' said Sunay, playing with the gun in his hand. 'But there are still one or two things I wish to say, just so our viewers in Kars won't be unduly alarmed. After all, some may have believed the rumours in the papers. Kadife, please look at this gun's magazine clip.' He removed the clip, showed it to Kadife (and, for effect, to the audience as well), then refitted it. 'Now, did you see that it was empty?' he asked with the assurance of a master illusionist.

'Yes.'

'But let's be absolutely certain about this,' said Sunay. He took out the clip again, and now, like a magician about to saw a woman in half, showed it to the audience again before snapping it back in place. 'Finally, let me say a few words on my own behalf. A moment ago, you promised you would shoot me with a clear conscience. You

411

probably detest me for having staged this coup and for opening fire on the people, just because they weren't living like Westerners. But I want you to know that I did it all for the fatherland.'

'Fine,' said Kadife. 'And now I'm going to bare my head. Please, I want everyone to watch.'

Anguish flashed across her face; then, with a clean, single stroke, she lifted her hand and pulled off her scarf.

There was not a sound in the hall. For a moment, Sunay stared stupidly at Kadife, as if she had just done the utterly unexpected. Both of them then turned to the audience and gaped like acting students who'd forgotten their lines.

All of Kars gazed in awe at Kadife's long, beautiful, brown hair, which the cameraman finally summoned the courage to show in tight focus. When he had found the nerve to zoom in on her face, it became clear that Kadife was deeply embarrassed, like a woman whose dress had come undone in a crowded public place. Her every movement bespoke a terrible pain.

'Hand me the gun, please,' she said impatiently.

'Here you are,' said Sunay, holding it by the barrel. 'This is where you pull the trigger.'

When Kadife took the gun in her hand, Sunay smiled. Everyone in Kars expected the dialogue to continue.

Perhaps Sunay did, too, because now he said, 'Your hair is so beautiful, Kadife. Even I would certainly want to guard you jealously, to keep other men from seeing it.'

Kadife pulled the trigger.

A gunshot sounded in the hall. All of Kars watched in wonder as Sunay shuddered violently – as if he'd really been shot – and then fell to the floor.

'How stupid all of this is,' said Sunay. 'They know nothing about modern art. They'll never be modern!'

The audience expected Sunay now to launch into a long death monologue. Instead, Kadife rushed forward with the gun and fired again, and again. With each shot, Sunay's body shuddered and lurched upwards. And every time it fell back to the floor, it seemed heavier. She fired four times in smart succession.

There were still many who thought Sunay was only acting. They were ready for him to sit up at any moment and deliver a long, instructive tirade on death; but at the uncommonly realistic sight of his bloodied face, they lost hope. Nuriye Hanım, whose admiration for theatrical effects surpassed even her reverence for the script itself, now rose to her feet. She was just about to applaud Sunay when she too saw his bloody face and sank fearfully back into her seat.

'I guess I killed him!' said Kadife, turning to the audience.

'You did well!' shouted a religious high-school student from the back of the hall.

The security forces were so preoccupied by the murder they'd just witnessed on stage that they failed to identify the student agitator who'd broken the silence. When Nuriye Hanım – who'd spent the last two days watching the awesome Sunay on television, and who'd decided, before the announcement of free admission, to sit in the front row irrespective of the cost in order to see him up close – broke down in tears, everyone else in the hall, and everyone else in Kars, was forced to accept the reality of what they had just seen.

Two soldiers running towards each other with clownish steps pulled shut the curtains.

No One Here Likes Ka

Four Years Later, in Kars

As soon as the curtain was closed, Z Demirkol and his friends arrested Kadife 'for her own safety'. Removing her through the stage door into Küçük Kâzımbey Avenue, they pushed her into an army jeep and headed straight for the central garrison, to put her into the old shelter where they'd kept Blue during on his last day on earth. A few hours later, all the roads to Kars had reopened. Several military units rolled in to suppress the city's 'little coup' and met with no resistance. The governor, the military chief of staff and a number of other officials were dismissed for dereliction of duty; the small band of conspirators who had staged the coup were arrested, along with a number of soldiers and MİT agents, who protested that they'd done it all 'for the people and the state'.

It would be three days before Turgut Bey and İpek were allowed to visit Kadife. On the day she was taken away, Turgut Bey knew in his heart of hearts that Sunay had died on stage, but he was still hopeful that nothing would happen to Kadife. All he wanted was to find a way to take his daughter home. But when midnight came and went, he capitulated and walked home through the empty streets, arm in arm with his elder daughter. İpek went straight up to her room, and, as she unpacked her suitcase, putting the contents back into her cupboard, her father sat on the edge of the bed and cried.

Most Kars residents who'd watched the events unfold on stage would discover for certain that Sunay had died after his theatrical death throes only when they read the *Border City Gazette* the next morning. After the curtain closed, the audience at the National Theatre quietly filed out, and the television station would never again mention the events of the past three days. But, as Kars was well

414

accustomed to military rule and to the sight of police and special operations teams chasing 'terrorists' through the streets, it wasn't long anyway before those three days ceased to seem 'exceptional'. And, when the general staff office launched a full inquiry the following morning, prompting the office of the prime minister's inspectorate to spring into action too, everyone in Kars could see the wisdom of regarding the 'staged coup' more as a strange theatrical event than a political one. Their fascination lingered over such questions as: if Sunay had just shown the empty clip to a live audience, how could Kadife have shot and killed him with the same gun?

I have referred several times already to the inspecting colonel sent by Ankara after things had returned to normal, so my readers will have deduced my indebtedness to this man and his detailed report on the 'theatrical coup'. His analysis of the gun scene confirms it was more a case of sleight of hand than magic. Since Kadife refused to speak to her father, her sister or even her lawyer, much less the prosecutor, about what had happened that night, the colonel was obliged to undertake the same sort of detective work I would do four years later: interviewing as many people as he could (although it would be more accurate to say that he took their depositions), he finally satisfied himself that there was no rumour or theory that had escaped his attention.

There were, of course, many theories which suggested that Kadife knowingly and wilfully killed Sunay Zaim, without his genuine permission. To refute these allegations, the colonel showed it would have been impossible for the young woman to switch guns or replace the empty clip with a loaded one so quickly. Furthermore, despite the amazement Sunay's face registered with every shot, the fact remains that searches carried out by the armed forces, the inventory of Kadife's personal effects at the time of her arrest, and even the video recording of the performance all confirm that she was in possession of only one gun and one clip.

Another popular local theory had it that Sunay Zaim was shot by a different gunman firing from a different angle, but that one was laid to rest when the ballistics and autopsy reports came back from Ankara to confirm that all the bullets in the actor's body had come from the Kırıkkale gun in Kadife's hand.

Kadife's last words ('I guess I killed him!') had turned her into something of an urban legend. The colonel saw them as proof that this was not a case of premeditated murder; but, perhaps out of consideration for the prosecutor who would open the trial, the colonel's report digressed to give a full discussion of premeditation, wrongdoing with intent and other related legal and philosophical concepts. Still, he wound up alleging that the true mastermind – the one who had helped Kadife memorise her lines and taught her the various manoeuvres she would deftly perform – was none other than the deceased himself. In twice showing the audience that the clip was empty, Sunay Zaim had duped Kadife and indeed the entire city of Kars. Here, perhaps, I should quote the colonel himself who, not long after the publication of his report, took early retirement. When I met him at his home in Ankara and pointed to the rows of Agatha Christie books on his shelves, he told me that what he liked most about them were their titles. When we moved to the case of the actor's gun, he said simply, 'The clip was full.' A man of the theatre would hardly have needed to be an expert magician to trick an audience into taking a full clip for an empty one; indeed, after three days of merciless violence visited upon them by Sunay and his cohorts in the name of republicanism and Westernisation (the final death toll, including Sunay himself, was twenty-nine), the people of Kars were so terrorised that they would have been prepared to look at an empty glass and see a full one.

If we follow this line of reasoning, it becomes clear that Kadife was not Sunay's only accomplice. After all, Sunay had gone so far as to advertise his death in advance; and if the people of Kars were so eager to see him kill himself on stage, if they were still prepared to enjoy the drama, telling themselves it was just a play, then they, too, were complicit.

Another theory, that Kadife had killed Sunay to avenge Blue's death, was refuted on the grounds that anyone handed a loaded gun with the express notification that it was empty could not be accused of using it with intent to kill. There were those among Kadife's Islamist admirers and her secular accusers who maintained that this was precisely what was so crafty about the way Kadife had killed Sunay and then refused to kill herself, but the inspecting colonel held that this was to confuse art with reality.

The military prosecutor stationed in Kars accorded the utmost respect to the inspecting colonel's meticulous report, as did the judges, who ruled that Kadife had not killed for political reasons.

They found her guilty of negligent homicide and lack of forethought, and sentenced her to three years and one month in jail. She would be released on parole after serving twenty months. Under Articles 313 and 463 of the Turkish Penal Code, Colonel Osman Nuri Çolak was charged with establishing a vigilante group implicated in murders by unknown assailants; for this, he received a very long sentence, but six months later the government declared a general amnesty and set him free. Part of the condition of his release was that he was not to discuss the coup with anyone. However, it was far from unusual for him to go to the officers' club of an evening, meet up with his old army buddies, have a few drinks, and then declare that, 'whatever else had happened', he had at least realised the dream of every Atatürk-loving soldier. Without undue rudeness, he would accuse his friends of bowing to the religious fanatics for want of courage.

A number of other soldiers and officials involved in the coup tried to portray themselves as well-meaning patriots or helpless links in the chain of command, but the military court was unmoved: they, too, were convicted of conspiratorial collusion, murder or use of state property without permission and held for a time, before being freed under the same general amnesty. One of them, a young but high-minded, low-ranking officer who turned to Islam after his release, published his story ('I Was a Revolutionary, Too') in the Islamist newspaper *Covenant*, but his memoirs were censored for insulting the army. By then it was common knowledge that the goalkeeper Vural had been working for the local branch of MİT as soon as the revolution was 'staged'. The court also found that the other actors in Sunay's troupe were but 'simple artists'. Funda Eser had gone on the rampage the night her husband died, levelling wild accusations against every person who crossed her path, threatening to denounce them all. When it was established that she had suffered a mental breakdown, she was sent to the psychiatric wing of the Military Hospital in Ankara, where she spent four months under observation. Years after her discharge, she was to become famous throughout the country as the voice of the witch in a popular children's television cartoon. She told me that she remained grief-stricken over the slanders that had prevented her husband (whose death she now termed a 'work-related incident') from taking on the role of Atatürk, and that her sole consolation was to see how many of the newest statues of the great man show him striking poses created by her husband.

Because the inspecting colonel's report had also implicated Ka in the coup, the military court summoned him as a witness. After his failure to appear at two hearings, they charged him with obstruction and issued a warrant for his arrest.

Every Saturday, Turgut Bey and İpek visited Kadife, who served her sentence in Kars. During the spring and the summer, when the weather was fine, the kindly warden gave them permission to spread a white tablecloth beneath the mulberry tree in the prison's spacious courtyard, and they would while away the afternoon, eating Zahide's stuffed peppers with olive oil, offering her rice meatballs to the other inmates, cracking and peeling hard-boiled eggs, and listening to Chopin preludes on the Philips cassette-player that Turgut Bey had managed to repair. To keep his daughter from seeing her sentence as a cause for shame, Turgut Bey insisted on treating the prison like a boarding school, a place through which all proper folk had to pass at some stage. Occasionally, he would invite along friends like Serdar Bey, the journalist. One day Fazıl joined them on a visit, and Kadife said she'd like to see him again. Two months after her release, this man four years her junior became her husband.

For the first six months, they lived in a room in the Snow Palace Hotel, where Fazıl now worked as a receptionist. But by the time I visited Kars, they had moved with their baby to a separate house. At six o'clock every morning, Kadife would take their six-month-old, Ömercan, to the hotel; Zahide and İpek would feed him and then Turgut Bey would play with his grandson while Kadife busied herself with hotel business. By now, Fazıl had decided it was better not to be too dependent on his father-in-law, so he had two other jobs. One was at the Palace of Light Photo Studio and the other was at Kars Border Television; he told me with a smile that his job title was 'production assistant', but really he was nothing more than 'a glorified errand boy'.

As I've reported, on the day of my arrival the mayor gave a dinner in my honour. I met Fazıl at noon the next day at his and Kadife's new apartment on Hulusi Aytekin Avenue. As I was gazing out at the enormous snowflakes bouncing softly against the walls of the castle before sinking into the dark waters of the river, Fazıl innocently asked why I'd come to Kars. Thinking that he might say something about the way İpek had turned my head at the mayor's dinner, I panicked and launched into a long, and somewhat exaggerated, account of my interest in the poems Ka had written while in Kars and my tentative plans to write a book about them.

'If the poems are missing, then how can you write a book about them?' he asked in a friendly, well-meaning voice.

'That's as much of a mystery to me as it is to you,' I said. 'But there must be one poem in the television archives.'

'We can find it this evening. But you spent the whole morning walking around every street in Kars. So maybe you're thinking of writing a novel about us, too.'

'I was just visiting the places Ka mentioned in his poems,' I said uneasily.

'But I can tell from your face that you want to tell the people who read your novels how poor we are, and how different we are from them. I don't want you to put me into a novel like that.'

'Why not?'

'Because you don't even know me, that's why! Even if you got to know me and described me as I am, your Western readers would be so caught up in pitying me for being poor that they wouldn't have a chance to see my life. For example, if you said I was writing an Islamist science-fiction novel, they'd just laugh. I don't want to be described as someone people smile at out of pity and compassion.'

'Fine, then.'

'I know I've upset you,' said Fazıl. 'Please don't take offence. I can tell you're a good person. But your friend was a good person, too, and maybe he even wanted to love us, but in the end he committed the greatest evil of all.'

I found it difficult to hear Fazıl imputing 'evil' to Ka's alleged denunciation of Blue, and I could not help thinking that it was only because of Blue's death that Fazıl had been able to marry Kadife. But I held my tongue. 'How can you be so sure that this allegation is true?' I asked finally.

'Everyone in Kars knows it,' he said. He spoke with warmth, even compassion, and took care not to blame either Ka or me.

In his eyes, I saw Necip. I told him I was happy to look at the science-fiction novel he had wanted to show me, but he explained that he wanted to be with me when I read it. So we sat down at the table where he and Kadife ate their evening meals in front of the television and read the first fifty pages of the novel Necip had first imagined four years earlier, and which Fazıl was now writing in his name.

'So, what do you think? Is it any good?' Fazıl asked – but only once, and apologetically. 'If you're bored, just leave it.'

'No, it's good,' I said, and read on with curiosity.

Later, when we were walking down Kâzım Karabekir Avenue, I told him truthfully how much I liked the novel.

'Maybe you're just saying that to cheer me up,' said Fazıl cheerfully. 'But you've still done me a big favour. I'd like to reciprocate. So, if you decide to write this novel, it's fine to mention me. But only if you let me speak directly to your readers.'

'And what do you want to say to them?'

'I don't know. If I can think of what to say while you're still in Kars, I'll tell you.'

We parted company, having agreed to meet at Kars Border Television in the early evening. I watched Fazıl race down the street to the Palace of Light Photo Studio. How much of Necip do I see in him? Could he still feel Necip inside him in the way he had described to Ka? How much can a man hear another's voice inside him?

That morning, as I had walked through the streets of Kars, talking to the same people Ka had talked to, sitting in the same tea-houses, many times I almost felt I *was* Ka. Early in my wanderings, while I was sitting in the Lucky Brothers Tea-house, where Ka had written 'All Humanity and the Stars', I, too, dreamed about my place in the universe, just as my beloved friend had dreamed. Back at the Snow Palace Hotel, as I went to pick up my key, Cavit the receptionist told me I was rushing 'just like Ka'. As I was walking down a side-street, a grocer came out to ask, 'Are you the writer from Istanbul?' He invited me inside to ask whether I could write that all the newspaper reports four years earlier about the death of his daughter Teslime had been false. He talked to me in just the way he must have talked to Ka, and offered me a Coke, just as he had offered one to him. How much of this was coincidence, how much was just my imagining? At one point, realising I was on Baytarhane Street, I stopped to look up at the windows of Sheikh Saadettin's lodge, and then, to understand how Ka felt when he visited the lodge, I ascended the steep stairs that Muhtar had described in his poem.

I'd found Muhtar's poems in Ka's Frankfurt papers and took this to mean that he'd never sent them to Fahir. But it must have been only five minutes after we were introduced that Muhtar, proclaiming Ka to have been 'a true gentleman', described how, during his visit to Kars, Ka had been so taken with Muhtar's poems that he had volunteered to send them to a conceited Istanbul publisher with a covering letter praising them to the skies. He was happy with the way his life was going: although the Prosperity Party had been shut down, he was sure to be the candidate of the new Islamist party the next time there was an election, and was confident of a time to come when he would be mayor. Thanks to Muhtar's warm, ingratiating manner, we were able to visit the police headquarters (though they didn't let us see the basement) and the Social Insurance Hospital, where Ka had kissed Necip's lifeless head. When Muhtar took me to see what was left of the National Theatre, and the rooms he had converted into an appliance warehouse, he conceded that he was 'partly to blame for the destruction of this hundred-year-old building', and then, by way of consolation, he added, 'At least it was an Armenian building, and not a Turkish one.' He showed me all the places Ka had remembered whenever he found himself longing to return. My thoughts remained with Ka as we walked through the snow, and through the fruit market. As we walked down Kâzım Karabekir Avenue, Muhtar pointed out the hardware stores one by one. Then he led me into the Halil Paşa Arcade, where he took his leave after introducing me to his political rival, the lawyer Muzaffer Bey. The former mayor reminisced at length about the city's glory days during the early years of the republic, just as he had done with Ka, and, as we proceeded through the gloomy corridors of the arcade, a rich dairy owner standing in front of the Association of Animal Enthusiasts cried, 'Orhan Bey!' He invited me in and flaunted his remarkable memory by describing how Ka had visited the association around the time of the assassination of the director of the Education Institute, and how he had gone off into a corner and lost himself in thought.

It was difficult to listen to his description of the moment Ka had realised he was in love with İpek, just as I was about to meet her at the New Life Pastry Shop. It was, I think, to calm my nerves, to ease my fear of being swamped by love, that I first stepped into the Green Pastures Beerhall to down a raki. But the moment I sat down across from İpek at the New Life Pastry Shop, I realised that my precaution had left me only more vulnerable. I'd drunk the raki on an empty stomach, so, instead of calming me, it had set my head swimming. She had enormous eyes, and just the kind of delicate bones I like. As

I struggled to make sense of her beauty – although I had been think-ing about it incessantly since first seeing her the night before, I had yet to fathom its depths – I inflamed my own confusion and despair by reflecting that I knew every detail of her time with Ka and the love they'd known. It was as if I'd discovered yet another weakness in myself. It was a painful reminder that, while Ka had lived his life in the way that came naturally to him, as a true poet, I was a lesser being, a simple-hearted novelist who, like a clerk, sat down to work at the same time every day. Perhaps this is why I now gave İpek such a sympathetic account of Ka's daily routines in Frankfurt: how he'd got up every morning at the same hour and walked the same streets to the same library, to sit and work at the same desk.

'I really had decided to go to Frankfurt with him,' said İpek, adducing several facts to prove it, including the suitcase she'd packed. 'But now it's hard to remember why I found Ka so charming. That said, out of respect for your friendship, I would like to help you with your book.'

'You've already helped enormously. Ka wrote a brilliant book about his time here, and that was all due to you,' I said, hoping to provoke her. 'He filled several notebooks with a minute-by-minute account of his three-day visit here – the only gap being the last few hours before he left the city.'

She proceeded to fill that gap with astonishing frankness, conceal-ing nothing, it seemed. I could not help but admire her honesty as she offered her own minute-by-minute account of Ka's last hours in town, what she had seen with her own eyes, and what she had guessed about the rest.

'You had no solid proof, but you still decided not to go to Frank-furt?' I asked, again by way of provocation.

'Sometimes you sense something in your heart and simply know it's true.'

'You're the first one to mention hearts,' I said. As if to make up for this, I told her what I had gathered from those letters Ka had writ-ten but never sent from Frankfurt: that Ka had never been able to forget her; that he'd been utterly distraught, needing two sleeping pills every night for a year after his return to Germany; that he would regularly drink himself into a stupor; that, walking the streets of Frankfurt, he couldn't go five minutes without seeing a woman in the distance whom he mistook for İpek; that, until the end of his life, he'd spent hours every day musing on the happy moments they'd spent together – the same film repeatedly playing in slow motion in his head; that he'd been overjoyed every time he'd managed to go even fifteen minutes without thinking of her; that he'd not had a relationship with any other woman until the day of his death; that, after losing her, he saw himself as 'not a real person at all, but a ghost'. When I saw her face succumbing to her compassion even as it silently begged, 'Enough!', when her eyebrows rose as if pondering a puzzling question, I realised with horror that I wasn't pleading my friend's case but my own.

'Your friend may have loved me a great deal,' she said. 'But not enough to come back to Kars to see me.'

'There was a warrant out for his arrest.'

'That needn't have stopped him. He could have appeared in court as ordered, and that would have been the end of the matter. Please don't take this the wrong way, he was right not to come, but the fact remains that Blue managed to make many secret visits to Kars to see me even though there'd been orders to kill him on sight for years.'

It pierced me to the core to see that, when she uttered Blue's name, her hazel eyes lit up and her face filled with a melancholy I could tell was entirely genuine.

'But your friend wasn't most afraid of the courts,' she said, as if to console me. 'He knew very well what his real crime was, the reason why I didn't come to the station.'

'You've never offered a shred of proof he was actually guilty of this "crime",' I said.

'All I have to do is look at your face. You're carrying his guilt for him.' Satisfied with her clever response, she put her lighter and her cigarettes back into her bag to let me know our interview was over.

Clever indeed. I held up a mirror forcing me to see what she could see: that I was jealous not of Ka, but of Blue. Once I had admitted this to myself, I knew I was defeated. Later, I would decide that I'd over-read her – all she'd intended was a simple warning not to let my guilt get the better of me. She rose to put on her coat (how tall she was, aside from everything else).

I was confused. 'We'll see each other again tonight, won't we?' I said. There was no call for me to say this.

'Of course, my father is expecting you,' she said, and moved away with that sweet walk of hers.

I tried to feel sorry that in her heart she believed Ka was guilty. But I knew I was fooling myself. As I sat there invoking 'my dear, departed friend', I had really intended only this: to speak of him wistfully, and then, little by little, to expose his weaknesses, his obsessions, his 'crime', then finally to blot out his noble memory as I boarded the same ship with her to embark on *our* first journey together. The dreams I'd entertained during my first night in Kars – of bringing İpek back with me to Istanbul – now seemed very distant; faced with the shameful truth, all I wanted now was to prove my friend's innocence. Did I know for sure that, of the two dead men, it was Blue rather than Ka who had provoked my jealousy?

Walking through the snowy streets of Kars after nightfall only darkened my mood. Kars Border Television had moved to a new building on Karadağ Avenue, just across from the petrol station. It was a three-storey concrete affair heralded on its opening as a sign that Kars was moving up in the world. Two years on, its corridors were as muddy, dark and dingy as any in the city.

Fazıl was waiting for me in the second-floor studio. After introducing me to the eight others who worked at the station, he smiled affably and said, 'My colleagues wanted to know if you'd mind saying a word or two for the evening broadcast.' My first thought was that this might help with my research. During my five-minute interview, their youth programmes presenter, Hakan Özge, said unexpectedly (perhaps at Fazıl's direction), 'I hear you're writing a novel set in Kars.' The question threw me, but I managed to mutter a non-committal answer. There was no mention of Ka.

We then went into the director's office to examine the shelves lined with videotapes. The law required that they be dated, so it wasn't long before we were able to locate the tapes of the first two live broadcasts from the National Theatre. We took them into a small, airless room and sat in front of the old television with our glasses of tea. The first thing I watched was Kadife's performance in *A Tragedy in Kars*. I must say how impressed I was by Sunay Zaim's and Funda Eser's 'critical vignettes', not to mention their parodies of various commercials popular at the time. At the scene in which Kadife bared her head to reveal her beautiful hair before killing Sunay, I paused, rewound, repeated, trying to see exactly what had happened. Sunay's death really did look like so much theatre. I reckoned that only the front row would have had any chance of detecting whether the clip was full or empty.

When I put in the tape of *My Fatherland or My Headscarf*, I quickly realised that many elements in the play – the impersonations, the confessions of the goalkeeper Vural, Funda Eser's belly-dances – were no more than little side-shows that the troupe must have inserted into every play they performed. The roaring, shouting and sloganeering in the hall, to say nothing of the age of the tape, made it almost impossible to work out what anyone said. But I rewound several times in my attempt to hear Ka recite the poem that had come to him on the spot and would later be titled 'The Place Where God Does Not Exist'. Miraculously, I was able to transcribe most of it. When Fazıl asked me what could possibly have made Necip jump to his feet while Ka was reciting the poem, and what Necip could have been trying to say, I handed him the sheet on which I had jotted down as much of the poem as I'd been able to hear.

When we got to the part where the soldiers fired into the audience, we watched it twice.

'You've been all over Kars now,' said Fazıl, 'but there's another place I'd like to show you.' With slight embarrassment, but a certain air of mystery too, he told me that the place he had in mind was the religious high school. The school itself was closed, but since I was probably going to put Necip in my book, too, it was important that I see the dormitory where he had spent his last years.

As we were walking through the snow down Ahmet Muhtar the Conqueror Avenue, I happened to see a charcoal-coloured dog, and when I realised that this must be the dog Ka had written the poem about, I went into a grocer's to buy a hard-boiled egg and some bread. The dog wagged his curly tail happily as I quickly peeled the egg for him.

When Fazıl saw that the dog was following us, he said, 'That's the station dog. I didn't tell you everything back there, maybe because I thought you might not come. The old dormitory is empty now. After the coup, they closed it – they called it a nest of terrorist and reactionary militancy. Since then, no one's lived there, which is why I've borrowed this torch from the station,' he added, shining a beam of light into the anxious eyes of the dog, still wagging his tail.

The old dormitory had once been an Armenian mansion before it became the Russian consulate, where the consul had lived alone with his dog. The door to its garden was locked, but Fazıl took me by the hand and helped me over the low wall. 'This is how we used to get

425

out in the evenings,' he said. He pointed to a large, high window. Slipping through the paneless frame with accustomed ease, he then turned around to light my way with the torch. 'Don't be afraid,' he said, 'there's nothing in here but birds.' Inside, it was pitch dark: many of the windows were boarded up, and the glazing in those that had it was so caked with ice and dirt that no light came through them, but Fazıl forced his way to the stairs with ease. He climbed fearlessly, but kept turning around like an usher in a cinema to show me the way. Everything stank of dust and mould. We went through doors that had been kicked in on the night of the raid, and past walls riddled with bullet holes; overhead, pigeons flew in a panic from the nests they had built in the elbows of hot-water pipes in the corners of the high ceilings of the top floor, where we walked among the empty, rusting bunkbeds. 'This one was mine, and that was Necip's,' said Fazıl. 'On some nights, to make sure we didn't wake anyone with our whispering, we'd sleep in the same bed, watch the stars and talk.'

Through a gap in one of the top windows, we could see snowflakes sailing slowly through the halo of the streetlamp. I stood there, giving them my full attention, my deepest respect.

'Necip used to watch them from his bed,' said Fazıl much later. He pointed down to a narrow gap between two buildings: on the left – just beyond the garden – was the side wall of the Agricultural Bank; to the right, another wall, the back of a tall apartment building. The two-metre gap between them was too narrow for a street and so best described as a passageway. A fluorescent tube on the first floor cast a purple light on the muddy ground below. To keep people from mistaking the passageway wall for a street, a 'No Entry' sign had been erected on the middle of the wall. At the end of this passage, which Fazıl said had inspired Necip's vision of the 'end of the world', there was a dark and leafless tree. Just as we were looking at it, it suddenly turned red, as if it were on fire. 'The red light in the sign of the Palace of Light Photo Studio has been broken for seven years now,' whispered Fazıl. 'It keeps going on and off, and every time we saw it blink from Necip's bed, the oleander tree over there looked like it was on fire. Necip would frequently dream of this vision all night long. He called the vision "that world" and on mornings after sleepless nights, he'd sometimes say, "I watched that world all night." He had told the poet Ka about it, and your friend had put it into his poem. I figured this out while we were watching the tape, and that's why I brought you here. But your friend dishonoured Necip by calling the poem "The Place Where God Does Not Exist."'

'It was your friend who described this landscape to Ka as "the place where God does not exist",' I said. 'I'm sure of it.'

'I don't believe that Necip died an atheist,' said Fazıl carefully. 'Except, it's true, he did have doubts about himself.'

'Don't you hear Necip's voice inside you any more?' I asked. 'Doesn't all this make you afraid of turning into an atheist so gradually that you don't even notice, like the man in the story?'

Fazıl was not pleased to learn that I knew of the doubts he'd expressed to Ka four years earlier. 'I'm a married man now, I have a child,' he said. 'I'm no longer interested in such matters.' It must have occurred to him that he'd been treating me like someone who'd flown in from the West to lure him towards atheism, because he immediately relented. 'Let's talk about that later,' he said gently. 'We're expected at my father-in-law's for supper, and it wouldn't be right to keep them waiting.'

But before we went downstairs, he took me to a grand room that had been the main office of the Russian consulate. Pointing at the table, the chairs and the broken raki bottles in a corner, he said, 'After the roads opened, Z Demirkol and his special operations team stayed here for a few days so that they could kill a few more Islamists and Kurdish nationalists.'

Until that moment, I'd managed to keep this part of the story out of my mind, but now it came back to me with a vengeance. I had not wanted to think about Ka's last hours in Kars at all.

The charcoal-coloured dog had been waiting for us at the garden gate and followed us back to the hotel.

'You look very upset,' said Fazıl. 'What's wrong?'

'Before we go in to eat, would you come up to my room for a moment? There's something I'd like to give you.'

As I took my key from Cavit, I looked through the open door of Turgut Bey's office and saw the bright room beyond, saw the food spread on the table, heard the dinner guests talking, and I felt İpek's presence. In my suitcase I had the photocopies Ka had made of the love letters Necip had written to Kadife four years earlier, and, when we reached my room, I gave them to Fazıl. Only much later would it occur to me that I wanted him to be as much haunted by the ghost of his friend as I was by Ka's.

Fazıl sat on the edge of the bed to read the letters, while I returned to my suitcase to take out one of Ka's notebooks. Opening it up to the drawing of the snowflake I had first seen in Frankfurt, I saw something that a part of me must have recognised a long time ago. Ka had located 'The Place Where God Does Not Exist' at the very top of the left side of the 'Memory' axis. This suggested to me that he had been to the deserted dormitory Z Demirkol and his friends had used as their base at the tail-end of the coup, that he had looked through Necip's window and so had discovered, just before leaving Kars, the true origin of Necip's landscape. All the other poems on the 'Memory' axis referred to his childhood, or to his own memories of Kars. So now I too was convinced of the veracity of the story all of Kars had always believed to be true: after Ka had failed to persuade Kadife to give up the play, and while İpek was still locked in his hotel room, he'd visited Z Demirkol in his new headquarters, where the latter was waiting for Ka to tell him Blue's whereabouts.

And I'm sure I looked just as dazed as Fazıl did at that moment. The voices of the dinner guests floated faintly up the stairs; the sighs of the sad city of Kars rose from the street. Each lost in his memories, Fazıl and I bowed to the unassailable presence of our more complex, passionate and authentic originals.

Looking out of the window at the falling snow, I told Fazıl that it was getting late: we really should go down to supper. Fazıl left first, loping off with a hangdog expression, as if he'd just committed a crime. I lay down on the bed and imagined Ka's thoughts as he walked from the National Theatre to the dormitory; how he must have struggled to look Z Demirkol in the eye; how, unable to furnish the exact address, he must have ultimately driven in the car with those who'd been sent for Blue, to show them the way. And what sorrow I felt to imagine my friend pointing out the building in the distance. Or was it something worse? Could it be that the 'writer clerk' was secretly delighted at the fall of the sublime poet? This thought induced such self-loathing that I forced myself to think about something else.

When I went downstairs to join Turgut Bey and his other guests, I was undone anew by İpek's beauty. Recai Bey, the cultivated, bibliophile director of the telephone company, did his best to lift my spirits, as did Serdar Bey and Turgut Bey. But let me pass quickly over this long evening, during which everyone treated me with the most gracious solicitude and I had far too much to drink. Every time I looked at İpek sitting across from me, I felt something come loose inside me. I watched myself being interviewed on television; to see my nervous hand gestures was excruciating. I took out the little dictaphone I'd been carrying around Kars to record my hosts and their guests giving me their views on the city's history, the fate of journalism here, and the night of the revolution. I did all of this dutifully but unenthusiastically, in the manner of one who no longer believes in his work. As I sipped Zahide's lentil soup, I began to imagine myself as a character in a provincial novel from the 1940s. I decided that prison had been good for Kadife; she was more mature now, more assured. No one mentioned Ka – not even his death – and this broke my heart. At one point, İpek and Kadife went into the little room next door, where little Ömercan was sleeping. I wanted to follow them, but by then your author had 'drunk a great deal, as artists always will'; I was too drunk to stand.

But I still have one very clear memory of that evening. At a very late hour, I told İpek that I wanted to see Ka's room, number 203. Everyone at the table fell silent and turned to look at us.

'Fine,' said İpek. 'Let's go.'

She took the key from reception. I followed her upstairs. The room. The window, the curtains, the snow. The smell of sleep, the scent of soap, the faint whiff of dust. The cold. As İpek watched, still keen to give me the benefit of the doubt but not entirely trustful, I sat on the edge of the bed where my friend had passed the happiest hours of his life making love to this same woman. What if I died here? What if I declared my love to İpek? What if I just stayed here to look out of the window? They were all waiting for us; yes, they were all waiting for us downstairs at the table. I babbled a bit of nonsense that amused İpek enough to make her smile. I remembered her giving me an especially sweet smile when I uttered the mortifying words that I told her I had prepared in advance: 'Nothingmakesyouhappyinloveexceptlove . . . neitherthebooksyouwritenorthecitiesyousee . . . Iamverylonely . . . ifIsaythatIwanttobehereinthiscityclosetoyoutilltheendofmylifewouldyoubelieveme?'

'Orhan Bey,' said İpek. 'I tried hard to love Muhtar, but it didn't work out. I loved Blue with all my heart, but it didn't work out. I believed I would learn to love Ka, but that didn't work out, either. I longed for a child but the child never came. I don't think I'll ever love anyone again; I just don't have the heart for it. All I want to do now is look after my little nephew Ömercan. But I'd like to thank you anyway – even though I can't take you seriously.'

For the first time in my presence, she hadn't said 'your friend'. She'd used Ka's name, and for this I thanked her effusively. Could we meet again, at noon the next day, at the New Life Pastry Shop, just to talk about Ka a little longer?

She was sorry to say she'd be busy. But, still determined to be a good host, she promised that she and the rest of the family would come to see me off at the station the following evening.

I thanked her and then confessed that I hadn't the strength to return to the dinner table (I was also afraid I might start crying), whereupon I threw myself on the bed and passed out.

The next morning I managed to leave the hotel unnoticed and spent the day walking around the city, first with Muhtar and later with Serdar Bey and Fazıl. As I'd hoped, my appearance on the evening news had put the people of Kars at ease about talking to me, so I was able to gather many essential details that clarified the end of my story. Muhtar introduced me to the owner of Lance, Kars' first political Islamist newspaper (circulation: seventy-five). I also met the retired pharmacist who was the paper's managing editor, though he arrived for our meeting quite late. The two men went on to tell me that the anti-democratic measures launched against it had sent the Kars Islamist movement into retreat, and even the popular demand for a religious high school was waning. Only after they had finished speaking did I remember how Fazıl and Necip had once plotted to kill this ageing pharmacist after he had twice kissed Necip in an odd manner. The owner of the hotel who'd denounced his guests to Sunay Zaim was now writing for the Lance, and when we turned to a discussion of recent events, he revealed how thankful he'd been that the man who had assassinated the director of the Education Institute four years earlier had not been from Kars, a detail I'd somehow managed to forget. The assassin, he said, had turned out to be a teahouse owner from Tokat. It was later proved that he had committed another murder around the same time using the same weapon. When the ballistics reports came back from Ankara, the man from Tokat was charged with the murder, and he confessed he'd come to Kars because Blue had invited him. An affidavit submitted at his trial claimed he had suffered a nervous breakdown, so the judge sent him

430

to the Bakirköy Mental Hospital, and when they released him three years later he decided to make his home in Istanbul, where he now ran the Merry Tokat Tea-house and wrote columns on the civil rights of headscarf girls for *Covenant*.

The cause of the headscarf girls in Kars had been greatly weakened four years earlier, after Kadife had bared her head. Although it now showed signs of resurgence, so many girls involved in the court cases had been expelled, and so many others transferred to universities elsewhere, that the Kars movement had yet to display the dynamism of those in Istanbul. Hande's family refused to see me.

The fireman with the strong baritone who'd been yanked into the television station the morning after the revolution to sing Turkish folk songs had gained such a following that he was now the star of his own weekly programme on Kars Border Television, *Songs of the Turkish Borderlands*. They taped it on Tuesday night and aired it on Friday evening; the music-loving caretaker from Kars General Hospital (a close personal friend and one of His Excellency Sheikh Saadettin's most devoted followers) accompanied him on a rhythmic saz.

Serdar Bey, the journalist, also introduced me to 'Glasses', the young boy who'd appeared on stage on the night of the revolution. The boy, who'd been forbidden by his father ever to appear on stage again, even in a school play, was now a full-grown man, but he still worked as a newspaper distributor. He brought me up to date on the Kars socialists who depended on the Istanbul papers for their news. They still admired the Islamists and the Kurdish nationalists who were prepared to lay down their lives to oppose the state, and they occasionally issued indecisive statements that no one bothered to read. These days, their activities amounted to little more than sitting around bragging about the heroes they'd been and the sacrifices they'd made as younger men.

It seemed that almost everyone I met on my walks around Kars was waiting for just such a hero, someone ready now to make the large sacrifices that would deliver them all from poverty, unemployment, confusion and murder. Perhaps because I was a novelist of some repute, the whole city, it seems, had been hoping that I might be that great man for whom they'd been waiting. Alas, I was to disappoint them with my bad Istanbul habits, my absent-mindedness and lack of organisation, my self-regard, my obsession with my project, and my haste. What's more, they let me know it. There was Maruf the tailor, who, having told me his life story in the Unity Tea-house, said I should have agreed to come home with him to meet his nephews and drink with them. I should also have planned to stay two more days in order to attend the conference of Atatürk Youth on Thursday evening. I should have smoked every cigarette and drunk every glass of tea offered to me in a spirit of friendship (I almost always did!). Fazıl's father had an army friend from Varto who told me that in the past four years, most Kurdish militants had either been killed or thrown into prison; no one was joining the guerrillas any more. As for the young Kurds who'd attended the meeting at the Hotel Asia, they'd all abandoned the city, though at the Sunday-evening cockfight I'd seen Zahide's grandson the gambler, who had greeted me warmly and shared some of his raki, which we sipped surreptitiously out of tea-glasses.

By now it was getting late, so I made my way back to the hotel, plodding slowly through the snow like a traveller without a friend in the world, laden with all its sorrows. I still had plenty of time before my departure, but I was hoping to leave without being seen, so I went straight up to my room to pack. As I was leaving through the kitchen door, I met Saffet, the detective. He was retired now but he still came every night for Zahide's soup. He recognised me straight away from my television interview and said he had things he wanted to tell me. Back at the Unity Tea-house, he told me that while he was officially retired, he still worked for the state on a casual basis – there was, after all, no such thing as retirement for a detective in Kars. He'd been dispatched because the city's intelligence services were keen to know what I was trying to dig up here. (Was it to do with the 'Armenian thing', the Kurdish rebels, the religious associations, the political parties?) Smiling graciously, he added that if I could tell him my true business, I'd be helping him make a little money.

Choosing my words carefully, I told him about Ka; I reminded him that he had followed my friend step by step around the city during his visit four years earlier. And I asked what Saffet remembered about him.

'He was a man who cared about people, and he loved dogs, too – a good man,' he said. 'But his mind was still in Germany, and he was very introverted. No one here likes Ka these days.'

For a long time, we remained silent. Hoping that he might know something, but still apprehensive, I asked about Blue, and discovered that a year ago – just as I was now here asking about Ka – several young Islamists had come from Istanbul to ask about Blue, the enemy of the state. They had left without finding his grave, probably because the corpse had been dumped into the sea from a plane, to keep his burial site from becoming a place of pilgrimage.

When Fazıl came to join us at the table, he said that he'd heard similar stories. He'd heard that those young Islamists were following the same path Blue had taken on his own 'pilgrimage'. They'd escaped to Germany, had founded a fast-growing radical Islamist group in Berlin, and, according to Fazıl's old classmates from the religious high school, had written a statement – published on the first page of a German-based journal called *Pilgrimage* – in which they'd vowed revenge against those responsible for Blue's death. It was this group, we guessed, that had killed Ka. So perhaps the only existing manuscript of his book was now in Berlin, in the hands of Blue's Pilgrims. At least, that's what I imagined as I gazed out at the snow.

At that moment, another policeman joined us at the table to tell me that all the gossip about him was untrue. 'I don't even have grey eyes,' he insisted, although he'd never worked out why that should have been a reason for Teslime not to marry him. He'd loved her with all his heart, and if she hadn't committed suicide, they would certainly have wed. It was then that I remembered from Ka's notebooks how, four years earlier, Saffet had confiscated Fazıl's student identity card at the public library. It occurred to me that both Saffet and Fazıl had long forgotten the transaction.

When Fazıl and I returned to the snowy streets, the two policemen came with us – whether in a spirit of friendship or out of professional curiosity, I couldn't tell – and, as we walked, they spoke unbidden about their lives, the emptiness of life in general, the pain of love and growing old. Neither had a hat, and when the snowflakes landed on each man's thinning white hair, they didn't melt. When I asked whether the city was now even poorer and emptier than four years earlier, Fazıl said that everyone had been watching a lot more television in recent years, and that, rather than spending their days sitting in the tea-houses, the unemployed now preferred to sit at home watching free films beamed from all over the world by satellite. Everyone in the city had scrimped and saved to buy the white dishes that were now hitched to the edge of every window. This, he said, was the only new development in the city.

433

We stopped at the New Life Pastry Shop, where we each bought one of the delicious nut-filled crescent rolls that had cost the director of the Education Institute his life: it would be our evening meal. When the police had ascertained that we were heading for the station, they said their farewells, and, as Fazıl and I walked on past the shuttered shops, the empty tea-houses, the abandoned Armenian mansions and bright shop windows, I looked up from time to time at the snow-laden branches of the chestnut and poplar trees above streets randomly illuminated by the odd neon light. We took the side-streets since the police weren't following us. The snow, which had shown signs of abating, now began to fall more heavily. It may have been the emptiness of the streets, or my pain at the prospect of leaving Kars, but I began to feel guilty, as if I were somehow abandoning Fazıl to a solitary life in this empty city. Hanging from the bare branches of two oleander trees were icicles that had intertwined to resemble a tulle curtain. In a nest of ice I saw a sparrow fluttering; it took off into the swirls of giant snowflakes and flew over our heads. The blanket of fresh, white snow had buried the empty streets in a silence so deep that we could hear only our own footsteps and breathing. The longer we walked, the more laboured and thunderous our breathing became; the shops and houses remained as silent as a dream.

I stopped for a moment in the middle of a street to watch a single snowflake fall through the night to its ultimate resting-place. At that same moment, Fazıl pointed above the entrance of the Divine Light Tea-house: there, high on the wall, was a faintly lettered poster, now four years old:

HUMAN BEINGS ARE GOD'S MASTERPIECES
AND
SUICIDE IS BLASPHEMY

'This tea-house is popular with the police, so no one dared touch that poster,' said Fazıl.

'Do you feel as if you're one of God's masterpieces?' I asked.

'No. Only Necip was God's masterpiece. Ever since God took his life, I've let go of my anxieties about atheism and my desire to love God more. May God forgive me.'

The snowflakes were now falling so slowly that they seemed suspended in the sky, and we did not speak again until we'd reached the station. The beautiful, stone station house – the early republican building that some readers might remember me mentioning in *The Black Book* – was gone now. It had been replaced by a typical cement monstrosity. We found Muhtar and the charcoal-coloured dog waiting for us. Ten minutes before the train's scheduled departure, Serdar Bey arrived with some back issues of the *Border City Gazette* that mentioned Ka. Giving them to me, he asked me to take care not to say anything bad about Kars and its troubles, the city or its people, when I wrote my book.

When Muhtar saw Serdar Bey bringing out his present, he nervously, almost guiltily, handed me a plastic shopping bag. Inside was a bottle of cologne, a little wheel of the famous Kars cheese, and a signed copy of his first poetry collection, vanity printed in Erzurum.

I bought my ticket and a sandwich for the little dog my friend had mentioned in his poem. The dog wagged his curly tail happily as he approached me, and I was still feeding him the sandwich when I saw Turgut Bey and Kadife rushing into the station. They'd only just heard from Zahide that I'd gone. We exchanged a few pleasantries about the ticket agent, the journey, the snow. Turgut Bey reached with embarrassment into his pocket and pulled out a new edition of *First Love*, the Turgenev novel he'd translated from the French while he'd been in prison. Ömercan was sitting on Kadife's lap and I stroked his head. His mother's head was wrapped in one of her elegant Istanbul scarves, and the snow it had collected was falling from the edges. Afraid to look too long into his wife's beautiful eyes, I turned back to Fazıl and asked him whether he knew now what he might want to say to my readers if ever I was to write a book set in Kars.

'Nothing.' His voice was determined.

When he saw my face fall, he relented. 'I did think of something, but if you don't like it . . .' he said. 'If you write a book set in Kars and put me in it, I'd like to tell your readers not to believe anything you say about me, anything you say about any of us. No one could understand us from so far away.'

'But no one believes everything they read in a novel,' I said.

'Oh, yes, they do believe it,' he cried. 'If only to see themselves as wise and superior and humanistic, they need to think of us as sweet and funny, and convince themselves that they sympathise with the way we are and even love us. But if you would put in what I've just said, at least your readers will keep a little room for doubt in their minds.'

435

I promised that I would put what he'd said into my novel.

When Kadife saw me eyeing the station entrance, she came towards me. 'I hear you have a beautiful little daughter called Rüya,' she said. 'My sister isn't coming, but she asked me to send greetings to your daughter. And I brought you this memento of my short theatrical career.' She gave me a photograph of herself with Sunay Zaim on the stage of the National Theatre.

The stationmaster blew his whistle. I think I was the only one boarding the train. One by one, I embraced them. At the last moment, Fazıl passed me a plastic bag; inside were the copies he'd made of the videos and a ballpoint pen that had once belonged to Necip.

By now, the train was moving, and it took some effort to jump into the carriage with my hands so full of gifts. They were all standing on the platform waving, and I leaned out of the window to wave back. It was only at the last moment that I saw the charcoal-coloured dog, its pink tongue hanging from its mouth. It ran happily alongside, right to the end of the platform. They all disappeared into the thickly falling snow.

I sat down next to the window and looked through the snow at the orange lights of the last houses of the last neighbourhoods, at the shabby rooms full of people watching television. As I watched the last snow covered rooftops and the thin, quivering ribbons of smoke rising from the broken chimneys, I began to cry.

April 1999 – December 2001